I S L E

J E S   D O R Y

◆ FriesenPress

Suite 300 - 990 Fort St
Victoria, BC, V8V 3K2
Canada

www.friesenpress.com

SUMMARY: Isle is a captivating story of a typical teenage girl, Eleanora Stone, who is thrust into a hidden world that has been awaiting her since birth. The secrets of her mysterious past will begin to unveil themselves as she encounters magic, danger, forbidden love, and power she never believed to be possible.

ISBN
978-1-4602-7526-9 (Hardcover)
978-1-4602-7527-6 (Paperback)
978-1-4602-7528-3 (eBook)

1. YOUNG ADULT FICTION / FANTASY / DARK FANTASY

Distributed to the trade by The Ingram Book Company

For my everything

My name is Eleanora Ada Stone. I was moved from home to home for seventeen years. I am now living on this godforsaken island in Maine. I was being kept from a world of secrets.

I have abilities.

1

"We're moving *again*!"

I couldn't believe it. And yet there was my Aunt Ada, packing another cardboard box.

"Yes, we are," she said—the start to a dialog that Ada and I had become very familiar with.

"Four months!" I squealed, my hands open in a slight plea. "We've only been here four months Ada!"

"Come on Nora! Where's your sense of adventure? Traveling is exciting! How many girls your age can say they've seen as many parts of this country as you have?" She was trying to sound positive.

"I wouldn't know." I crossed my arms burning my eyes into the side of her head.

We've never stayed around one place long enough for me to make any friends. I took two of the liquor store cardboard boxes.

Gripping them in frustration, I stormed to my room where I sat staring at my belongings for a few moments, frozen, unsure of why I had taken my belongings out of their boxes to begin with. It had been almost eighteen years, and we'd lived in twenty-five different homes across the country. I opened my closet and began stuffing my sweaters and jeans into the first box. Once filled, I taped it shut and wrote 'NORA' across the top in marker, then shoved the box closer to the door where it met Ada's bare feet. Her toes were decorated in thin gold rings and her nails were always manicured; this week they were painted a deep blue. I gave her a sour look then opened the flaps of the second box. I heard Ada sigh.

"Look, sorry we're moving again. I promise this will be the last time." She stood in the doorway with her arms crossed.

"So far Ada, that's been a promise you haven't been able to keep."

Ada turned her gaze to the floor fiddling with her rings, defeated by my comment.

"I don't understand why we bother having things or renting apartments, or with me attending school. Really, we should just buy a van and live on the road. At least I could say I am a wanderer, a nomad. Because that's exactly what we are." I scrawled 'NORA' across the second box. "Sounds better than 'We're moving *again* because my aunt's free spirit got the best of her *again*.'"

Ada raised an eyebrow at me as she played with the feathers wrapped in her hair. She'd had those since I could remember. Two grayish blue feathers twisted in a thin gold thread.

"I think you're really going to like this next place," she tried to reassure me as if it would be something different.

"Oh yeah, you think? Where are we going next? Chicago, Brooklyn, Los Angeles, Canada—"

"Mmm, close."

My cheeks flushed with heat.

"*Canada!* You're taking me to Canada?" I took a deep breath trying to calm myself. "It's like we're always on the run, witness protection style, and now we're leaving the damn country, Ada! Unbelievable."

Ada pinched her lips at the choice of my words, saying nothing of it.

"I just think that getting out of these cities we've always lived in won't necessarily be a bad thing. Besides, it's *not* Canada."

Ada walked over to the battered roadmap of the continental US that was tacked to my wall. We'd found it at a garage sale, and on it I had marked all the places we'd lived and visited. I watched her pull it down and hand it to me, her finger pointing out the spot. Our next home was so tiny it was completely obscured by her fingertip.

"Stone Isle, Maine," she smiled with an odd sense of excitement in her voice that I had never heard before.

I sharply tracked my gaze from the map to her and back.

"You're moving me to an *island*?" I spat and stared in utter astonishment at this tiny green dot near Nova Scotia. I found myself lost for words.

"Oh come on, it's not that bad. It's the island we're from." She smiled, exiting my room. I heard her yell down the hallway of our small apartment, "Get ready for some serious change, girlfriend!"

"Yeah," I called back. "A change to some serious isolation!"

Where we're from? Why on earth would she want to move back to that island, a place with the heavy memories of losing my mother and her parents out at sea? Ada and I were the only ones to survive the rough storm that took everyone else that night. I was never sure if my father was amongst the dead or living. She claimed to know very little of him, and that was that. I wasn't able to squeeze much else out of her in regards to him or my family over the years no matter how hard I pressed.

I studied the little green island that kept disappearing when I put my pinky over it. Folding the map back into its creases, I stuck it into my canvas bag and lay down on the cold wooden floor.

Stone Isle. An island.

By the next morning, our apartment was packed, and I looked at the five boxes that contained nearly everything I owned. Aside from a small twin-sized bed, an old blue chest Ada found at the same garage sale where we'd found my map, and the worn step stool that I used for a nightstand, this was it; this was my life—no more, no less. It fit in five medium-sized boxes. *Pathetic*, I thought. I was gazing between the stacked boxes and the folded old map peeking out of my bag when a strange man walked into my room and startled me.

"Excuse me, ma'am. I'm with the moving company. Are these boxes ready to go?"

He was a short man with a pudgy nose and a circular patch of hair missing from the top of his head. He took out a dark handkerchief from his back pocket and wiped the sweat from his brow while awaiting an answer. The name stitched on his tan work shirt read 'Jack'. I nodded. He picked up three out of the five boxes in one armload. *Well, doesn't that just put things into perspective nicely?* He turned to walk out of my room and the back of his shirt read 'Jack and Son Moving Services - Coast to Coast'. I wondered if he knew that he'd have to paddle our boxes in a boat to an island.

Before I knew it, the apartment was completely empty, and I felt no attachment to it. Ada, on the other hand, always had to have her sentimental moment, and she walked around the empty rooms one more time, savoring the feeling of the place. Slinging my bag over my shoulder, I left her and made my way to the car.

It was a dreary March day in Washington DC, and the lingering algid undertones of a winter slipping away hung in the air. The wind funneled through our street, taking dried leaves and pieces of trash. Today was the last day of classes before the start of spring break, and it still looked like winter. A few girls I recognized from class walked by our packed old hatchback Volvo with a moving truck parked behind it. They stared curiously in my direction with lips slightly parted as if they had questions.

Believe me, I thought, *I don't think I'd be able to answer them even if you asked.*

Intentionally avoiding eye contact, I hopped in the front seat and slammed the car door behind me. I watched as the girls disappeared from the rearview mirror. Ada emerged, locked the front door, and then slipped the apartment key through the brass mail slot in the door. I watched her gracefully move towards the moving truck, where she spoke with Jack. I noticed another younger guy, maybe mid-twenties, sitting in the passenger seat of the truck, and guessed this was Jack's son. The three suddenly laughed and Ada stepped back, waving as the small truck filled with our belongings pulled away.

"Where are they going? Shouldn't they be following us?" I said when Ada opened the driver side door and sat down.

She rooted around in her bag.

"Um, oh there you are!" She pulled out the car keys, dangling them in the air. "They know where they're going, besides they have other deliveries to make before they make ours. They anticipate getting to Maine tomorrow. Anyway, it's quite the drive, so get comfortable."

"How long exactly is this drive?" I thought again about the little green dot on my map.

Ada picked up a small handheld GPS that she kept propped between the cigarette tray and gear shift and programmed it for Stone Isle, Maine. A monotone voice spoke: "Stone Isle, thirteen hours and twenty-eight minutes to your destination."

Wonderful.

Washington began to fade from view in the car's rearview mirrors, and the thirteen-plus-hour trip to nowhere had officially begun. Every few hours we stopped for gas and to stretch out our legs, and when Ada was exhausted, I'd take over the wheel. We pushed our way through the heinous bumper-to-bumper traffic of the metropolitan states. We finally pulled off in Lowell, Massachusetts, where Ada found a little motel off the highway. The motel was vacant— not a single car occupied the parking lot. Ada and I exchanged looks of uncertainty before heading inside. An elderly woman sat at the front desk watching late night television. The image reflected off of her glasses.

"Room for two please?" Ada said while yawning.

"Thirty-five dollars." The woman barely looked up from her little television set as Ada rummaged through her purse and pulled out three tens and a five. The woman handed Ada a heavy key with a red tag and continued on watching her show.

"Okay great, well uh, thank you." Ada gave me a look that said, 'awkward.'

We grabbed our overnight bags and made our way down the tight hallway, as the fluorescent lights above us hummed and flickered.

"Ah, here we go, room one-ten." Ada yawned. We didn't even bother changing out of our clothes before crashing onto the beds.

I awoke to light streaming through the motel's thick maroon curtains when a sharp knock came behind the door. It took me a minute to remember where we were.

"Housekeeping." It was a woman's voice.

"Still sleeping!" Ada moaned.

"Okay ma'am, I'll come back later."

It was eleven, and we still had about five and a half hours of driving left. My eyes felt heavy as I rolled off the bed and made my way to the bathroom. It was a tiny bathroom. Stepping over the toilet was the only way to close the door. The bathroom barely needed a light. The bright neon orange shower curtain practically glowed. Pushing it back, I turned the faucet and stepped into the cold chipped tub. I sat in the dry end of the tub and watched the steaming hot water slowly make its way to meet my skin. As the water level rose, I was slowly immersed. I had to admit that the heat was soothing.

Thoughts of the tiny island spilled obsessively through my mind. How come Ada had never told me much about it? Trying to remember past conversations, I realized that whenever the subject of her childhood was brought up, Ada tended to avoid giving me direct answers. Instead, she would say things like, "Oh Maine, it was a boring place to grow up" –or– "It's really not that interesting, Nora. We grew up in a silly little town." I suppose I could understand why Ada never divulged much of the past, the pain of losing her immediate family must have been difficult to speak about. I filled

up my lungs before submerging my head under the surface of the
water. A low buzzing sound filled my ears as I lay there staring at
the surface of liquid above me when I heard voices. *We're coming
for you. We're coming for you,* followed by a pounding sound that
vibrated the surface of the water. I almost jumped out of the tiny
tub while choking on a mouthful of water. Ada was at the door. I
looked around the tiny bathroom. What the hell was that?

"Nora! I have to pee! Are you almost done? Come on!"

My fingers were like red prunes.

"One minute," I said slightly paranoid.

The stiff bleached white towel was barely big enough to wrap
around me. I stepped out of the tub to open the door. Ada and I
squeezed past one another.

"Wow, talk about a tiny bathroom," she said, closing the door
and giving a sigh of relief from behind it.

Yanking open the dusty curtains, my eyes adjusted to the vicious
sunlight. There really wasn't much to see except a parking lot mostly
empty of cars, a dumpster, and a few finches pecking the asphalt.
I began to dress and heard Ada turn on the shower. Running my
fingers through my hair, I braided it back and then pulled out my
laptop. Well, at least this place had free Wi-Fi. I began researching
Stone Isle, Maine and clicked the first link that I pulled up.

> Stone Isle is about nine miles long and four and
> a half miles wide. Much of Stone Isle is owned
> by Eldergrove National Park. Sixty locals cur-
> rently live on Stone Isle and during the summer
> months, the island's population can increase
> to three hundred or so. Most of the locals work
> in the fishing or lobstering industry. Stone Isle
> has a fairly small school system held in a local's
> private home. The island's school embodies pre-K
> through eighth-grade and currently has enrolled

six students. The island's six high school students travel to and from school by boat to neighboring islands or attend boarding schools. Stone Isle and many of its fellow surrounding islands have yet to receive cellular towers but hope to see progress in the next few years. Landlines are still widely used on Stone Isle, and service is dependent on weather.

You have got to be kidding me, I thought. *She is trying to kill me. Or drive me insane.*

It took me a moment to register what I had just read. I looked at my thin white phone lying on the bed. No cellular towers. Landlines. My guess was that there wouldn't be internet unless we were going to rely on dial-up. This island was a mass of land stuck in prehistoric time. Not that I had friends who texted me, but I nursed a faint hope that someday my phone's chime might indicate a text from someone other than Ada.

Goodbye, computer, goodbye cellphone, goodbye any chance at a normal life.

I closed my laptop and lay back on the polyester motel blanket. The idea of six high-school students commuting an hour by boat sat numbingly in my mind, and I visualized rowboats full of students stuffed into life jackets, paddling their way across rough seas to get to class. Well, they'd have to change that number to seven—seven high-school students commuting by boat to school—unless Ada had other plans for me, like boarding school.

Interrupting my thoughts, Ada casually stepped out of the bathroom, bent over, and began to aggressively towel-dry her hair. She looked up at me through a parting in her hair.

"What's up?" she asked.

"I was curious if you were planning on getting me my very own rowboat, or if the high school was going to provide me with one along with school supplies?"

"What?" Ada threw me a confused look.

"Or if we were going to have to revert to times of writing letters and possibly even dial-up internet?"

Ada stopped drying her wild hair and stood up. "What are you talking about?"

I rolled over and propped my head up on my hand. "I just finished reading that all six, well now *seven*, high-school students on this massive island commute to school by boat, and that while cellular towers have yet to be built, they do hope to see progress on that front in the next couple years. You know, nothing out of the ordinary."

"Sarcastic, are we? Don't worry, Nora. I'm sure there is a yellow painted ferry that will charter you to and from school," she said. "As for cellphone towers, who needs towers when you have string and tin cans?"

Funny, I thought.

I rolled my eyes and lay back, taking my cellphone with me. I pressed down on the top button until a 'power off' screen came on. I slid the arrow to the right and watched it turn off.

Goodbye technology, goodbye social media, goodbye hopes of having a boyfriend or friends or anyone beside Ada message me. Goodbye, world.

"Come on, gloomy girl," she said. "It's already one thirty, we should get going!"

Ada took the wheel first, and we began the second half of our journey. Ada and I had little interaction during our drive. I was too angry at being shuffled to yet another home. However, what interaction we did have was heated on my behalf.

"Why are we moving back here?" I asked, pressing my forehead against the cool window and watching my body heat fog its pane.

"I think it's about time we get back to our roots," Ada spoke as if rehearsed.

"Our roots? Ada you've kept me displaced for almost eighteen years and now what, you want a community? Friends? Family?"

At this Ada bit the inside of her cheek and I regretted mentioning the word family. I was her only family, according to her stories.

We continued to drive into the dead of night and Ada sipped her cheap gas station coffee and hummed blissfully to radio tunes eventually lulling me to sleep.

When I opened my eyes Ada was driving on a gravel road, pulling up alongside a small building. I saw a sign that read Ferry Landing and another that read Stone Isle Boat Service with the fees and times listed below. I lowered my window, and the thick smell of salt filled the car. I could hear the ocean moving and breaking somewhere near us. I watched as an outside light flickered and buzzed before turning on. A man walked out of the little building, and Ada stepped out of the car.

"Hello ma'am," he said over the sound of crashing waves. "I'm awfully sorry, but we're closed. Next ferry leaves at seven in the mornin'."

He was a tall man with a big belly and a thick mustache that obscured his mouth. He was turning around to go back inside when Ada found her voice.

"Eric?"

The man casually turned back and eyed Ada as he thumbed his blue suspenders.

"Eric *Turner*?" she said.

"I'm sorry, ma'am, but do I know you?" he said, squinting in our direction.

"It's me! Ada, Ada Lane! Rebekah's sister, we—"

"Ada? But it can't be! Ms. Lane, is that really you?"

Rebekah. I rarely heard Ada mention my mother's name, and here she was casually offering it to a man I didn't know.

"Yes it is," she walked over to him. The man gave her a cautious look until he realized it really was Ada, then I watched the two embrace like old friends. I sat perplexed.

"Oh my dear girl, it's really you!" he said while squeezing her in his beastly arms. "I haven't seen you since, well I can't even remember. You haven't changed a bit, darlin'."

"You either, it's just wonderful to see you, Eric!"

Eric slapped his belly. "Well, I did add a few pounds since I last saw you, still eatin' Mary's cookin' n' all."

Ada laughed. "How is she? I hope she's still making those chocolate ganaches."

The man gave a low, hearty laugh. "Every Saturday night for church on Sunday. What a nice surprise to see your face again. What brings you back to the island?"

"We're moving back," she said.

"By God, you might be the first person ever to move *back* to the island." He laughed again. I felt my brow crinkle, wondering why Ada wanted to move back to an island it sounded like most people were dying to get away from.

"Well anyway, I'm glad to hear it," he said. "This island could use your laughter again." Then he pinched Ada's cheek as if she were a little girl.

"Eric, I want you to meet someone."

Ada brought him closer to the car and I opened the door, slowly stepping out. The man studied me as Ada began the introduction.

"Nora, this is Eric Turner. He runs the ferry to the islands around here including Stone Isle, Eric this is—"

"Wait just a darn minute." Eric threw up a hand to pause Ada. "No, but it can't be. I know who this is."

He walked over to me and put both hands on my shoulders, studying my face closely. His fingers were round like sausages and his mustache even thicker in close proximity.

"You brought her back?" Eric glanced to Ada then returned his heavy gaze upon me, "I mean, you're back? Rebekah's little girl? You're a spittin' image of your mother, you know. She was a real beauty, just like you."

He smiled but a hint of sorrow entered his glacier-colored eyes and a tinge of pink bled into his weather-beaten cheeks.

I couldn't help but smile back at his comment about my mother. "You knew her?"

"Did I know her? Lord knows I knew that girl! Ada and Rebekah use to almost give me a heart attack every mornin' takin' them two troublemakers to an' from the mainland."

Ada laughed.

"Troublemakers you both were," he said, waving his plump index finger in her face. Then he shook his head. "Boy, will Mary be thrilled to learn you two came by."

Ada's cheeks blushed as she smiled with embarrassment.

"Um, Eric, is there any way you can take us to the island? I know it's late, but it's been a pretty long journey for us to come home." She batted her eyelashes, locking her gaze with his. Listening to the undertones in Ada's voice I knew she wasn't entirely referring to the thirteen-hour journey here.

"I'll bring you coffee in the morning," Ada said in a playful sing-song. I watched Eric shake his head as if his brain had frozen.

"Oh darlin' anything for you and Rebekah's girl. What'd you say your name was again?"

"I didn't. It's Eleanora, but I go by Nora." I extended my hand.

"Nora," he said. He shook my hand (along with my arm and shoulder). "Alright Ms. Nora, you ever been on a ferry before?"

I shook my head.

"Come on then, let's get you both home." He patted me hard on the back. "Let's get you both home." He headed for the dock. The word sounded so inviting. *Home.*

I went to get back into the car.

"Uh Nora, we need to *unpack*," she said. "The car stays."

"What do you mean, 'the car stays'? How are we going to get anywhere?"

Ada called back over her shoulder.

"Eric!"

"Yes, Ms. Lane?" He said.

"Can I leave the car parked here? I'll be back in the morning with your coffee to take care of it."

"Take care of it? I said. "What do you mean take care of it? Where's it going?" I tried again.

"Of course, you can," Eric said, having to raise his voice over the rising wind. "I'll be on the ferry when you're ready."

Ada turned back to me. "There are no vehicles on the island. We walk or bike to get anywhere," she said, "or run—and I am not getting rid of it, just leaving it at a parking lot reserved for residents of the island."

Seven high school students, commuting by boat, no cellphones or high-speed anything, land lines, and now no vehicles. I waited for Ada to mention that there was no electricity or plumbing either. I scowled and flung my bag across my body and made my way to the ferry.

I'd never been on a boat—or to the ocean—before, and I suddenly felt anxious. The sea looked black, and the only thing I could see out in the distance was a small light blinking slowly. I walked down the creaking dock, and Eric offered me his hand, helping me aboard. The sea felt alive as it moved the little ferry back and forth like a toy boat in a bathtub. I caught myself on a rail when the boat was hit by a wave.

"Better grow some sea legs, girl," Ada said.

"Why?"

"Uh, because we're moving to an island!"

Right.

Ada gave me a playful punch in the shoulder and guided me to the front where we leaned over the guardrail together and looked down at the inky black surf splashing the side of the boat. The light in the distance continued to blink slowly, and I watched as it disappeared and reappeared.

"That," Eric said, pointing in the direction of the light, "is where we're going. Alexander Point. Alright, hold on tight!" Eric sounded the horn and the ferry began vibrating as its engine went full speed.

"Home sweet home," Ada said into the salty wind.

I stared at the blinking light. *Home sweet home*, the words echoed in my head. I'd never heard Ada use these words before, but the feeling she gave me by saying those simple words caused the hairs on my arms to stand on end. An eerie chill swept over me, and I pulled my jacket tighter around my body.

The boat was rocked by another wave, and I squeezed myself a little tighter staring out at the dark sea.

2

The blinking light grew closer and closer, and I learned it was a lighthouse. I'd never seen one before. It was mesmerizing. I felt it calling, wanting to bring me to the comfort of its direction, the way a siren would lure sailors. The air was thick with salt, and every now and then a bit of water misted our faces. Ada went to what I learned was the captain's bridge to go catch up with Eric, and I was left to my thoughts. I wondered what this island was going to do to my life. Would I even meet anyone? Why were we coming back, why now? Something about this move tasted different than all the others, something tasted permanent.

Resting my body against the rail, I leaned as far over as I could. The island's black silhouette was becoming larger and larger as we approached. Eric began slowing down the ferry, and we coasted near a white dock that glowed under the stars. I heard scurrying footsteps, and I turned to see Ada practically run to the side of the boat to help Eric tie ropes. They pulled the ferry perfectly side-by-side along the dock. I remained frozen, watching the light of the towering lighthouse continue its rounds. Ada jumped out of the boat and Eric handed our bags to her one-by-one. Something felt strange as I stared at the long white dock; my feet felt weighted, cemented in place.

"Well Nora, welcome home," Eric said, flinging one arm wide to present the island to me.

I didn't say anything back, only looked at the dark, unknown mass of land. My stomach began to coil uncomfortably.

"Well? Come on, Nora," Ada said, her voice as bright as the moon.

Eric helped me out of the boat.

"I'm sure I'll be seeing you sooner than later." He gave me a wink then began untying the rope from the dock to set the ferry free again. Ada waved.

"See you in the morning, Eric!" Ada called over the sound of the engine.

"Yes, ma'am. Lookin' forward to it, Ms. Lane." Eric then sounded the horn and pulled away.

The ferry began its journey back to the mainland, and suddenly I wanted to jump into the sea and swim towards it. The feeling of being trapped on this island made its way to my chest and increased my heart rate. I leaned down and picked up two bags, not taking my eyes off the little ferry. The moon lit our path to land, and I trailed behind Ada. The wooden planks beneath my feet creaked as I stepped from board to board. The sound of the ocean's breaking waves felt haunting, and I turned one last time to see the ferry's light vanish into a thick fog that had appeared out of nowhere. I made my way closer to Ada. She looked at me and wrapped her arm around my shoulders. I took a deep breath of salty air. Ada's eyes had become more vibrant in color here, sage green and shining brilliantly.

"You know, you really do look like your mother, especially here," Ada said.

We walked through a small boathouse with nets and ropes hanging along the walls. Two rocking chairs covered in cobwebs stood as though they hadn't been sat in for years. A breeze tunneled its way through, moving them gently. When we exited the boat-house, an old home stood not far from another long walkway that linked to the lighthouse.

"Is this where we're staying?"

The house was large for the two of us.

Ada sighed. "Yep, this is home."

"It comes with a lighthouse?"

Staring back and forth from the home to the old lighthouse, I realized I had seen this place before. It was in various photos I had stumbled across when scanning the Internet at the motel. I watched the tall structure in amazement. Ada and I had always lived in tiny apartments and now here we are moving into a home that came with a lighthouse.

"I don't understand how we can afford to live here," I said.

Ada smiled.

"This house has been in our family for over two hundred years. It's where your mother and I grew up. Nora, I'm still waiting for the big elephant-in-the-room question, which you have yet to even mention."

I stared blankly in her direction.

"Stone Isle?" Ada raised an eyebrow in my direction. "Seriously?"

I stood silently not understanding where Ada was going with this.

"What about Stone Isle?"

"Eleanora Ada…" She paused for effect. "Stone? Come on, girl! I thought I raised you to be more inquisitive than that."

"So what? My last name and the name of the island have something in common. That doesn't mean much to me, Ada. Besides, it doesn't make me like the idea of living here."

"Nora, this is your island. Your father's side founded and settled here hundreds of years ago. Then others, including our family, eventually settled here too, buying bits and parts of the island. Not only is this house your home, this entire island is. The trees, the dirt, the woods, the cliffs, the sea, the air, all of it is your home."

I stood aghast. Dumbfounded. And angry.

"You're kidding right?" I shrugged her hand off.

"I wish I were, but I'm not." Ada glanced towards the tree line and then reached to the top of the doorframe where she slid her hand back and forth until she felt something. She pulled it down and opened her hand to reveal a copper-toned key. Ada wiggled it into the doorknob, and we both heard a loud click, followed by the door slowly swinging open.

"Ada."

My aunt stopped before entering the home and turned to look at me.

"Why now?" I said. "Why did you bring me back here now? Is this really about coming back to our roots, or is there something else you're not saying? Why not when I was little, why did you hide Stone Isle from me? How *could* you?"

Ada turned towards the entryway of the home and froze, she didn't want to look at me.

"I hid this all from you because I had to. Horrible memories took place here for me, Nora. I lost my sister and my parents, and in order to survive, I had to take you, knowing you would never know them, and leave to make us a life away from this island. But I knew I couldn't hide your roots from you forever, and I promised myself I would bring you back before your eighteenth birthday." Ada looked over her shoulder at me. "That's why."

"And my father? I thought you knew nothing about him. You failed to mention he left me an inheritance of an island. What *else* do you know?" I spat the words out angrily. I could tell Ada was hiding more, so much more from me.

"What else do you know about my father, Ada?" I asked more aggressively.

"Nora, I'm not getting into this tonight." Her words sliced through the air. I looked back to the water. Questions upon questions had begun to build in my mind.

The house was dark with only a little moonlight filtering through the dirty windows. We entered the kitchen. Ada flipped a light switch up and down.

"Oh, dang it."

Ada put down her bags, opened a cabinet and fumbled around.

"What are you looking for?"

"Matches," she said. "I can't see anything."

"I knew it. No electricity on this damn island either, right?" I glared at her.

"What? Of course there's electricity, has been since the early seventies." Ada said continuing to fumble. "It's remote, but it's not part of the eighteenth century. I called the Eldergrove Electrical Company yesterday to turn it back on."

"They're right there, Ada." I pointed to a red box on the right side of the cabinet. It was apparent that I had better night vision than Ada. "I think you need glasses."

Ada analyzed my face curiously for a moment, then pulled out the matches and a tall white candle.

"Perhaps," she said, blowing the dust off the matchbox and sliding the little red cardboard box open. It took her a few strikes to light the match, but once lit, the little flame softly illuminated the kitchen.

Ada pulled out another candle. "I'll call again in the morning and get the electricity turned on. Until then, a candelabra ambiance it is."

She lit three more, placing them around the kitchen and handed one to me.

"Here, you'll need it to find your room."

I didn't move.

"Well? Aren't you curious to look around?"

As I picked up my bag, the hand holding the candle trembled. I walked slowly, careful not to blow out the flame. The candle engulfed me in a little bubble of light as things appeared and disappeared around me. The stairs were at the end of the kitchen, and I made my way up. The wooden banister was smooth and cool as I slid my hand along it. The second floor was pitch black, for all the doors were closed. I walked down the hallway until a doorknob made of black metal caught my attention. I held the flame closer, and the light revealed engravings of delicate vines and leaves. I ran my fingers over it, then turned the knob and pushed open the door.

The room had angular ceilings, and two windows allowed the moonlight to spill onto the wooden floor. The ceiling was vaulted and a black metal-framed bed took up most of the space. A nightstand with a lamp carved from driftwood sat on the right side of the bed, and a wooden chest sat at its end. The chest resembled a larger version of my blue one. On the other side of the room stood an old desk with a wooden chair. The desk was bordered by empty shelves built into the wall. There was a tall pair of double doors, which I assumed was the closet. Stepping into the room, I decided this was it. I didn't bother looking at what lay behind the other doors in the hallway. I liked this one. I put my bag down on the bed. The air was musty. I attempted to open the window. At first, it was stuck, but after wiggling and banging it a bit with my fist, it cooperated and slid open. I took a closer look at the bed frame and realized it matched the doorknob. Black metal twisting and turning like vines. I sat in the desk's chair and slid my hand over its dusty smooth surface. The drawers were locked when I tried opening them. The chest, too, I found was locked.

Wonder if Ada knows where the keys are?

The breeze picked up a bit and slammed the bedroom door, causing me to jump. I placed my hand over my racing heart when I caught my reflection in a tall mirror that was hidden behind the open door. I walked over to it. The glass was tarnished with copper stains, and the bottom right corner was cracked. I looked at myself.

You look just like her. Eric and Ada's words rung in my mind.

I stepped closer to the mirror analyzing my face. I held the candle closely and felt its warmth on my freckle splattered cheek. My eyes appeared to have taken on a sapphire blue tone like my mom's, no longer a dark gray. I blinked hard, stunned, as I watched them change back to their murky color. *Impossible.* I blinked my eyes a few more times, but they remained their usual dark hue. *What the hell was that?* I walked back to the bed and begun unpacking my overnight bag. I didn't have much and wasn't sure when the moving men would arrive with our things. I undressed and pulled on my vintage silk nightgown I had found in a thrift store.

The breeze moved the sheer curtains, and they gently rolled in and out. It was enchanting to be able to hear the ocean from my bed, a sound I was positive I could get used to. My cellphone fell from my bag and onto the soft, pillowy comforter. I turned it on and waited patiently. I watched the antenna bars, hoping for some kind of signal, but there was none.

I turned it off and tucked it back into my bag. I pulled out my toothbrush and a travel-sized toothpaste and left the room to find the bathroom. Turning out the bedroom door, I ran into Ada and quickly jumped backward, startled.

"Whoa, you okay?" Ada said.

"Yeah, sorry I didn't hear you come up the stairs. My nerves are a bit on edge at the moment. Actually, I thought I just saw my eyes—" My heart continued to race.

"Your eyes *what?*" Ada raised an eyebrow.

"It might sound crazy, but I thought I just saw my eyes change color for a moment in the mirror."

"That *is* crazy," Ada said, as she looked into the bedroom I had begun to settle into. "So, this room, huh? You like it?"

I gave her a nod. "I do."

"Have you checked out any of the other rooms? There are five bedrooms on this floor."

"No, I didn't, this was the first one I opened. I'm not even sure where the bathroom is yet," I said, holding up my brush and toothpaste for her to see.

"Right," she said.

Uncomfortable vibes radiated off Ada as she walked around the bedroom with her arms crossed. She ran her fingers over the bed and then made her way to the window where she peered out.

"Did you open this?" Ada looked back at me.

"Um, yeah. Were you expecting someone else to have?"

"No, just want to make sure it was originally closed."

"Should I pick a different room?" I asked, a little unsure now of my decision.

"No, no, this one is just fine." She turned and looked at me. "It was Rebekah's, your mom's."

I didn't reply. There was an awkward silence, and then Ada broke it by taking a deep breath.

"Come on, let me show you where the bathroom is. The water isn't working, I tested the kitchen sink. I brought you this."

Ada handed me a big mason jar filled with water. "There's a hand pump just outside the house. I'll fiddle with it in the morning to get the water going too." Ada led me down the hall to the very last door and opened it. She then lit another candle for me.

"Here you go," she said, extending her arm.

"Where are you going?" I asked as she exited the bathroom.

"Oh, I'll be reacquainting myself with my old room," Ada smiled and pointed to the door next to mine.

Nodding, I watched Ada head down the hallway before dipping my toothbrush in the glass of water to soak the bristles. I put the toothpaste on my brush and begun brushing my teeth. The scrubbing sounds filled my entire head, and a few times I stopped, listening carefully to the dead silence of the night. The island had me on edge. It was far too quiet for comfort. I was used to the hustle and bustle of busy cities: ambulances, fire trucks, neighborhood traffic, and taxis. I finished quickly and spat into the sink. The water was refreshing. I cupped my hand and poured out some water then splashed my face. There weren't any towels yet, so I wiped my wet face and hands on my nightgown and blew out the candle. As I turned to walk out of the bathroom I thought I saw my eyes change color again in the mirror, but when I blinked, they were back to their murky gray. This was a definite sign that I needed sleep.

Walking quietly down the hallway, I passed my room and went to knock on Ada's door. The candle's flame in my hand flickered. Before I could knock, I noticed the door was cracked open and I peeked in. Ada was sitting on the end of her bed incredibly still. I lightly tapped the door frame and her eyes sharply looked right at me, startling me. They almost appeared black for a second, but before I could really register much in her dimly lit room, they were back to their sage color.

Her voice was soft and distant. "Come in."

Ada's cheeks were glistening.

"That's okay," I said. "I was just coming to say goodnight."

"Oh, well goodnight, darling. See you in the morning."

I glanced at her one last time and then closed the door.

My room was chillier than before. I quietly closed my door and locked it. Something about this house had planted a seed of paranoia in my mind. I pulled the old skeleton key out of the lock and set it on my nightstand, then slipped under the sheets and tried to close my eyes. The sheets had a musty scent. I burrowed beneath them. Muffled weeping came from the room next door; Ada was having a tough time returning to her once full and now empty home, I thought. I closed my eyes and forced myself to fall asleep.

Nora.

I awoke to the faint sound of my name being spoken. It was the middle of the night. I lay frozen. My nerves jangled. I listened for Ada. The sound of her sobs was gone. Deciding that I had heard nothing, I closed my eyes again trying to push away the paranoid thoughts. Then, ever so quietly, I heard it again. This time, I flung my eyes open and watched as the curtains waved in the breeze. After scanning the room multiple times, I stood up and closed the window.

The moonlight had vanished, the temperature had dropped drastically since I had gone to bed, and before tucking myself back under the covers, I pulled on a pair of wool socks. I peeked through the curtains again, and what I saw was the eeriest yet most heavenly view my eyes had ever fallen upon. The sky appeared to take the form of a thick blanket, stitched together by heavy clouds that swallowed the world. A ghostly glow from the trapped moon filtering through the seams. A thick fog began to seep in from the tree line, covering the earth like a ghostly dream. I had never seen anything like this before, and goosebumps crawled down my arms. I was pressing the window down once more, making sure it was secure, when out of the corner of my eye, I saw someone. A dark human silhouette appeared to be trapped in the fog for an instant but then vanished.

Oh, shake it off, Nora. Your eyes are just playing tricks on you.

I locked the window and tugged the curtains together. Getting back into bed, I tucked myself as far under as the sheets would allow me to go and forced myself to think of other things, anything but the dark silhouette and my name being whispered. After convincing myself that my imagination had gotten the best of me, I finally fell back to sleep.

The warm sun poured through the sheer curtains and began heating up my room. I awoke and stayed in bed until I had the energy to pull myself to my feet. I heard voices downstairs, followed by the front door slamming. I grabbed the key from the nightstand and opened the bedroom door. I walked down towards the sound of a kettle's angry whistle. This was a sure sign that Ada was up. The house appeared different in the daylight, friendly, natural, and inviting. Much of it was plainly decorated in different shades of whites and neutrals.

"Morning!" Ada said in a more cheerful tone than she had used to say goodnight.

"Good morning."

"You sleep okay?" she asked, pulling the kettle off of the stove. "Got the electricity and water up and running, thank God."

"Kind of, I kept waking up. Just not used to sleeping here, I suppose."

She put a mug in front of me and poured hot water over a teabag. I watched the berry color stain the steaming water when I remembered waking up to the sound of my name. I must have been over-exhausted and incredibly paranoid. My mind was probably desperate for sounds; I was so used to sleeping in the music box of city life. Holding the warm mug between my hands, I turned and noticed all of our boxes were in the living room.

"I see all our stuff came."

"Yep, I took Eric coffee this morning and the movers were there, waiting. So Eric helped me load them on the ferry and bring it all back." She took a sip of her tea. "Complicated not having a car or a road to and from the mainland."

"Or civilization," I added under my breath.

I began taking my boxes upstairs. Unlike the moving guy, I could only carry one at a time, and right when I was about to take the last box upstairs Ada stopped me.

"About last night, I'm sorry if I made you feel uncomfortable. Nothing can really prepare you for returning to a place that was once filled with the people you loved. I suppose I thought I would handle it differently."

"I understand. But why Ada, if the pain is still here, why are we back?" I asked adjusting the side of the box onto my hip.

"Just tired of finding my way out there. I also want you to get to know your real home, where your parents are from, where your lineage is rooted. It might even help you understand yourself a bit more."

"Understand myself a bit more?"

"Here," Ada pulled two keys from her pocket.

"One's for the chest and the other's for the desk. I figured you may want to open them. All the keys for the house are in this kitchen drawer." Ada pointed to a long thin white drawer.

Ada walked over and tucked them into my nightgown pocket. "Whatever is in those drawers and chest is yours. She would have wanted you to have all her things."

I thanked her and made my way upstairs.

3

After placing the last box on the desk, I fished in my pocket for the two keys. They were small, old keys similar to the one that locked the bedroom door. I took a guess and picked one to unlock the desk drawers. The key effortlessly entered the hole, and a sliding click followed, allowing the top left drawer to pull open. A few items were scattered around inside: a seashell, some old pencils and paint brushes with chew marks, and an old spool wound with thin blue string. I couldn't help but smile to learn that my mom had chewed her pencils the way I did. Next, I opened the right drawer. There wasn't much except a few feathers my mother must have collected; they looked similar to the ones Ada wore in her hair. I picked one up and took in its silver blue color, then closed my eyes and brushed it across my face. This was the first time I'd ever felt close to her. I sat there for a moment, wishing she would walk into the room, imagining the sound of her voice yelling up the stairs and tunneling through the halls, but no one came, and no such sound broke the silence.

Pressing my fingers against the drawer, I began closing it when a sound of something rolling around caught my attention. Pulling open the drawer as far as it could go I looked in, but the drawer sat empty aside from the feathers. As I slid the drawer back and forth the banging of a rolling object continued. I reached towards the back of the drawer, touching what felt like the end, but when I pressed my fingers against it, the back panel tipped over and a small blue marble escaped, stopping amongst the feathers. I moved my hand around in the back of the drawer and felt paper. I pulled out the paper bundle of two old letters wrapped in a thin leather strap. I heard the sound of Ada's feet beginning to move up the stairs, and I quickly shoved the letters back into the drawer, shut it, and stood up, making my way towards the bed. Ada's face peeked in.

"Everything okay?" she asked, searching the room. "Need any help?"

"No, I'm fine. Thanks, though." I cleared my throat.

She left, and I decided to wait until later, when Ada was asleep, to pull the letters back out. I wanted my first insight into my mother's life to be private. I ripped off the packing tape from a box and began putting my books on the empty shelves. I took out the only photo I had of my mother and placed it on my nightstand.

I like your room, Mom.

I took out my clothes and put them away in the closet along with some hodgepodge art pieces Ada and I had collaborated on. Before I knew it, the room began to look like a lived in bedroom, and it was my favorite one so far. Next, I opened the window and allowed the ocean breeze to sweep through the room. The drawer with letters burned in the corner of my mind, and every now and then I became antsier to read them. Taking out the other key, I opened the chest for a distraction. It was filled with clothes, another pillow, and a large quilt that had the letter R stitched in the corner. These were the first of my mother's belongings that I had ever held in my own hands. I unfolded the heavy quilt and draped it over the end of my bed. I ran my fingers over the stitched R, then packed everything else back in the trunk and closed it.

"There," I said out loud. My room was done.

I lay belly-down on the bed, propping my head on my hands and staring at the desk's drawer once more. Maybe I could read just one? Swinging my legs off the bed, I got up and opened the drawer.

Arbitrarily picking out one letter, I folded it in half and tucked it in my pocket, then pulled on a sweater and walked down the hall. The minute I touched the banister, I heard Ada's voice.

"Nora?"

Damn, so close. I turned on my heels and went right back to Ada's room.

"Yes?" I said.

"Where are you going?" she asked with an eyebrow raised in my direction.

"Outside."

"Done unpacking already?" she asked.

"Yeah, for now," I said, wondering when we would move again.

"Okay, but please don't go far and come back soon." Ada's voice sounded concerned.

This was a new Ada. She never worried *before* about where I was going or what I was doing, really. She never before told me not to go far or come back soon unless she had an event or special dinner planned. There appeared to be no other living beings in close vicinity. When we'd lived in cities, I had never needed to report to Ada and could come and go when I pleased, within reasonable hours. In the kitchen I peered out the window and saw that the sun was beginning to break through the scattered clouds, causing the sea to shimmer.

Yep, this place looks dangerous alright. Right up there with the projects of Detroit.

I stepped onto the porch barefoot and took a deep breath. The air was invigorating and, for once, it felt refreshing not to inhale city fumes but rather salt, dew, and plant life. I made my way down a small winding path to the beach and stared out across the water. The sea was an endless dark blue with a few small boats scattered along the horizon. The beach was entirely made up of stones, not sand as I had imagined it would be. I bent over and picked up a black porous stone and smelled it before tossing it into the white cap of a small wave. I bent down to pick up another when I heard a sneeze. A boy wearing a red flannel shirt was hunched over about twenty yards down the beach.

"Bless you," I said, loud enough for him to hear me.

The boy froze, looked in my direction and sat up.

"Sorry, I…bless you!" I said again, even louder, this time, thinking he hadn't heard me.

We looked similar in age, and he had ashy blonde hair. As he cautiously stood up I noticed he was holding a fishing net in his hands. He looked at me with wide eyes and then began to collect his things without saying a word. He stuffed the net under his arm and grabbed a red bucket full of what I imagined were tools. He eyed me up and started to walk away.

Awkward.

Maybe Ada was right to be worried. This place was apparently full of bizarre introverts. I continued walking along the beach until I found what appeared to be the most comfortable spot to sit and pulled the letter from my pocket. The envelope was a creamy shade of ivory and addressed, in elegant cursive, to Rebekah.

Bringing the envelope close to my nose I inhaled; the scent was that of aged paper like the kind found in old library books. A wax seal was on the back with the letter S stamped into it. I flipped open the envelope, pulled out the letter, and a black feather fell out. I picked it up and unfolded the paper.

Rebekah,

Words can't explain the emotions I have at the moment for you and for our soon to arrive child. I cannot wait to meet her, and I hope she will have your eyes. I cannot wait until the day comes when I find myself holding you once more. I know things aren't what we would like, for it's impossible for us to spend every minute of every waking day together;

however, I promise that we will find our piece of heaven someday, and there we will be free to love. No more secrets, no more hiding, no more fear. I read your list of baby names and I agree on "Eleanora." Nora for short is perfect. You and our little Nora are my world, and I will do everything in my power to see you soon.

Forever,
Alexo

Dried watermarks speckled the letter. She had cried when reading this and caused the ink to run. I was confused as to why this Alexo couldn't be with her, and what he meant by hiding and fear. I thought he'd fled and left her. I thought he was a deadbeat. I read the letter again. His words were full of love, not that of a man who would leave his expecting lover. I folded up the paper and stuffed it back into its envelope and into my pocket. Perhaps Ada didn't know the whole story?

Or perhaps she's been lying.

I sat a little longer, tilting my head back and soaking up the sun, watching the fishermen on their boats, and digging my toes under the pebbles into a layer of sand. Fear seemed an odd thing for lovers to feel. Did my grandparents not like him? Was he running from the law? I scanned the shoreline and I saw the boy again in his red flannel hiding behind a tree. I sat up quickly and pulled my sweater tightly to my body, then stood up, staring back in his direction.

"Nora!" Ada's voice spilled through the air.

I looked over my shoulder and waved my arms. She was standing on the porch with her arms crossed, staring in my direction. I looked back towards the tree line searching for the red flannel boy, but he was gone.

I began making my way back down the path and towards the white home. I knew I couldn't have been gone for more than a half hour, so what was Ada's issue? She didn't budge from her waiting stance until I got within five feet of her.

"Where were you?" she asked, looking around.

"Sitting by the water," I said.

Ada put her arm around me and swept me back inside. Once we got into the kitchen I shook her arm off. The envelope fell from my pocket and landed by Ada's feet.

"Where did you get this?" Ada picked up the envelope and held it in her hands.

"I found it in my mother's room. Why were my parents hiding, Ada? Why weren't they free to love? And what are *you* hiding from *me?*"

"You shouldn't have found this." Ada ripped the envelope in half. "It's in your best interest."

"What the *hell* is your problem these days, Ada?"

"Watch your tone, little lady."

Ada snapped a finger in my face. This was not the Ada I knew. She was sounding and behaving bewilderingly unlike herself. A small finch landed on the windowsill, and Ada whipped her head in panic towards it.

"Damn it!" She went to the sink to fill up a mason jar with water and chugged it.

"Maybe moving here wasn't the best choice, Ada. You're not acting like yourself at all. I'm getting the feeling that you've been hiding things from me, and it's starting to freak me out."

The finch cocked its head, staring at Ada through the glass. I watched Ada take her fist and lightly pound the glass, shooing it away.

"It's just a finch, Ada. Nothing scary there! We've lived in way more dangerous places, and never before have you behaved like this." I pointed to the window. "There's barely anyone on this island! What the heck is stressing you out?"

She turned to me and raised her voice to a parental level. "Nora!"

I stormed out of the kitchen and up the stairs back to my room, but before slamming the door I yelled back at her.

"Is this why you brought me to this stupid island? To confine me! Cut me off completely from civilization? There are prisons for that, Ada!"

I slammed the door then heard the kitchen door slam back in response. The kitchen windows gently rattled. Clenching my pillow tightly in my fisted hands I screamed into it. *CRACK.*

I looked back at the mirror—its corner had shattered. I made my way to it kneeling down and picking up one of the shards. My eyes flickered quickly in the reflection of the sliver of glass. I dropped it. My fingers trailed over the tarnished broken corner when an unseated flake nicked my index finger. A small bead of blood fell onto the wooden floor. Did I do this? I sucked my finger, keeping my eyes fixated on the glass when suddenly they changed again; this time, the reflection of my eyes were black. *Nora.* A hissing voice, as if it was coming from the mirror, spoke my name. I pushed myself back in a panic, small pieces of glass stuck to my legs. What was happening? The voice vanished like a gasp of air and I quickly snatched the key off the nightstand and locked my door. My heart beat rapidly and my body became hot. Ada was keeping much from me. I felt hot and irritated in my own skin. My blood boiled. I paced angrily around the bedroom. My whole body felt as if it were overheating. I ripped off my sweater and threw it against the mirror. Lies, everything was feeling like a lie. I opened the desk drawer and took out the other letter. This envelope wasn't addressed to anyone. When I pulled the folded paper out I noticed the handwriting was different, not like the elegant cursive in the last, but more like mine.

> *Sister,*
>
> *I wanted to tell you that Alexo and I just welcomed Eleanora Ada Stone into the world, and she is beautiful. I can't wait for you to meet her. She has my eyes,*

34

*but more importantly, Alexo's spirit and smile. We
have nicknamed her Nora for short. I wanted you to
know that if anything should happen to me, I made
Alexo swear to hand Eleanora over to you. I want you
to raise her, take care of her, and love her. I know
you will. I want to continue on with our plan to
escape these islands, and I cannot thank you enough
for risking your life for us, for Nora. We are currently hiding in hopes that we won't be tracked. We
are planning to travel through the night and make
our way back to Alexander Point in three days' time.
From there, we'll continue on with Nora. I love you
with all my heart and am terribly excited to bring our
little Nora back to meet her aunt and cousin. I miss
you, sister, and I hope this letter makes it safely into
your hands.*

Rebekah

I was stunned.

*Alexander Point? That's the lighthouse, that's here! What cousin?
Ada never mentioned any more family. Did my father have brothers
and sisters?*

My thoughts were even more disorganized and frustrated than
before. What was the big issue? What were they escaping from, and
what did Ada do to help? Where and why were they in hiding? My
chest felt tight. I lay on the bed with the letter pressed against my
heaving body and cried, cried from frustration until tears weren't
able to form anymore. I had no control over my body and mind.
My emotions were simply devouring me. As I lay there, exhausted
from crying, the heat of the sun began to warm my room and eventually lulled me to sleep, a sleep filled with terror.

I woke up later to a crisp, cold breeze that had filled my room.
The sun had already set. Had I slept the day away? The night was

frigid and dark. It had gone from a cool sunny early afternoon to a frigid dark night. It smelled like rain was about to roll in. I got up and pulled on a flannel. Attempting to shut my window, I saw a figure standing in the yard, looking in my direction. I quickly backed away from the window. My heart began to race.

–Nora–

I heard my name being whispered *through* the window. I started to panic and felt afraid to move. My body shook with a minor adrenaline rush. It was the voice from last night. I peeked back out of the window, and the figure was still standing there.

Oh, Ada, I thought, *please walk into my room right now, please. I'm so sorry we fought.*

I wanted to yell her name but couldn't find my voice, my throat dry and webbed with fear.

–Nora–

It was a female voice. Soft yet insistent. Sliding down with my back against the wall, I began to crawl towards the door.

–Nora, come outside–

The voice bounced around in my room, and I rolled over, looking in every direction for the girl I was sure must have somehow entered my room. The voice was musical and inviting, and at the same time, it made me feel like I wanted to obey, ought to obey, *needed* to obey. I lay there on the floor, pressing my knees to my chest and willing whatever it was to go away.

–Nora, I can tell you everything you want to know–

I couldn't escape her voice no matter how hard I pressed my hands over my ears.

–I can tell you what those letters mean. I can show you what you really are–

I panicked. I was being watched. The paranoia that I'd been feeling since I stepped foot on this island was real. I began crawling over to the window, listening, interested. She had something I wanted, answers. But what did the voice mean by *show you what you really are?*

The breeze pushed the letter off of my bed, and it slid across the floor towards my feet. Picking it up, I looked at my mother's handwriting. Did this stranger really have the answers to my questions? The curiosity was beginning to burn somewhere inside me. Somewhere between the layers of fear and wonder emerged a bit of bravery or stupidity, and I decided to go see the stranger.

Grabbing a jacket and slipping on some shoes, I tucked the letter under my pillow and took the skeleton key off of the nightstand. For the first time since I had slammed the door on Ada, I unlocked it and pulled it open. The hallway was dark and soundless. I stood still, listening for Ada, but heard nothing. Her door, next to mine, was closed, and I slowly turned the handle, cracking it open to peek inside, but her bed was empty. I pushed the door open further and looked around the room. The clock sitting on her nightstand read 9:45. Why hadn't she woken me up for dinner? My stomach growled. Where was she?

I backed out of the room, closed the door, and turned around, only to come face to face with Ada. My back slammed against her door.

My heart might have suffered a small attack at that very moment. I hadn't heard her come up the stairs. She stood there wrapped in a robe, her legs covered in goose bumps, and her hair wet and knotted on the top of her head. I hadn't heard the shower or any noise coming from the bathroom.

"Where are you going, Nora?" Ada asked, looking down at my shoes, keeping the space between us tight.

"I uh, I couldn't sleep, so I thought I'd go for a walk," I said, unnerved at Ada's appearance.

There was something about the way she was watching me that started making me feel uneasy. She was hiding something, and I could see it in her eyes.

"Ada, just now outside I—"

"I'm sorry about earlier," Ada said in a serious tone taking a step back, giving me space to breathe.

She opened her hand and a black porous stone lay in her palm, identical to the one I had held earlier in the day. She handed it to me.

"Thought you might like this."

I took it from her and caught a hint of salt in the air. Had she been in the ocean?

"Like it?"

"Um-yes, thanks." I squeezed the stone in my hand.

"I think we should get to bed." Ada cleared her throat. "It's getting late, and I'm pretty tired."

I sensed it was an instruction, not a suggestion.

I slid out of the confining space between her and the door and she followed me into my room. The hairs on my neck stood on end.

"What happened here?" Ada stopped to examine the mirror.

"I don't know. Well, I think," I stopped.

"You think what?" Ada raised her look to me.

"I think I did it, but I'm not sure."

"How do you think you did it, but you're not sure?" Ada crossed her arms.

"I screamed and it cracked."

"That's absurd Nora. Something must have hit it."

I was beginning to feel insane, so I dropped it. I was being lied to. "And," I continued, "and I saw someone in the backyard. A woman calling my name."

"What?" Ada said, this time, raising her eyebrows as if questioning my sanity. I raised mine back to her, questioning her legitimacy. I had expected Ada to freak out, but her voice was nonchalant as if the idea of me seeing a stranger wasn't alarming.

"I'm sure you didn't see anyone," she dismissed the idea.

"This mirror, however, was your great-grandmother's Nora." She changed the subject back to the damn mirror.

"I know what I saw. My eyes changed color again Ada, the mirror cracked when I screamed and I saw someone in the backyard!" My voice spat with agitation.

Ada walked over to the window and pushed aside the curtains. "See," she spoke as if slightly annoyed, pointing out the window. "No one. I think someone needs a little shut-eye."

"No, there was someone standing there. I heard her."

I charged over to the window but there wasn't anyone standing out there. My lips parted as I leaned out the window, aggressively scanning the tree line and acreage.

"What do you mean you heard *her*?" Ada's attention was caught.

"Yes, she was saying my name, calling me to her." I leaned further out of the window searching. I felt Ada's hand on the small of my back, I jerked and banged my head against the sash.

"Jeez!" I rubbed the tender spot on the back of my head.

"You're pretty jumpy, Nora. You didn't see anyone. Let's get ready for bed, okay?" Ada's voice was compelling—the way the stranger's voice had been. "You didn't see anyone, my dear," her voice soft and tranquil.

A wave of exhaustion washed over me. Maybe she was right. Maybe I do need sleep. I obeyed, slipped off my shoes, and crawled into bed. Ada leaned in and kissed my forehead. She made her way out of the room and closed the door.

"Sleep, child." Ada whispered from the door.

Through the fog of exhaustion hazy thoughts still lingered. Where had the stranger in the yard gone? Was I the one who shattered the mirror? My eyes, they were black. The voice returned to my dreams.

−Nora, Nora, Nora, I can show you what you are. −

4

"Good morning." Ada's soft voice woke me up.

I stretched out and opened my eyes, taking in the stream of morning light flowing into my room.

"What time is it?"

Ada was folding the sweater I had thrown at the wall yesterday in anger. The broken glass had been cleaned up, but the crack in the mirror remained.

"Seven," she said.

"What?" I asked dazed, my head still feeling foggy with distant dreams.

"It's seven o'clock Nora. I started some tea and made breakfast. Join me?"

I yawned and stretched again before kicking off the sheets. Ada disappeared into the hall, and I stood up, bending side to side and cracking my knuckles. I peeked out the window and saw that the bluebird sky was clear, not a single cloud lingered there, and the ocean reflected the welcoming color. I pinned up my hair and made my way to the kitchen.

A sweet aroma wafted through the air. Ada had made steaming hot oatmeal drizzled with honey and cinnamon. I grabbed a bowl from the shelf and helped myself while scanning the kitchen and living room for her.

"Ada?"

"Out here." Her voice traveled in from the front porch. "Join me. Grab a sweater from the hooks. It's chilly but refreshing."

I grabbed a frumpy old sweater and flannel and layered up. I grabbed my bowl of oatmeal and a cup of tea then made my way outside.

"Breakfast with a view." Ada gazed out towards the ocean. "Pretty amazing."

"Indeed." I took a sip of tea which warmed my insides.

Ada smiled.

"I read another letter." I stared at her holding the warm mug between my chilled hands.

Ada sat silently almost appearing dumbfounded for a moment.

"Why would my mother have sworn my father to hand me over to you if something were to happen to her? Why couldn't I stay with my father?"

"Nora," Ada spoke. "I don't know the answer to that question." Then she averted her eyes from my gaze.

"Yes you do, Ada! You have all the answers. I can see it. I can see you lying to me, hiding things from me. What the hell is going on? Why have you brought me back to this island?"

"I understand how I may seem. You are right, you know. I *am* keeping certain things to myself for the moment, and you have every right to demand answers from me, but Nora, can you give me four days? Four days for me to settle and do what I need to do, then we will sit right here and I will answer your questions. Please."

She said this with an almost desperate tone in her voice.

I gripped my mug and ground my teeth at her response.

"For what it's worth, Ada, I've moved from city to city, have been taken out of schools and shuffled around this country without ever getting a decent explanation and I thought, well I *thought* it was just a fluke in your wiring. But you know what? All those moves, all those dumb explanations, are starting to feel like lies. Lies upon lies.

Four days Ada, that's all I am giving you. And then I want answers, truthful answers, or I'm getting the hell out of here."

I couldn't even look at her. I was in disbelief with her, with myself, with everything.

"Thank you," Ada whispered, closing her eyes for a moment. "So, any plans today?" She sipped on her tea. Her mood swung drastically from pleading with desperation to nonchalant.

I looked at her, my brows lifted.

"Oh yeah, loads of them. There seems to be so much to do here that I don't even know where to begin. Not to mention the unlimited freedom I seem to get here."

Ada looked distracted and a little uncomfortable, unwilling even to rise to the bait.

"I'm going to go visit someone for most of the day," Ada said into her mug.

"Oh yeah?" I said. "Who?"

"An old friend. I'm not even sure if she still lives here, but it's worth a try." Ada shrugged her shoulders. "So, I was curious if you wouldn't mind spending most of the day here alone."

"So I'm not invited then. Is she a part of the secrets too, Ada?"

I looked at Ada but couldn't read her expression. I had never not been invited along anywhere Ada had gone before.

"Err, not this time. It's just one of a few things I need to do before we have our conversation in four days." She smiled.

"You know what?" I took a sip of my tea. "I definitely don't mind spending the day alone and away from this new you. No offense, but I liked the old Ada better. I felt I could trust her."

Ada winced at that and turned away slightly. I could see her cheeks turn a subtle pink.

"The only condition is that I *really* need you to stay at home, or near the house. Can I ask that of you?"

I stood up and slammed my mug on the wooden banister. Tea jumped from the mug and splattered on the painted white wood.

"Please Nora. Please just do as I ask for the next four days, please. I know I am asking a lot with zero explanation, I *know*, but please, Nora." She looked shockingly nervous.

Most of that morning I spent exploring the house, opening doors I'd yet to open, finding all the nooks and crannies. The house had five bedrooms, two bathrooms, and about a hundred perfect places for hide-and-seek, if I were still into that sort of thing. I reorganized the living room, moved coffee tables, chairs, and couches around until the *feng shui* felt just right. I lounged on the couch, staring mindlessly towards the sea, when someone strolling by the water caught my attention. Perking my head up with curiosity, I made my way to the porch. It was the boy I had seen yesterday, only this time he didn't have on a red flannel, but a green one. I put my mug down on the porch banister and began making my way down the sandy path to the pebbly beach. The boy caught sight of me and picked up his pace.

"Hey!" I said, trying to catch his attention, but he ignored me. "Hey you!"

He looked over his shoulder and began to walk even faster.

What is this guy's problem?

"Stop! Do you live here?" I yelled, beginning to jog and suddenly feeling desperate for human interaction. He too began running. I ran down the beach after him. "Wait!"

He wouldn't stop.

I was running as quickly as I could when my foot caught an edge of driftwood and I went down hard with a loud cry and scraped both knees.

Cursing, I rolled over, wiping sand and blood from my legs. Further down the beach the boy had stopped and turned around to look at me. I stood up and began hobbling back towards the house, feeling like an idiot for chasing him. *What has gotten into you, Nora?*

That's when he finally spoke.

"Are you okay?" he said.

I looked back over my shoulder then turned back the way I had come.

What a jerk.

I heard his footsteps on the pebbles as he approached me.

"Hey look, I'm sorry. It's just I thought…well, never mind. I'm Eben."

"Gosh, nice to meet you, Eben," I said and continued walking towards the house. I was both annoyed with him and embarrassed.

"I *do* live here, to answer your question," he said, perhaps hoping it would slow me down. "A few properties that way actually." He pointed behind us. "Not too far."

The blood from my right knee trickled down and wrapped around my heel. I took the sleeve of my sweater and tried dabbing it.

"Here, let me help," Eben said, catching up to me. He placed his hand on my shoulder. I saw a crib, a mobile made of sticks, hands disappearing over the railing, a crow with black eyes perched outside of the window, a door slam.

I stopped.

"Hey, you alright? Blood make you queasy?" He smiled, "Come on," and led me to the water. "Salt. It's the best thing for cuts, at least that's what I'm told. It cleans it right up!"

He crouched down, cupped his hands, filling them, and then began rinsing my knees while occasionally glancing up towards me. I scowled as salty water burned my cuts.

I'd never experienced salt water in a wound before, but Eben just smiled at me, his eyes the color sage just like Ada's.

"There. See?" Eben smiled.

I looked down, and my cuts were now puffy and white, no longer oozing blood. I continued watching. The gashes appeared to already be sealing.

"Guess salt water does do the trick, huh?" I said.

"Nice to meet you," Eben said, pausing while reaching out his hand. His wrist and hand had scars, and the skin looked callused and rough.

"I'm Nora," I said reluctantly shaking his hand, thinking of the recent vision. "And well, thanks."

"So you just moved here then, huh?" Eben said, looking towards the white house.

"Yeah, my aunt used to live here."

Eben wrinkled his brow curiously.

"Really?" Eben said. "Are you sure?"

"Well, that's what I'm told," I said, annoyed. "Why?"

"Well, it's just that this home has been vacant for at least a hundred years. It's a historical site really, for tourists. There aren't any tours inside or anything, but they pass by on the daily ferry during the summer season. It's part of the island's attraction," Eben smiled. "In a few months you'll be sick of seeing the little ferry tugging along these parts with touring, deer-eyed paparazzi who for some reason find this place interesting. But then again it brings life to this place and gives us jobs, aside from fishing."

"And lobstering," I said.

"Ah, I see you've done your research."

"Is that what you do?" I asked. "Fish?"

"My father is a fisherman, runs his own boat, and I do too, a little, but I specialize in making nets and braiding rope for the crew and selling my nets to other fishermen. Crafty like that." Eben held out his hands and flexed them open, showing me his callouses.

"And your mom? Is she a braider or a fisherman?" I asked.

"Don't know, never met her. She left after I was a babe. I'd like to think maybe she's out there running another fishing boat." Eben looked out over the horizon.

"Oh, I'm-"

"Nah, no apology needed, happened seventeen years ago. I'm pretty over it."

"Oh, we're the same age," I said.

"Yeah? You're seventeen too, huh?" He stuffed his hands into his pockets awkwardly.

"Yeah, but I'll be eighteen June fourteenth."

"Nice, I'll be eighteen in two days. Amazing how you moved here just in time to celebrate it with me!" He smiled. "It's nice when your birthday falls during spring break, even though we don't get those warm temps."

"Right, spring break." I had forgotten we had moved here right before it started. I wondered what kind of rumors would spread in my former high school about my sudden disappearance.

"So you'll probably be going to our high school, huh?"

I swallowed hard, my stomach knotted with the thought of entering yet another school system.

"Don't sweat it! I'll show you the ropes, so to speak."

There was something sincere and genuine about Eben that made me feel a little flushed.

"What school do you go to?" I asked.

"Stonington. It's on Deer Isle. Small class, but fun. You can meet some of the kids if you come to my birthday celebration! So you're coming right?"

"Um, I don't know." My cheeks felt warm. "I'm not really a party kind of person."

"Oh no, it's not like a rager or anything, we're Plymouth kids, girlie! Just a bonfire on the beach down that-a-way at sundown." He pointed towards the direction I had chased him in earlier. "So, you wanna come?"

"Sure, I guess."

Eben's face lit up. "Great! Well, listen I gotta get back to work before Pops gets home. I'm workin' on a new kind of braid."

"Oh, how exciting!" I said with a hint of sarcasm in my voice. Eben smiled and began walking away. "See you in two days, Nora. Nice meetin' ya, and welcome to the island."

I waved. "Oh Eben, wait!"

He spun around, listening.

"What you said earlier, about my house being vacant for over a hundred years, are you sure?"

"Well, I'm no older than you, but there are a lot of rumors about the Alexander Point home and that ol' lighthouse, lots of legends. But who knows, people get so bored here sometimes, I think they make stuff up to entertain themselves." He shot me a winning smile.

"Right. Okay, well, see ya."

When I turned back towards the lighthouse, goosebumps crawled up my arms.

I walked through the boathouse all the way to the end of the long white dock and sat down. The sun felt warm, and I peeked over my shoulder to make sure I was alone before pulling off my sweater and unbuttoning my flannel. I lay down on the wooden planks, taking in the remainder of the late afternoon sun. My mother's letters and Eben's words danced in my mind. Nothing made sense. The home couldn't have been vacant for over a hundred years. Maybe Ada and her family weren't very neighborly and kept to themselves. Ada and my mom had lived here growing up, right? Or perhaps Ada was lying and hiding something about this too. However, even Eric claimed to remember the days watching the two grow up. Eben must have been mistaken. He was probably right about one thing though, people on this island were probably so bored out of their minds that they had nothing better to do than make up stories. God knows I would. The warm sun sank into my pale skin.

"Nora?" I heard Ada's voice break between the meditative ocean sounds.

I propped myself up on my elbows and looked back. Ada was standing at the opposite end of the dock with a brown paper bag in her arms.

"Are you insane? It's like forty-five degrees out! Button up before you get sick."

"Forty-five degrees? Are you sure? Feels a heck of a lot warmer to me." I sat up and buttoned my flannel.

Ada threw me a curious look. The temperature was one thing Ada and I could never agree on. I didn't feel temperature the way Ada did, or anyone else for that matter. All our lives, when she was freezing, I was more than comfortable. Ada had once told me that my body temperature was abnormally warmer when the school nurse called her in, reporting a 110-degree fever, and I felt perfectly fine. I was removed from that school only a few short days later. Ada claimed that she wouldn't have me attending a school where the nurses couldn't handle a slight fever.

"You're lucky I kept my bra on, Ada. I entertained the idea of going topless since this island seems pretty uninhabited. Should have just got downright naked, maybe even a taken a dip." Ada smiled and turned.

"I wouldn't judge," she said. "Now come help me. I picked up some groceries for dinner."

I stood up and followed her back to the house.

"Where'd you get the groceries?" I asked.

"The mainland. My friend took me on her boat, so I figured I should take advantage and pick a few items up for the house and dinner."

"Her? Does your friend have a name? Does she live on the island? Was it good to see her again?" I started questioning, taking a pack of chicken and putting it in the freezer.

"Put that in the fridge, I was planning on making it for dinner tomorrow night, and yes it was nice to see her. Of course, she has a name. It's Edel, and yes she lives on the island. It's been too many years." Ada said, smiling to herself.

"Will I get to meet Edel? Or, do I have to wait three days?"

"Soon. What'd you do today, besides tan in your undergarments?"

"I rearranged the living room like five times, explored the house, and met someone today." I quickly stated.

Ada's eyes widened in my direction. "Oh did you?"

"I don't know why you stress so much, he seemed like a perfectly normal person, sort of."

I thought of Eben running.

"He?"

"Yes he, on the beach. His name is Eben, he's my age and lives a few properties down, at least that's what he said. I didn't leave our beach area, so take a breath, Ada." I said trying to calm her stressed expression but the expression didn't fade.

Silence cut the air between us and for a moment I watched her, half expecting her to freak out, but she didn't.

"Nolan's son," she said.

"Oh, so you know him?"

"I knew his father, a fisherman here on the island." There was a *slight* change of tone in her voice as if she'd begun to relive a painful memory.

"Well it's his birthday in two days, and he invited me to a bonfire on the beach. It's really not that far away. Can I go?" I asked, looking at Ada as I put the eggs one by one into a wired cage shaped like a hen. She stayed silent a while and stared out the window.

"Nora, I don't think it's—"

"Oh please, Ada! I've never been invited to a party or had the chance to make friends. Come on, he's really nice. I bet you'd like him."

Ada inhaled deeply and smiled. "Okay sure, but I'll walk you at least half way."

"Awesome. Thanks!" I dropped an egg on the stone floor. The shell shattered and the yellow yolk and clear egg whites tunneled between the cracks.

Ada handed me a wet rag. "Pull yourself together," she said. "It's just a bonfire."

I smiled.

Over the next two days I pressed Ada with questions, but she continued reminding me that I had three—then two—days left until all my questions were answered. I asked about my father, my mother, the obvious peril the letter revealed them to be in, and I even asked about the house. Ada avoided and danced around the questioning or continued disappearing off to visit her mystery friend, Edel. The sun began to set, and I knew I'd be off to Eben's bonfire soon. Ada and I sat quietly at the dinner table, and I pushed around my rice, making shapes as I chewed chicken.

"You still want to go?" Ada asked, breaking the silence.

"Yes, still need to walk me?"

"Yes."

"Ada, Eben mentioned something odd the other day."

"And what's that?" Ada picked up her knife and cut into her chicken breast.

"He mentioned how this house had been vacant for over a hundred years before we moved in, but then he said that there are many rumors and stories attached to this property and island."

Ada chewed her chicken, attentively listening to me.

"Well, I just don't understand, if you grew up here, how it could have been vacant for so long. You and mom *did* grow up here, right?"

"People on this island are so bored that they love to make up stories and nonsense for entertainment," Ada said.

I chuckled.

"What's so funny?"

"Eben said the same thing."

Ada sweetly smiled as if that pleased her.

"See? And yes, Rebekah and I grew up here. We just never really mingled with many people on this island before, kind of kept to ourselves, but this home *has* been vacant for coming up to eighteen years. No more than that, though."

"Right," I said turning my eyes to the setting sun over the water.

"Anyway, I'm going to go grab a jacket and then we can head to the bonfire. Thanks for dinner."

I placed my plate in the sink and ran upstairs, grabbed a fleece-lined jacket and stopped to look in the old mirror. My eyes suddenly flickered again to the bright blue I had seen the first night we came here and then they quickly changed back.

What the...

I stared at myself, blinking my eyes over and over again until Ada's head popped into the room.

"Ready? What are you doing?"

"I keep seeing my eyes change color when I look into the mirrors of this house!"

"Are you sure you feel well enough to go to this bonfire?"

"I'm not making it up!" I pinched my lips in frustration.

"Good, then let's head out before I change my mind," she said, zipping up her cargo coat. I tied my hair back and followed her down and out of the house.

The evening air was nippy, and a light breeze blew off the water. I pushed my hands into my fleece-lined pockets and hugged my shoulders into my body.

"Chilly tonight," Ada said.

"Yeah, a bit."

We walked silently down the shore listening to the water kiss the beach when a warm amber glow began to appear in the distance and the sounds of laughter and voices were being carried by the wind. Ada and I walked towards a fire encircled by maybe six or seven people. I stopped for a moment before we took another step. My stomach twisted with nerves.

"Something wrong?" Ada looked at me. "Shall I leave you to walk from here? Don't want them seeing your aunt walking you to the party?" She smiled.

"I don't care if people see you, I just got nervous is all. I've never gone to a party or gathering before." I felt the blanket of introverted feelings begin to tighten around me. I really wouldn't have minded just turning around and going home and curling up in my bed with a good book and hot tea. My heart began to thump and my eyes locked on the fire.

"You'll be fine, Nora. You know, I think this may even be good for you."

"I hope so."

"Meet you here in a few hours?"

I looked at Ada and nodded.

"Nora?" Eben's voice broke into my ears.

I looked to Ada for one last look of reassurance, but she was gone. I turned and watched her silhouette disappear into the darkness.

"Hey!" Eben's hand tapped my shoulder. "Come on, fiesta's this-a-way." He walked me towards the fire. "You came alone?" Eben said looking behind us.

"No, my aunt walked me half way," I said, looking back over my shoulder scanning for Ada once more.

"Nice."

"Yo Eben, catch!"

I placed my forearm over my face as an object hurled right in my direction. Then I heard Eben grab it out of the air.

"Hey man, be careful!"

The other boy ran over to us. He had blonde hair and light blue eyes, and his shoulders were broad like Eben's.

"Nora, this is Joe. He works on my pop's fishing boats scrubbing the decks. Joe, this is Nora. She just moved here."

"Attractive introduction, you really know how to flatter a guy," Joe said. He stretched his hand out to shake mine. His hand was just as large and calloused as Eben's and I shook it, trying to match the firm grip.

"Nice," Joe said. "I like a girl who can match a handshake instead of givin' me the ol' dead fish." I raised my eyebrows as Joe made a mocking girlie handshake in the air.

"Okay, Joe that's enough," Eben said, pushing him aside.

Five other friends hung around the fire: two girls and three boys, all focusing their attention on the *new girl* being brought into their tight little circle. Eben offered me the can in his hand.

"It's okay if you don't drink. Joe's older brother hooks us up sometimes."

I'd never drank beer before and couldn't see how one beer would do much anyway. I took the can.

"Just one," I said.

Eben smiled. His sage eyes were lined with rings of fire.

"Okay cool, so guys, this is Nora, she just moved here from…" He turned to me. "*Where'd* you move from?"

"Washington DC."

"Seriously?" Eben choked on his beer. "This is a change of scenery for you then for sure, huh?"

I nodded as he continued, "Okay, okay, guys this is Nora. She moved from Washington DC and lives in the old Alexander Point house."

"Really?" asked one of the other boys.

"Really," I said and took a sip of beer.

"Right, so Nora, this is Mark, Kyle, Lana, Brian, and Wren."

They all shot me smiles, some head nods, and a couple of waves, except for Lana, who studied me without any reaction.

"It's about time! Eben here hasn't shut up about meetin' ya!" Brian laughed, and I could sense Eben's chest tighten.

"Welcome to the island," Mark said, holding his can of beer up, "the island where dreams come true!", he sang.

"Thank you?" I questioned, raising my beer in response, and taking a sip. The beer tasted bitter washing over my tongue.

Eben grabbed a beer from a cooler and was coming back towards me when Kyle walked over and cut him off.

"So you live in that creepy house, huh? No one's lived there for, well, as long as I've been alive. What's it like, any paranormal activity sightings yet?"

"Um, no?" I said, looking over his shoulder at Eben who was engaged in a conversation with Lana.

"Oh Kyle, leave her alone!" Wren said and walked over holding her hand out to me. "Wren," she said, smiling. "Like the bird."

Wren, like Joe, had bleach-blonde hair, but hers was long— almost down to her waist—and she wore a knitted purple hat with a pom-pom on top.

"Nora," I said.

"Welcome, cool to have another person our age on the island. Not many of us here. Actually," she said looking around at the group, "this is it."

"Well thanks," I said. "Yeah, I read that online. Slim population." I took another sip of my beer.

"Well, we work with what we got. Winters can be bleak. Just cold, wet, dark, and honestly it turns into a ghost town. Only the hardy-stubborn fisherman and their forced families stay, like mine." Wren smiled. "So if you're not a fisherman, I know I may sound like I'm jumping to conclusions, but as a Washington DC transplant, why move here?" Wren asked. "No offense but most people try to leave the island, not come here."

"My mother and aunt grew up here, and *she* wanted to come back." I kept it short and sweet because I still didn't know the real story myself.

"Your mom?" Wren asked.

"No, my aunt. My mom died when I was an infant."

"Sorry to hear that, but now I see the connection between you and Eben!" Wren twirled her finger in the air.

"I don't think there is a connection. He's just being nice is all."

"Yeah, right! Eben here is a nice guy but he also just does *not* talk to girls! Poor Lana over there has been trying to get him to notice her since the fifth grade. No success. But I admire her effort." Wren pressed her beer to her lips and took a sip. "And Mark has been trying to date Lana for forever it seems, but she pays him no attention because of Eben, and Brian has had a 'secret' crush on me for forever, but everyone knows about it, including me, so really it's not a secret. Oh, and Joe is Eben's best friend and my ex-ish."

"Huh." I barely knew the girl and she voluntarily gave me the Spark Notes on the group's gossip.

"So no boyfriend then?" I asked trying to contribute to this conversation.

"Nah! *So* over this scene." She waved her hand towards the group again. "I'm waiting until I'm outta here to meet someone. But I can vouch that Eben is a gem, so be good to him." She winked in my direction. "Plus, I'd love to see Lana get shut down." She made an explosion sound and gesture with her hand as if a firework or bomb went off.

I felt uncomfortable. I crossed my arms and continued sipping my beer. Joe stumbled over and linked his arms around Wren's waist.

"Baby, give me a kiss for old time's sake."

"Old time's sake? We broke up like yesterday!"

Wren rolled her eyes and shoved him off. He laughed and grabbed her hand, leading her away. She looked back at me.

"Men," she said, shaking her head. "So dumb! Might as well get some entertainment while I'm stuck on this godforsaken island!"

My jaw parted, and I felt incredibly innocent and naïve compared to Wren. Lana popped her hip in apparent annoyance as Eben ended their conversation and made his way over to me.

"So Wren got a hold of you already, huh? I'm sure she spilled the circle's beans to ya. She's always desperate for new company." He smiled.

"So they…" I pointed in Wren and Joe's direction, as the two were now making out and giggling near the beer cooler. "Are they a couple still, or?"

"Who knows! Those two have a strange relationship. One minute they fight like cats and dogs then they're dreamy lovebirds the next, but we don't have much to work with on these islands. So we tend to keep the same relationships for years, even if they aren't the healthiest. Everything here is about familiarity, and familiarity is what's most comfortable, ya know?"

"Right." It was all I could say because, no, technically I could not relate at all; the only thing familiar in my life was Ada.

"About earlier," Eben continued as he clenched his beer. "You know, the whole running away from you thing. I feel pretty stupid, I just thought—"

"You just thought *what*? That I was a ghost or something?" I asked with a big smile.

"Maybe." Eben took a huge gulp of his beer.

"Seriously? A ghost? Like Casper?" I started laughing.

"I know it sounds lame. It's just, I didn't know anyone had moved into the Alexander Point house, and well, people on this island are superstitious and have tales about your place, you know?"

"No, I *don't* know, actually. Like what kind of tales? Enlighten me." I placed a hand on one hip and raised an eyebrow to him, mimicking the eyebrow Ada always flashed me.

"Well, there's a legend that these beautiful women lived in that house—"

"And you *ran* because of beautiful women? Come on Eben!"

"Let me finish, woman," Eben smiled and wrapped his arm around my waist, pulling me close to him.

I tensed.

"Oh, sorry." He smiled and released his grip.

"It's okay, go on! I'm *dying* to hear about these beautiful women." I smiled to mask my nerves.

"The legend of the Sereni women."

"Stop right there!" Brian said loudly overhearing our conversation. "Washington DC here doesn't know about the legend?" My cheeks burned with slight embarrassment. "Oh come on, tell us all birthday boy! We all love a good legend."

"Fine!" Eben shoved Brian off him and Eben cleared his throat.

"The legend of the Sereni women." Everyone settled, sitting on chunks of driftwood. I sat beside Eben noting Lana's possessive gaze.

"They say these islands were first inhabited hundreds and hundreds of years ago by these so-called Sereni women. They were women of extreme beauty, kind of like the sirens of Greek mythology. They killed men—any man to get involved with a Sereni woman somehow, someway, would come to a fatal end."

"Have any last wishes, Eben?" Wren spoke in the swankiest voice I've ever heard.

Everyone's composure lasted momentarily before they broke into laughter. Eben wrapped his hand around me and pulled me in closer.

"This gets pretty scary Nora, just want to make sure you feel safe," Eben smiled and I playfully shoved him with my shoulder.

His eyes were splashed with speckles.

I felt my body tense again. He smelled of smoky earth and salty sea.

"Seriously." He loosened his grip and continued on. "Since the mid-1800s there have been many recorded mysterious deaths on this island alone including fourteen shipwrecks and fishing boat wrecks total. Men have gone missing never being seen again, captains and crews, distracted by some kind of force pulling them off course, or so they claimed. Bodies have been washed up on these very shores or discovered in the forest with their flesh ripped open as if huge beasts had mauled them. There was even a rumor that these women were immortal, with eyes the colors of vibrant precious stones."

I froze thinking about my reflection in the mirror. Then Eben gazed into my eyes.

"Your eyes," he whispered tilting my chin up and I held my breath, "look normal to me." He smiled and continued.

"These women, the Sereni, could never die unless killed, and some are said to have lived hundreds of years, maybe even thousands. Being with one was how a man would find euphoria, but once seen by these goddess-like creatures, a man would become her prey, lost to her forever."

"Sounds good to me," Joe smirked and Wren pushed him off the log into the sand mouthing the word *men* to me.

"There have been recorded sightings here on Stone Isle and on others. The sightings have been more recent. The older generation here believes that something is changing. That the tides are shifting so to speak. Hikers and tourists have recently reported strange ghostly women in the forest near *your* home."

Everyone's eyes turned to me.

"Have you seen anything?" Wren asked, her eyes wide.

I sat still thinking about the strange woman lurking on the outskirts of our acreage, calling my name.

"No," I whispered, not wanting to be made a spectacle of.

"Boring," Lana finally spoke.

"During the night sometimes, the lights inside the lighthouse or your house would be on with ghostly shadows drifting around. Reported cries and screams have been heard coming from your property. They say there is a curse about a child born under the blood of a blue moon or something. Sacrifices and blood spilled on your shore." Eben was speaking directly to me now.

"Stop!" Wren squealed, "No more! I can't take it. I won't be able to sleep tonight and poor Nora has to return to that house you are ranting about with blood and shadows and ghostly women."

"Oh come on baby," Joe swooned her, "it's just a legend!"

Suddenly two hands grabbed my shoulders and I screamed turning and punching whoever it was right in the face.

Brian laid there with blood trickling from his nose. I shook off the paranoia.

"Serves you right— " Wren laughed, "—for scaring her!"

"Great reflexes girlie," Brian smiled as he wiped his nose with his sleeve.

"I'm sorry." I tried to help him up until I caught a hint of the metallic blood and stepped back.

Eben's hands wrapped around my waist. Everyone laughed. The hairs on my arms rose. I wanted to be pulled in closer to him. Something unnerving settled in the air. In no time, everyone was back mingling and I could hear the sizzling cracks as cans of beer were opened.

"It's just a story," Eben whispered to me. "But, silly as it may be, that's why I ran from you. When I saw you, you were the most beautiful girl I'd ever seen walk this island, and then I remembered the legend, and I thought I was seeing a siren. I have never seen anyone roaming the Alexander Point beaches before, so I ran."

Eben stopped and looked at me.

"You have *got* to be kidding me," I spoke, flustered thinking there may be some truth to all this.

"I know, stupid story huh?"

Eben laughed nervously. Then he casually wrapped his arm back around me. I'd never had a guy hold me before. I felt oddly protected within his arms. I pressed my nose against his flannel and inhaled the scent of smoky earth and cedar. My heart mellowed, I could feel his hand slide from my hip to my lower back, pulling me in. I buried my face into his jacket when his calloused hand gently touched my chin, leveling it with his. He wanted to kiss me, and to my surprise, I was going to let him.

My breath felt tight as he closed in when suddenly the flames of the fire roared and began burning out of control, spitting in all directions. Everyone screamed and began to flee. The flames lapped the air and pops and bangs came from the wood. Leaves from a nearby tree shriveled in the heat, and Eben covered my face quickly with his flannel and we both ducked as a piece of burning wood flew over our heads. His hands grabbed my cheeks, his forehead pressed against mine.

"You okay?" Suddenly I fell into a string of images; of cloaked figures, a baby's birth, blood, hands grasping, strange symbols carved into flesh, the mobile of wood and a crow watching, swaying.

"Nora," Eben's hands shook me bringing me back to that moment, "did you get hit?"

"Nora!" Ada's voice bellowed into the chaos, and I looked over Eben's shoulder to see her running in our direction.

"Are you okay?" she asked, pulling us both up. As soon as I saw her face the flames died.

Eben looked from Ada to me confused, and I totally forgot I had told her to meet me in a few hours.

"I've got to go." I looked at Eben and wiggled myself from his arm. "Look, thanks for inviting me. Oh, and uh, happy birthday."

Ada backed away, staying a few feet in the distance as she watched Eben intensely. She seemed unable to take her eyes off him and Eben stared back, fixated.

"Let's go, Ada," I said yanking her arm. "Why are you *staring* at him like that?"

Ada shook her head and began walking. "Huh? Oh, nothing."

"Are you okay," she looked at my head.

There was a small cut from the flying wood.

"I'm fine."

"Did you…" Ada leaned over and sniffed. "Were you drinking?" She gave me a crooked smile.

"I had *one* beer. I know, I'm grounded," I said, jumping to conclusions, but Ada laughed.

"Whatever, I'm just glad you had fun." Ada wrapped her arm around me and looked back at Eben one last time. He hadn't moved. He watched us until we disappeared into the darkness.

Lying in bed I thought of how the flames had lashed out the moment Eben pulled me in for a kiss, the string of thoughts that flooded my mind, sirens and their eye color, voices and sacrifices, and how Ada appeared at the very moment the flames died down. I shook my head and hit the pillow, beginning to feel the paranoia set in once more.

Get those stupid ideas out of your mind, Nora. There are no such things as ghosts—or sirens.

5

I was startled awake. It was morning. My dreams vanished into oblivion.

"Hey, Nora!"

I sat up quickly, feeling sweaty and disoriented.

"Norrrraaa..." A male voice from outside my window was playfully dragging out my name. There was nothing ghostly or sinister about *this* voice.

I got of bed and opened the window. I blinded myself with the sunshine and threw my arm up over my eyes. There, mid-way down the path to the beach, were Eben, Wren, and Joe.

"Want to come sailing with us?" Eben yelled.

"Morning Sleeping Beauty!" Wren yelled, still clinging on to Joe as she wiggled her fingers in my direction. "Won't you come with us? Please!"

I yawned and nodded.

"I'll be down in a moment." I banged my head on the window sash.

God! Seriously, again?

Rubbing the back of my head, I shut the window. I pulled on some jeans and a thermal shirt, slipped into a pair of clogs and stuffed a sweater in my bag. I felt excited to see Eben again. I quickly combed my hair, ran to the bathroom, brushed my teeth, took one last look in the mirror, and ran downstairs where I almost plowed into Ada.

"Holy moly, girl!" she exclaimed as she spilled some coffee onto the floor.

"Sheesh, I'm sorry, Ada." I grabbed a flour sack towel, quickly dabbing the floor.

"I would offer you a cup, but I don't think you need it at the speed you're moving this morning."

"Coffee? You never drink coffee." I grabbed a muffin off the counter and ripped it in half, leaving the rest for Ada.

"I know, but I found my father's old percolator in the cabinet, and so I borrowed some coffee from Edel."

I stopped chewing, half expecting Ada to have a meltdown or something.

"Oh, it's fine. Kind of nice actually, for a moment it felt like he was back in the kitchen brewing his morning cup again. Memories are a bittersweet thing."

Her cheeks became slightly pink and her voice sounded stuffy for a moment as she looked up.

"Anyway, your new friends have been there for almost a half hour trying to wake you up. I invited them in, but they seemed kind of timid."

"Well, Eben told me a little about the legends of Alexander Point. He said these so-called Sereni women settled here hundreds of years ago and they would lure men to their deaths, and ship and boat wrecks have happened because of them, sacrifices, screams coming from this house and the lighthouse! You know? I mean you should have seen Eben's face when he first saw me on the beach. He was shy of passing out, ran like a bat outta hell in the opposite direction. Honestly, Ada, you are so right. People are bored out of their minds here! The best part is that they believe it's true! For all they know you're a siren yourself."

"Fascinating." Ada sipped her coffee. "He say anything else?"

"Nope, then well—" I stood quietly watching Eben laughing with Wren and Joe out of the window.

"Then what?" Ada stood beside me watching the three friends.

"Well, then he wanted to kiss me. I almost landed my first kiss, Ada!" My cheeks were warm remembering the smell of his flannel and the safety net of his arms cast around my waist.

"Were you going to let him?" Ada peeked in my direction, smiling.

"I was until the fire erupted and you came out of nowhere. *That* wasn't awkward or anything." I grabbed the coffee from her hands and took a sip. It tasted bold and bitter.

"Well, maybe that was a sign? Maybe you and Eben shouldn't get involved like that yet. Why tie yourself down right away? Get to know him first."

I raised an eyebrow in Ada's direction.

"Anyway, are you gonna make them wait forever?" She gestured her mug in their direction.

"I guess I should go. We're going sailing."

Ada paused as if thinking twice about something. She watched Eben.

"Please be careful, Nora. And be home before nightfall, okay? Promise me."

"Wow. Giving me a bit of freedom today, huh? Tomorrow's the day, Ada. I haven't forgotten." I leaned in and kissed her cheek before running out the front door.

"How is it that you look so pretty, even in the morning with no time to get ready?" Wren asked me as I approached the group. "I must learn your metropolitan secrets."

I smiled bashfully.

"How's your head?" Eben asked when I joined them. "Saw you bang it." He smiled.

"Fine," I said rubbing the back of my scalp.

"Have you ever been sailing before?" Eben asked.

"Nope." I hiked my bag higher on my shoulder.

"Well, this will be an adventure for you then!" Joe said.

The four of us walked down the beach until we reached a very small boatyard with a couple motorboats, a large fishing boat, and a tiny sailboat.

"We're all going to fit on that?" I asked.

"No!" Joe scoffed. "You and Eben are. Wren and I are in another dinghy. We're racing! The winds are perfect!" Joe said, practically jumping.

I stopped in my tracks.

"Racing? I've never sailed before, and you are making me race?"

"Ha, you'll be just fine, girlie." Eben tossed me a life jacket and took my bag, storing it in a dry seal compartment in the front of the boat. "Ready for your first sailing lesson?" He threw me a smirk as he clipped my lifejacket on and tightened the straps. His breath smelled of toast and bitter coffee.

"That'll do, good fit. It's my old life jacket, from when I was like, fifteen. You know, before I got all manly and buff." He flexed his right arm jokingly and I flexed my puny arm in response.

"Don't you worry, little sea-hopper," he said. "Someday you will be as strong and wise as I am."

He took a seat at the edge of the dock and began slowly slipping himself into the little boat.

"Okay, where to begin? First off, this is a sunfish," Eben said.

"That's the name of your boat?"

"No, that's the *type* of boat. This boat's name, if you must know, is *Stella*."

"*Stella*? Why?" I asked giggling.

"No idea, first name that popped into my head when I saw her. She was a birthday gift from Pops," Eben said, glowing slightly. "Right, so let's rig her up, shall we?"

I smiled, not understanding a lick of what he said.

"Hand me the dagger board," Eben said, pointing towards a board on the dock. I picked it up and handed it over.

"This goes *here*," he said and slipped it into a slit in the boat. I watched Eben unravel two lines that held the mast and sail. The sail was striped and beautiful when he hoisted it into the air. The sunlight filtered through the faded blue and green lines and peaked over its edges as it ruffled in the wind. I stood taking in the swaying hues of blues with my thumbs tucked into the armholes of my lifejacket.

"Lookin' stoic, Nora. Ready?" Eben sat staring at me with his hand outstretched in my direction.

I carefully ducked under the boom and sat on the edge of the cockpit with him. "I'm ready."

"Great! I'll be doing most of the maneuvering, but there are a few things you should know. First the word *jibe* When I yell 'jibe', know that the boom will be coming right for your head, so you need to duck and switch sides as quickly as possible or you'll get knocked off the boat with a pretty nasty bruise on your head."

I swallowed.

"Secondly, you're going to be my tiller girl, so basically I trust you with turning Stella where she needs to go. When I yell *right*, you turn the tiller to the *left*, and when I yell *left* you turn the tiller to the *right*. Opposites. Got it?"

Eben's smile was wide, and my own face felt like it showed a raw emotion of panic and excitement.

"Really? Can't I just focus on the jibe thing first?"

"Oh come on, girlie. It'll be fun, yeah?" Eben said, looking towards Joe and Wren. "Hey! You kids ready to race or what?"

"You betcha!" Joe yelled back, and I could see Wren smiling in my direction, quickly braiding her beach blonde hair. "Let's start at the third buoy and head towards the Seal Trap, yeah?"

"You're on!" Eben yelled back. I nervously held the tiller in my now sweaty hand.

According to Eben, the wind was perfect, and he helped me guide the tiller to steer the little sunfish towards the buoy.

"Lookin' like a pro," Joe yelled in my direction. "Looks like you have some Plymouth blood in ya after all!"

"Trying here, trying," I yelled back.

Wren dipped her fingers in the sea and splashed Joe.

"Okay, well on the count of three. One!" Eben's voice boomed looking towards me. "Two!" He tightened a line in his hand. "Three!" The wind suddenly filled the sail and the four of us were off.

"Right!" Eben yelled, and I turned the tiller to the left. "Good, Nora!"

A wind curtained with microbeads of salt water splattered our faces. There was a thrill of speed. I glanced over at the other sunfish. Wren was Joe's tiller girl. I saw the two quickly duck under the boom and change sides.

"Left girlie! Jibe!" Eben yelled and we both swung under the boom and quickly sat down on the other side. "Nice." Eben glanced over. "You okay with the tiller?"

"I'm getting the hang of it!" I belted over the wind.

Both boats were on par, racing into the wind, side by side.

"*There!*" Eben yelled. "That's where we're headed, Kimball Island, Seal Trap."

The water thrashed, and I clutched the side of the boat for balance while gripping the tiller. I heard Joe yelling over the wind to Wren. Adrenaline accentuated the tension as both boats exchanged leads, battling to win. The mass of land became closer and closer. I could feel Eben's body tense in excitement, like a little kid at a theme park.

"Jibe!" he yelled, and we ducked under the flying boom and switched sides, the sail refilled with the wind. We took the lead, and Eben let out a loud hoot. I focused on the point of the island when I felt Eben's hand touch mine. Instantly Ada's face, streaked with tears, saying goodbye to an infant in a crib, flashed in my mind.

The little hands swatted the empty air looking for her. The wooden mobile swayed and the crow in the window cawed. I quickly removed my hand almost letting go of the tiller. The boat abruptly jerked and Joe and Wren took the lead.

"What! What was that sea-hopper? You okay?" Eben asked, quickly turning to me.

"Woo! Who's king of the island now, suckers?" Joe yelled back with both arms in the air as they reached the appointed finish line and began to slow down.

"Nothing, I-I'm fine. My hand slipped. Sorry." I watched Eben's eyes soften as his cheeks pulled back in a smile.

"No worries! You killed it, Nora. Not bad for your first time, eh? Told you you were going to be fine! Nice work." Eben held out his fist for a fist bump.

I sat, numb, thinking about the vision I had just had.

"Hey don't leave me hanging, girlie!" I lifted my hand and pounded his.

"Okay, let's switch," he said. "I'll bring us into shore from here, just be mindful of your head!"

We switched spots and I watched as he skillfully brought us towards the beach. Eben and Joe both rolled up their pants, jumped out, and pulled out the dagger boards. I followed suit, took off my clogs, rolled up my pants, and hopped out. I was mid-calf-deep in the freezing Atlantic water. The four of us hauled the two sunfishes onto the sand. Eben loosened the sail and then pulled out a little bag from where he'd stowed my backpack.

"Brought us some cheese and this awesome sourdough bread Wren's mom makes. Want some?" He looked at me and offered the half loaf of bread. I ripped off a piece and helped myself to a cleaved piece of white cheddar.

"Thanks," I said, shivering and offering the chunk of bread to Wren.

Joe quickly gathered driftwood and started a small fire on the beach. We crowded around it warming up our numb toes.

"Nice job, Nora!" Wren sang, skipping over to me with two wool plaid blankets. "Oh yeah, Momma's bread. She's famous on the island, mainly because she's the only baker that lives here full time." Wren smiled and ripped off a piece of the loaf and took a few chunks of cheese.

There we were, the four of us sitting together, watching the slate blue water, heating our toes, and enjoying the simplicity and warmth of the fire. The beach was dressed in beautiful dark stones and pieces of driftwood. The trees behind us were a wall of dark evergreen. Seagulls fussed in the skies, and salt-masked air caked our bodies. There was a comfort all around us on this piece of earth.

Maybe this right here is what Ada missed about life out here, that feeling of having a little piece of earth all to yourself.

We spent most of the afternoon roaming Kimball Island, collecting tidbits of treasure from the sand: rocks, sea glass, and small pieces of driftwood. Before we knew it, the sun was setting and Joe and Eben were preparing the two little sailboats for our journey home. Warm amber light streaked the sky as the four of us, rich with a silent and underlying contentment in life, set sail once more back for Stone Isle.

When we arrived, we undressed the boats and tied them in. Wren and Joe grabbed their belongings and headed out. Eben offered to walk me back to Alexander Point. With a wave to Joe and Wren, we turned and began the walk back.

"You're right," I said. "They are a weird couple, or whatever it is they are."

"Told ya," Eben said stuffing his hands in his pockets. "Hey listen, about the other night, sorry if I was a bit too forward, sometimes with a few beers in me—"

He was speaking of the kiss we'd lost.

"It was fine. I mean, I was okay with it, you know." I glanced in his direction. "But, if I could be honest with you..." I was thinking about what Ada had said in the kitchen. "I just moved here and right now I want to make friends." I felt his spirits dip and I nudged my shoulder into his side.

"No, I get it." He wrapped his arms around me, and I pressed my cheek against his chest, taking in the scent of salty smoky flannel.

"Friends," I said looking up to him.

"For now." Eben's cheeks turned a nice rosy pink. "Anyway, I'm out fishing with my pops and Joe for the rest of spring break, so I'll be seeing you in school, huh?"

"Yeah, I guess so, unless I'm being sent to boarding school or something."

"Hope not, that would suck majorly! How am I supposed to convince you to kiss me if you're that far away?"

I smiled.

We both reached the bottom of the path to my house, and I began making my way towards Ada who was sitting on the porch reading. Eben waved to her before he turned and began making his way home.

"Have a good time racing?" Ada asked, watching Eben disappear behind the sand dune.

"Yeah, how'd you know we raced?" I asked.

"Most kids here do that sort of thing. Your mom and I did," Ada said, keeping her eyes down and nose buried in her book.

"Obviously. Well I'm going to shower and change." My clothes were damp and the salt that caked my skin was beginning to prick and itch.

I made my way upstairs, dropped my bag in my room, and then headed into the bathroom. I turned the shower on and let the steam cloud the space as I stripped down. I cracked the window open, welcoming in the stream of cool air when I spotted someone on the beach staring in my direction. It definitely *wasn't* Eben, but a smaller framed figure draped in a long dark cloak. He or she suddenly tilted their head towards the lighthouse. I quickly backed away from the window and wrapped a towel around myself, then opened the bathroom door to see Ada down the hall entering her room.

"Ada!" I gasped.

"What? What's wrong, Nora? You look like you saw a ghost!"

"There's someone on the beach watching the house Ada, look!" I grabbed Ada's hand and practically dragged her back to the bathroom, forcing her to look out the window, but no one was there.

"I see," Ada said, looking at me once more with concern.

"What? I swear! I just saw someone, someone wearing a long black cloak or something with a hood covering their face. What kind of people wear grim-like outfits on this island, Ada? Are we near a mental ward? Maybe there was a breakout?"

At this Ada sparked an uneasy look for a split second, then softened her eyes in a rehearsed and *understanding* way.

"Nora, just take a shower. You may need food, all that sun and salt's got to your head. I'll go start dinner right away." Ada left the bathroom quickly, not allowing me time to reply.

She was beginning to make me feel crazy, as if I were seeing things, hearing things. *Was* I seeing things? My heart thumped against my ribs, and I peeked back out of the window—sure enough, the figure was gone. I grabbed my growing-out bangs and felt like ripping them from my scalp.

"Damn it!" I banged on the wall with my fist feeling furious, the towel dropping around my feet. I stepped into the shower. The hot water burned and stung my skin as I inhaled the steam that was now being masked by the aromas of lavender soap.

Just breathe Nora. You are not crazy. You are not seeing things. You are not hearing things. Something is not right on this island, and Ada has until tomorrow to tell the truth.

Ada and I exchanged very little dialogue that evening, and after dinner, I washed my plate and made my way to bed. The day spent with Eben, Wren, and Joe out on the water and in the warm sun began to sink into my bones, easing me into exhaustion. I cracked the window open for fresh air then I tucked myself under the heavy comforter. The night air had a wood smoke scent to it. Somewhere along the coast, someone was having a fire. I was beginning to regret not letting Eben kiss me on the beach this afternoon, but a part of me thought Ada was right, I should get to know people a bit more on the island. The candle by my bed flickered and then blew out with the next breeze that entered my room.

You are not crazy. You are not seeing things. You are not hearing things. Something is not right on this island.

I repeated these assurances until, before long, I was asleep.

–Nora–

I may have been only asleep for a couple hours when my eyes flung open again to the sound of my name.

–Nora–

It was the same voice as the other night.

–Nora–

This time, I ripped the covers off and swung my legs over the side of the bed, stepping into my clogs. Without hesitation, I looked out the window and there, in the mist, stood the figure, watching me. This one was not the same as the cloaked individual I saw earlier.

–Nora–

My name echoed throughout the bedroom.

–Nora, I can explain everything. Come outside, Nora–

The sky rumbled as the storm began its performance.

–The fire growing out of control was no accident, Nora. Someone caused it. I was watching. I can tell you if you listen–

Someone caused the fire to grow out of control?

I was beginning to feel insane but oddly justified all at the same time. I was right, something was not right or normal about the bonfire explosion.

What has Ada been hiding from me?

I tiptoed on the wood flooring, desperately not wanting to wake Ada. I did not want her to interfere and get between me and the answers this stranger had. I quietly worked my way out of the bedroom and down the hall. I paused before my hand made contact with the banister and listened for movement. Ada rolled over in her sleep. I could hear her mumble something then settle, falling back into a deep sleep. This stranger was the confirmation that Ada had been keeping secrets from me for a long time. The thought of being lied to by the one person I trusted for so long burned to an unimaginable degree. If I wanted answers, if I wanted to know the *truth*, I would have to go out and find it.

I quietly put pressure back on the balls of my feet and headed down the wooden staircase and through the kitchen. For a moment, before reaching my hand out to touch the brass doorknob, a surge of apprehension took over my body. Running back upstairs and hiding under my covers quickly crossed my mind until I remembered the letters and the one Ada had torn up.

You can do this, Nora. You want answers right?

Yes. I do.

Then go to her.

But what if it's a trap? What if the island is filled with psychopaths?

Tomorrow Ada will explain everything, right?

Will she? Or will she lie?

You know something is not right, we both know. Go.

My mind battled itself, and then with a deep breath, I twisted the doorknob and stepped outside.

The air was thick, and fog had swallowed almost everything in sight. This island was officially giving me the creeps. I could hear the ocean crashing behind the curtain of fog. Rain began to fall, and I wondered if Eben was out there already with his dad and Joe thrashing around in the stormy waters. The drone of the lighthouse filled my ears while it desperately tried to shine for those out at sea, but I doubted if its light could break through the thick walls of barricading fog. Something moved in front of the lighthouse, but the motion was so subtle I wasn't sure if I had even seen anything at all. The island began to swell with its secrets. What if the tales of the Sereni women were true?

–Nora–

My hands tightened in my fleece-lined pockets as I heard her voice again.

–Come, Nora, come–

Her voice was unnerving, yet everything about it was enticing, luring me to go to her. I wanted to do nothing but submit to the string of elegant musical notes. The thought of Ada lying to me for seventeen years was a painful discovery. Bitterness and distrust began to root itself in my body. She was never honest with me, and out of resentment, I took a step off the porch into the rain. Walking slowly around the corner of the house, I saw the stranger standing near the tree line. She was there, and very real. I watched her for a moment, unsure if she had seen me, then her face angled towards me, indicating that I had been officially spotted. My resolve strengthened with every step I took towards her across the soggy ground. The stranger was no taller than me and waited, meticulously still, a marble statue smiling with parted peach lips.

"Don't be afraid Nora, I won't hurt you."

Swallowing my fears, I spoke. "Who are you?"

No reply.

"How do you know my name?"

The silence continued for another moment, and then she looked at me curiously as if something were obvious, but not.

"I know more than just your name, Eleanora, don't you?"

The sky rumbled.

"Oh my," she said as though to herself. "The rumors are true; you *have* been kept in the dark."

I took another step, opening my mouth and preparing to either question her or defend myself—I wasn't sure which—when she held up a bony finger and pressed it to her lips, silencing me. A lump formed in the back of my throat constricting my voice. I grabbed my throat, unable to form sound. She then smiled and the restriction released, my voice returned. I stared at her in horror. What the hell was she? The rain began to fall harder, and I pulled my hood tightly around my face. The girl never flinched. She stood in the ice-cold downpour and continued to look up into the stormy night sky. Her face was becoming clearer the longer I observed her. Her milky skin was painted with dark freckles like mine that fell over the bridge of her nose, down the sides of her neck, across her collarbones and over her shoulders. Her eyelashes were dark and long, and rain streaked her skin, cutting into the corners of her mouth as they pulled back into another smile. It was a haunting sensation to watch her. Her bone structure appeared delicate, her arms thin and her collarbones protruding sharply. It looked like with only a little-applied pressure she might break. Every inch of her persona appeared in the frailest of states. She was indeed a beautiful creature, an enchanting creature, and a ghostly creature. At that very thought, I took a step back. Eben's story played in my mind like an old broken record. I took another step back. Was she a siren? Were the tales true? Her eyes flashed in my direction, noting my retreat.

"Oh, don't leave Nora. I have so much to share with you, so much you *must* know, you *must* see."

Thunder roared and my body tensed. I obeyed her and stayed, frozen. Her eyes widened and their pupils dilated in my direction as if they were magnetically pulling me towards her, keeping me near. My feet felt heavy and glued to the earth. Even if I had wanted to, I wasn't going anywhere. A grisly breeze swept between us, and I wrapped my jacket tighter around me. The girl didn't seem to feel the cold the way I did. My hands were wet and beginning to go numb. As she watched me, I could tell her mind was moving rapidly. Her vibrant eyes quickly flickered back and forth from me to the sky to the tree line near us. I opened my mouth, searching for the bravery to speak again, to say something, *anything*, when her cold thin fingers made the first contact and pressed against my lips. The gesture was alarming. She raised her face and looked to the gradually darkening sky, not taking her fingers off my lips. Suddenly blackness devoured her eyes and her lips parted and a harsh voice, unlike the one I had heard her use, slithered past her lips.

Bring her to us. Bring her.

I tried to back away, terrified, but my feet stayed glued, my voice once again taken.

It was growing darker, and the clouds grew thicker as they pulled over us like a soft blanket filled with nightmares and secrets. A chill began at the base of my tailbone, shivering its way up my spine. The wind picked up once more, howling aggressively. Her eyes, black and glassy, reflected the dark gray of the clouds. Then she snapped her face towards me and her eyes flashed to a vivid amethyst—the way my eyes had shifted in color. Something in my chest ignited heat in my body, and I turned my gaze from her. She placed her hand over my chest and spoke words I did not understand. The immense burning sensation continued, building and spreading like wildfire through a field of dried brush on a hot summer day. It boiled my veins and coated my throat. No amount of swallowing could push down the intensity.

"You are awakening," she said trailing her fingers across my lips and looking satisfied. "So much power hidden. It is your birthright to know, to feel what you truly are." She pulled my face in and planted her lips on mine.

"What are you doing?" I shoved her, then leaned over coughing, hitting my chest.

"Undoing what Ada worked so hard to do, freeing you. Lighting your soul on fire."

She stood barefoot in a shallow puddle. Her nails were painted a deep oxblood red, her toes were wiggling, but the rest of her body remained perfectly composed. In the rain, her thin cotton dress stuck to her skin revealing her flared hipbones. Her breathing was thin but quick—twice the pace of mine. She reminded me of a hummingbird. Was she nervous?

"Any minute now."

"Any minute *what*?" I said, wiping the rain from my eyes so I could see her more clearly.

The rain began to fall harder than ever, and I felt disoriented.

"Don't fight the sensation Nora, free yourself. Learn who you truly are, girl!" She spoke a little louder this time. "We've been waiting for you, waiting for so long for you to come back."

She waited again for the sound of thunder to speak.

"At the first sound of thunder, we'll start running, got it? It's harder for *them* to track us in the rain. We aren't the only ones looking for you, Nora. Then you'll see, you'll see how very different you are. You'll see what you are." Her lips pulled back in glee.

"Track us? Who's tracking us? What is going on?" I remembered the letter from my mother to Ada; she mentioned being tracked.

The thunder fell silent and so did she. Did she not want someone to hear us, perhaps Ada? The girl spoke as if the sky was going to give us a signal, as if it was going to fire a shotgun and a hunting spree would begin. I felt helpless and forced by her manipulating voice to stay with her. I waited, waited for her, waited for *something* to happen—waited for answers.

"You said you had answers for me!" I yelled finding my voice. "What happened at the bonfire? What were my mother's letters about? Who am I? Tell me the truth!"

She leaned in and whispered into my ear. "You must experience your power first before I give you answers, Nora. Ready to finally understand?"

"Understand *what*?"

"Everything."

Then she placed her palm on my forehead and suddenly, somehow, I could feel Ada fling her body up in bed.

"Nora!" Ada screamed.

"It's too late, Ada." The girl whispered, hissing towards the house.

The burning sensation and thoughts were quickly replaced with nausea, and a current of energy swept through my body. Every joint tingled, every finger and toe felt electrified. I had never felt this alive before. The sky deeply growled, and then it let out an ear-piercing CRACK. The sky flashed, and thunder shook deep in my bones and through the trees.

I heard Ada's window slam open. "Nora! Don't!"

The woman who had lured me ran into the woods, and before I knew it, I was right on her heels running, following her, disappearing into the dense forest of the island.

We ran. She led and I followed. We ran through knee-high ferns, and the soft moss stained the bottoms of her feet. Mud splashed up the back of our legs.

My heart pounded. My mind remained surprisingly calm and focused, momentarily uncluttered of the hundreds of questions. The wind ripped past my ears, brushing the sides of my face, pulling my hair back. I could breathe, for the first time ever, I truly felt like I could breathe. My lungs expanded to their full capacity as I dove into freedom. I broke through some sort of shell that I hadn't even known existed around me. The girl was right; something began awakening inside me. A gear of an intricate machine had turned, and for the first time, the mechanism began to function properly.

Run! Run! Run! I chanted over and over to myself. I looked down and realized that the speed we were both running at was not humanly possible.

I began to feel like I was caught in an uncontrolled chase and had the sensation that I was being followed. I glanced behind me but saw no one. As the paranoia of being chased set in, I began to move even faster. Rain showered me, and trees blurred by. The girl was the only thing I could keep in focus. Her feet looked as if they barely touched the ground, her bony shoulder blades pulled back so far they appeared to be touching. Thoughts of Ada, my mother, Alexo, the letters, Eben, the bonfire, this girl, running, the Sereni tales, and this island flooded my mind. I faintly heard water running, splashing angrily as it hit smoothed-over rocks, and the sound grew louder and louder.

I searched for where it was coming from, and then dead ahead, there it was—water. The girl jumped and somehow flew over the wide body of a lake. Her arms lifted in the air like parachuting wings and she glided down, landing softly on the other side, then turned back to watch me. This was all impossible, absolutely impossible! *How did she do that?* I wanted to stop. I wanted to dig my heels in the dirt and come to a halt but I couldn't.

"Don't stop, Nora. Jump. You can do this!" Her voice rang in my ears.

I was locked into my speed and officially feeling I had lost my mind. Humans could not jump like that, even animals couldn't jump like that. The lake looked black, brewing with the storm, and I started to get tunnel vision. My legs began gaining even more speed as I gauged the distance.

Stop, Nora! Stop! Reason entered my thoughts.

You know you have always been different! Do this! Find out the truth!

Why do this, Nora? Why? Why take the risk, you don't even know this girl. Go home. Go back to Ada. Just hear out Ada tomorrow, you only had to wait one more night.

She has been lying to you your whole life. It wouldn't be any different today or tomorrow. If you want answers, jump!

Suddenly the girl's voice interrupted my battling mind.

–Stop thinking, Nora. Feel everything–

I *wanted* answers. My eyes watered with fear as I took my last step and jumped, swinging my arms wildly through the air.

The angry water splashed underneath me. I was airborne. For a split second, I closed my eyes and stopped breathing, waiting for the moment I would painfully slam into the water. Instead, I landed hard on earth and began rolling. The girl's cold hands stopped me and stood me up.

"Next time, keep your eyes open." She winked in approval.

The ground teeter-tottered and my knees buckled as I tried to regain the feeling in my legs. I turned and looked at the distance I had leaped across.

"See what you've been missing out on!" Her whimsical laugh echoed through the trees, and I watched her take off again in excitement.

What am I?

"Come on, Nora. Keep up!" The voice trailed off again into an airy unnerving laughter that twisted my stomach.

The sky rumbled and streaks of lightning flashed through the trees followed by another ear-piercing crack. My legs began to move. I felt weightless and astonished at my own speed. The forest blurred past us, and we worked our way through the trees. I listened to her laughter echo through the forest when, out of the corner of my eye, I thought I saw something. Someone else was near, but when I looked, no one was there. I glanced in the other direction and thought I saw another woman before she vanished.

The laughter disappeared. The girl looked back, her face no longer inviting and pleasant but filled with fear and angst. Her eyes had shifted to black.

"No," she hissed.

I started feeling sick and my stomach contracted violently.

"Hurry!" she said, looking past me.

I looked back to see what she was seeing—there in the distance were two figures chasing us through the trees. Their appearance was wolf-like, their eyes yellow and teeth bare, snapping the air. Next, two other women appeared beside me, where I thought I had sensed someone earlier.

"Keep running, we'll take care of them," said one of the women.

The two women slowed down, and I turned to watch one of them fling one of the wolf-like creatures into a tree then leap in front of the other creature. She pivoted, threw the creature to the ground, reached down and tore its arm from its socket. My stomach convulsed at the sight of blood and the sound of cracking bones. I felt lightheaded. I heard the woman's voice again.

"Eleanora, look out!"

At that moment, my foot caught a raised root and I fell. Another wolf-like creature sailed over my head and collided in mid-air with the girl I had been chasing. I hit the ground hard and rolled violently, unable to stop. My world spun like a kaleidoscope. I crashed. Something shifted in my lower back and an excruciating pain shot down my legs.

Everything went black.

6

A drowning sound of voices began to fade in and out, and I was unsure exactly how long I had blacked out for. My entire body remained numb and paralyzed. I recalled clearly slamming into an unforgiving object, and I remembered a painful break somewhere in my back, but at this moment, I felt nothing. My heart began pounding harder and harder as my breathing reflected a pattern of sheer panic. The side of my face lay pressed into the soggy earth.

The ground smelled of fresh rain and rich black dirt. The copper taste of blood seeped into the corners of my mouth. I had bitten my cheek. Listening carefully, I could hear the movement of life under the moist soil. Voices continued fading in and out. How long would I lie here before the end? Would someone help me, or were they planning to only watch? Where was the girl I had followed? I should have listened to Ada. I remained motionless, hidden behind the darkness of my bruised eyelids. The white sound of buzzing began to disappear, and the voices became clearer. Their tone was low and urgent. Something was wrong.

Perhaps I was in the terrible state I imagined myself to be, perhaps they weren't sure what to do with me, what to do with my body. Would they leave me here alone, lost in an unknown location in the woods to die? How would Ada find me? Would anyone find me? Would anyone aside from Ada even bother to look for me on this forsaken island? The island wasn't large, but I had no idea where

I was. Someone passing by, perhaps a hiker on a warmer day, like in Eben's tale, would discover me and bring my bag of flesh and bones home to the sheriff's office. Did we even *have* a sheriff's office? The voices were starting to get louder and more distinct. I recognized the airy voice of the girl I had followed; she began to speak but was cut off by another woman's voice that sounded more serpent-like, hissing angrily as she spat words.

"What were you thinking, you *wretched* girl? We were supposed to be bringing her back to them *unharmed*!"

A third voice, harsher and raspier, said, "How was she supposed to know they were hunting nearby? *You* were supposed to be protecting the perimeters while Vivienne moved her to us! We had orders, Iona, and you didn't follow through on your end!"

"I *was* protecting the perimeters! I'm not sure how they slipped by unnoticed, but they did!" snapped the serpent-like voice I now knew belonged to Iona.

"At least all three were finished off, but we need to make sure we cover our tracks. I'll go burn the bodies now," the raspier voice said, followed by feet shuffling in the leaves.

"They know. They know that Eleanora is back." Iona sounded nervous. "We had to move her from that house before they discovered its location. There are only a few safe houses left here."

An eerie silence replaced their conversation. Then the back of a cold hand touched my face. My cheek twitched.

"What are we suppose to do with her now? She doesn't even know what she is, or who she is. I cannot *believe* Ada kept her in the dark this long. Why would she do this to her? Rebekah couldn't have wanted this," said Vivienne.

"You don't know *what* she wanted! Perhaps this was part of their plan," Iona said.

The contact was refreshing, calming, and reminded me that I was, at the moment, still alive. They were speaking of my mother. It sounded like they all knew her. I needed answers. I gathered that

I was different, but what was I? I wanted to see what these women looked like. Struggling, I attempted to move my upper body, but the pain caused me to groan as every inch of my body slowly emerged from its numbed state.

"Don't move child!" Iona said, her voice sharp as hands restrained me.

"Your magic is wearing off, Iona. It isn't strong enough!" Vivienne said.

"I'm working with what I've got in this bloody forest!"

Even if I'd wanted to, I couldn't move. A number of cold hands pressed against my shoulders, and I was carefully rolled over onto my back. Something popped in my lower back, and I let out another agonizing moan, this one I was sure echoed through the trees. A cold hand forcefully pressed against my mouth.

"Shh, shh, shh, it's okay," said Vivienne. "Quiet, please, they might hear us again."

"As if she knows who 'they' are Vivienne," said the third and as yet unnamed voice.

I tried opening my eyes, hoping my vision would restore itself. Dark shadows of bodies were hovering over me. I blinked, trying to clear my vision.

"She must have broken something," said the third voice. A thin scent of burning flesh, blood, and bones wafted through the air.

"What an unpleasant aroma they give off," Iona said.

"You don't say, broken huh?" Vivienne almost sounded shocked and curious.

"You basically fed her to the wolves, Vivienne, what go into you?" Iona said while coughing, as the smoke of the fire wafted in our direction. Iona was sounding rather protective of me, and she reminded me slightly of Ada. "Simply repulsive," Iona complained again referring to the odor. "The incantation will take a minute! She'll be fine and heal quickly. What'd you expect running for the first time at that speed and then being attacked? And here I'm limited to roots and elderberry to heal her, no tonics, nothing!"

"It's amazing how she doesn't even know *anything...*" Vivienne's voice trailed off into an unsettled tone.

I heard a crunching sound that I gathered to be the roots and berries being mashed into my skin. I could not make sense of anything. What I believed to be Iona's hands pressed even harder into my side as words in a foreign tongue hissed through the air. A warm sensation spread over the surface of my skin until a sudden sharp stab nipped my side and a current of immense heat shot through my body. The burning feeling returned and traveled down my back, flaring out into my thighs. Every muscle quickly contracted, my heart raced at a pace I had never felt before. My toes and fingers clawed into the soft ground. A painful, maniacal scream exploded from my mouth. Someone's forearm aggressively pressed into my mouth trying to muffle the sound.

"Ach, she bit me!" said the third voice.

The sweltering feeling ran deep, deep into my bones, deep into every muscle, as the sounds of my own heart flooded my ears. I could feel my throat pulsating and my lungs grew tighter with each breath. Tighter and tighter until I was *gasping* for air, and every breath became more painful like shards of glass being ground into my lungs. I had no control of my body, of my mind, of the insanity. Tears flowed down my muddy cheeks, my body jolted with electrifying currents, and my back arched in agony. Clenching my jaw, I bit my raw cheeks, again bringing up the taste of blood. Next, my legs violently trembled and a seizure overtook me. My nerves were in shock, sparking and sending eradicating messages across the field, wanting to put an end to this. Then voices were gone, and I was left alone in the mind-twisting field of my own war zone, fighting to get through this pain, fighting to stay alive.

Then, just like when a child blows out the candles on her birthday cake, the flames were gone and there was silence.

Hyperventilating, I lay on the ground like a diseased animal, gently whimpering and waiting for its suffering to finish it off. Motionless on my back, I could feel rain on my skin. Sweat gently beaded my forehead. But the pain was gone. I lay in shock that it was all over.

"I will take her from here." Iona's threatening voice faded into the distance.

I surrendered into her arms.

7

Pricking goosebumps made their way up my arms as I rubbed them with my hands in a bid to keep warm. I stood in a dark damp room, unsure how I had arrived there, listening to the sound of water dripping. I could faintly hear the sounds of a sea in turmoil crashing somewhere outside the walls. The air smelled of sea and mildew. I began to wander as my eyes adjusted. A thin stream of light from a small barred window filled the room. I followed the light, watching as specks of dust glittered. When I heard the abrupt flutter of a bird swooping nearby, I ducked. A crow. Squawking, it soared high above into the shadows of endless stone arches. Its feathers were oily and lustrous, and its beady black eyes caught the light. I was standing in a tower I did not recognize. I heard a loud surge of electricity, and the crow squawked again. High above me an enormous spotlight began to slowly rotate. I was in a lighthouse. Tugging my thin sweater around my body, I made my way through the space. My focus moved upward once more towards the loud light. The crow rocked back and forth, silently watching me, seemingly interested in my every move. My foot bumped into something soft. I quickly took a step back and saw at my feet a dark blanket covering something. Whatever the blanket concealed wasn't moving. I reached down and touched the cold damp fabric. The crow squawked louder. My heart found its way into my throat and pounded in my ears.

I tugged at the blanket.

Underneath was a thin female body lying on the stone floor. She was quite still, possibly even dead—no, her teeth were chattering. Her skin was sunken and stretched across her bones. She was barely dressed; what was left of her clothes were falling apart at the seams. Black characters were branded into her forearm and exposed back. Pale scars ran down her throat, legs and arms. The crow screamed as I pulled the blanket back a bit more. I wanted to see her face, but it remained hidden behind a layer of her long dark hair. She was tightly curled in a fetal position, looking defeated. Her arms pressed into her chest and the knuckles of her hands were bony white. They appeared to be clenching something that was starting to leak through the creases of her fingers. The sound of her teeth chattering faintly began to slow. Something about her felt familiar. I bent over and started to push the hair off her face when a woman's voice broke the silence.

"You can't save her."

Abruptly, I withdrew my hand and looked over my shoulder. A female figure broke from the shadows of the lighthouse and walked towards me. Her face was hidden under a dark cloak, but the sheen of her deep red lips glistened as she smiled. The woman reached out her hand, and an invisible force moved me aside. Her skin appeared clammy and cold, lined with dark veins and what appeared to be scarred bite marks. I watched as she waved her outstretched arm over the body.

The girl's long dark wavy hair pulled back and gently tucked itself behind her ear. The image horrified me, and I let out a low gasp while gripping my hands together. It was me—an older version of me—but there was no mistaking it.

By now my eyes were fully adjusted to the dim lighting of the room, and I noticed the body (my body) covered with rings of bruises. Gashes and bite marks painted the fair skin; the hands continued to grasp onto something that started to pulsate and release dark liquid.

The insides of my stomach started to turn as bile accumulated in my mouth. I slowly took steps backward, away from the horrid sight. The longer I beheld the body, the emptier and colder I felt. A distant beating sound grew louder and louder. Like tribal drums they bounced off the walls and echoed throughout the tower. The cloaked figure was nowhere to be seen. The crow squawked and landed on the exposed shoulder of the prone body. It looked at me carefully then began to peck at her hands, removing bits of flesh.

My nose caught the overwhelming scents of spoiled meat and death that ruined the air. The dark liquid from the thing in her hands was now gathered around her in a pool. The crow's repetitive pecking resulted in the girl's hands slowly giving in and opening. There lay a muscle, the muscle that allows us all to make thoughtless, rash decisions, allows us all to feel, allows us to be exposed, allows us to become breakable, to become strong. It rolled from her hands and stopped short of my feet. It was her heart. *My heart.*

The chattering of her teeth finally came to an end, and I watched her rib cage release its last breath of life. I rubbed my eyes. I wanted to wake up, this was not real. None of this was real. I needed to find a way out. The corpse's eyes flung open suddenly and they were piercing and black, full of painful hatred. Frantically, I began to move away, not knowing where to turn or how to escape this nightmare. The drumming of her heart continued echoing louder and louder, blaring across the lighthouse. The sickening laughter of the strange woman in the cloak danced through my ears.

"One must die. One must die. One must die." Her voice chanted over and over, screaming, laughing, and singing manically through the tower.

Suddenly more voices began to layer in hissing and snapping.

"Relentless power."

"Strong bloodlines."

"A child of Lamia."

"Prophecy."

"Come to us Eleanora. Come!"

My pace quickened, searching for the source of voices, faster and faster and turning into a trot as I heard her beginning to scream. The corpse. The more she screamed in horrifying agony, the tighter my chest became. I was gasping for air, no longer able to breathe. I was being suffocated, deprived of air, my lungs tightening, and I fell onto the hard stone floor knees first. Strange warmth began flooding my chest. I looked down and saw that thick dark blood was soaking through my clothes. I put my hand on my chest and felt the indentation wherein my heart once beat.

I slowly turned my gaze over my shoulder, blood stringing my fingers.

The girl's eyes, violent and black, stared at me, her head dropped back, her mouth open and she shrieked my name.

8

Opening my eyes, I sat up, clutching my chest. It was wet. I frantically looked down expecting to see blood staining my hands, but
instead, I found myself in a thin cotton nightgown that was stick-
ing to my body with sweat. My heart raced and I looked around
me, not recognizing where I was. I tried collecting my thoughts. In
dreams, you normally cannot remember how you arrived, but as I
sat there panting I remembered Vivienne, remembered Ada slamming open the window yelling, and I remembered running at an
astounding speed. I thought of Eben out in the stormy seas and
then of the ruined body I had dreamt of on the lighthouse floor and
the crow picking the flesh off its hands. The corpse with my face.
One must die. One must die. One must die... Then I thought of the
wolf-like creatures, one flung broken against a tree, another having
its arm torn off.

The smell of burned fur and flesh lingered in the back of my
throat. I leaned over and vomited on the floor.

I groaned and looked around, wiping my lips against the linens.

I had been placed on a long thin mattress covered in cotton
sheets that smelled of lavender. Candles lit the room, and their light
bounced off a wind chime that hung in the corner. It was made
of sea glass, driftwood, and tiny mirrors. I shifted my weight and
looked around. The room had green ivy that had overtaken one
of the walls completely. Next to the ivy sat a small wooden table

covered in old books with a copper watering can on the window-sill above it. The room had a dark wooden desk with a blue chair. Picture frames and a glass jar filled with stones, seashells, and paint-brushes sat on the desk.

Where am I?

The bare wall closest to the desk had a few uncanny sketches of what looked to be mythical creatures, strange flowers with remedies written in thin pencil, and animals. I noticed another chair posi-tioned close by me. Whoever occupied it had been watching me as I slept. A chill ran down my spine and panic fluttered in my chest. The lingering smell of vomit wafted by my nose.

My breathing quickened as I tried to recall *anything* of what might have led me to this room, and then the silence was inter-rupted. The glass doorknob rattled, and I watched it turn until it came to a stop. The door creaked open just enough to see whatever it was peeking in at me. A vibrant green eye, no more than a foot above the doorknob, widened in fear upon seeing me awake. The eye vanished, and the door slammed shut. Footsteps shuffled behind the door, and I heard whispering. I began scooting myself nervously into the corner of the room. The doorknob began to turn again, and this time, the door swung open. Closing my eyes, I scooted as far back as I could until my back hit the wall. I was trapped.

"I hope Yael didn't wake you." A woman's kind voice spoke.

I opened my eyes, and there stood a woman with a girl pinch-ing her nose while looking at the yellow bile I had vomited. The woman smiled.

"Oh my," she said, finally seeing the vomit. "Well, not to worry, we'll clean that right up."

The girl disappeared for a moment and returned with a sponge, rag, and pail of water. Without a single word she quickly cleaned the vomit while the woman continued speaking.

The woman fixed me with a stare. It wasn't hard or accusing but it was certainly intense. She was striking. She had a small-framed body like Ada and wore a flowing dress that faded from a midnight blue to a light gray and brushed the tops of her bare feet. Her hair was black as ink with a thick silver streak that lined her face and emphasized her prominent facial features. Her eyes matched Yael's vibrant emerald green.

Eben's words strung through my mind. *"There was even a rumor that these women were immortal, with eyes the colors of vibrant precious stones."*

"My, how you look *just* like her." Her lips curled up into a smile, flashing a set of pearly white teeth.

I didn't have to ask who she meant.

"You must be hungry, deary." she said as Yael finished cleaning the floor. "Come on, let's get you something to eat."

Yael swiftly spun around with the pail in hand. Her waist length black hair swayed back and forth as she disappeared off down the dark hall.

"The kitchen is just down the hall when you're ready," the woman said then she followed behind Yael.

Rolling onto my knees, I pushed myself off the woven mattress and stepped onto the stone floor. I had been dressed in a long t-shirt looking nightgown, my clogs by the door and my jacket hung beside it. I tugged at it, pulling it up to reveal my legs and hips. I touched my lower back to see what damage remained from my fall in the woods. Nothing. There was nothing there to indicate I'd been hurt at all, not a scratch, not a bruise, nothing.

Did I imagine the entire thing?

I stood up and rocked my hips back and forth and felt no pain. If it did happen, could I have really healed that quickly? I wasn't sure anymore; everything felt like a confused, rudderless nightmare. Moving my way out of the room, I stopped when I caught my reflection in a small hand held mirror lying on the desk. I picked it up and looked at myself. My eyes were even bluer than before, deep and cold like the pacific waters. I blinked to see if it was an illusion, but they stayed quite blue this time. My skin appeared fairer and my hair richly darker than usual. At a glance, I may not have even recognized myself. A pan banging in the kitchen broke my concentration. I placed the mirror down and headed towards the sounds.

The hallway was long and empty. The walls, like the bedroom, were made of stone. The kitchen was dimly lit, and Yael sat on the counter with her legs dangling off as she carefully watched her mother. She couldn't have been more than a couple years younger than me. As I moved into the room, Yael hopped off the counter and stood beside her mother.

"Sorry, we've never had a guest before! Come on Yael, say hi, you know how long we have been waiting for her!"

Yael threw me a quick smile.

I took a seat at the wooden island in the middle of the kitchen and watched them. The kitchen was warm and comforting, with a roaring fire in the woodstove and copper pots and pans hanging from a rack on the ceiling. The window sat over a deep white sink. The moon reflected off a large body of water outside. Where was I? Perhaps, it was the lake I jumped over? Was I near the lighthouse? I felt a sudden poke on my shoulder and turned to find Yael handing me a ceramic cup filled with tea that smelled of fresh herbs.

"Thank you."

Yael only exchanged a curious look, said nothing, and turned to her mother. The woman gave Yael a wink whilst pouring herself a cup of tea.

"Ma'am, I should—"

"Ma'am? Please, child! I'm not that old!" She paused, thought a moment, and then chuckled to herself. Her laugh reminded me of Ada—who I knew must be worried sick, frantically looking for me, blaming herself for my disappearance.

"My name is Edel," Her voice was gentle, sweetly interrupting my frantic thoughts.

"I'm Nora," I said. "Look, I need to go home, my aunt is going to be…" Then it dawned on me that this was Ada's friend.

"Eleanora, I know who you are, and you cannot leave at the moment. Trust me, Ada knows where you are. Bottom line is that you're safe now. Iona brought you here. You were lucky too, you could have died tonight, or worse."

What on earth could be worse than death? I shook my head and I could feel a wry smile work its way through the stunned shock I was in.

"What is it, dear?" Edel addressed me smile.

"It's just that everyone seems to know me, my name, my mother, what I am…"

"It's a small island. But beyond that, the questions you have, and there must be many of them, will all be answered soon. The question at the moment though is 'who are we?' Am I right?"

"That would be a start, I guess," I said, but there was a giddy irrational anxiety bubbling up in me that I couldn't quite get in front of.

Was Edel involved with the women in the woods? The thought that I'd been kidnapped quickly entered my mind. Was I ever going to see Ada again? What about Eben, Joe, and Wren? Where was I being kept hostage? Was I even still on the island? I wanted to stop this stomach-twisting merry-go-round I was being forced to ride with no instructions. The uncontrolled pressure of questions flooded my mind as I tightened my lips while pressing my tongue against my teeth. I gripped the end of the kitchen island, focusing on having my questions come out calmly and slowly, but the effort had no success. I could feel Edel's eyes on me.

"Can you please just explain to me what the *hell* is going on!" My voice sounded close to a shriek.

Edel didn't seem surprised with my outburst.

"Who are you two? What are you two? What am I?" I continued, looking back and forth between the two emerald pairs of eyes that now watched me almost in amusement. I hated how they watched me. It started to frustrate me how neither responded, just observed. The anxiety boiled over into anger.

"Tell me, how it is you know me! How did I end up here, in your house? Why am I this person people have been waiting for!"

Still no response from either, and my frustration grew worse.

"Fine. Who were the women in the woods then? How is it you all know my mother?"

Yael moved closer to Edel the angrier I became.

"What is *happening* to me?" My voice grew louder, and I watched as Edel maintained her elegant composure.

"I already *told* you, dear," Edel said. "Your questions will be answered soon, it's just not my place."

"Seriously? Not your place? Whose place is it then! When? *When* will they be answered?"

I heard a bell go off.

"Toast is done," was the only thing Edel said.

Sucking in a deep breath, I tried calming myself. The toast smelled slightly burnt, and she got up gracefully, floating to the other end of the room, taking the toast out and putting it on a small white plate. She brought it over to the counter with a little jar of jam and placed both items in front of me. A cautious wide-eyed Yael handed me a butter knife, her expression slightly fearful.

"I am not hungry," I spoke through clenched teeth.

"Well, you're missing out if you don't at least try it. Yael made the jam from our garden." Edel said, proud of her daughter. "It's blueberry. Oh, you like your toast a little burnt, right? Your mother did," she added, shrugging her shoulders, disapproving of the toast.

Yael tapped on her mother's shoulder, and Edel turned around. Yael must have been thirteen or fourteen, so why wasn't she speaking? The girl began to make hand signals to Edel, and I understood. Yael was mute.

"Okay, okay," Edel said and turned to me.

"Yael would like to know if the blueberry jam is okay? If not, she has also made wild raspberry."

"No, I mean, yes it's fine, thanks." The truth was I couldn't care less about the flavor of the damn jam.

"Yael doesn't speak," Edel said with a hint of sadness in her eyes. "But she can hear. In fact, she has a gift for hearing. She simply can't speak."

Normally I would have felt compassion towards the girl as I watched Yael gently spreading the jam over her own piece of toast, but at the moment, my sympathy level was at an all-time low. All I wanted was to know what was going on, and every question that I had asked so far had been ignored. Edel read my frustration and immediately began to answer my rising thoughts again.

"Look Nora, I know a lot of things have happened to you within the past twelve hours, and we do owe you a lot of explanations, about everything. About your whole existence really, but we aren't the appropriate ones to answer these questions. You need to be patient, please," Edel said with a more serious tone.

Yael stared at her mother, and Edel took Yael's toast, breaking off a piece for herself. Yael licked the jam off the end of her fingers and then froze, narrowing her eyes sharply and turning her face to look at the front door.

I became nervous with the way Yael sat perfectly still, too still, to the point where even her breathing stopped for a long moment. Yael turned to Edel and the two shared a moment of silence; this time, no signing was exchanged.

"We have company," Edel said, breaking the silence and looking in my direction.

I listened, but I couldn't hear anything, just the breeze causing a branch to lightly tap the kitchen window. Yael searched my face, wondering if I could hear what she was hearing, and I shook my head. She slightly narrowed her vibrant green eyes at me and then I heard it.

–Try–

A light voice strung through my ears, the way Vivienne's did, but it wasn't Vivienne's voice. Somehow I knew it was Yael.

–Try, Nora–

Her lips never moved, and I open my mouth stunned when I heard her voice again.

–Can you hear me, Nora–

Her words trailed off into a whimsical giggle, and I stared fascinated, not knowing how to respond. Her voice was so vibrant, sweet and high pitched. When she stopped *speaking silently*, the voice I'd heard left a ringing in my ears.

–If you can hear me, Nora, then maybe you can do what I can do. Answer me back, Nora–

Edel noticed something happening between Yael and me.

"You can hear her, can't you?" Edel asked stepping closer to me.

I sat still, my shoulders stiff, my chest tight. I was hearing voices. I was hearing the voice of a mute child. I was losing my mind.

"Nora, can you hear her?" Edel spoke louder, almost stumbling over her words in shock.

"Yes, *yes* I can hear her! This isn't normal, this can't be!" My hands trembled.

–Don't be afraid, it's okay–

Yael smiled.

–Maybe you can hear what I'm hearing then? Why don't you try–

Yael gestured towards the window.

Perhaps I hit my head harder than I anticipated when I fell. Perhaps I was still in the nightmare and I hadn't awoken yet. I pinched my own skin. Yael laughed again.

–You're awake Nora, you're not in a dream. This is real. Go on and close your eyes, sometimes that works when I can't focus–

Obediently closing my eyes, I listened as Yael's soft hand touched my arm. At that very moment I began to hear *everything*. Someone's quick little breaths, Edel's fingers tapping on the kitchen island impatiently wanting to know what was happening between us, the candles in the other room sizzling as they ate through their wicks and a fan's blades turning slowly as it moved the air around the other room. Standing still, I began realizing what was happening to me, I had the ability of magnified hearing of some sort.

–Pretty amazing ability, huh? Now try to focus outside–

Ability?

Focusing on the branch that tapped the window, I closed my eyes. The sound grew into a heavy thumping. I was able to hear each individual leaf shake as if they were being combed by the wind. Some type of animal padded around in the grass nearby the house, and I could hear the water outside gently lapping the beach. Then something foreign filled my ears. I heard footsteps. The feet were cracking branches and crunching leaves as they walked quickly in our direction. They were coming closer and closer. Two voices that were faintly mumbling to one another made their way to my ears. The conversation sounded serious and intense. My eyes widened as the voices became clearer.

Ada!

–Yes, That's right! It's Ada–

Yael 'yelled,' causing me to jump out of my chair.

"You can hear everything I am thinking?" I said, and she nodded with a satisfying look of contentment.

I turned to Edel. "She can read minds?"

"No she can't," Edel said. "Well not everyone's. She can't read my mind even if I am trying to send her something. But I can hear her."

I pressed my palms against my temples, squeezing my head. I began feeling dizzy, looking back and forth between Edel and Yael and unable to block the intricate sounds I was now being exposed to. Tap. Tap. Tap. My heel fluttered in frustration against the wooden floor.

Do these people not realize how freaking crazy this is for me? I am hearing voices like some sci-fi crap on television or in a fantasy book.

I felt even more stir-crazy and uncomfortable in my own skin unsure of what I'd experience next.

"But how is that possible?"

"Nora, we don't know how or why our abilities behave the way they do. My guess is that you two have a lot more in common than you think. It's called a mind connection, only common amongst Lamians and Shapeshifters. The way your..."

Edel seemed to catch herself and simply stopped talking. She closed her eyes and turned placing her hands on her low back. She had said too much.

"My mother?" I said. "What *about* my mother? What the hell is a Lamian? This is freaking insane!"

What was beginning to happen to me? Ada was almost here, I could hear her voice, but I knew she was nowhere in the range of normal hearing. I quietly listened again, trying to settle my mind and ferocious heart. She was even closer now, she was running.

"Ada's been in on this too, all these years? Does she have abilities?", I asked, my heel hitting the wooden floor with more force as I tapped it with growing anger.

"You all have left me in the dark for seventeen years. Alone, in the dark about who I am, hiding what I am. Am I even human, Edel? What am I?"

My skin had begun to feel irritated and itchy. I raked my chest with my fingers leaving fiery red lines. Edel had yet to turn back and face me.

"*Look at me*, Edel!"

Edel unnaturally turned around and looked straight at me. Her face warned caution. I was becoming aggressive, upset, angry, and feeling out of control.

"Nora, I think it's only right if we wait for Ada. Okay dear? She is almost here. You heard her!"

"So that answer is a no! I am not human? Am I whatever you said earlier, Lamian or some kind of shapeshifter?"

"Please Nora," she exchanged looks with Yael. "I only think it's right if you hear it from Ada."

"Ada had seventeen *years* to tell me this stuff!"

My face flushed scarlet. I was a stranger in my own skin. I had never felt this kind of anger in my life. Fury and confusion grew. Its sensation was an overwhelming concoction of hate. The only things I knew—the only things keeping me remotely calm—was the following litany.

My name is Eleanora Ada Stone. I was moved from home to home for seventeen years. I am now living on this godforsaken island in Maine. I was being kept from a world of secrets.

I have abilities. I am not human.

I do not know what I am.

I kept repeating it to myself over and over.

I felt insane.

Tightly shutting my eyes, I continued listening to Ada who was now very near. She had been hiding an *entire* world from me. The only person I had ever trusted had lied to me for seventeen years. Who was she really? Was she even my aunt or was that a lie too? Was the lighthouse really our home, or was she hiding me there?

Yael's face reflected her awareness of my fuming thoughts and my repetitive chanting. I watched as she slid off of the island and stepped behind her mother.

"Stop, Nora. You'll be getting all your answers momentarily! Please, try and relax. You don't know what your abilities make you capable of. Try to remain calm, emotionless."

"*Emotionless?*" The word was like pulling the pin from a grenade. "That's the state I've been forced to live in all my life, Edel!"

My vision started blurring as flashbacks crossed my mind. Moments of *almost* experienced emotions quickly being suppressed by Ada: I fell off a bicycle, but before a single tear could escape my eyes, Ada had scooped me up and told me to calm down, stay emotionless, the pain would pass; or the time when a girl in school threw a rock at my head as Ada was picking me up from school, calling me a freak, but before I could turn around and run at her, Ada had grabbed me, calmed me down and told me to walk away, turn the other cheek. Flashes like a picture book of emotionless moments flickered in my mind. I had been trained to live in a numb state. Trained to hide from my true self.

Anger was consuming me like a wild animal, clawing, snapping, and foaming at the mouth. I focused on Edel's voice feeding me what felt were *more lies*. I could trust no one. All of it was a lie. My life was made up of lies. I wanted the truth, and I wanted it now. Ada had always kept me moving around so I could never feel emotions, build friendships, feel attachments or even discover what I was. Was this because she was afraid of the unknown with me? Afraid to see how I'd react? Afraid she wouldn't know how to *control* me? Then I saw Edel clasp her hands at her neck. My thoughts were volatile, a stream of concentrated poisonous liquid.

–STOP IT NORA! STOP IT! MOMMY CAN'T BREATHE!–

Yael blared through my mind like a bullhorn.

Edel gripped the side of the counter with one hand and the other was at her chest, her face quickly changing colors, and Yael clung to her in panic. I backed away scared, unsure of what was happening to Edel. I couldn't have done that; it was impossible. I never touched her! Edel coughed and scraped for air as she lay down on the kitchen floor in her daughter's arms. Yael threw me a look of resentment as she gripped her mother for dear life. Edel finally began to catch her breath, and tears ran down Yael's flushed cheeks.

I backed away in horror from a murder I'd almost accidentally committed. I bumped into a chair, knocking it over, and it smashed onto the kitchen floor.

"Edel, I..." The words couldn't come out of my mouth. "I am..."

"Stop her," Edel instructed Yael.

Yael stood up and started to walk towards me.

"Don't come any closer." I put my hands up and Yael flew backward into her mother's arms.

I looked at my hands. *I was dangerous.* I was terrified. I could feel my blood pulsing in my neck and arms. I turned and ran out the front door. I didn't know where I was on the island. I had no control over my own body, my mind, and my thoughts weren't private anymore.

The lake was the only place I could think of running to, and I fell into the sand. Gripping my knees to my chest, I let out all the tears that had been backed up for the last seventeen years.

Wake up! Wake up! Wake up! Come on Nora wake up! I pleaded to myself.

This was surely a nightmare. For the first time, I felt incredibly alone. I wanted and needed my mother more than ever. I was a child again, pleading, lost, hurt and vulnerable. The tears continued breaking through, and I could scarcely breathe as I tried muffling the sounds against my knees. I had no memories of crying before. My chest heaved, and I was still unable to catch my breath. Screaming cries began to fill the still peaceful night air.

My body swelled with suppressed emotions. Thoughts of Ada and our fabricated life together flashed through my mind. Thoughts of the photo by my bedside. Ada and my mother were both extraordinarily beautiful, just like these women. They both had vibrant eyes; my mother had beautiful Pacific blue, and Ada a sage green. My mother's smile was lovely and mesmerizing—so what happened to me?

My eyes were never vibrant, only a dark gray-blue, and my skin didn't seem as fair or as flawless as hers or these women but spilled on by constellations of dark freckles. My hair was a plain brown that was bunched up like a knotted nest filled with tangles on top of my head. What was wrong with me? New truths were beginning to unravel. I shivered.

My name is Eleanora Ada Stone. I was moved from home to home for seventeen years. I am now living on this godforsaken island in Maine. I was being kept from a world of secrets.

I have abilities. I could kill someone without meaning to. I do not know what I am.

I am dangerous.

9

A timid hand brushed along my shoulder. I looked up to see Ada's face as she sat down beside me. We sat in silence for what felt like an eternity.

"I royally screwed up," Ada finally said.

"Ya think?" I was consumed by the intensity of all that had happened.

"Your parents and I thought we were doing the right thing when we decided to hide you."

"Ada, you all have kept me in the dark, flat out lied to me about everything. Everything!"

"Their intention behind all that was for me to keep you as far away from this world for as long as I could. We've been tracked ever since I left this island with you bundled in my arms. I had to leave everything, everything behind, except you." There was a break in her shaky voice. "You think I *liked* being nomadic? No never, I'm a homebody at heart. I like placing down roots and staying in one place longer than several months. I kept you moving from town to town so you wouldn't get comfortable. I did it to keep you alive. And I knew that one day you would be filled with hate for me. I was honoring your parents' wishes in wanting to give you your best chance before I had to bring you back here. God only knows how many nights I stood by the windows of our apartments watching to make sure we were safe while you slept soundly in bed."

"So why did you *have* to bring me back here?" My mind felt numb.

Ada took a deep breath.

"I noticed your powers coming out in small ways, mostly when you were asleep. The rattling of objects when you experienced nightmares, flickering of lights when you felt excitement or anger. And your eyes. I have seen them change before, but I had to keep my mouth shut."

"If it's safety you all were so concerned about, why keep me in the dark, why lie? Why keep me vulnerable like that?" I said. "Y'know what, Ada? I'm kind of overwhelmed right now if you can imagine that. I can't even come up with the words. You try being lied to for seventeen years, thinking you're living a normal human life and the best that your aunt could provide you after your parents' death. I mean, did they even die, Ada? Everything, *everything* to me feels like a lie right now. I've found out about abilities I can scarcely imagine! I almost killed your friend, Edel, right in front of her daughter whom I flung back shortly after using some invisible force! I am dangerous, and you kept that from me! Why?"

I pressed my hands against my temples and took a deep breath.

"There is something happening to me. I don't feel in control of my body, especially when I get upset. It's as if something inside of me wants me to hurt the nearest person. Is that feeling normal? I am terrified right now. Terrified of myself. I'm scared to even think! What am I?"

I picked up a smooth oval stone, squeezed it in my hand and threw it into the lake. Ada closed her eyes and silence sunk into the space between us. I could feel a small ember of annoyance. Rather than let it smolder and kindle into something else, I broke the silence.

"No more lies. I want answers now."

She wouldn't look at me and stared fixated towards the horizon of the lake.

"You don't know how many times I've played out this conversation over and over in my mind. Hundreds, thousands, ever since the first time I held you in my arms, knowing that someday I would have to answer this question on my own to a child who will view me as deceptive, with every right." Ada said. "That story Eben told you isn't far from the truth, well, the part about men being lured to their death is a bit of a stretch if you ask me. We are Sereni, part of a supernatural race that has been on this planet for over three thousand years, semi-descendants of a particular woman, Queen Lamia, an ancient Queen of Libya. Our bloodline, however, extends from her through Merrow, who was the most powerful siren to ever walk the earth or swim the seas.

"Merrow's was only one of seven pure bloodlines drawn from Queen Lamia that descended from the depths of the darkest waters of various parts of the world. Some bloodlines were killed off during hundreds of years of bloodshed, war, and curses, but there are still four strong lines remaining. At least that is what we know."

"You've lost me already." I was so frustrated.

"I know, I know, I'm doing a poor job, but please be patient with me. I'm trying here, okay? It's a lot to suddenly put on your plate. I thought I was going to have more time before this conversation. I wanted to introduce all of this slowly to you, not like this. I am just as stressed to expose you to any of this as you are anxious to learn about it. You don't understand yet the weight you are about to feel. I mean—"

Ada sealed her lips as if she had said something wrong, revealing something I was not yet supposed to know. I glared at her, and she could sense my anger.

"No more lies." I hissed slowly in her direction.

"You are a siren, just as your mother was before you. Just as I am. Ours is an entire world that humans aren't aware of. Very few of them, in fact, know we exist, very few. There has been documentation of myths and stories in ancient literature and text, but even so, a lot of that documentation is fantasy."

"Sirens?" I stared in disbelief. "I remember you reading me Greek myths when I was younger. I thought they were strange. And I remember the sirens."

"Yeah, the closest I ever came to starting this discussion with you. But I just couldn't. I'm sorry."

"We're sirens?"

She looked troubled and I felt, again, that she was holding something back.

"Sereni, yes. It's not like the stories. But all stories start somewhere. We aren't exactly luring sailors to their deaths, like in some depictions, nor are we part fish or bird like in other tales, but we do exist. Those stories are all twisted versions of the truth, but it is the only bit of documented history we have out there in the world." Ada sighed.

I began digging my toes into the sand as a lump developed in my throat.

"I think it's best if we start at the beginning." Ada took a breath, sitting up more comfortably and just like that she began the tale.

"There once was a queen, Queen Lamia. She was born into this world over three thousand years ago to a very poor farmer and his wife in the wild-grained fields of Libya. It is said that the spot of earth where Lamia was born, where the bloodbath of birth was spilled coming from her mother's womb, was left barren for all eternity. No matter how hard the farmer would work the land or how deep he would dig to remove the topsoil, no seed could or would grow. The farmer told his wife that the child was a demon, that the Gods had punished them, and that she must be killed before she was strong enough to defend herself. The farmer's wife refused to kill their only child, and outraged at her husband's wishes, she sliced her husband's throat in his sleep that night, for she feared, if she did not kill him, he would kill Lamia. You see, Lamia was born with very unusual gifts, gifts of control and seduction that began to blossom as she aged.

"Lamia grew to become a devilish and crafty child, showing signs of demonic behavior as she proudly started bringing home animals she had tortured and killed, befriending poisonous serpents in the fields, and speaking an attractive language she claimed the serpents had taught her. The farmer's wife became afraid of what had become of her daughter. The farmer's wife prayed every night to the Gods for the protection of her and Lamia, to rid her of the devil inside her daughter's heart. When the farmer's wife showed signs of worry, Lamia would embrace her mother and say, 'Don't fear me, my beloved mother. I will always protect you and will never allow harm to come your way, and someday I will be queen and will give you all the jewels and gold you desire.' Lamia's mother embraced her daughter's gifts as part of everyday life until the night she witnessed a scene that placed fear in her heart, even fear for her very life.

"On the night of a terrible storm, a shrieking scream stirred the farmer's wife from her sleep, and she ran to Lamia's room where she found the linens empty with no daughter in bed. She knew something was not right, and when she heard another yelp, she ran to the window where she watched Lamia kill a poor farm boy who lived down the road. She watched Lamia whispering, in a serpentine tongue, words she could not understand as she handed the boy the knife. With fear in his eyes and tears flooding his face, the boy sliced his own throat against his will, as she had done to her husband once seventeen years ago. She watched as a large black serpent, lingering at Lamia's feet, began to consume the boy's body. Lamia bent down and stroked the serpent when she saw her mother in the window. The farmer's wife fell to her knees and prayed to the Gods to protect her from Lamia. That night Lamia took her own mother's life, allowing the serpent in to consume her mother's body. She partially kept her promise to her mother, however; for her bones, when stripped from flesh and dried, were eventually dipped in the purest gold and laced with jewels before being buried beneath the red earth."

Ada stopped her story for a moment to examine me. My eyes were wide with shock and my arms were lined with goosebumps but I said nothing, and so she continued.

"Lamia grew stronger and stronger with age, and upon her twentieth birthday, she met a man dressed in silk garments. Lamia and he crossed paths during her daily walks to the market where she had been visiting a woman by the name of Inessa, a witch who practiced the dark arts of magic. With the skill of persuasion, Lamia drew the man into conversation, and he revealed to her that he was, in fact, an ocean god called Nethuns. At which point, Lamia unleashed the full irresistible force of her seductive powers at Nethuns, enslaving him utterly. Every night he would leave the bed he shared with his wife, Amphitrite, and venture to a cave on the Sirte shores of the Mediterranean where Lamia became his mistress. Nethuns promised to make her Queen of Libya, granting her immortality and three sons who would become the future Kings of Libya in return for her silence. And in time three sons were indeed born to Queen Lamia, and all three shared the dark abilities of their mother. They drank the blood of animals and people, and had venomous teeth, the powers of shapeshifting and the use of dark magic.

"Lamia was pleased with her sons, and in time, she became the queen of Libya. She hid her family's dark secrets until one night when Amphitrite—a powerful Goddess in her own right—followed her husband to the cave where the two met every night and found Queen Lamia and her husband together. The wrath of Amphitrite was terrible. She cast her husband from Lamia's bed and sent him from the cave in terror. When alone with Lamia, she cut off her legs, replacing them with the bottom half of a serpent. The goddess then stripped Queen Lamia of her title and went out in search of Lamia's demon sons, who she killed and beheaded. She then brought the heads back to Lamia's cave and tossed them to Lamia's coiled body.

"The Goddess then took seven drops of her own blood and seven from Lamia and created seven women. The Goddess told Lamia that she had created seven of the most beautiful women, so beautiful, that even amongst the gods, they stood in extraordinary magnificence. And furthermore, as these women walked away with beauty drawn from Lamia's blood, her own beauty would wither and die. No man or beast would ever love her again, and even the people she once ruled over would forget her existence. Queen Lamia was left to perish alone in that very cave over a hundred years, forgotten and festering in her own feelings of jealousy, resentment and anger towards the Goddess and towards the seven women created from her own blood who stripped her of her beauty, her crown, and what remained of her humanity. These seven women became known as the Seven Sereni Women, or sometimes simply the Seven."

I felt numb. "So we were created from the blood of a demon?"

"Well, so legend has it," Ada said. "But legend is legend. Who knows for certain? But remember that in the legend we were created in the image of the Goddess Amphitrite to ridicule Queen Lamia. However, even the Goddess could not anticipate the furthest consequences of her revenge."

Ada wiped the sand from her hands, crossed her legs, and sat up straighter before continuing the tale of Queen Lamia and the Seven.

"Disfigured and bereft, Lamia would sing to soothe her soul in the dead of night, using the language of the serpents. She would hold the skulls of her slain sons, promising them they would not be forgotten and that she would one day bring them back into this world and that they would be stronger than ever.

"One evening, a fisherman near the cave heard her serpent song, and attracted by her voice, he walked into her cave. 'Why have you entered here?' Lamia asked from the shadows, not wanting the fisherman to see her disfigurement. Her hair had fallen out. Her once beautiful amber eyes were now black, and her skin had grown a pale ghostly white with dark protruding veins running down the front of her arms, and hard scales lined the back of her arms and sides of her face.

"The farmer replied, 'I followed the most beautiful voice to ever reach my ears, and I have come to seek your hand in marriage, for a woman with such a voice must sing to me every night.' Lamia was flattered, and without thinking she slithered out of the shadows to greet the first man to have shown her even a glimmer of compassion since she had been disfigured and disgraced. But when the fisherman's eyes adjusted to the cave's dim light, he saw what she had become.

"In his horror, he foolishly denounced her. 'Twisted demon! Abomination. Who could ever love such a foul and hideous creature?' Stung by his words, Lamia's battered heart beat all the faster as she coiled the man in her serpent tail and bit his neck, watching her venom, like black ink, web and spread through his body until it killed him. She tossed his corpse into the ocean and retreated back to her cave. From that night on, she would sing to lure man after man into her cave, each professing love for the woman who sang so beautifully, each recoiling at the sight of her. Most she caught and killed and tossed back into the sea. But a few survived her deadly kiss and, half dead and blind from the venom raging in their veins, wandered deranged upon the Sirte shores. And so rumors were spread of a honey-voiced demon who lured men to their doom. And so once sought-after fishing waters were abandoned.

"Until one day when the story reached the ears of a sailor named Keto. Strong and capable, he took his ship along the Sirte shores in search of this monster. But it was not madness that drove him, for he too was part demon and sought his kind. He docked his ship and waited until nightfall, and when he heard the song of Lamia on the salty night air, he followed it to her cave.

"Keto entered the cave and called out to her. 'What a beautiful voice you have. Surely you must be a Goddess in exile. With a voice such as yours, you must become my bride.' Keto heard her hissing

laughter from the corner of the cave though he could not as of yet
see her. 'So you say, deceitful wretch. You have no idea how many
men have entered this cave drawn by the same lust as yours.' But
Keto was not deterred. 'I doubt it not,' he said, "for I have heard
tales from past suitors, indeed such tales are spreading far and wide.'
Lamia hissed at the thought. 'Now, come into the moonlight,' Keto
said. 'Come and I will show you how different I am. Come and let
me see you!'

"Lamia slithered out into the moonlight with her teeth bared,
ready to spring at the bold suitor, but even as she emerged, Keto
transformed into a large black snake and twined himself around
her. For the first time since her doom, she loved again. Keto listened to ten nights of Lamia's cries and stories of what the Goddess
Amphitrite had done to her and her three sons. She poured her
broken vengeful heart to Keto, and Keto soothed it with sweet serpentine words of his own.

"Soon Keto gave her three sons who were again released into the
world. They were powerful and dark-hearted, and like Keto and
Lamia, they too possessed an uncontrollable thirst for blood. They
had dozens of children, after their first powerful three, and when
mature, these later children walked from the cave in human form
and disappeared into the world of men.

"When the Goddess heard fell rumors of the evil wrought by
Lamia's reborn sons, for that is how they represented themselves, she
revisited Lamia in her cave. There she was shocked to find Keto and
Lamia surrounded by dozens and dozens of nests with empty shells
of eggs. She sliced off their heads, burned their bodies and destroyed
a nest of still-warm eggs. The Goddess then went in search of the
children of Keto and Lamia, calling upon the Seven and the children of the Seven to help her in the hunt. This was the start to
how many of the bloodlines were lost. It marked the advent of war
between the Brood of Lamia and the Sereni Women.

"They say that the sands along the Libyan shores were once red, stained with the blood of the Brood and Sereni Women. The Goddess and Sereni Women killed many of the Children of Lamia; however, she could not find them all. One who always evaded her was the most powerful of them all, one of the first three sons that Keto gave Lamia. The Goddess sent Merrow, the most powerful of the Seven, who was said to have been born of blood from Lamia's very heart, to kill him. His name was Alexo Iskander, your father."

"What? Wait, wait, wait." I put my hands up stopping Ada from saying another word. "My father was a son of Lamia and Keto?"

"Yes, he—"

"I thought you said I was a siren?"

"You are Sereni, Nora. A direct descendant of Merrow through your mother."

My head was spinning. "But…"

"Merrow, the most powerful of the Seven, is your great great grandmother."

I was silent for a minute, trying to bring all of this into focus. So much of what she had finally disclosed was so incredible that I didn't know where to start. *My great great grandmother.*

"Hang on, that's only five generations," I said.

"Right," said Ada.

"But you said Lamia was queen three thousand years ago."

"Yes, that's true," she said. I could tell she was wrestling with what to say next. "Nora, the Sereni do not age in the way that, well, *mortals* do."

"You mean I'm immortal?"

"No, we're mortal in that we can be killed. But we don't diminish with age, and we can heal ourselves of many wounds in ways that humans can't."

"And Lamians?"

"Mortal as well. Neither Sereni nor Lamians diminish, though both can be killed."

"And I am?"

"Both. You, Eleanora Ada Stone, are second generation Lamian descended from Alexo Iskander, and a fifth generation Sereni descendant of Merrow, the Sereni tasked with killing him."

"And I can live forever." I was still trying to wrap my mind around this.

"Nora, we all age. What that means for *forever*, who can say? Forever never arrives. Lamia herself and Keto are both dead. Surely they had a stronger claim on immortality than either of us."

Just then, some part of the tension inside me broke, and the prospect of everything Ada had just told me struck me as so out-landish that I could not help but start giggling. It was a nervous slightly manic laugh, but I couldn't get it under control. And when I saw the hint of a smile on Ada's face, I didn't want to stop. It was hard being mad at Ada.

"I know," she said. "It's crazy. It was different for your mother and I because we were raised with this knowledge. I can't imagine how—"

"Wait, how *old* are you?" I felt a flutter in my chest, knowing that her answer would shift the foundation of the world I grew up thinking I knew.

"How old do I *look*?" She gave me a deliberately coy, corny smile.

"Forty-seven," I said though as far as I knew she was thirty-seven and she didn't even look that. Now that I thought about it, she looked more or less as she did in the photo by my bedside taken seventeen years ago.

"Ouch!" she said, feigning insult. "Well, I guess forty-seven is pretty good all things considered. I will turn five hundred and thirty-two this summer. I've always thought there was something wise and dignified looking about white hair, but I have a lot of waiting to do yet."

I was stunned.

"It's a lot to take in," Ada said, sensing the blow she'd just dealt me.

"What happened with Edel? I nearly killed her, didn't I?"

Ada looked grim.

"Yes," she said. "It's not your—"

"I'm dangerous," I said. "I almost killed a woman in front of her own daughter."

"Nora, *anything* can be dangerous if not used properly. You haven't been taught anything, and that's my fault."

I glared at her. My feelings of anger returned.

"Yes, but some things are intrinsically more dangerous than others, aren't they?"

I wondered if Ada could feel the heat simmering in my head.

"Okay, yes. That is true. As Sereni descendant, well it's complicated, but a purebred siren is one-quarter blood of Lamia herself, the rest being made up of blood of the Goddess. More divine than demonic. Those numbers change if a siren, well if a siren mates outside the Sereni race. And it does happen. Oh, I should say that there are male Sereni and so you're…"

Just get to the goddamned point! I was having a hard time focusing on what she was saying.

"…not the only half Lamian. There are others. But Alexo, he wasn't just *any* Lamian, he was a first born of Keto and Lamia, and therefore not simply Lamian but a full-blood demon."

I gripped my knees, bringing them closer to my beating heart.

"So I am more Lamian than Sereni," I said rocking back and forth.

"No, Nora," she said. "You're not. But you are more demon than divine. Which makes you *special,* maybe even unique at this point."

"Don't sugar coat it Ada. What it makes me is dangerous."

"Nora, your powers, all of them, can be controlled. But you must always be aware of them because you will live with them the rest of your life, fighting and yielding."

My chest swelled.

"And I'm afraid there's more," Ada said.

I didn't want to hear it.

"I almost *killed* her! I felt the overwhelming energy of anger, hate, and was suddenly unable to control myself. I wanted to hurt her and I was unable to stop that desire. That was the demon side of me, wasn't it?"

I was starting to panic, nervously scratching under my collarbone, digging my nails into my skin. I began to feel hot and itchy, an itch that no matter how hard I raked my skin could not be relieved. My chest heaved. I was afraid of my thoughts, of my body, and what I could do or whom I would hurt next, including myself.

Ada latched onto my body and tried to calm me, but I grew angrier and angrier the more she held me.

"Nora, there is more you need to know."

"Get off!" I shrieked like a tea kettle erupting. Ada flew back in the sand the way Yael had done. I was like a wild horse that Ada had repressed for years.

"Nora, *please.*"

I looked at her stunned. She was clutching her forearm and wincing.

"Oh God, Ada!" I snapped back to my old self, fearing what I had done.

"It's not you." Ada's eyes darted to her arm and she cringed. I could hear the teeth grind in her mouth. We both stood in the sand watching as something began to stain her skin. A black mark started to appear and like ink dropped in water it leaked through her fair pigment, forming strange symbols. Ada mumbled a string of painful words under her breath.

"Ada?" I said. "What is happening to your arm?"

"It's a glyph," she whimpered.

"A *what?*" I ran my fingers over the swollen skin.

"A glyph. It's like a tracking device You will have one too, the day you become eighteen. It's so they have an element of control. Son of a—" Ada bit her lip and grabbed her arm, hunching over.

"Who?" I asked and I cautiously lowered my voice in a paranoid whisper. "Ada, who exactly is tracking you?"

"The Elders, they know you're back. They want to see you."

"The Elders? Who the heck are they!" I stood up and took a step back from Ada. "Are they coming here now?" My eyes darted around the tree line and across the lake. I became afraid wondering if I could really trust Ada.

"Stop looking at me like I am an enemy, Nora! I have given my life and word to both your parents to protect you, and that is *exactly* what I plan on doing. I would die before I would ever let anything happen to you."

I knew I would be lost without Ada. My hands were bound. I had to trust her.

"I'm sorry, I don't know what came over me." I took a seat, looking at her. It was starting to become easy for me to lose control of my emotions. Ada rubbed her forearm and winced once more.

"Nora, there is more I need to share with you, but right now we have to go. The Elders aren't exactly patient."

"But who *are* they, Ada?"

The skin on her arm was red as if blistered and on the brink of bleeding.

"They are the oldest and most powerful Sereni alive. Nephthys was one of the Seven created from Queen Lamia's blood and is over three thousand years old. The other two, Milda and Nit, well, it's complicated in ways that aren't important right now. What is important is that the Elders rule the Sereni world and enforce what they see as the law. However, their loyalty has been a topic of question for over a thousand of those years or so. Their story will have to be told another time."

Ada ground her teeth again in pain as a drop of blood spilled from her forearm to the sand. She looked as though she wanted to reach out and put her hand on my shoulder.

"Please, I know it's a lot to ask after what I've done to you, but please trust me. I know I have disappointed you, but I need you to trust me right now, this very minute. We need to go. I will explain and answer any questions when we come back, okay?"

I said nothing more and stood up, brushing the sand off of me.

Ada grabbed my hand, but I jerked it out of hers, and I knew this action was like taking a small blade and piercing her heart. We both walked back together towards the stone cottage in silence.

10

When we got to the cabin, Edel and Yael were there and waiting for us. A third woman I had never met emerged from the shadows. All three were dressed in hooded cloaks that left half their faces in shadows. The one I did not know held up her lantern directly in my face. The light shone off her lips, which were slightly parted in a cynical expression. She tilted her face up towards me, and her eyes flashed a brilliant amber. She slowly pulled back her hood then looked to Ada.

"Took you long enough," she said, turning the hand that held the lantern and showing the dark angry welt on her forearm.

"*Lia.*" Ada sounded as though the name left a bitter taste in her mouth. "It's been a while."

Lia sneered. "Not long enough." Then she turned to me. "Eleanora, I presume."

She had two cloaks draped over her unmarred arm, and before I could reply she threw one at me, then tossed another to Ada.

Ada swung her cloak gracefully around her body and pulled the hood over her head, buckling three brass clasps. The cloak thrown at me looked similar. It was heavy, lined with some kind of animal fur on the inside and around the collar. Mine had one brass clasp instead of three like Ada's. I fastened it and pulled the hood over my head like everyone else. My body felt cozy inside the draping fabric.

Lia began to cover her face again and threw me a withering glance.

"What an honor to finally meet the *one*."

I looked to Ada and mouthed the words, "The one?"

Ada looked very tired. "Like I said, I have more to share with you. For right now, just trust me please."

"She doesn't *know*?" Lia smirked. "Boy, is *this* going to be a rude awakening."

I glared at Ada.

Lia pulled back her shoulders and stood frozen with her one arm stretched out and her palm facing the starry night sky. No one moved. She closed her eyes and became very still, not even a strand of hair swayed in the breeze. Then her nostrils flared as if she caught a hint of something foul in the air. She made a low hissing sound that ran chills through my body. Her eyes flung open and they were no longer a warm glowing amber, but black and smoky. The blackness had swallowed the entire whites of her eyes. She looked possessed by something dark, the way Vivienne had.

"Let's go," she said and began to run.

"She is being controlled right now," said Ada under her breath.

"By who?" I tugged my cloak.

"The Elders." Edel's voice sounded raw and gravelly; the first words I had heard her speak since I had almost killed her. I noticed Edel had a painful looking glyph raised on her forearm as well.

We all began to run, following Lia into the forest.

We entered the forest line near the cottage, and a wall of fog greeted us, swallowing the trees. The thick cloud added a certain element of haunting beauty to the woods. Within minutes, our world had turned white, and at times, the unnerving environment left me tense for fear of losing the group. I kept close to Ada. It began to grow significantly colder as the fog grew thicker. For once the temperatures affected me. My teeth chattered. The thick icy air ripped through our throats. I pulled the collar of my cloak tightly around my neck as we ran into the unknown.

My mind raced with questions about the Elders, about the stories of Queen Lamia, Merrow, my mother, and my parents' death. There were moments when the fog was so thick I stopped, lost in a sea of haze, listening for someone, *anyone*, a footstep, a breath, when Ada's face would appear inches before mine and she would snatch up my hand to lead me. We came to a sudden stop in front of a dark wet wall made of stone—a cliff. I touched the icy surface and looked up. It was an enormous cliff that towered over us, disappearing into more fog.

Now what?

Lia stood next to me, staring up at the wall. She reached out her hand and stroked the surface, hissing in a foreign tongue. Little chips of rock began to rattle, falling to our feet, and then the ground began to tremble. I backed up against Ada who didn't budge. Like an intricate lock, the wall began to move, banging and sliding stone forming stairs. I blinked in amazement, touching the steps. Lia began running up the stone staircase. Yael quietly raced up behind her and Edel followed. I stepped back, timid of stepping on the charmed stairs.

Ada pushed me back towards them but I remained still. "Did that seriously just happen?"

"I know this is a lot," Ada said. "I get it, but we need to move. The steps won't last forever."

"What do you mean they won't last?"

Dark heavy cloaks whipped about, making loud snapping sounds in the air overhead. I timidly took a step towards the staircase.

–Climb!–

Yael's voice sounded in my head.

Yael was half way up the staircase watching me. My feet found their courage, and I began making my way up the first couple stairs. Slowly, I began to climb, feeling exposed and afraid.

"Faster, Nora!" Ada yelled from behind me.

I looked over, and within seconds, she leaped over me and ran up fifteen or so stairs.

"Let this idea of fear go. It's only preventing you from moving, and you *need* to move. Trust me, you don't want to be on this when it begins to crumble." Ada's idea of a pep talk.

"What do you mean let go of fear? Like I'm choosing to be afraid. I *hate* this, all of this."

Ada jumped back down to the step above me and placed her hands on my shoulders. "Nora. I know what I have done to you, I know that you don't trust me, that you even hate me, but you need me right now to survive. Do you understand? So please, for the moment cut the attitude and trust me. Move!"

I angrily watched her, wanting to go home, back to the white house where I had made friends and where Eben was waiting for me. I didn't want to be here with her and in this freak world she suddenly thought appropriate to introduce me to.

"Nora!" Ada's voice rose as she tried grabbing my hand.

I took a step back down evading her grasp and *away* from Ada. I looked up, past her, at the other three cloaked figures standing above us on different steps watching.

"Bring her to us!" Lia's voice ripped the air. But it wasn't her voice—not the voice she had near the cottage; the Elders were communicating through her.

"Nora *move*!" Ada whispered intensely.

"Bring her to me!" The strange voice boomed again.

My chest felt tight and my cheeks burned. Ada's eyebrows furrowed in annoyance as she snatched my hand and started yanking me up the stairs when a sudden tremble began beneath our feet.

"Nora!" Ada released my hand to hold her balance. "Move!"

The staircase had begun to crumble. Edel and Yael ran quickly after Lia, and Ada and I began to scramble. Below me, there was nothing but exposed air. The fog had devoured the forest. Crumbling chunks of stone fell to the earth. Then the realization that I was maybe a hundred feet above ground unleashed a nervous panic. The sharp wind howled by my ears, and my hood flew off my head. Suddenly the step below my feet crumbled and I began to fall. My stomach quickly moved into my throat, and I waved my arms in the air when Ada grabbed my hand pulling me up the next step.

"*Now* will you listen?" she fumed.

Sweat lined her forehead. I nodded obediently. She let go of my hand, running to the top of the staircase, and I followed. Sounds of loud bangs came from underneath us as the staircase continued breaking off into chunks and vanishing into the fog. I caught the sound of laughter through the crashing of stone and I looked up to the ledge, it was Lia. A sudden surge of anger boiled up. The same dark energy that had taken me over when I attacked Edel revisited my bones.

The dark demon inside of me stirred, and I began tearing up the staircase like a lion spotting its prey. I was no longer in control of myself. Something inside of me moved effortlessly throughout my body, the sensation was seductive, and the idea of seeing pain sprouted a seed of pleasure in my mind. I wanted to *hurt* her. Within seconds, the last step collapsed, and as though through a red fog I somehow found I had Lia pinned down by the throat, holding her tightly as her head dangled off the ledge and her curly dark hair waved violently in the exposed space.

"Well, well." The Elder's voice rattled her tongue. Lia gasped, fighting for air as we both heard the last crash coming from beneath the fog. "You *are* the child of a demon. Run by your desire to hunt. To kill."

Her black possessed eyes burned a hole in me. The rain made her lips glisten, and I realized where I recognized her from—my dream. She was the one watching me as I watched myself die.

She let out a deep ticking growl. I started to release my hand, realizing what I was about to do— afraid of the darkness within me—when I felt a sudden blow to my stomach and I flew into the air. Lia watched me flip and then sent a second searing blow into my ribcage, while grabbing and twisting my wrist and slamming me into the hard wall. My vision was going in and out. I realized I was now hanging off the cliff, weaving in and out of consciousness. I clenched her wrist with my hand.

"If you want to play like a demon," said Lia, "then you better prepare yourself, Eleanora Stone, and kill when the moment presents itself."

My wrist felt limp and broken. Helplessly I dangled there, digging my nails into her cold veiny skin. I watched the black smoke fade from her eyes as they shifted back to amber brilliance.

"Lia, *enough!*"

A new voice, a male voice, though I couldn't see the source.

Lia pulled me up and threw me to the ground like a rag doll. Folding into a fetal position, I coughed, trying to breathe while clenching my wrist with my other hand. I watched her walk away towards another figure. My vision was shaken up, and my head throbbed. Then I saw him for the first time. He too was cloaked. I watched as he grabbed Lia by the chin, pinching her cheeks in as he whispered to her. Lia's hands clenched by her side in what looked like pain. He sounded angry, and then he let her face go, pushing her aside. He was tall and his skin glowed as fairly as Lia's did from under the oxblood cloak. Lia followed him and stood a few feet behind. I watched her as she wiggled her jaw.

"We don't have time for these games," he announced. "The Elders are growing impatient."

He glanced in my direction. There was silence. I felt a hint of fear when he spoke, and now his eyes burned into the side of my face. I stayed there a moment longer, watching as he began to close in on me. Yael's small fingers and Ada's hands grabbed my shoulders, picking me up. I flinched at the pinching sensation of my wrist.

"What the heck has gotten into you, Nora?" Ada spat. "You're going to get yourself killed. Please let me protect you right now until you're ready."

I might have been ready years ago if you had only bothered to tell me.

My cheeks burned with embarrassment, and I pulled my cloak back over my shoulder with my one working hand. The man watched me carefully from the corner of his eye.

–Aston, his name is Aston–

Aston? I thought to Yael. *Who is he?*

–Aston and Lia are twins–

We struck off into the wilderness again, Lia and Aston moving gracefully together, Lia still a few steps behind her brother.

Are they Sereni?

–Yes, they are Sereni-Lamians. Like you–

So Yael knew then. I guess it was obvious, after what I had done to Edel.

We trekked through the snow, and the temperature grew bitter, warranting the need for these cloaks.

–Arctic weather. It travels wherever the Elders roam–

I wrapped my arms around my body inside my cloak. My wrist throbbed the entire way, causing me to break into a sweat. Ada noticed.

"We'll have to send for Iona. She can heal that quickly."

"Iona?" I recalled the name.

Just then Aston held his hand up and Lia stood still, no longer trailing. He looked over his shoulder to make sure Lia did not move. This was the first time I got a clear glimpse of his profile. He looked just like Lia, fair with dark hair, but with dark, honey brown eyes.

–You find him attractive, huh?–

I felt embarrassed and frustrated knowing that my thoughts around Yael were no longer private.

–He is very dangerous, Nora. They both are–

Dangerous, this is how Yael explained Lia and Aston to me—two people who were a mix of Sereni-Lamian blood, like me. I was labeled dangerous. Yael had been dissecting and observing this world silently her whole existence. Aston walked quietly, and I listened as his feet crunched in a light layer of fresh snow. Our breath had become visible, and I wrapped the cloak even tighter around my body. I watched as Aston stretched out his arm to me.

Everyone in the group stopped and watched his gesture. He scanned my appearance, and without a fight, I obediently walked a few steps forward. I felt like I was on display. When I was close enough, he raised his hand, almost touching my face. Unintentionally I flinched, thinking of how he had grabbed Lia. I closed my eyes in fear of contact, but he only pulled open my cloak and took my wrist in his hand. Aston studied my face as he felt my injured wrist between his hands. Then he spoke so that only I could hear.

"I have a wretched sister," he said. "Here." He pressed both of his hands around my wrist then without warning he squeezed his hands so tightly I gasped. Immense heat wrapped my wrist. The pain was so overwhelming that my eyes began to roll to the back of my head as my knees buckled. Aston caught me in his arms. I blinked tears from my eyes.

"Better?" he asked.

Aston helped stand me up and looked at my wrist, moving it back and forth. The pain was gone.

"Iona, won't be necessary," he said over my shoulder to Ada.

"Thanks," I whispered.

Aston nodded, searching my face once more before turning away.

For a moment, I thought I saw him smile. Could he hear my thoughts like Yael? I felt Yael, Edel, and Ada close in on me.

Lia's voice broke the silence.

"It's them."

"How far?" Aston asked.

Lia took a deep breath, and her nostrils flared again like she could smell them coming. Could she?

"Any minute."

No one moved.

"Nora, listen to me carefully." There was a desperation to Ada's voice I found unsettling. "Do not speak unless spoken to. Do not move unless told to move, and do not look into their faces."

An overpowering scent began to fill the air that stung the inside of my nose and throat. A nerve struck me, and I nervously moved behind Ada, peeking over her shoulder, watching as three shadows appeared through the fog. The tallest figure must have been Nephthys, she led the other two, Milda and Nit. Aston and Lia made the first motion as they knelt to the ground with their heads bowed. Yael was gripping Edel's hand so tightly that her knuckles were white. Everyone else gracefully followed Aston and Lia's lead, except me. Then a hand gripped my just-healed broken wrist and yanked me down to my knees, which crunched into the cold crispy snow.

I shot Ada a look, but she looked back at me square on with such seriousness in her eyes that I did not argue.

"Stay still!" she whispered.

I mimicked everyone and kept my head down, but I couldn't help looking up at the figures slowly approaching us. They glided eerily over the snow and arrived short of Aston. The tallest leaned over and put both hands on his shoulders, raising him to his feet. The hooded face then seemed to kiss Aston's left cheek and speak something very softly into his ear. Aston nodded, then looked at Lia who stood up and turned. He then looked directly at me and walked over, standing before Ada. She moved out of the way without a word being exchanged, and Aston stepped in front of me. This time his face was inches from mine, and I began to feel flushed.

"They want to see you," he spoke quietly.

Everyone watched and Ada looked anxious. I noticed Edel
pulling Yael in closer as I stepped around Aston and walked towards
the three hooded figures. Lia glanced at me, her eyes changed again,
no longer amber, but black and violent. I looked away, stopping a
few feet short, facing the tallest. Her face was hidden behind a dark,
tattered, heavy hood so that only the end of her chin was visible.
The skin on her chin looked raw and thin, as if decomposing. I
quickly turned away, remembering what Ada had told me about
looking at their faces. I didn't want to see any more of what hid
beneath that hood. My body began to feel cold, my heart heavy,
and a feeling of immense weakness swept through me. I felt slightly
sedated as if I could no longer protect myself. She walked closer to
me—with my head down I noticed then that she was barefoot—
stepping through the snow. The skin of her feet was white, tightly
wrapping her prominent bones and tendons as dark veins streaked
them. Her toenails were gray and brittle. I was frozen, hard, scared,
and iced over. I tried not to look into the hood and stayed focused
on the snowy ground. The snow began to illuminate and shimmer
so brightly it became blinding, so I closed my eyes. Then a soft
flowery voice strung through my ears.

"Eleanora Ada Stone, lineage of Merrow, daughter of Rebekah
Lane and Alexo Iskander Stone. Yes, yes I see the bloodline strong in
your veins. What an honor to finally meet you, child. We have been
looking forward to seeing the one hidden for so long. My name is
Nephthys, and these are my sisters Milda and Nit."

Milda and Nit were now circling me and muttering words under
their breath.

"Tell me, Eleanora. Have you always felt different from those
humans you have been forced to live amongst?" She said it as if disgusted by the idea.

"I suppose, a little different," I spoke quietly, my voice subtly
shook, and my tongue felt heavy and wary.

"Only a little different? Modest." She darkly let out a curt laugh, and I could hear the other two chuckling beside her, echoing her words.

"Modest... only a little... different...amongst humans..."

"I see you've been experimenting with your unknown abilities," Nephthys said.

She turned and faced Edel's direction. "Death seems to be near wherever you go."

Edel touched her chest and Nephthys paused, glancing between Yael and me.

"Mind connection, fascinating," Nephthys acknowledged.

"I didn't intentionally—"

"*You*, Eleanora," she spat, and then quietly returned to her sweet flowery voice, "have within you very powerful forces, very dark forces. Ones that will attract your enemies, enemies who also have been waiting for you, who have been looking for you, who want you. Ultimately the choice is yours as to which light you want to strive in."

I swallowed at her last words.

"You can become very useful to us, Eleanora."

Nit and Milda chimed in. "Yes, yes, very useful, very useful."

I had no idea what she was talking about and felt like I wanted to scream.

"Your abilities are yet unclear, but time will tell us all. Control of your emotions will also come with time, but until then, you will be assigned someone who will be watching you very closely. Someone who knows better than to take you and try to hide you."

"*Very* closely," Milda hissed in my other ear, her breath bitterly cold.

That was enough.

"I can take care of myself."

An invisible force struck me across the face, and my tongue clove the roof of my mouth.

"You *will* obey us!" Nephthys said. "And you will *not* interrupt me again."

My tongue released itself, and I clenched my cheeks tightly, feeling humiliated.

Nephthys held up her thin hand and curled her fingers, summoning someone behind me. Turning, I caught a glimpse of Aston making his way over without a word.

"No!" Ada yelled from behind as she attempted to charge in our direction, but she was flung back by an invisible force, the way I had pushed Ada in the sand. Edel rushed to Ada's side and restrained her.

Nephthys glided aggressively towards Ada. "How *dare* you think you can intervene now? You should have thought about this *seventeen years ago* when you foolishly took her! The child was to be brought to *me*!"

"*You* would have killed her!" Ada spat. The veins in her forehead and neck strained.

"Maybe so," Nephthys said under her breath.

"Fool," Milda hissed.

I tried to yell to Ada but my voice was lost and my throat tightened. Nephthys continued on as she lifted both her hands and my right arm numbingly rose and my fingers reached towards Aston. Our hands clasped forearm-to-hand with immense pressure and I winced at the pain, but Aston never flinched, never showed a sign of weakness. Even though his stature looked cold as stone, I could see a flicker of confusion enter his eyes. He was not prepared for what was to come. Nephthys waved her hand over ours, and a burning sensation began to coil through our bound limbs. Nephthys began whispering words, chanting something I could not understand, over and over. Aston's eyes were locked penetratingly on mine, then the burning pain was too much and I screamed.

"Let go! Stop it! Ada!"

Ada tried once more to get up and hit an invisible wall which flung her back into the snow. The more I yelled, the louder

Nephthys chanted and the more our bound hands burned. Then, without the blade of a knife present, I watched as three matching characters began to cut into our forearms. First, an X. Nephthys hissed. Underneath the X a deep painful line began to split my skin slowly, filling with black liquid. Finally, a sharp hook began to burn and carve into our forearms below the line. The black liquid filling the fresh cuts turned to blood, dripping onto and staining the crisp white snow at our feet. Nephthys touched my right cheek, and pins and needles made their way through my mouth and down my throat.

"Now," said Nephthys, "shall we see if the prophecy is true?"

"Prophecy?" I gasped, feeling heavily sedated.

Nephthys sighed and cast a baleful glance towards Ada. "*That* vulnerable."

The Elders began to encircle us, and I could feel the sharp cold air being kicked up.

"Relentless power," said Nit.

"A pure soul," countered Milda.

"Resentful, *very* resentful," hissed Nephthys in my ear.

"Darkness will be visiting in the dead of night," said Milda.

"Human friendships, oh but there is one, one that is different?" Nit sounded disgusted, confused.

"Yes, I see the one. Perfect," said Nephthys.

"You will be surrounded by much pain, child," said Milda.

"You will create much pain," added Nit.

"A child of Lamia," hissed Milda.

"Is she the one? Does the bloodline reveal it?" Milda asked.

"There *is* a chance," said Nit. "I must look closer."

"Heavy decisions will be made," whispered Nephthys harshly into my ear. "Are you prepared to see death? To cause death? For blood to stain your hands?"

"Strong bloodlines," Milda told Nephthys. "Too strong."

"Threatening," Nit said. "She could be *it*."

"Let's kill her now." Milda's voice was bloodthirsty.

"Yes. Yes!" Nit was practically squealing. "Let us taste her!"

There was silence for a moment. Then Nephthys spoke.

"A direct line of the queen herself. A demon. A child of Merrow. The bloodlines have gone untouched. Look at me."

I tried my hardest to resist.

"Look at me!" Nephthys yelled.

My neck twisted against my will, and I yelped in pain. My eyelids were pulled back, and I was forced to see her face. Forced to see what lay beneath her hood. Her skin was marbled, waxy and thin. Her eyes, an arctic blue, were hidden behind narrow slits. She resembled a corpse. I felt frozen in place. My temples pounded and my heart beat rapidly.

Nephthys pulled away quickly, hiding her face behind her hood once again. She grabbed my hand and studied my palm.

"We must be careful with this one." She pulled my hand close to her hidden face, then a long black tongue licked my palm. "She *is* the one the prophecy speaks of."

Goosebumps traveled under my skin. My eyes grew heavy, and as if a powerful drug had just been injected into my veins, I was dragged unwillingly towards sleep. My knees buckled, and my body collapsed into Aston's chest. The ground by our feet was now red. Soon my world was stained red as I fought to keep my eyes open, clutching onto him.

"Please," I whispered. "Don't let them take me."

11

I floated around in dark liquid. My lips began to part. I inhaled gently to breathe, but instead of air, salt water entered my mouth and began filling my lungs. My body began to jolt, fighting for breath. I gripped my throat, kicking my legs, trying to find a way out, but I couldn't. My chest began tightening, and my ribcage restrained my lungs from expanding. I screamed, but no one could hear me. I was alone in darkness. Alone to drown. The water was alive and began to pull me down, drawing me further into darkness. My ankle was shackled to a never-ending chain. Looking up towards a hazy abyss of space, I gave one last scream. Any air that I might have had left escaped, flowering bubbles to the surface. The force of the current pulling me down stopped and everything went still. Silent.

A small stream of light shone through the surface, and I felt nothing, nothing but peaceful silence. This was my last moment. The tides would be taking me soon, taking me to a distant shore, taking me from this world. I thought of Eben and the laughs shared with my first few friends—sitting on a deserted island basking in the warm glow of the setting sun. I tried to relax within the fear of the unknown. The gentle surface of glowing light began to shimmer.

I was ready to accept my fate, ready to let go. My eyes closed for the last time. I felt the stroke of fingers along my cheek when the clasp around my ankle released. I opened my eyes. A body made of fair skin and dark hair wrapped itself around me, pulling me to the surface.

Mom?

I faded into its ghostly arms.

My body rested on a hard earthen surface. My ears were ringing, and I kept my eyes closed. Slowly, after I gained back my hearing, I opened them again. A blinding white light greeted me, and I squinted. The warm sun sank into my skin. I stared through narrow slits until things began to regain their definition. I was in the woods somewhere, with no trace of the body of water I had just drowned in. No trace of the pale-skinned figure who had hauled me to the surface.

Why would I be placed in a barren forest, in the dead of winter? A holly bush nearby sat vibrant green with crimson berries. Frost kissed the ground. I began to shiver, watching my breath escape. I rolled over and felt my damp hair, coated with frost, crunch and peel itself from the earth. I watched the branches of barren trees swaying in the sun.

Why a forest?

I heard laughter. I sat up, looking around for the source of the sound. The laughter began to grow louder—a man's profound voice laughed along with a woman's. The woman began singing a song and I listened.

"Oh little child so small and sweet
stay this way forever with me
through the tides and across the seas
you will always be a part of me."

There was something distant and familiar about these words. Perhaps I had once heard them in a dream. I'd just crawled over to some dead bushes and peered through the barren branches when I spotted them. The woman and man were not even twenty feet from me. They laughed whilst holding something bundled in animal hides. The woman kept repeating the song over and over again as the man hummed and smiled. They looked happy, cooing and making faces at a sweet little child.

The man pushed the woman's fur hood back and kissed her forehead. She was my mother, and the man was my father. Then it occurred to me that the child squirming around in their arms was me. This was the first memory I'd ever had of my family, and I wanted to hold on to this moment as long as possible. It all felt like a distant dream. I'd never had a memory of my family before. I have only ever been cursed with dreams, waking up in sweats, fighting to fall back into the same dream so I could see her again. She was truly beautiful, just like the only photo I had. The sun beat on her dark wavy hair, her eyes a pacific haunting blue, and her laughter and song seemed to fill the deadened forest, bringing life amongst the wintered trees. It was contagious. I smiled, listening.

I never knew what my father looked like before. I had no images of him. He was a striking man with prominent features. He didn't look like a demon, but a kind and gentle soul. He was tall; even sitting next to my mother, he towered over her. His arms wrapped around the both of us, and he played with my mother's hair, twisting it in his fingers. His hands looked strong. They truly loved each other. They looked content and lost in bliss.

The two were entertained by something I was doing. Silently I watched my mother pick a dead branch off a nearby bush and wave it in my face. She raised her arm high in the air and let it go. I quickly shifted my weight, watching as my laughing came to a stop. I froze.

The branch hovered in mid-air above my small face.

I reached as far as my little arms could go, squeaking with laughter at the suspended object. My eyes wide as I watched myself, I moved even closer for a better look. The branch slowly began to come back to life. The dried out branch turned a rich brown and little buds appeared, twisting open into green leaves. My parents and I stared in amazement as it flourished in mid-air. My little arms stretched and swatted for the branch. When I couldn't reach it, my laughter came to an end, and my eyes shifted to black in annoyance. The branch then wilted once more to its original state and then broke into pieces. My mother flinched, looking at my father, who had gone stiff and cold as stone.

"She is strong, Alexo. She will survive."

"She is a demon, Rebekah, because of me. I have burdened her with this. How I had hoped she would be born with only your blood running through her veins. We were fools, Rebekah, fools. They will look for her until the end of time."

"She *will* survive, Alexo! She will grow to learn and strive to stay within the boundaries of light. Use her power for greatness. I know this."

"How do you know this? How?" There was a slight desperation to my father's voice. "They will find her, Rebekah. She is the key to their destruction. She is the prophecy. How long do you think they will allow her to live? It is only a matter of time."

"Gytha showed me the vision." My mother kissed my forehead. "Even if they do, she will become stronger than they could have ever imagined or hoped to control. She will carry out our legacy and fulfill the prophecy, Alexo. You must believe this to be true!"

"A vision." My father sighed, "visions can change, my love."

My mother embraced my small body kissing my forehead once more.

I wanted so much to be part of this moment, to be held in the arms of my mother. I crawled even closer, trying to see more of their faces. Something snapped under the pressure of my hand, a twig. Alexo's face whipped in my direction, and for a second, I locked eyes with him. It was like looking into a reflection, I had his dark, moody eyes. His face spilled with patches of dark freckles and his hair wild and untamed.

Can he see me?

Apprehensively he stood with my mother, scanning in my direction. She looked frightened and quickly swaddled and hushed my giggles, bundling me close to her chest.

"Alexo."

He placed two fingers on her lips and listened. His eyes shifted to black. Something was wrong. I could feel the tension in the air.

"Is it Ada?"

My right ear twitched, hearing feet pounding into the earth, and I turned to see Ada running straight at me until, like a ghost, she flew through me. My body shivered with an overwhelming icy sensation. I turned to watch the three. Ada handed my mother a small paper bag, and my mother handed me to Ada.

"Eben?" she asked, but Ada looked back at her numbly, grabbing me and taking me into her arms.

"They're coming," Ada said in a raw voice. "We need to move!"

"Save her." These were the only words my father said, and within the blink of an eye, the three vanished.

I stood up.

"Wait! Wait, please. Mom!" I called out into the barren forest. Pushing forward, I tripped over the thorny bush that had hidden me, scrambled to pick myself off the ground, and ran to the spot where the three had been standing. I searched frantically around, but they were gone. Was my mother referring to my friend Eben? What was the prophecy they spoke of? My head was spinning. Who was coming? Who was after me?

My heart thumped against my heaving chest. I spun around only to see a barren forest in every direction. Flurries began to fall from the sky, and frost glistened on the trees and branches. My family was gone forever along with their secrets. I was so close to them. I fell to my knees and lay down gripping the ground, crushing the pieces of the broken branch in my hands while breathing in hints of lavender. I took a piece of the branch and shoved it into my pocket.

It was all too real, the pain of being so close and losing them pierced my heart. Tears began to spill down my cheeks as I blinked furiously, trying to wipe and clear my eyes. I began to hear snarling and snapping sounds closing in, claws scraping the hard wintery grounds. I turned and saw five wolf-like creatures running towards me along with cloaked individuals.

One was Lia, her teeth bared.

I began to run. They were after me. It was a dream, an illusion. My body was frozen, iced over, and I fell towards the earth and back into the black waters, shackled once more.

I didn't have the will to fight, the will to live, the will to become a part of this world filled with painful memories, lies, secrets, prophecies, demons and darkness. I had nothing to live for. I never had. I am empty. I am lost. The chains began to slowly tug at my ankle again, and I let them drag me without a fight. Whoever they are, they were going to kill me. This seemed inevitable.

Slowly I began to lose consciousness and, without a struggle, closed my swollen eyes. Floating in a sea of icy water felt soulfully deadening. My heartbeat began to slow its pace, and this time I wanted the numbing sensation to sweep through my entire body and mind, freezing me right where I was and allowing my soul to break free, to go home where I was once wrapped by the love and protection of my parents.

I opened my mouth, about to welcome the icy cold water into my lungs, when something brushed against my body. Eben's face appeared before mine—he was swollen and ghostly white, floating in the sea. His eyes were closed and bubbles lined the edge of his forehead. The silhouette of another body floating beyond him caught my attention. It was Yael, and like Eben, she was chained and unconscious. Her little fingers gently twitched; she was barely alive.

Then I realized Eben and Yael weren't the only ones. Four other bodies were chained in the water surrounding us. Edel, Ada, and Lia were all there amongst hundreds if not thousands more bodies, everyone unconscious, chained, and floating eerily with swollen skin. Like a sea of kelp ebbing and flowing with the ocean current. The numbing sensation I had almost given myself over to lifted and was replaced with anguish. I touched Eben's face with my hand. He didn't move. Even in the water, I could almost smell the bonfire and earth on his blue flannel.

Something hard slid along my collarbone, and I jerked back. A thin necklace had been placed around my neck and from it hung a key. Grabbing the key and snapping the necklace, I began making my way to Yael, but I was painfully jerked back by the shackle at my ankle, I looked down and a little cloud of blood formed. That's when I realized that my aggressive movement had triggered something, for we were all being dragged down towards the sea floor. Far below was a writhing mass of serpents and corpses—the corpses of dead humans—pulling and hauling us towards them. Their black consumed eyes gazed up at us avidly from the abyss and their teeth flickered dimly in the gloom as they dragged us down.

Terrified, I doubled over and clutched at my ankle, rattling the key in the shackle lock, my hands trembling, my lungs beginning to tighten. A loud *click* stopped even the serpents for a moment of stillness, and then they began hauling as hard as they could at the chains. Everyone was sinking faster and faster. I kicked hard, swimming to Yael. I grabbed her ankle, released her, and pushed her up to the surface. Her body floated peacefully towards the light. Eben was second, and the current began to move with more power. I watched Eben float towards the white light. Then I grabbed Ada's hand, shook it, but there was no sign of life. I released her ankle and pushed her after Eben and Yael's distant bodies. Turning around, I could feel my chest beginning to restrict even more, but I kicked, I fought through the current to Edel, fumbling with the key. My hands now violently shaking—the key entered the little hole, and the clasp opened. Edel was released. Forcing my legs to kick as hard as they could, I made my way towards Lia.

The current grew stronger and stronger, and I had to thrash in order to reach her. I wasn't sure if I would make it. The muscles in my legs burned and cramped. I let out a scream, grabbing her waist and pulling my way down her body to her ankle, unlocking the clasp, setting her free. As I tried pushing her body to the surface, her eyes flung open and were midnight black.

The gazes of the Elders were on me. Lia grabbed my arm, tearing into my skin with her sharp, rust colored nails. Another cloud of blood began to engulf us. My attempt to scream in agony was muffled by water. The pain swept through my arm, into my shoulder and down my back. With her other hand, she stabbed her nails into my side and began dragging me down to the corpses. She wanted me dead, *they* wanted me dead—the Elders.

The last thing I saw as my vision dimmed was Lia's beautiful dark hair awash with blood.

Someone grabbed my other arm and jerked me upwards. My eyes flickered open. Lia spun around and hissed. A deep ticking sound came from her throat. Her nails carved down my arm and across my chest, like razors slicing my skin.

All went dark.

Aston.

12

I woke up with sweat soaking through my clothes and sheets. My head pounded along with my heart, registering my environment. I was back in Edel and Yael's home. The window was cracked open and a warm breeze swept through the bedroom. A glass of water sat on the nightstand. I snagged it. My mouth felt sticky and dry. I gulped down every last drop without breathing, but it didn't quench the burrs and tickles in my throat. The sun was blinding, triggering a searing pain that shot across my brow and into my pounding temples. I pressed the palms of my hands against them.

It felt surreal to wake up from the nightmare to a beautiful day. I lay back down, closing my eyes when I heard the crinkle of paper. A folded note had been tucked beside my pillow.

Nora,

I have no doubt you have questions. In fact, I'm sure you have many, and you are probably even angrier with me. I'm sorry you had to go through what you did last night. I warned you, I had more to tell you. I suppose it was the Elders' way of tapping into your mind. I watched your mother go through it once, the Elders didn't trust her, knew she hid great secrets. They are only supposed to practice that ritual if they find you a potential threat of some kind like they did Rebekah. They wanted to see what kind of powers you are hiding, what abilities you have in store and who you care most about in your life so they will have tools to use against you in the future. They left you in the snow and disappeared without saying a single word to any of us.

They will come for you again.

We'll speak more when I come back. Edel, Yael, and I went to the mainland to gather some things since we will be staying with them for now. Most of your belongings have been brought here overnight. We can't go back to our home, not yet.

-Ada

P.S. You have a visitor. Hope he's still there when you wake up.

A visitor? Eben! I placed the note on the windowsill and got out of bed. I yanked off my sweaty nightgown and tossed it onto a small stepladder that sat vacant in the corner of the room. All my clothes had been brought here from the house at the point and stored neatly in the closet. For once I had actually really looked forward to settling down in a home for more than a few months.

A white linen curtain hid the closet. I pushed it aside, sliding the metal rings along a long wooden rod. I grabbed the first pair of jeans I saw. Yael must have helped with the organization of my clothes because nothing was stored higher than my chest level. I slipped into a shirt and a rather ugly toffee colored sweater that was missing a few buttons and had a hole under the right underarm: another one of Ada's hand-me-downs that I couldn't part with.

"Why don't you throw that old thing away, it's hideous! I put it in the donation pile for a reason," Ada had said as I was making my way to the bus stop for school. But I couldn't, there was something wonderful about this old sweater that wrapped me in a safety net of cozy fibers.

The corner of my mother's face caught my attention. Her photo lay under a small burlap album that Ada and I had made together over the past years. Pulling out her photo, I stared at her face once more.

I now know you smelled of lavender, Mom.

I placed her picture on the bedside table and turned to revisit the closet and the long old mirror hanging in its center. The mirror's edges were rusty, and the glass stained in certain parts like the one in my mother's room; however, the reflection in the mirror was exactly the same, a vision of sheer plainness. Taking a blue hair tie from a little basket on the shelf, I tied my hair back in as decent of a braid as I could manage.

"Well, that's as good as you're going to get."

Eben was waiting for me, and I wondered how he had found me at Edel's home. Maybe when they were collecting our things, Ada had seen Eben and given him directions.

'Oh, hey Eben! Just wanted to let you know that we can't stay at this house anymore. Nora had to go through some life-changing stuff, like learning that she's not human, so if you want to see her please go to the following address, but be careful not to upset her or she could unintentionally kill you. Okay? Great! Have a lovely day, dear!'

I thought of sailing, and how I just wanted to get away and out of this world. Maybe he could take me today, we could leave and never come back. For the first time, I had felt like myself when I was with someone, simple and content within my own skin, none of this Sereni and Lamian crap, no Elders, no abilities, no magic, just a simple life of fishing and sailing. My body temperature spiked from thoughts of my nightmare: the prophecy, my mother mentioning Eben's name and the sea of beings chained.

Flipping over my sheets, I took a deep breath and tried to make everything look somewhat tidy as I stole one last glance around my new temporary room with its stone walls and overgrown ivy. Quietly closing the bedroom door behind me, I made my way down the hall to the kitchen. The house felt empty, no noise hinted that a visitor was anywhere on the premises. The only sound I heard were my clogs against the wooden floors. Was he still here waiting for me? I reached the arched entrance to the living room and cautiously looked in—no one. I went in and looked around more thoroughly. Still no one.

"Eben?" I called out. Had he gone? I checked the kitchen.

"Eben?" I opened the back door and stood on the porch.

"Eben!" There was not a soul in sight, just a few blackbirds picking in the garden that took off startled at the sound of my voice.

Why would he leave?

I slammed the screen door behind me. *I could really use the comfort of a friend right now. I just want to feel sane again.*

"Eben?" A voice spoke.

I spun around. It was Aston. He was leaning against the very archway I had only just walked through. He had an entertained smile.

"You sounded desperate for a moment," he said with a smirk.

"Desperate for sanity. Yes, you could say that." Flattening down my sweater, I watched him carefully.

"Well, hate to disappoint you, but he's not here. However, on a lighter note, it's good to see you survived the Elders and my sister for that matter." Aston scanned his eyes over me, trailing them up and down my body.

My cheeks began to tingle, and I knew I must have looked a bit flushed. Aston was no longer hidden behind a dark cloak, but instead was looking fairly normal. He had on jeans, a navy blue

Oxford shirt with the cuffs rolled, and his hair sat somewhat messy as if styled to look that way.

"Not so friendly of a sister you've got there," I said, massaging my wrist where I still vividly felt her nails digging in and ripping open my flesh. To my surprise, my fingers ran over bumps, and I looked down at my wrist wide-eyed. There, faintly on my skin, were three thin scars. *This can't be. Wasn't it a dream?*

Aston was watching, and I quickly twisted my wrist over.

"Well yes, she's rough around the edges," he said. "Always desperate to please the Elders."

"That's the understatement of the year. She seemed to have it out for me from the first moment I met her. Do you know why? I mean, what exactly did I do to her?"

"You exist," he said. "That's more than enough for Lia."

"Exist?"

"If you want my opinion, I think you look nice." Aston changed the subject with a smile.

"Excuse me?"

"Well, you said earlier 'that's as good as you're going to get,' and I just wanted you to know you look nice is all."

Great, now he was listening to me behind closed doors. Whatever happened to privacy? Apparently that doesn't exist on this island.

I rolled my eyes.

"Look, I know the Elders dubbed you my protector or whatever, but I don't need your services, okay? And honestly, I'm out of here the first chance I get. I'm not getting myself involved with you people with freak abilities." I waved in his direction and turned towards the kitchen, but he was already at the island leaning on his elbows before I could take a step forward.

"Ah! How did you do that?"

"You actually think this is something you can run from?" He raised one eyebrow.

"I'm hoping."

"Well, I really hate to disappoint you," he said suddenly only inches from my face, "but you can't." He leaned in bringing his lips to my ear and whispered. "This is who you are, Nora, what you are." He pulled away, watching me.

"You know nothing of what or who I am, Aston. None of you do!"

"You're right, I probably know as much about you as you do." My cheeks burned with anger.

"But thus far I have been able to gather that you are defiant, hard-headed and temperamental," he said bluntly.

"Excuse me?" I stood shocked.

"Look, I know it's a lot to take in, and I was only swinging by to make sure you were okay after last night." Aston lowered his voice into a subtle serious tone, and we began to walk clockwise around the kitchen's island, Aston trailed his fingers over the countertop.

"The thing is Nora, you aren't playing in your human world anymore. This is a whole different game with different animals and rules, and you don't quite understand how it works yet. What you need to come to terms with is that, no matter how far you run or where you hide, this world will find you. You can't hide. You never could. Your aunt did a hell of a job concealing you, but it wasn't sustainable, now was it?"

"I said I'm fine." I looked him dead in the eyes.

"Fine. You are indeed very fine, beautiful in fact, but here's the deal, I'm still not going anywhere. I can't." He smiled again and I took a step back.

Beautiful?

"Yeah, I get it, because it's the Elders' orders, right?"

Aston pushed up his left sleeve. "It's because we are *bound*, Nora." I had already forgotten about the characters the Elders branded us with. I looked at my left forearm. It matched Aston's. How could I have missed this while getting dressed?

"Besides, outside of the Elders binding us, I actually feel responsible for you now. Someone has to be." He spoke flatly.

"What do you mean "has to be", and what are you smiling at?" I stopped contributing to this ridiculous dance. I grabbed the kettle and began to fill it with water in the sink.

Suddenly I felt the slight weight of his body against my back and the corner of his mouth brushed against my ear.

"How *human* you are," he whispered.

I grabbed a knife that sat in the sink and turned around, gripping the wooden handle in my hand, but he was sitting at the kitchen table, watching me. My chest heaved as my heart began to race. I had felt him; he was just behind me, right?

"Did you really plan on using that? Because you'll need to be a lot faster than that. Not that you aren't capable of speed, of course. Lia found *that* out first hand, didn't she?" Aston smiled, and I gently placed the knife back in the sink, feeling shaky and agitated. I shook the feeling off and turned back to filling the kettle.

"How human I am? What's *that* supposed to mean? Tea?" I shakily placed two mugs down.

"Just that Ada did a good job, but there was no way you would have been able to hide it much longer. And no thanks on the tea." He had an amused look on his face. "Nora, you don't need to be scared of me."

"I'm not! Do you want water or something?"

"No."

I began to feel hot under his gaze, so I took off my sweater and could feel his eyes watching me. I placed both forearms on the sink, needing a moment to breathe. I was starting to feel sick. I stared at the markings on my arm when I saw his forearms frame mine. His body leaned against mine, and I turned around, our hip bones pressing against each other.

"Look, I don't understand how this world may work yet, but I *do* know that invading my space isn't winning you any points on me liking you."

The corner of his mouth pulled back but he didn't back off.

"Y'know, I am trying to be a hospitable, friendly human since this is clearly an undesired arrangement," I said, annoyed and flustered. "And what the hell is the big deal with humans? Why are you and the Elders so disgusted? I am a human you know, and so are my friends!" I spoke defensively thinking of Wren, Joe, and Eben.

"Who said I was disgusted with humans?" Aston said. "I don't have a problem with them. Why should I? The Elders, well, that is a whole different situation and a long story. As for *you*, you are the furthest thing from human, I'm afraid. You may act like one, you may have been groomed to behave like one, but you're not. There is no part of you that is human. As a matter of fact, the laws of genetics being what they are, *I* am more human than you are."

I wasn't going to rise to that bait. I didn't know enough to argue. Ada had left me in the dark. Here, however, was someone who seemed to know the score.

"Tell me," I said.

"Tell you what?" He was back on the other side of the island watching me.

"Everything. The story of the Elders and humans for starters. You just said it was long, and since I'm trapped on this landmass time is exactly what I have. Does it involve my parents?"

"No not directly," he said.

"What about the prophecy?"

"That's a whole other kettle of fish, and yes that does have to do with your parents, obviously."

"Tell me everything. If your job is to look out for me, it's time I wasn't fumbling around in the dark."

"Your water is about to boil." He pointed at the stovetop and sure enough, the kettle began to whistle.

"Is that another one of your abilities? Being able to predict things like a boiling kettle?" I took the angry kettle off the burner and opened the pantry in search for some tea, knowing Edel had some. I placed a bag of mint tea in the ceramic mug and began to pour the hot water over it, watching as the aromatic fragrances and earthy dyes escape the bag. I was feeling antsy and uncomfortable at the silence between the two of us. After my tea had a decent color I turned around, opening my mouth to insist he tell me the story of the Elders, but he was gone.

I placed the pot back on the stove and turned with my mug to look for him. He was standing outside on the back porch, looking out towards the lake. I softly swung open the screen door and stood beside him.

The view was beautiful, and I closed my eyes soaking up the glimmer of sunshine. It was the first time I had seen the lake during the day, and the air still held a hint of salt. We couldn't have been far from the ocean.

"I will tell you the story of the Elders," he said without turning to look at me. "But first, I believe we started off on the wrong foot."

"Okay."

"I didn't ask to be bound to you, and it wasn't the way I envisioned meeting you. I'm sorry you feel trapped here on this island and feel such strong anger towards me, to Ada, and, well, your whole life at the moment, I suppose. I cannot and will never understand it completely, but I sympathize with your frustration. However, once I feel you are well trained and able to protect yourself, you'll be on your own, and I'll do my best to figure out how to reverse the bind, if I can."

My stomach tightened at his maturity, which left me feeling like a complete jerk. I wondered what he meant about reversing the bind. The thought of someone reassuring me of his or her absence left an unsettling feeling in my chest.

I thought about asking him what it meant to be bound, but I didn't want to get off topic if he was willing to fill me in on the rest.

"Look," I said. "I've been through a lot these last few days and half of the time I can't tell if I'm delusional or not, awake or asleep. I don't mean to be taking it out on you, really. I just don't know how to handle everything at the moment."

Aston smiled. I pushed up my body next to his, sipping my tea casually.

"Walk with me," he said. "And I'll tell you the story of the Elders."

Aston walked towards the lake, and I followed. He shoved both hands into his pockets, and we began to walk side by side.

"Do you know the story of the Seven and Queen Lamia?"

"Yes, it's the only story Ada has shared with me so far."

"Right, well Nephthys was one of the Seven created from the blood of Lamia. She is the last one that we know of still alive since the days of Queen Lamia. She's over three thousand years old."

Aston looked at me. His skin looked cold, but his eyes grew warm as he began the story. My stomach grew tighter the longer he watched me, so I looked away, foolishly blushing.

"After the Seven were created from Queen Lamia's blood, they dispersed over time in search of their own corners of the world where each could build their family and life. They tried to love and marry humans, but each time the human found out she was not human, nor that aged the way they did, they had to flee. Their human lovers began to hunt these women believing them to be witches, wanting to burn them at the stake and kill their "cursed and demon children". These women had become lonely and sad so that the Goddess Amphitrite came down and visited each of the Seven, presenting them each with a suitable Sereni man. A man whom they could spend the rest of their lives with. This pleased *six* of the Seven. The seventh, Nephthys, refused her chosen partner and promised her current human lover that she would never leave his side. She had found her love and was loved in return.

and Nit in their present incarnations. It is said that each of
ee now carry or possess an object of some sort, devised by
that both contains and safeguards their powers and sustains
mmortality. Tales have it that if these objects were ever to be
ed, all three would be stripped of their abilities and rendered
. Who knows if that is true, however.

ce Milda and Nit were no longer truly daughters of
hys, the three of them became known as the Elders.
e three sisters traveled across lands and seas to pay a visit
other three Sereni women, Amena, Linnea, and Miksa.
hys wanted them to join her in a great war to destroy human-
ieving all of humanity to be cruel and filled with greed as the
whom she had once invited into her home. Amena, Linnea,
iksa, horrified at the corpselike abomination that had once
heir sister and her two ghoulish sister-daughters, all shut
hys out.

iksa, the last of the remaining Seven to be visited, went so
to accuse Nephthys of giving way to madness and corrupt-
erything about herself that had made her Sereni, branding her
er two thrall monsters no longer children of the Goddess.
ut Amena, Linnea, and Miksa underestimated the power of
te that drove Nephthys in her quest for revenge, and in the
f night it is said that Nephthys visited each one and drove
ry dagger, a relic of power Nephthys took from Inessa, not
hrough their hearts, but those of their mates and children.
agger absorbed the Sereni powers and passed them on to
hys. Unsatisfied with the murder of her once sisters, she then
d their villages, killing and capturing most of their Sereni
es and murdering every human they crossed paths with along
ay, beheading and hanging men, women, and children. The
then forced every surviving Sereni descendant to their knees
nding their unquestioned fealty under pain of death.

"Now Merrow, your great great grandmother, traveled to the
Labrador Sea where she was married and promised to a Sereni man
named Argon. That is how your family ended up here on these
islands. Symi remained in the Mediterranean Sea; Miksa created her
home in the Bering Sea off the coast of Alaska; Nessa traveled to
the Greenland Sea; Amena traveled to the Black Sea; Linnea moved
to the White Sea; and Nephthys to the Norwegian Sea where she
settled in a remote fishing village in the Faroe Islands. The vicious
cycle of war continued for the Seven. Humans hunted the Sereni,
the Children of Lamia continued to hunt and kill Sereni, and the
Seven—including the Goddess Amphitrite—continued fighting to
protect their race. After over a thousand years of war between the
Lamians and Sereni and their descendants, thousands of Sereni and
Lamian Children were killed and burned; the only ones from the
original Seven to have survived these wars were Nephthys, Amena,
Linnea, and Miksa."

"Wait," I said. "How did my great great grandmother die?"

"Patience." Aston glanced over with a smile.

I might just die of patience at this freaking rate, I thought as I
sipped my tea.

"Nephthys was given two daughters by the human she fell desperately in love with. This man, Asger, was a fisherman, and the four
were inseparable. The aging human lover of Nephthys had to leave
on a fishing trip that would take him away from home for months.
Nephthys waited day in and day out for him to show up at their
doorstep once more, but months went by and he never showed.
Then an entire year had passed, still no return. Then one morning,
Nephthys and her daughters awoke to the sounds of a startling
crash. The three quickly dressed and ran out to discover that a
great ship, like the one presumably lost with Nephthys' husband,
had wrecked. The sounds of men screaming and drowning spilled
through the icy Nordic air. Most of the men died during this ship-
wreck, and Nephthys and her daughters sifted through the bodies

looking for their long lost loved one, but instead were greeted with one frozen and lifeless soul after the next.

"Five men, however, were discovered barely breathing, and Nephthys instructed her daughters to pull the men from the waters and bring them into their home, because every sailor, every fisherman, reminded Nephthys of Asger, her great love—a love she feared was lost forever at sea. The three took care of the men, exchanging their frozen clothes for warm dry furs and nursing them back to health.

"Now, according to the story passed down by Nephthys, upon waking up, the fishermen knew Nephthys and her daughters for what they were, for they had heard rumors of the ancient Sereni women and their magic, and they wanted their blood which was rumored to be concentrated with the ability to heal and give even humans temporary abilities. They were consumed with the idea of power, and in the dead of night, after Nephthys had prepared the men dinner with warm brandy to soothe their lost souls, the men attacked Nephthys and her daughters, repaying their kindness with murder. They drove daggers through both of the daughter's hearts—but failed to kill Nephthys herself, for the Seven were not easily slain.

"The villainous fishermen filled the brandy bottle with blood, hoping to sell it on the black market, and robbed the home of its precious crystals, gold, and provisions, before leaving the three women dead—or so they thought—on the floor of their home. They provisioned the one intact lifeboat from their crashed ship and started rowing for Askvol. The men didn't get far. Nephthys survived and with the ability to manipulate the elements she invited the most bitter winds of the Arctic Ocean to cross their paths, so all five men froze to death on their journey and the bottle of her blood was said to have been lost to the sea.

"Nephthys' heart began to grow black that day, and she traveled far and wide in search of a way to bring back her daughters.

One day, while roaming the streets of Tro
a man who gave her the name of a pow
Nephthys searched for a hundred years a
northern Russia for Inessa, while her daug
and snow. After many years, her search ca
finally crossed paths with Inessa. Nephthy
that, even among the practitioners of the
she asked the witch to resurrect her daught
ing that, if she brought her daughters back
daughters but return as mortal demons.

"Nephthys didn't care, she wanted her
thermore, Nephthys wanted the witch to
into three pieces so that she could ensure t
ters, even in demon form, would be connec
blood, abilities, and immortality. Inessa, wh
working with the dark arts, refused Nepht
would not tear a being's soul into three pie
deliver not only Nephthys but also her dem
of gruesome half death.

"According to legend, Nephthys was on
the Seven, with skin as white as milk, hair
Arctic Ocean, and eyes as crystal blue as den
play upon her vanity, also warned Nephthys
monstrous and terrible to look upon, and
love again.

"But Nephthys did not care about love
She wanted only her daughters and revenge
Inessa, it is said, had seen the look of reve
seen it in Queen Lamia's eyes when she was j

"Inessa again refused, but Nephthys thre
Inessa relented. After ninety days without sl
a way to resurrect the two girls and bestow
tions of Nephthys' twisted sundered soul.

Milda
the th
Inessa,
their i
destroy
mortal

"Si
Nepht

"Tl
to the
Nepht
ity, be
men v
and M
been
Nepht

"M
far as
ing ev
and h

"B
the ha
dead
an iv
only
The
Neph
burne
famili
the w
Elder
dema

"The Elders gained mass power through fear and their dark ability to harvest the powers of Sereni rebels and dissidents. The Elders had become the most powerful beings in the Sereni world—some say more powerful than the Goddess herself who, throughout the slaughter and madness, has remained absent. It is said she abandoned the remaining Seven for she never expected such evil and betrayal from any of the Sereni.

"The only telling blow that struck Nephthys and her sisters after their ascension was at the hands of the being who had granted them their horrible half-lives to begin with: Inessa. Enraged by the evil unleashed by the Elders, she articulated a prophecy, cursing the three of them to a future doom. This is what she foresaw:

"'During a blue moon, a child will be born. She will become the hidden child and emerge from the ashes of darkness. Her bloodlines pure and powerful. The hidden child will be the end of destruction, the end of our pain, and will return us to our haven.'"

"When Nephthys heard this she uttered an insane scream of fury, but before she could behead Inessa, the witch vanished in a cloud of dark smoke—never to be seen again. Since then Nephthys has killed every Sereni child born on a blue moon."

Aston rubbed the back of his head. "Pretty intense, our history. Still following?"

I nodded, and he continued.

"From that day forth the Elders were, and still are, the strongest and most powerful beings controlling the Sereni World, laying the laws, claiming to be protecting us from the Lamian children and humans, and cultivating powers. They forbid all interaction with humans, and any interaction revealing our world to humans is punished under the laws of the Elders. The only problem is, we live in a world of humans, and there aren't many of us left. Eventually, our survival will depend on them."

"Why? Why aren't there many of us left? Thousands of years, there must be many of us, right?" I asked.

"The Elders claim that the Lamians and humans have destroyed our race, but some have other theories. Unexplained Sereni disappearances with no bodies to be found have raised many questions. Some say that the Elders are capturing and cultivating powers. In order to stay powerful, the Elders must continue regenerating by cultivation. Some also believe that the Elders control the Lamians; that they have some truce or deal with each other. Some even suggest that Alexo may have sold their loyalty to the Elders in return for protection under their umbrella of power. However, that is something we may never know."

We had walked entirely around the lake and were approaching Edel's cottage again.

"So, there you have it. The story of the Elders." He cleared his throat. "Its heavy, but this is all a part of your lineage so it's best you know."

"And Merrow, my great great grandmother, how did she die?"

"Merrow, it is said, died in a battle with the Lamian Children in what is now Nova Scotia."

"Descendants of the three reborn sons of Lamia, you mean."

"That's right. Lamians claim any descendant of the Three, no matter how distant, as children of Lamia—much in the same way that the Elders claim any descendant of the Seven as Sereni. Then there are folks like you and me, who are both. There are enough of us, and we are sufficiently powerful, that neither side is willing to cast us out and give us over to the other."

"So much hate," I said.

"It's true," he said. "Two blood enemies each circling the other, waiting for the balance of power to finally shift. That's where you come in. You were the child born under the blue moon. You are the prophecy."

"But I don't understand. If the prophecy foretells that I will be the downfall of the Elders, why am I still alive? What am I missing?

I was completely in their power just last night. Why wouldn't they have just killed me in front of all of you?"

Aston leaned against a tree. I could hear someone distantly approaching Edel's home from the other direction. I assumed Aston could hear it as well. He didn't seem alarmed and so I let him keep talking. "There are two things you need to know about Nephthys," he said. "The first is that she is insane. Perhaps she always was. Maybe the grief of losing her husband, then her daughters—her actual daughters, that is—drove her to madness. And it could be that having your soul served up like cake simply isn't a good idea. Whatever the reason, she is crazy, and everyone recognizes that."

"What about Milda and Nit?" I asked.

"If you want my honest opinion, Milda and Nit are just names. Nephthys is the Elder. One twisted soul served up on three plates."

A sick shiver crawled up the back of my neck. "And the second thing?"

Aston thought a second before answering. Whoever was approaching Edel's place grew nearer.

"Well, the second thing is that, even though she's insane, she's still shrewd. She's learned how to harvest the powers of her enemies. In fact, it is how the Elders have managed to hold dominion over the rest of the race and at the same time maintain a stalemate with the Children of Lamia. If she had killed you last night, everything would go back to the status quo, and she's not satisfied with the status quo. She wants complete dominion over the Children of Lamia as well. Perhaps she feels that once she is no longer fighting a war on that front that she can turn her full wrath to the world of man. Who knows? Like I said, she's insane."

"Okay, you've lost me. Why would she let me live?"

"She *plans* to kill you. I have no doubt about that. But she'll only do so when it will benefit her the most, which is to say when your powers have fully flowered. She is likely hoping that the power she gets from you will be enough that she can turn the tide against the children of Lamia once and for all. She will strike when your powers are at their prime, when she can reap the highest potentiality you possess. That is why they assigned me to you; that is why they bound us—to speed up your development and to control you."

I heard the screen door open and turned to see Ada standing on the porch.

"Nora, what are you doing out here alone?"

Aston had vanished and I felt an odd pang in my chest.

Ada's eyes darted around the property's perimeter, and then she beckoned me to come back inside. I didn't fight her this time. I had begun to understand where her worries were rooted, and so I followed, without resistance, back into the kitchen.

"I thought Aston was supposed to be here."

"He was."

"Oh." She sounded shocked. "Well, did you get to know each other a bit?" She eyed me, interested.

"Kind of."

Ada watched me for a moment, expecting me to say more, but then decided to leave it alone, and instead said, "So, about last night—"

"Aston shared with me the story of the Elders. He also told me about the prophecy."

Ada stared blankly. "Did he really? Well, that's a lot to take in. I suppose I'll have to thank him. He relieved me of that heavy weight."

"He also mentioned a bind. He said something about being bound, and that he would find a way to unbind us. What's he talking about? Is that what the Elders did last night to us? Is that why we have these matching markings now?" Ada's gaze dropped to her hands, and I sighed as I ran my finger over the new tattoo on my skin.

"Last night the Elders forced a bond between the two of you, a bond I have only ever witnessed once before." Ada looked upset.

"Well, what's that mean?" I egged her on. Ada was nowhere near as forthcoming as Aston, perhaps because of her long years as my guardian.

"It means that they bound your souls. Every fiber of your being is bound to Aston." Ada stared at me silently.

"What do you mean they bound our souls? What the—" I sat down on the stool trying to understand what in the heck this meant.

"It means that you two are bound for eternity. It means that Aston is and will be in your life whether you like it or not. He has taken a piece of your soul, and you have a piece of his. The Elders use this dark magic, this strategy, to control a possible threat. Knowing that you are the hidden child, the prophecy, you are their largest threat. It is a way to control you."

Aston had said the same thing though he didn't get a chance to expand on it.

"Well, what if we break it? Isn't there a stupid hocus-pocus spell or some ability to do that?" I began to hyperventilate, for the thought of my soul being bound to someone left me claustrophobic. "Ada, I want you to break it."

"I can't," Ada said, her voice lowering to a whisper.

"Well, let's find someone who can! In the story of the Elders, there was a witch named Inessa. Let's find her!" I busted out, hardly comprehending what she or I were saying.

"We never use dark magic, Nora. Didn't you learn something from the stories?" Ada raised an eyebrow in a you-should-know-this fashion. "A bind cannot be broken, it's an eternal promise."

"Promise? There was no promise. I didn't promise a goddamned thing. What happens if we attempt to break it? Aston said he would find a way. This can't be a good thing, Ada." My stomach tightly knotted, and for a moment, I thought of Eben. Silence filled the room, and a black crow landed on the branch outside the kitchen window. It ruffled its feathers, twitched its head and then, with its hoarse voice, cawed loudly into the dampening air.

"It *can't* be broken. And if you or Aston attempt it, it will kill the both of you." Ada's gaze floated from the crow to me. I sat there on the stool, nervously gripping my hands, stunned.

"What?"

"When the Elders discovered that your mother had become pregnant with Alexo's child, the highest form of power of the Lamians, they bound her to a man named Finn Gray. You must understand that the Elders have motives for everything they do and your mother and father knew this. Finn was held captive by the Elders and when rumors spread that you were born on the night of a blue moon—"

"They killed her," I said as it all finally became clear to me. "They didn't even have to find her; they simply killed Finn, and in doing so killed her."

"Yes," said Ada.

The crow gave another angry call and took flight for the trees.

"And now," said Ada, "If they catch Aston and torture him, you will feel every bone breaking, every laceration, every lashing, every nightmare, everything. It takes time for the connection to strengthen. That's why they have left Aston free and assigned him to you. It will strengthen the bond between you, but it will also help bring out your other abilities, and that's what they are most interested in. Nephthys will not rush. She will bide her time."

"Terrific," I said. "That's just great."

"You are the purest and strongest line to Queen Lamia and so the power you possess is unimaginable. But you mustn't give it to them, Nora. You must never give them what they want. If you do, they will destroy everything, including us."

I pressed my forehead against my hands, feeling the sudden weight of the world on my shoulders.

"This is the secret your mother discovered about the Elders hundreds of years ago. If we were stronger in power or numbers, we might have had a fighting chance had we chosen to follow your mother's path."

I remembered the dream where I was listening to my parents. This was it. They wanted me to eventually destroy the Elders.

"So what about Aston and I?" I asked. "What's going to happen to us?"

"I don't know, but a bind not only binds the soul, it binds everything, Nora—your feelings, your emotions, pain, pleasures, sometimes even memories overlap. Everything you feel, think, or desire, he will know, and you will know of him. Every ounce of your being and every ounce of his are now entwined."

I stood up and paced, thinking of my parents' faces, and stared at the black tattoo and scars on my arm.

"Ada, after I passed out I had some very disturbing dreams. Is there a chance that those dreams could have been, I dunno, *real?*"

"What do you mean real? I know dreams can *feel* very real at times, but—"

The scars on my wrist tingled and I pulled my sleeve down.

"After you passed out the Elders simply dismissed us and Aston carried you back here himself. You didn't *go* anywhere, only in your thoughts."

As Ada spoke I looked at my sleeve, then down at my shoes.

"What about all the blood?"

"What are you talking about?" Ada froze.

"From our forearms, during the binding, the snow around our feet was red with it."

Silence.

"You didn't *see* it?" I asked.

"You never bled, Nora. Perhaps the pain was so intense that you were hallucinating," Ada said with caution in her eyes. "They know they can cause you immense pain if you begin to fill your mother's shoes, but until then they want you alive, just long enough to cultivate your powers or turn you to join them or kill you." Ada picked up a brown paper bag that she'd brought back with her. She sat it on the counter and pulled out a sack of red apples.

"Immense pain through Aston? I don't even know the guy!"

"You will," she said. "He will be your greatest and closest ally. Treat him well. Your life rests in his hands and his in yours, Nora."

"Are you freaking kidding me? This is the twentieth century, Ada. I feel like I'm in an arranged marriage!"

"I know it must feel that way, but it's not. No one is saying that you have to marry him, but you should learn to like him."

I rolled my eyes.

"Look, their attempt at torturing you through visions and memory was to try and awaken any abilities you have dormant inside of you, to get a reaction, but instead they found nothing, they couldn't see anything. You somehow protected your mind and let's just say their foundation was shaken. You put a heck of a lot of fear into Nephthys' mind. Fear of the unknown."

The thought of the Elders fearing me was inconceivable. I was a girl who could fit her life in five boxes, the Elders were supernatural three-thousand-year-old beings—or three aspects of one three-thousand-year-old being. So far I knew that I had the ability of speed, which everyone here had, and the ability to bring pain to someone to the point of death, mind connection with Yael, and impeccable hearing. What else would I be capable of? I could barely control the abilities I'd already discovered.

"How many abilities do you have?"

Ada's eyes lit up like she'd been waiting for me to ask. I could not help but smile.

"We all have one or two abilities that we are born with and that are usually passed down through bloodlines. Aside from the obvious speed, I somehow was lucky enough to have the ability of persuasion and altering one's thoughts and feelings."

I laughed. "The ability of persuasion, oh come on, really?"

"Don't laugh, Nora," Ada spoke with a very serious tone, locking her eyes with mine.

My world suddenly became cold and dark. The sensation in my fingers turned cold like ice and I watched as my skin started to stain with blotchy red spots.

—Fight her, Nora— A hissing voice from the depth of my soul.

—Kill her—

My tongue vibrated against the roof of my mouth like the tail of a rattlesnake.

—You can control yourself—

Another voice had entered my mind

—You love Ada, don't hurt her—

I twitched my neck in agony, battling my mind.

"Nora!"

I snapped awake to the sound of Ada's voice, my eyes sharply looking at her.

"You see what I can do?" She smiled, pleased with herself.

"Yeah, I see." I rubbed my right temple. I was deeply afraid, afraid of myself.

"You okay?"

"Yeah, headache is all."

Ada filled a glass with water and handed it to me with two little brown pills. "Here"

I placed the two pills on my tongue and swallowed.

"What about Lia? Why does she hate me?" I asked.

"Don't underestimate her, she's intelligent and very powerful."

"Yeah and apparently crazy."

"Since her parents died, Lia has become a struggling soul. She can't seem to decide what light she's going to walk in. She has pledged her loyalty to the Elders, and because of their high interest in you, well, let's just say her dislike for you will only grow. Everyone knows that Lia hungers for power and walks a very fine line." Ada stopped for a moment as she bit into a grape she'd chosen from a fresh bunch.

"Why would she want the attention of the Elders? They are freaking gross. She can have them if she really wants. I didn't ask for this!" I said, placing my forehead to the countertop.

"She's addicted to power. You see, the problem with abilities and power is that some become consumed, addicted to it like a drug. Addicts crave more and more power, and the craving is never satisfied once they have tasted it. Some, like Lia, abuse it."

"What do you mean, *abuse it?*"

"There are accusations about Lia, accusations of murdering humans in her frustration and hunger. Once you allow a demon to take hold of your mind, you slowly are consumed by it unless you are aware and can control it. The demon that all Lamians possess, thanks to Queen Lamia, is a very powerful one. She's a wildcard at the moment; no one knows what will happen with her."

My arm hairs rose under my sweater. I thought of Lia, of her eyes changing from amber to black. The memory of our encounter made me feel incredibly uncomfortable. Ada threw one of the grapes from the bunch at my forehead, and at this, I broke into a little smile.

"Enough of all this creepy, dark talk. Let's try and focus on something more positive. Aston! He's a good guy. He's nothing like Lia, trust me. He has a lion heart like your father. Give him a chance and get to know him a bit more! Anyway, you'll be spending a lot of time with him, so at least make your first friend out of the situation." She laughed in a very twisted way.

"I already made my first friend," I said defensively, "Eben."

Ada ignored me.

"Speaking of which," I said. "When can I go see him again? We're supposed to be starting school together."

"You won't be seeing him again, and you won't be starting school with him."

"What? You're sending me off to boarding school then, aren't you? That's the only other option here I've read."

"You won't be attending *any* school, Nora."

"What?" I sat there staring blankly. "Did you just say I'm not going to school? I'm not graduating high school!"

"We aren't *human*, Nora. And at the moment, we have bigger fish to fry. For example, instead of English or history class, you will be training day in and day out with Aston, and you will be taking it seriously. So your education has shifted to education in your real history, abilities, survival, and fighting. On a lighter note, I think it sounds way more exciting than math class, don't you? Besides, we cannot guarantee your safety in a school anymore. And what would happen if you inadvertently showed ability amongst humans? It's really for your safety, babe."

"Holy cow, Ada! I'm in total shock. I mean, I get it. My life is a little more important than a high school career, but seriously, I didn't expect that news. I'm not gonna lie, I can't say I'll miss it."

"I figured you and I would see eye to eye on this one," Ada smiled.

"And Eben?" I asked again.

"Nora, I can't have this conversation right now. I just can't."

"What do you mean *you just can't?*"

Ada put her hand up, her chest inflated and hardened with air as if she couldn't breathe. She was hiding something, yet again. I huffed, tired of constantly being at crossroads of secrets with Ada recently.

"Are we ever going back to the other house? I wanted to gather some of my mother's things."

Ada's expression became serious once more as she shook her head, at a loss for words.

"But I really want some of those things back. I've never had any-thing of hers before."

"Right now we can't go back. The Lamian trackers who hunt by scent are out looking for us, and apparently during the night of your escapade, our scents were spotted near that part of the island. They know the general area we were staying in, so I grabbed what I could, risking trackers and all, and made it back here safely with Edel."

She pointed to a box on the kitchen table, and I walked over quickly to open it. Inside was the quilt that I had laid across the bed, a few bird feathers and the black porous rock Ada had given me.

Ada looked out the window. The beautiful sky had turned gray again, and a light rain began beading the glass.

"I'm sorry we had to leave that house." The corners of Ada's eyes gently filled up with tears. "It really was stupid of me to think they would never track us there. That I could pick up where I left off."

"It's my fault, I didn't listen to you. I didn't stay close." I reached out and held her hand, squeezing it in reassurance that we were going to be fine.

"I had no choice but to bring you back here, Nora. And I am so sorry for that. You can only run from the Elders and from Lamians for so long."

Ada's left hand touched my cheek, and for a moment, I was living Ada's memory. She was running through the woods with something bundled in her arms. It was the same child bundled in furs—me—from my lucid dream of my parents. I watched her searching and choosing paths in the forest. I could feel the fear in her chest. Sounds of hissing howls filled the sharp winter air. Ada removed her hand from my cheek and stepped away from me.

"I tried so hard to keep you away from here, but I couldn't." She glanced at me. "On your eighteenth birthday you will come of age to the Elders, your abilities strong, and you will be marked with the glyph. I couldn't continue playing pretend with you out in the human world for long. It was better for us to be here where we are with our own kind, with individuals who could help fight and protect you, than out there always on the run. We risked dying alone in their world with no protection." Ada grabbed me, holding on tightly.

This was the first embrace we had shared since our old life. I warily wrapped my arms around her. The top of my head became warm and wet with her tears.

13

The next morning, I woke up in a slight panic from dreams of Lamian trackers and the sound of wolves howling in my ears. The cottage was filled with warmth, and I could hear Ada and Edel speaking secretively in another room. Yael's thoughts were mumbling on about what she wanted for breakfast as she putzed around the kitchen. Her thoughts were my primary motivation to get out of bed, for they made me realize how hungry I was. My stomach growled angry tunes, and I grabbed my robe off an old rusty nail by the door and made my way to the kitchen. Living here wouldn't be so bad, I reassured myself.

"Morning Yael."

She quickly stood up, banging her head on an open silverware drawer.

–Owww!– She rubbed her head and looked at me with an embarrassed grin.

"Sorry, I didn't mean to scare you." I reached forward, pulled her in, her body's frame slender and bony in my arms.

"Sorry about yesterday, with your mom, and you." I kissed the top of her head. She looked surprised at my gesture.

–It's okay, we're fine. But, the Elders did a good number on ya, huh?– Yael searched my forearm for markings. – Can I see it?– She wiped white powder from her apron.

I scrunched up my sleeve and watched as Yael's gaze fell to my tattoo.

–You're in a pretty good mood for what happened to you the other night.– Yael shifted her focus back to wiping her hands.

–Well, considering I just learned I won't have to attend high school anymore, the Elders and others want me dead, and that I have abilities and am part demon, yes you could say I'm in a good mood. Living the teen dream is all.–

Yael laughed as she picked up a small index card and studied it.

–Good, well in between all your interesting discoveries, I'm making sweet potato pancakes, so I hope that's part of your teen dream–

She handed me the card; on it was a recipe she was following.

One pound of sweet potatoes, peeled. I looked into the sink at the pile of peeled orange potatoes. *A half cup of all-purpose flour*—Yael had managed to get this ingredient all over herself and the counters—and on the recipe went.

–I know. I heard, hence the reason I came straight away to the kitchen–

–Well, isn't your hearing developing quickly, huh?–

–Can I help?–

I put the note card down on the counter and attempted to take what looked like a very heavy ancient mixer out of her hands.

–Sure! You can start by telling *him* over there to stop staring at you the way he does. It's kind of weird–

Aston was sitting on the couch in the living room, from which he had a clear view of the kitchen. My cheeks felt warm as I stood there, feeling naked in my robe. He had been sitting quietly, watching me.

"Good morning," he said with a pleasant smile.

"What are you doing here? Uh, I mean, good morning." I felt flustered. I couldn't understand why he made me feel this way.

"Breakfast, of course. Yael makes the best pancakes in town from what I've heard." He raised one eyebrow at me and went back to reading a newspaper that was lying on the coffee table in front of him, *The Stonington Courier.*

Yael beamed.

"Right." I eyed him, questioning his response, then quickly left the kitchen.

–Why didn't you *tell* me he was here?– I yelled at Yael.

–Geeze, I didn't know he was *that* big of a deal– She giggled. –He's right though, I do make the best pancakes–

–Oh, shut it–

Quickly walking to my room, I passed Edel and Ada again talking in secret, and I thought I heard Eben's name being used in conversation.

"Oh Nora, Aston's here to see you. He's out in the—"

"Living room!" I threw my hands up in the air. "Yeah, I know, just saw him!"

I slammed the door behind me and quickly began putting clothes on.

What's wrong with you, Nora? Why are you freaking out? Just yesterday you didn't even want his company.

I threw on clothes that were lying around my room. I pulled down my hair, brushed it out and braided it back. I reached to open my door when the doorknob twisted on its own. My heart stopped, then Ada's face peeked in.

"Ugh," I gasped, my chest pounding.

"Everything okay?" Ada looked at me, her eyebrows screwed up in confusion.

"You look very…" Ada paused studying my outfit, "thrown together?" She ended, questioning my ensemble.

"I just wanted to throw some clothes on. No big deal. Why, do you not like it? Should I change my shirt? I'm not sure what to wear." I began to rummage through the closet when Ada cut me off.

"Whoa, whoa, Nora. Slow down. I've never seen you like this before. This can't be because of Aston, is it?"

"I don't know! I guess after finding out that our souls are bound I'm not sure what to feel anymore! I'm just nervous. I was comfortable making friends with Eben, so I don't understand why Aston makes me feel so—"

What *did* he make me feel?

"So *what?*" Ada crossed her arms.

"Confused. Insecure even?" I looked away.

"Ah," Ada said. "You're feeling attracted to Aston aren't you? Nora, that's normal. He is an attractive young man, and you and he share something now that no other being can: your souls. Attraction is inevitable, really."

Ada smiled and grabbed me by the hand, sitting me down on the bed beside her.

"I was going to wait until this evening, but I'll give it to you now." She put her hand in her pocket and pulled out a necklace and handed it to me.

"Your necklace?" I asked, holding it in my cupped hand.

"No, actually this was your mother's. I still have mine on." It was a match to the one she wore. "Our mother gave them to us when we were maybe your age. It was the only thing Rebekah left me when she handed you to me. It's for you."

The necklace was a thin gold chain and two small gold charms hung from it: they looked somewhat similar to the markings on my forearm. Ada helped me put on the necklace.

"What are these markings?" I tucked my chin in looking at the thin wiry charms.

"This one means protection," she pointed at the prong charm, "and this one," she touched the incomplete angular fish shape charm, "inheritance, in regards to our ancestral spiritual power. They are rune symbols." Then Ada grabbed my forearm, "Just like these symbols here that bind you and Aston. They are powerful symbols that hold great meaning.

"*Gebo*, sacrifice and gifts. For every gift, your bind will bring you a curse." Ada explained each rune character, working her way down my forearm "*Isa*, ice or stillness. Ice is attractive and deceitful, it can lock life beneath a surface and lull a soul to sleep until it reaches death. *Laguz*, the rune of becoming, emotion or unconscious mental power and mastery of emotion. Communication between souls, the conscious and unconscious minds."

"I feel cursed." I closed my eyes and squeezed the charms.

"Find a way to see the light in all this." Ada touched my cheek.

"Ada, I haven't forgotten about Eben, you know." I opened my eyes, longing for the normality of his company.

"I know, I haven't forgotten either, trust me."

"I'd like to see him again."

But Ada didn't reply, she only stood up, smiled again, and led me out of the room.

"It's because he's human, isn't it?" I whispered in the hall. "I was once human too, Ada."

Ada stopped and lowered her voice.

"No, you weren't. Right or wrong, you were only taught to believe you were. Besides, it's *not* for that reason. But you'll see him again, I promise."

Ada's eyes fluttered with thought.

By now Yael had made an entire batch of thick pancakes drenched in butter and maple syrup. She was stuffing a pancake into her mouth and watching Aston out of the corner of her eyes as syrup lined her lips.

"No pancakes for you?" I asked, noticing he had an empty plate sitting in front of him. "Thought that's why you're here."

"No, I'm actually here for you."

I then heard Yael. –I made all these pancakes and suddenly no one is hungry. Humph!–

"Oh, what smells divine? Yael made pancakes? I'm starving!" Ada bellowed.

"Me too!" Edel chimed in.

This pleased Yael.

"You're here for me? What do you want with me?" I took a pancake and began eating it a tear at a time.

"To get to know you, train, become friends? I figured we'd go for a walk and work on some abilities? Yael told me that you have the ability of mind connection? Nice tool to have."

I shot Yael a sharp look.

—Whaaatt, he awwskked meehh— How was it that her *inner* voice was muffled by pancakes too?

"And that you almost asphyxiated Edel," he said. "Internal suffocation—classy. Sounds a little Elder-ish. Of course, it was unintentional." He folded up the newspaper he had been reading and set it aside.

At this Yael tilted her face down.

—I think I need to make more pancakes—

She got up, avoiding eye contact with me.

"Yeah great," I said to no one in particular, suddenly annoyed. "Well let's go then, off to training camp!"

He got up and opened the back door for me like a gentleman.

"See you later, Yael." He winked, and her cheeks reddened a bit.

With the door open, the sunlight filled the room and I squinted, making my way to the outside. We quietly walked together, and I didn't think to ask him where we were going, but he led me towards the forest saying nothing. We walked a while in silence and he casually kept his hands in his pockets, kicking leaves as he walked, occasionally turning to glance in my direction.

"Curious as to where we're going?" he said.

"Does it matter? I'm becoming accustomed to surprises these days."

He laughed. "I bet you have. I heard you're quite the runner?"

"Me?"

"Come on, let's see what you've got." He nudged his shoulder into mine. "I'll start and you try and keep up, okay?"

Great, I thought, remembering how the last chasing experience had ended for me. My hands became sweaty and I grew slightly nervous, not wanting to encounter a tracker again. I wiped them on the side of my jeans and watched Aston.

"What are you looking at? Don't your hands ever sweat?" I said defensively.

"Don't worry, I'll take it easy on you," he said.

He took off, and within seconds he was a couple hundred yards away.

"Whoa, *so* impressive!" I sarcastically yelled. I bolted after him, and within another few seconds I was by his side.

"Show off," he muttered with a smile, rolling up his sleeves. I stared at the markings on his arm. My chest swelled and I began to feel butterflies creeping into my stomach. My legs felt like jelly, and I wobbled as my knees gave out. Aston caught me by the waist and then released me quickly.

"Right, takes some getting used to. We need to strengthen your sea legs, girl."

"Yeah," I softly agreed, my heart racing as his hands held me upright.

We zipped in and out of the trees together, and once in a while, I would catch up to him. It was as if he was running a mapped course. Obstacles included jumping over streams, and when he found a family of foxes we ran alongside them. It was fantastic, like something straight from a dream.

The forest was alive, blurring by me in different shades of vibrant greens. If I'd known I could run like this all my life, I would have been doing it every day for the last seventeen years. It made me feel free and weightless. My heart felt full and content. We must have covered miles, perhaps the entire island. I continued mimicking his movement, racing and catching up. He laughed when I'd get close, and then would take off in another direction. For a moment, we were just children playing in the woods together, when suddenly he disappeared.

I froze in my tracks and listened very carefully. My body tensed, and I had no idea where we were. I began searching for him but found nothing until I heard earth being stepped on and I turned meeting him face to face. In surprise, I stepped backward. My heart skipped.

"Your cheeks are turning pink, Ms. Stone."

"Well, I was just running a thousand miles per hour."

"Something, I might add, you are very natural at. Doesn't surprise me." He took a step closer, and I took another counter step back. "I'm curious to see how good your senses are."

"My senses?" I asked, watching as he placed his hand in his pocket and pulled out a long piece of black fabric.

"May I?" He held up the fabric with both hands.

"You want to *blindfold* me?" My voice cracked nervously.

"Only for a moment, if that's alright with you? I promise nothing will happen to you. Nothing will ever happen to you."

I nodded, biting my lower lip. Aston's hands carefully covered my eyes. I could feel the warmth of his chest close to mine. My fingers held the soft fabric in place. It was the second time he had felt so close to me. His scent lingered with notes of the salty sea, like Eben, accompanied by the smell of earth after a rainfall. Suddenly a new feeling was introduced, one that I had never experienced before, I shifted my weight between my feet. Uneasy. I held my hands, wondering what was going to happen.

"Listen carefully." Aston's breath warmed the back of my neck, sending chills down my spine. My neck hairs rose. "A tracker can smell your trail days after you've passed through. We have a highly evolved sense of smell. We can intricately distinguish even the smallest traces of scent: a being's natural fragrance, the type of tree you brushed against, time, emotions, how fresh a snowfall is, even in the ocean masked by salt we can track anything; however, blood is the strongest scent of them all." I felt the warmth of his breath on my lips. "Find me, Nora."

I raised my right hand and tried to touch where I had felt him last, but I touched only air. He was gone. Taking my first step with a feeling of insecurity, I thought of Yael and how she had introduced me to a world of extraordinary sound. Quietly, with my eyes closed tightly behind the blindfold, I stood there in stillness like ice, listening to my surroundings. The trees were the first to come alive. I felt the warm sunspots that broke through the canopy as they speckled my skin. A small animal nearby nibbled on what sounded like vegetation. Then several hearts beating rapidly came into range. As I listened to the animals rustling in the forest, I tuned into a slower, stronger heartbeat—a heartbeat that belonged not to an animal, but a person.

The sound flooded my ears, and for a moment, I was confused as to whether or not it was my own. Placing my hand over my chest, I felt it simultaneously pulsating with the heart I could hear. I walked towards the sound slowly, trying not to trip on roots or uneven ground. As I got closer, the beating grew louder and louder, echoing in my ears. I reached out my arms, swiping into the empty blackness that engulfed my world. The ground was questionable with every step. I wobbled here and there but never lost complete balance. The more I trusted the darkness, the more I trusted Aston, the more I trusted my senses and the faster my pace grew.

I jogged steadily until my hands came into contact with a cool rough surface of stone partially covered with moss. I leaned in until the tip of my nose touched the damp moss. I could smell Aston's scent lingering and trail off to the left. Hovering my nose over the surface, I followed it while trailing my fingers lightly against its texture. Slowly I transitioned, allowing my sense of smell to lead the way. Aston's scent grew slightly stronger—an indication I was on the right path. The more time I spent in this world of darkness, the more my mind embraced it, the more my other senses slowly began to flourish.

The scents of the woods were in full bloom. The trees were moving in the breeze, and I could hear the wood bending and squeaking. With this new discovery, I began to trust myself even more. I decided then I could tentatively run. I began to pick up the pace as I followed a trail of Aston's scent. This newfound awareness was sensational and natural. I felt like a hunter. I *was* a hunter.

I knew I was weaving in and out of the trees without seeing them. His scent began to grow stronger and more potent, and the stronger it became, the faster I ran. He was near, very near, when suddenly it was as if a blade had severed the strand of his scent. I braked hard on my heels. My weight rocked back and forth, unstable; I heard waves furiously crashing below. Pushing up my blindfold, I found myself at the edge of a cliff. I felt lightheaded and collapsed. I scooted away from the edge and lay down on the damp grassy earth. I panted, listening to the ocean's voice roaring below, beckoning me. I could feel the force of the crashing dark waters pulling me, wanting me.

The waves slammed into the sides of cliff walls as it covered and uncovered a rubble of rocks at the base. The possibility of me flying blindfolded off a cliff crossed my mind.

That would have been…interesting.

Rolling over and pushing myself up to a seated position, I edged closer to the edge until my legs dangled in the open air. The strong salty flavors of the sea filled my nose. I closed my eyes. The dense air was suddenly masked by Aston's aroma.

"Now that was impressive," he said.

I didn't bother to turn around and look at him. I watched the dark magnetic slate blue colors of the water. The wave's white crests appeared and disappeared, swallowing everything in their path. Aston sat down, letting his legs dangle next to mine.

"Would you have saved me?" I asked.

"I would have. I was watching."

I looked at him, my cheeks pink.

"I've never seen anyone track so quickly like that before, especially without an ounce of training, *and* blindfolded. I'll admit I purposely set you up for failure. It's haunting to think of how strong your abilities are without any training or knowledge of them for seventeen years."

"There was something that just felt natural about it for me, like it was ingrained into every fiber of my being. Why could I never feel them before coming here, out in the human world? You would think *something* would have broken through, right?"

"It's the island, us, everything. Being around us with our abilities helps. All of it has begun to wake your abilities, you can't stop the domino effect now. It's exactly what the Elders want." He spoke quietly. "Your abilities are something you will never be able to escape again."

"I wouldn't want to."

There was silence as if this satisfied him. Aston took my forearm in his hands and gently ran his thumbs over my markings.

"How exactly *did* you follow me, Nora?" He asked.

"At first, I listened. I listened a while, and the woods began to feel alive, and I sifted through sounds until I found your heartbeat, then I caught your scent, and so I followed that trail."

"My scent, really?" He asked.

"Yes, well you *did say* we had a highly developed sense of smell."

"When I say 'we' I mean the Lamian side of us, you understand? That's where the ability to hunt and track by scent comes from, not the Sereni side. Lamians and Shapeshifters are the only two species that have a powerful sense of smell like ours."

"Shapeshifters? As in—"

"As in beings able to transform into an animal. Yes."

I narrowed my eyes at his last words and took a moment to let the idea of Shapeshifters sink in.

"By the way," Aston said, "what did my scent smell like to you?"

I leaned in close, pressing my side into his body. Aston's jaw line tightened with tension. I stopped when my nose hovered over his neck and inhaled. The tension of his body heightened the longer I stayed. Closing my eyes, I listened to his deep slow heartbeat speeding up. I quickly pulled away. Something deep inside me suddenly became incredibly uncomfortable, a hunger sparked.

"The sea, the woods after a rainfall, fear, and—" I stared at him, his eyes were wide and his pupils dilated watching me as he listened.

"And?"

"Hunger," I said. I turned my gaze back down to my hands, then to the ocean as heat rose into my chest and face.

"I live by the sea," he said to break the strange tension that had just sparked between us.

He pointed in a direction over the water where I assumed his home most likely was located.

He turned his face to look at me.

"You really are different from anyone I've ever met," he said.

"I've never met anyone like you either, let alone been bound to anyone, that's a first." The words slipped from my mouth.

"You know what it means?" Aston asked, slightly shocked.

"To be bound? Yes, Ada explained." My mouth became dry.

"Yeah." He pulled his knees to his chest, crossed his ankles and sat there.

We sat in silence together, understanding and accepting our destiny.

"Aston, you mentioned the other day you could find a way to break the bind. Ada told me you couldn't because if you try, we'd die."

Talk about some serious Romeo and Juliet crap. Instead of poison and killing ourselves in the name of love, we'd kill ourselves if we ever wanted out of this situation.

"I know, you looked *so* upset the other day, I didn't know what else to say." He quickly added, "I can feel you, you know." He glanced at me from the corner of his eye.

"What do you mean, feel me?"

"Your emotions," he said. "When you have nightmares, when you wake up, when you are angry or scared. I feel them all."

The privacy bar just dropped even lower.

"Right."

"You're scared," he said.

"Sometimes. I'm scared of—"

"Yourself, I know. I won't let anything happen to you, Nora."

And it was reassuring to hear him say so.

Most of the afternoon we lay on the grass and because he was curious, I told him everything I could remember about all the cities and apartments that Ada had dragged me to. The human world of which I was no longer a part. We picked wild berries and purchased a few oysters from a fisherman he knew. The old man taught me how to shuck an oyster, and to my surprise, I actually enjoyed the buttery flavor. I wondered if the fisherman knew Eben, but I kept my thoughts about Eben to myself. We exchanged stories until the sun was beginning to set over the ocean, painting the sky with hues of purple and red. We sat there for some time watching the colors change before my stomach interrupted with a growl.

"Oysters and berries aren't exactly filling," Aston smiled. "I need to get you home. You're hungry again, and these woods aren't as friendly as they seem once the sun is gone." He threw me a half smile, but something in his eyes told the truth. These woods hid Lamians, Sereni, Shapeshifters, and who knew what other secrets.

We ran back together. I had no idea where I was. I stayed close beside him. In a few minutes, we had covered much of the island's terrain and Aston had me back at Edel's front doorstep. From the stoop, we watched the sun vanish over the tree line.

"Hey, am I going to see you tomorrow?" I asked before turning to enter the stone cottage.

"Thought you didn't *like* me?" He grinned. Aston stepped up and stood inches from me looking over my face. "I'm looking forward to the sun rising, Ms. Stone." He brought his hand close to my cheek, almost touching me.

Instinctively, I closed my eyes the way I had done with Eben, but when I reopened them he had vanished. The scent of the salty ocean and forest loam vanished with him, but the smell of hunger was stronger than ever. There, on the ground beside my feet, was the black fabric he'd used to blindfold me earlier. A small seashell was bundled within the fabric. I held it to my nose and observed the dark forest with a smile tugging my lips back.

The front door to the cottage swung open.

–Nora? I thought I heard you–

Yael searched the front yard, and I pushed her into the cottage, but before closing the door behind us, I glanced one last time, knowing that I was being watched, if not by Aston, by someone. My stomach growled again. Yael had saved me a plate from dinner. I took a few bites and then headed to my room.

I slid open a box of matches I had found on a shelf and lit a few candles as I thought of Aston. My forearm tingled, and I ran the tips of my fingers over our binding mark—and the three scars which looked whiter and had become sensitive. Grabbing the nightgown off its hook, I slipped it over my bare, bony body, released my knotted hair, and stared at myself for a moment in the mirror. There was a distinct change beginning to happen. I felt different, and I thought maybe, maybe tonight my father's dark, gritty, prominent features had softened and I looked a bit more like my mother. I picked up the photo of her and kissed the glossy print.

"Night," I whispered as if she could hear me.

Crawling into bed, I wrapped myself in the soft cotton sheets and tightened them around me like a cocoon. My imagination took off, and I pretended Aston was accompanying me around the island until I began to fall asleep. I imagined his arms wrapped tightly around me, and for a moment, I almost felt the lucid thought come to life. Lips touched the back of my shoulder. Quickly, I opened my eyes and rolled over: nothing.

I was alone.

14

That night was the first time I dreamt of running. I ran through endless fields of forest masked with winter under a bright moon. The sounds of howling filled the crisp night air, and I was free. My hair waved wildly in the wind, and the dark dense woods echoed with life. Something entered my peripheral vision. I glanced over. There amongst the trees, a white wolf ran parallel to me. The charms that Ada had given me began to burn and sear my chest.

I woke up.

Stretching in the morning light, I quickly began forgetting the details of my dream, but I reached up and felt the charms. They were cool in my palm. I rolled over and was greeted by the black blindfold on the pillow next to my face. A sudden excitement to see Aston held me in suspense. I closed my eyes and twisted the blindfold around my finger while soaking in the morning sun. The cottage sang its familiar tunes.

Edel and Ada were in the kitchen, once again quietly discussing something serious. Deciding to go see what the fuss was all about, I swung my legs out of bed and made my way down the hall, but as I entered the kitchen, the conversation vanished in smiles, and shop talk about the latest *Kinfolk* magazine and newest recipe Edel had found took its place. Tucking the blindfold in my pocket, I noticed a figure in the yard. Yael was in the garden repeatedly bending over every few steps, picking something. There was no sign of Aston yet, and I walked through the house to make sure this time, but he wasn't anywhere to be found. Perhaps he was outside with Yael, but when I went to open the back door to see, Ada's voice stopped me.

"He's not there either." Ada had a half smile spread on her face, and she leaned over her elbows on the island clenching a ceramic mug of steaming dark coffee.

"Oh," I replied.

"So you enjoyed your time with him then, yeah?" Ada asked as Edel listened into the conversation, pretending to read her magazine.

"It was fine," I said, not wanting to give Ada any ideas.

"Fine? That's what you have to say, just fine?" Ada questioned my answer.

"Yes, just fine." I shoved both hands into my nightgown pockets and looked at her dead on.

"Was he nice to you?" Ada asked, possibly worried about Aston's behavior.

"Of course! I mean it was fun too, Ada. Definitely different. We worked on my running abilities, smell and hearing," I added.

With this answer, she seemed more pleased.

"Smell huh? Well, good!" Ada said. "Is he coming today?" She took a sip of coffee and exchanged looks with Edel.

"He said he would." I watched the both of them. They always looked like they were hiding something from me.

"Oh, okay well let us know then." Ada walked out of the room, and Edel put down her magazine and followed.

"Wait!" I yelled before they disappeared. "It's been another day. Eben? He should be back from his fishing trip by now, and what, our house is just going to be vacant again with no answers?"

"Get dressed," Ada ordered.

"Why?" I watched Edel squeeze Ada's hand in an encouraging fashion.

"I need to show you something."

When I finished dressing, Ada was already waiting for me outside. The sun was now peeking through an overcast sky.

"Okay, I'm here," I said, giving Ada a smile, which she didn't exchange for one of her own.

"Good, let's go." Ada took off running and I followed.

It was the first time we had run together alone. Zipping in and out of trees, over a stream and up a hill, she was fast. It was a joy to run with Ada, to finally both be together in a moment of time where there was a subtle silence of honesty. Ada began to slow down as we arrived at our destination, then she stopped and crouched behind a small boulder.

"Get down." She whispered, looking at me.

I knelt down and crawled beside her. The earth was moist and the leaves wet. It must have rained last night. The island seemed to be trapped in a bubble of clouds and condensation. I peeked over the rock and down the hill and saw a small cabin with a steady stack of smoke emerging from the chimney. Cords of wood lined the right side of the home, and an old green rowboat sat in the yard.

"That night when you went to the bonfire for Eben's birthday, it was you and Eben who caused the fire to erupt."

I watched Ada, her sage eyes were intensely focused on the little house.

"What? Us?"

My cheeks felt warm, and butterflies fluttered from my stomach to my chest when I remembered how Eben's arm felt wrapped around me, and then Aston's face entered my mind.

Suddenly we heard voices. We crouched down a little further. Two men appeared from the woods and walked towards the home. It was Eben, accompanied by an older man who shared Eben's height, stride, and broad shoulders; this could only be his father. The two had shotguns slung over their shoulders, and the father was holding two trussed dead rabbits in one hand. I was so excited to see

Eben I wanted to jump and yell hello, but Ada's hand pressed gently against my shoulder. They were arguing.

"If you were paying more attention, boy, we would have gotten that bull," his father's boisterous voice belted in anger. "Honestly Eben, where the heck has your head been?"

Eben stuffed a hand into his pocket.

"It's that girl again, isn't it?" His father went on. "You've been looking for her, haven't ya?" His tone grew angrier. "I told you once before and I'll tell it to you again, Eben," his father stopped dead in his tracks and eyed Eben carefully. "Don't ever go over to that part of the island again."

"Those are just tales, Pop! Come on, you can't be serious!" Eben raised his voice in frustration.

"*Ever*, Eben! Do you hear me? I forbid it." Eben's father disappeared into the little house, slamming the screen door behind him.

Eben picked up a red-handled ax and began chopping a pile of wood out of frustration, muttering words of anger under his breath. He raised the handle over his head and split a log in half. I heard him huff as he picked up another log, slamming it onto the tree stump and repeated. We watched as Eben took his frustration out. He had been looking for me. He hadn't forgotten about me.

"What do you mean it was us that caused the fire?" I whispered. Ada watched him carefully with concern.

"He's my son," she whispered.

"What!" I forgot for a moment that we were in hiding. Ada pressed her hand against my lips. Eben stopped swinging the ax in mid-air, turned his face in our direction and scanned the tree line. We both ducked until we heard the ax split another log.

"He's your *son*?" I whispered. "He's my cousin!" I felt suddenly a little embarrassed about the feelings that had been growing inside of me for Eben, thinking that I had almost kissed him, that I wanted that moment with him. I leaned against the rock and lay my head back. Ada turned around and sat beside me.

"Nolan, Eben's father and I once knew each other."

"Once knew each other? You had a kid together, I would say you knew each other pretty well."

"It was a long time ago." Ada turned over and continued watching Eben split wood. I couldn't even look at him. I knew what his hands felt like, the scent of his skin, his broad shoulders, his smile, and how he called me 'girlie.' Why Ada, why?

"It was your energies that caused the bonfire to erupt, nothing more. Just raw power you both were beginning to ignite." Ada laced her fingers together. "No one knew about Eben except Edel and your parents. And Nolan, of course. I wanted to keep Eben safe and hidden from the Elders and this world, just as your parents wanted for you. He doesn't know what he is, unless his father told him, but I doubt that."

"I sure as heck know how that's going to feel when he finds out the truth."

Ada looked at me as if that idea of telling Eben hadn't crossed her mind.

"You *are* going to tell him, aren't you?"

She sat silently watching.

"Did Nolan know you were different?" I asked. "Don't the Elders live here on this island? Wouldn't they have known, all these years?"

"Yes. Nolan knows about our kind. We disappeared when I became pregnant. We hid together until I had given birth to Eben. No one knows exactly where the Elders live, Nora. No one has ever been there. But for the safety of our son, Nolan and I disappeared, hid as far away we could. We hid everything we were. I knew we couldn't keep that life a secret for long. Your mother was the only one who knew our whereabouts, and one morning I received a letter from her. I wanted to take Eben with us. The thought of you two growing up together was fantasy. Nolan needed someone, and I couldn't just disappear from his life with his child. He needed someone to love, someone to be strong for." Ada's voice cracked.

I had read that letter from my mother to Ada and remembered.

"You left your own son, your family, to protect me, didn't you?" Guilt washed over me.

"I had to, Nora. It was the only way I could keep you, Nolan, and Eben safe all at the same time."

All these years living with this secret must have been killing Ada. Every time she looked at me, every time she held me, taught me, disciplined me, or sang to me, she must have been thinking in her mind how she wished she were holding her own child. She pressed her chin against the top of her hand and looked at the simple life she had abandoned, just down the hill. The cabin screen door opened again, and Nolan walked out with two beers in his hand; he handed one to Eben.

"Oh come on, he's only eighteen," Ada muttered in disapproval. I rolled my eyes.

Nolan patted Eben on the back and switched places with him hoisting the ax. This must have been their 'manly' way of making up.

"He was only four months old the night I disappeared. I left Nolan a note under his favorite coffee mug." She began to rehash her memory. "I loved him, you know? Gosh did I love that man."

"And you don't anymore?"

"It's been almost eighteen years. How does one know anything after that kind of time? Besides, I can only imagine the anger he must have felt waking up realizing he was going to raise our child alone."

"You should go see him. You should see your son! He thinks of you, you know? He told me so. Told me that he likes to think that his mother is out there in the world running her own fishing crew."

"Maybe he's better off that way."

"If you don't tell him, I will. I know what that feels like." I pointed towards Eben. "He is so lucky to have not just one but *both* his parents alive! Besides, he probably will start figuring out soon that he has abilities if he hasn't already since the bonfire, and how is Nolan supposed to explain that one?"

"I know, I know," Ada whispered as if to herself.

Ada crouched down as Eben looked in our direction again, and for the first time, she looked terrified, terrified of her own life, wondering and contemplating the 'what ifs' in her mind.

The screen door slammed as Nolan went back inside.

"This is your chance! Do you want to know your son or what?" I attempted to stand up and yell Eben's name, but she yanked me down. I could feel her blood pulsating in her sweaty hands.

"If my parents were still alive, I would want to know. If you want, I can leave. I know the way back to Edel's, and I'll be safe." Ada's eyes were rimmed with tears, but she stood up, shook the dirt off her pants, wiped her eyes and, without a word, began to head down the hill.

"I love you," I whispered over the rock, and she looked back at me for a brief moment with a nervous smile. I was about to witness a family reunion, something I will only ever have in dreams. I stayed for a while watching, and when she was halfway down the hill, Eben took notice and traded the ax for his beer. I watched Ada and Eben shake hands and talk for a bit until I saw the beer slip out of Eben's hand. He wrapped his arms tightly around Ada, and she slowly, cautiously wrapped hers around him. The screen door opened and Nolan stood on the porch, realizing that Ada had come back. He didn't express much besides giving a hand gesture inviting her inside. Ada glanced back up the hill in my direction. She disappeared into the tiny cabin, and I slouched against the rock. I was happy for her, for Eben. I stood up and began to walk back. I felt alone. Ada had her family now; Edel had Yael, and I was still left parentless, a burden, and the reason others gave up their homes and lives. A single tear rolled down my cheek.

I needed to run.

I sank into Edel's white couch in the living room and tucked my feet under a pillow. The sky looked gray and heavy with an approaching storm. I closed my eyes and fiddled with my mother's charms, listening to the unsettling waves of the lake. I waited patiently for the familiar sounds of Aston's footsteps, but they never came. Before I knew it, the small round clock sitting on the mantle over the fireplace read seven o'clock. The evening had rolled around, and after endless cups of tea, a few slices of a fruit pie Yael had made from the berries in the garden, and about five magazines, I found myself pacing the house, fidgeting and orbiting the coffee table. Every now and then I peeked out of the windows for signs of Aston, but there were none. Darkness began to paint the sky, and the smell of Edel cooking dinner filled the home.

Ada was still gone.

"Mind setting the table?" Edel asked me while handing me a stack of plates and a mason jar filled with silverware.

I took the plates when a sharp pain pierced my side. I bent over, dropping the stack of white dishes and silverware. They crashed and shattered around my feet. I fell and caught myself against the table then sunk to the floor.

"Nora!" Ada walked through the front door at that very moment and rushed over. Images appeared in my mind: an alleyway, rain, pavement, bloodstained hands, nails, teeth, and two bodies lying on concrete. It all happened so fast, like in a flip-book.

"Nora! Are you okay?" Edel and Ada picked me up from the floor. I felt disoriented as another searing streak shot through my forehead and lodged itself behind my eyes.

I screamed in pain.

"What is happening!" Ada asked Edel who looked anxious.

"I uh, I don't know. I had a vision. Two bodies on the ground; it was raining. Pavement. It didn't *feel* like I was on the island anymore."

"Okay, okay, let's get you seated." Ada exchanged looks with Edel and they sat me in a chair at the kitchen table as Yael began cleaning up the pieces of ceramic and shattered glass off the floor.

I felt terrible, something was gravely wrong. What had happened to me? Edel quickly took out four more plates and set the table.

Ada felt my forehead. "Nora, I think that you—"

"I'm fine," I snapped trying to remember the images.

"Okay! No harm done! Chili time it is!" Edel handed Yael butter and bread to put in the center of the table while she carried over a crockpot of steaming red chili.

"This will hit the spot, Nora. Don't you worry." Edel smiled, but her eyes were lined with concern.

We all took seats and began handing around the food, making sure everyone got a little of everything. After we finished I excused myself from the table. No questions were asked. Yael was the only one who watched me, and I could tell she had been eavesdropping into my thoughts, but I paid her no attention. I couldn't stomach the chili after seeing blood and bodies so I excused myself from the table. Ada tried to speak, but Edel placed her hand on her shoulder and lightly shook her head.

I made my way to the bathroom and splashed my face with cold water, then brushed my teeth, spat, rinsed, and wiped my face with a towel. My room was cooler. The window creaked slightly, opening and closing in the breeze. I closed the door and lay on the bed. The storm finally broke through, and I watched as the falling rain beaded the window. The sky growled angrily, and I couldn't escape the competing thoughts of Aston, Eben, watching Ada get her family back, or the violent thoughts I had in the kitchen before dropping Edel's dishes.

Yael knocked on the door and slipped into my room, closing the door behind her. She lay down beside me and spotted the seashell from Aston lying on the windowsill. I handed it to her and she studied it for a moment.

–Where did you get this?–

She held it at arm's length between her thumb and index finger.

"Aston," I said.

–Pretty– She turned the shell around examining it.

"He said he lives by the sea."

–He likes you–

I remained quiet, hoping the conversation would not escalate. She rolled over on her side and propped her head up with her right hand looking at me.

–And you, you like him too– This was more statement than a question.

"We're bound Yael, who knows what's real between us."

Yael pursed her lips.

–I saw everything in the kitchen–

"I know."

–But, I couldn't make any sense of it, of any of it.–

"I'm not sure what happened, I've never experienced something like that before."

–Well, all I know is that it wasn't you–

I looked at Yael.

–You were in someone else's mind– Yael pointed to the Laguz rune on my forearm –Communication between minds, it's part of your bind. Perhaps, you were in Aston's mind–

Ada had explained this to me. I shrugged my shoulders wanting to forget what had happened in the kitchen. If I was in Aston's mind, then where was he? What exactly was he doing?

–Do you love him?–

Her question derailed me as she handed me the seashell.

"What? Who said anything about love! I barely even know him!" I defended myself, stunned at the idea of it.

–You don't have to know someone to love someone. Some people just know–

"You speak as if you have experience, little one." I smiled in her direction.

–No. I hope to someday, though–

Yael nursed a faint thought of love in this dark world, the way I had once about friendship in a lonely world.

Yael looked at me from the corner of her eye. Then she smiled.

–You remind me of my mom, the way she used to look at my dad or when she would speak about him–

I thought of Edel and the permanent look of loneliness that hazed over her eyes when not masked by a smile.

"What happened to your dad?"

Her childish smile vanished.

–My dad?– She repeated as if she hadn't thought of the idea for some time. –He died when I was young–

Her reply was short and clipped. We watched the rain begin to hit the window harder for a few moments.

"Do you remember him?" I asked her.

–I do, I was five when he died–

Her answers were quick and short, so I assumed this was the end of our conversation. I didn't want her to have to rehash painful moments in her life, but then surprisingly enough she went on to describe her father.

–He had green eyes and dark brown hair. He would make her laugh all the time. She barely laughs these days anymore, and when she does it's not the same laugh she had when he was alive. That laughter died with him–

She stopped speaking for some time again. The sky let out a vicious crack, and Yael's body burrowed closer to mine. Her bright green eyes looked towards the window.

–When storms would come in, just like this one, I used to be scared to fall asleep alone, and the only way I'd sleep was between them–

The sky let out another loud bang, and the thunder slightly shook the house. Yael's body pushed a little harder into my side.

–But they don't scare me anymore, well not as much– She corrected herself, looking at my raised eyebrows. –They're not so scary compared to other things out there–

"What is it out there that scares you more than thunder?"

–The Elders mostly, and the Lamians–

At the next sound of thunder, her face turned and pressed into the side of my arm.

–He was human–

I was caught off guard. Her father? Human? Yael's face released from my arm.

–The Elders had him killed. They weren't as careful as Ada and Nolan. They refused to hide, refused to live like that–

Her eyes looked directly into mine, and I fell into her thoughts, reliving memories, watching images like an old film as she continued her story.

–He was a math teacher at the high school on the main island where humans go–

"Yeah, I know. It's where I would have gone. Where Eben goes."

–One day when he was coming home from work, a tracker was sent to kill him. She had been following from the minute he left our home–

I could see Edel and Yael waving to this tall handsome man as he stood on the ferry. Eric was there, waving. He looked younger and thinner. It was slightly painful to live through her memories like this.

–Mommy and I used to always meet him at the dock when he'd arrive, but he never showed that evening. Later that night we received a phone call from the Swan's Island Town Police Department with some information about my father–

I watched Edel as if I was Yael sitting at the kitchen table and waiting for her to get off the phone. Edel had her back to Yael and the phone fell from her ear, hitting the stone floor. Edel buckled at the knees, falling to the floor, her heart painfully splintering. I tried to hold back the tears forming in my eyes.

–Mommy and I went right away to Stonington Island, and once the police brought us to the scene to identify his body, Mommy knew it was no accident. With just one look at him, she confirmed he was Robert James Hughes and we left–

Edel and Yael were guided back into the police car and taken to the dock where Eric stood waiting to bring them home. His eyes were glassy and his cheeks tinted red. He had already shed tears for them.

–The tracker followed him in his car and caused him to drive off the road into a telephone pole. The police claimed he died instantly, and so Mommy told me that he went peacefully. But, his body was found with unexplained gashes and bite marks. The police told us that some kind of animal must have scented the blood and unfortunately got to him before the police were able to, but they'd never seen animal marks like this before–

Flashes of her father's face and part of his arm before the police zipped up the black body bag flickered in Yael's mind. And though my stomach tightened, I couldn't look away from the memory. It was a horror scene I would never wish for anyone to see.

–It wasn't enough that he was killed, but Mommy recognized those gashes and bites and they weren't from an animal, but marks of a Lamian tracker. That night Mommy called to the Elders and she cried, screaming for them to bring him back. Instead, they punished her for exposing our world to humans. They said that she endangered our kind and it was forbidden–

Edel was on her knees in the snow before the same three hooded figures that had encircled me. They stood still as they watched her fall apart before them. I hated this scene with every bone in my body. Nephthys faced my direction and pointed directly at me.

Edel's face was mortified and her lips screamed the word "No!" I collapsed onto the cold snow gripping my throat.

—They took away my voice. They told my mother that I would never be able to speak again as a constant reminder to her of her wrongs. I wasn't born like this you know—

I was left numb and at a loss for words. How does one respond to the pain and suffering that this girl had experienced? I asked the only question I could think of to ask.

"Who was the Lamian tracker?"

I noticed Yael had revealed the tracker's gender in the story.

—Lia—

The nerves in my stomach suddenly shattered. Aston's sister had killed Yael's father and then lost control, I presumed, giving into bloodlust. My hands trembled with anger as adrenaline began to build. The more I thought of Lia, the more the flames on the candles cracked and flickered in the room. How could Aston have allowed something like this to happen?

—Aston and Lia are *both* very talented trackers Nora— Yael was watching my face but glancing at the fitful candles.

"Wait. Are there different kinds of trackers?"

—A tracker can be anyone who has the ability to track by scent, or has been trained to track, and the Elders have trackers of their own, to do their bidding. Those women who were trying to bring you to them in the woods were all trackers of the Elders. Except for Iona; you were lucky she showed up. She was the one who brought you here—

Yael watched as the jar of stones and paintbrushes tipped over and spilled across the desk.

—Nora, Aston had nothing to do with the murder of my dad— Yael placed her hand in mine.

—Listen to me, the Elders did offer him the job first, but he declined it. They were disappointed in him, and said they found him to be a weak link in their system—

He may not have killed him, but he could have prevented it if he knew about the task, I thought. Which was worse? My chest tightened; I had no idea Aston was a tracker for the Elders, and there I was exposing myself to him. I felt violated, a fool. I was bound to a traitor, someone who could have prevented that pain, and someone whose hands had killed.

–He isn't like Lia. They're incredibly different. Mommy says she's a bad seed. The only reason the Elders haven't killed her for breaking as many rules as she has is because she is excellent at tracking and hunting and completely loyal, loyal to their every bid and call–

"Why would they bind me to someone they believe to be a weak link?" I questioned, my body feeling hot, the markings on my forearm beginning to tingle.

–To give him a second chance.–

"A second chance?"

–Ada and Mommy have been up in arms about your bind to Aston because of this, because we are all vulnerable to Aston's decisions with you.–

This is what Ada and Edel had been discussing in private over the past few days, would Aston stab us all in the back like Lia had? Why wouldn't he? Betrayal to their kind runs in their blood apparently.

I was cursed.

–Nora, Aston is good. I know this, his heart is good.–

My cheeks tightened and I pulled Yael into my arms. My heart ached as if it had broken while reliving her story. I didn't know what more to add to this conversation. I ran my fingers through her hair. My shoulder began to feel warm and wet. She was silently crying for her pain, for her loss. Holding her until she fell asleep in my arms, I sang and hummed the song I heard my mother sing to me in my dreams.

> "Oh little child so small and sweet
> stay this way forever with me
> through the tides and across the seas

you will always be a part of me."

Yael's body soon twitched and her breathing became heavier; she was fast asleep. The painful knowledge she exposed me to spread through my mind, and my eyes began to swell as I watched her face lingering peacefully in a world of dreams. My hatred for Lia began to take deep roots though I had only met her once in the flesh. Suddenly an urge to do something rather strange crossed my mind, something that I had never thought of before in my life, and most certainly would have never dreamed of doing. Carefully leaning over, I allowed my inner demon to slip through. It's hissing voice whispered into Yael's ear as she slept.

"I will hunt her, Yael. I will hunt her, and I will kill her."

As I kissed her forehead, her hand opened and the seashell fell out onto the blanket. Aston.

The rain began to pound the window, but Yael took no notice. Her little fingers twitching reminded me of the dream I had as she floated in a sea of darkness. Gently pulling my arm from under her neck, I rolled her over and tucked her under a knitted blanket. Carefully crawling over her, I got out of bed and made sure the window was tightly shut to stop the rain from entering. I turned to make my way outside; I needed space to sort my thoughts. I slowly closed the door, watching Yael disappear behind the crack, then turned and ran into Edel.

"Is Yael with you?" she asked, me with an undertone of paranoia in her voice.

"Yes, she's fast asleep in my bed. It's okay. I don't mind, really," I said so Yael wouldn't be woken up and moved. Edel smiled, and I could see a little sign of relief on her face. I couldn't help but hug her. She was surprised with my action and then gently squeezed me back.

"Thank you for spending time with her, Nora. She really has become quite fond of you, you know."

Smiling without a word, I made my way past her down the hall. I needed to be alone. I sat on the back porch watching the storm and rehashing the memories and information Yael had shared with me. The rain began to fall harder, creating multiple small waterfalls off the roof. My lips pinched together tightly as I thought of the cruel restrictions this new world offered, restrictions I was forced to live within and obey, restrictions that, if tampered with, could result in death. A lump grew in my throat, knowing what my future would look like. Something had to change.

Lightning illuminated the sky and the lake's water stirred strongly. I stood up and reached my arms out, filled my cupped hands with fresh rain, and washed my face. A barrier broke, and I began to cry. I cried for the growing pains I felt. I cried for my life, a life that had suddenly been thrown off kilter. I had been dealt an unfair hand without instructions. Gripping my mother's necklace, I ripped it off in a moment of fury.

Why would you leave me here like this? Why?

If she loved me, if my father loved me, why didn't they fight for me, run further, hide for longer? How could they willingly hand me over, their only daughter, to someone and disappear from her life? I was a burden. A cursed child. I stepped down from the porch and threw the necklace as far as I could into the rain, then sank to my knees and lay down in the grass, letting the cold rain cover me. My body fumed with emotion that wouldn't stop. Ever since I'd first set foot on this island, I could so easily turn to a place of darkness, anger, and hate. Something about it was comforting and soothingly seductive. It felt easy and natural. I closed my eyes when I felt a body lay down next to mine. I didn't need to see to know who it was. He had come back. His head close to mine, he lay there in silence with me. Aston had felt me.

"Sorry I'm late," He said.

I wasn't able to form the words, only tears spilled from the corners of my eyes.

"Why are you crying?" Aston asked.

I sat up and pushed myself off the ground, my nightgown now muddy and wet as I stood, my body shaking with adrenaline in the rain. My hair was soaked and heavy as it slowly fell out of its high bun.

"Why didn't you tell me the truth about your sister, how she's a murderer? How she killed Yael's father? Or the fact that you *knew*, Aston. You knew and didn't stop it! Or, the fact that our bind is your second chance to prove to the Elders that you aren't a weak link!"

Aston was lost for words and watched me with an expression of disbelief.

"I heard the story, Aston."

He stood up without exchanging a single word.

"Do you *really* have nothing to say? You know, for a moment yesterday I almost forgot that you were forcefully bound to me, that you are just following the Elders' orders, for a moment I thought I felt something real. That you weren't just preparing me for them. I almost forgot this was your job." The outburst felt uncontrollable, my tongue sharp and vicious. "Would you like to figure out what else I can do? What other abilities I have, so you can go report to the Elders? Maybe they'll send Lia after me next if you don't do your job well!"

I felt irrational. This behavior wasn't me, allowing anger to control me, to smolder within me. Oh, but it felt good. The darkness was seemingly comforting to my soul.

Aston took a step closer to me.

"Nora, stop! I have been nothing but honest with you."

His hands outstretched as if to fend me off, backing me down. What made me more dangerous than Aston was how erratic my emotions were. Like a poisonous snake, it's always the new blood, the young ones, that are the most aggressive, the most dangerous; nature's way of giving the weakest, the untrained, the most protection.

"True, I didn't tell you about Yael's father, but that conversation had yet to take place and besides I said no to the job. I have been open about everything with you. I have been clear about my feelings toward Lia and clear on my thoughts of the Elders. And just like the job to kill James, I will not give them what they want with you either! Every little thing I've learned about you is between us, and I will figure out how to protect that information from the Elders when the time comes." He reached his arm out to touch me, but I sharply backed away. He withdrew his hand immediately. He was the trainer, and I the trainee.

"Nora, I couldn't do anything about Yael's father. I didn't know they had turned to Lia until it was too late. I tried hard to find her, to change the Elders' minds, but I couldn't. By the time I arrived, it was too late, Lia had struck and the trackers had fed."

He stopped for a moment and looked as if the pain of the memories had become overwhelming. His heartbeat pounded in my ears.

"And just like that damn night, it's because of Lia that I am late."

I searched his face curiously, but he wouldn't make eye contact with me.

"I had to go to the mainland to clean up another one of her *episodes*," he said in a disappointed tone.

"What do you mean by that?"

Aston grabbed his side, wincing slightly.

"What happened to you, Aston?"

But he continued his train of thought.

"It was in Stonington, near a movie theater."

His tone had turned serious, my mind rewound to the visions I'd had in the kitchen earlier, and I pressed my hand to my stomach.

"She just killed two people, didn't she?"

Aston looked shaken. "How did you—"

"Because I was *there*. I mean I wasn't there, but I saw it. Earlier, before dinner, I suddenly felt a sharp pain in my side." I looked at the side Aston had grabbed in pain, it was the same side that had folded me over in the kitchen earlier.

"I dropped a stack of dishes onto the floor, then fell into this vision of blood, rain, two bodies on the ground, teeth. It was Lia! And I was in your mind, wasn't I?"

Aston stood there pressing his hand to his side. I could see a little blood seeping through the fibers. He was speechless. I walked over and moved his hand, lifting his shirt to inspect his body. There were deep gashes along his ribs.

"Laguz." I hissed. "Our minds have the power to communicate, to see into one another. This is why you can feel me." I pushed up his sleeve and pointed to the third character down.

"Why, Aston?" I lowered my voice. "Why did she do it?"

"I am not sure *why* she does it. But ever since you got here, her impulsive craving for blood has gotten worse, it's uncontrollable. I am trying here, Nora!"

"Does she actually *drink* blood?"

"Yes. She does." Aston said softly.

"Do you?" I asked, widening my eyes.

Aston paused, looked away, and then back at me.

"I can survive on it, but before you start freaking out, Nora, you should know that all Lamians do. It's the demon we are all born with. Lamians can survive on food or blood. The stronger your demon, the thirstier and more powerful your hunger for blood can be. You will want to kill for it and it's only a matter of time until you begin your transition." Aston turned over the hand that had been pressing against his almost healed gashes, his palm red with blood. "At first, the scent will begin to smell sweet. This will awaken your demon. Then the burning sensation of hunger will begin to flower, coming from the depths of your soul, and eventually you will want to taste it. After that, the choice is yours. You control your thirst. My sister, can't. She allows her demon to control her, to drive her, to choose for her."

I swallowed hard, disgusted by the idea of tasting blood.

"Is that why I can feel hunger with you? A constant hunger?" I lowered my voice.

"No."

I looked apprehensively towards the forest that surrounded this cottage. Lia could be watching us for all I knew. I smelled the air like some kind of animal, but I caught no scent of strangers. Then it dawned on me.

Lia has been killing people to temporarily abate her hunger for the blood she actually wants: mine.

Aston noticed the discomfort beginning to seep into my eyes, and I could tell he saw that I had pieced it together.

"Nora, I will not let her touch you. Do you hear me?"

"Why haven't the Elders gotten involved?" I interrogated him. "Aren't they the *law* around here? Isn't she exposing our kind to humans when going on killing sprees?"

"Because she's valuable to them. She will bend to their will. She will kill when asked. She is desperate to please for power!" His voice was escalating in volume.

I took a few more steps away from him with my heels sinking into the soft earth.

"Don't look at me like that," he said, slightly wounded and ravening. "I am nothing like her."

"What if she's been watching us?"

Then I thought of Nolan and Eben and began to panic. I felt like a wide-eyed deer suddenly aware that a lethal predator was lurking nearby. The rain fell even harder, and it became more and more difficult to see him. I wiped my eyes, pushing the loose hair from my face.

There was a pause and then, without a warning, he approached me, pulled me into his arms, pressed his lips against mine. He held on to me tightly. My heart beat rapidly, and my body flickered with emotion. We stood there frozen, both uncertain, then Aston picked me up and I wrapped my legs around him, giving in and kissing him back. It felt like a moment I wanted to last a lifetime; I never wanted it to end.

It was my first kiss.

My fingers ran through his dark hair as he pressed his hands into my back, keeping his lips pressed against mine. The scent of the salty sea revisited my nose, a smell I had been subconsciously longing to taste. Aston pulled back for a moment and looked into my eyes, studying me.

"*That* is why you can feel my hunger."

My whole body shivered with a new kind of adrenaline, a kind I had never felt before. I pushed his hair off his forehead as he put me down and opened his hand. In his palm lay my mother's necklace. Aston held it up.

"You'll need a new clasp." He smiled and leaned in, kissing the side of my neck, running his hands down my ribs. "I've waited a long time for you, Nora. I've dreamt about the girl who was out there in the world, hidden. I've been waiting for your return and from the first moment I saw you, I couldn't stop dreaming about you."

He was right, there was something potent here, a connection that was unbreakable. Something changed inside of me, rooted, and for a moment, I forgot all the hate and fear I was building inside only seconds before we kissed.

Was loving Aston dangerous, or was loving me fatal? We were bound and cursed.

Was this part of the Elder's plan, would falling down this rabbit hole weaken us, was this the snare they planned to entrap us in? Aston sensed my stirring emotions and grabbed my hand.

"I don't know," was all he said, looking at my skittish eyes.

"Maybe this is exactly what they wanted," I spoke quietly.

"Maybe it is."

"Goodnight, Nora." Aston leaned in and kissed me.

I watched him disappear into the darkness.

15

The next morning, I awoke to the chatter and laughter of unfamiliar voices in Edel's kitchen. I tried to tap into Yael's mind, but I couldn't find her. The sky was gray with periwinkle hints in the clouds. I honestly didn't mind the weather, but the occasional sunny, warm day would be nice. I sat up and tipped the copper watering can into a small potted plant Edel had placed in my room. The shell and blindfold sat on the windowsill, along with my mother's necklace. I listened to the voices laughing in the kitchen, and I thought of Aston, wondering when he'd show. I thought of our kiss last night, and I buried my face into my knees. It was a bit dramatic, but a pretty top-notch first if you ask me.

Someone rapped at my door.

"Come in."

It was Ada.

"Good morning," she said slipping into my room and taking a seat at the end of my bed. "Sleep okay?"

"I did."

"Good, good. Now, about last night."

"I *know* what happened, Ada. I was in Aston's mind, our thoughts overlapped. He came over late in the evening, said he felt me, felt my distress or something. It's hard to believe how intimate and intense a bind can be." I sat cross-legged.

"Yes, being bound to someone is something no one could imagine unless they have experience with it. What happened then? What did you see?"

"Lia had what Aston called 'another *episode*.' She is satisfying her hunger by killing and last night she killed two humans in Stonington all because of me, Ada—because she wants me."

"Aston said that? That it was because of you?"

I tightened my lips and grabbed my mother's necklace. "Can you fix this? I broke it by accident." Trying to change the subject.

"Right." Ada took the necklace and a sip of her coffee. "This is what Marcia was just telling us in the kitchen. We fear the things that Lia may do. She is so power hungry and apparently festering with hate and envy for what you will become. Only time will tell I suppose. No one, not even Aston, can predict what her intentions could be."

"Who is Marcia?" I asked.

"Marcia and Jane. They are two more Sereni, and Jane is actually your age. She's dying to meet you." Ada smiled.

"Does she have some personal agenda to kill me too?" I sulked, uninterested in meeting another potential enemy.

"Hmmm. No, trust me, you're going to *like* Jane. Okay, hop on up, get dressed, and come meet our friends." Ada began to make her way out then turned. "Oh and Nora, work hard when training with Aston. The faster you develop your skills and abilities, the faster you can properly defend yourself and your mind, even from the Elders."

"I am trying, Ada."

"Good." She left the room and made her way back to the kitchen, which erupted with laughter once again.

I swung my feet off the bed, pulled my nightgown off and began to dress. I slipped into jeans and was pulling up the zipper when I heard a voice.

"Good morning."

I quickly spun around, my wild hair covering my breasts. Aston was standing on the other side of my room. I stood there, feeling naked. I crossed my arms over my chest.

"Good morning, sir." I could feel heat rising into my cheeks.

Aston smiled. He was holding a bag in his hand and dropped it on my bed.

"What's that?"

"Training clothes. I took the liberty of picking you up some since I highly doubt you had any of your own." Aston eyed my jeans.

I walked over and pulled the drawstring open seeing a bundle of black fabric. "Colorful."

"We don't want to stand out."

I pulled the drawstring closed when I felt his hands move over my skin from my hips to belly. I looked down at our identical marks, my breath tight. This was a feeling I had been longing for since last night. My heart slowed and my body laid back into his.

"I know I am being a bit forward here."

You don't say. I thought standing there in his arms half naked.

"I wanted to apologize again about yesterday and last night."

"It's fine, Aston. In my past life, I wouldn't have acted so intensely, but ever since coming to this place, my emotions feel out of control. They're strong, dark, and immensely overwhelming. I never used to be like this, I used to feel more in control of my mind, my body, and my thoughts."

"We'll get through this, Nora."

I felt the most intense connection to a human being that I had ever felt in my life; beyond anything I'd have thought possible.

"Okay well, I need to go," Aston said letting his fingers rake my skin.

"Wait, aren't we training?" I asked turning around to meet his gaze. My body felt cold with his release.

"We are. I'll be back to pick you up. I can't exactly walk out of your room with you." Aston smiled, taking my hand and kissing the back of it.

"See you soon, Ms. Stone."

I narrowed my eyes at his allure.

Aston escaped through the window and vanished into the forest. I knelt onto my bed and looked out the window, scanning the tree line when I saw movement within the shadows. I narrowed my eyes, but the movement had stopped. I thought I saw the glimmer of a pair of eyes watching me. An uneasiness began to sink into my bones. I closed the window and pulled the black fabric out of the bag.

Stop being so paranoid, Nora.

The bundle of black clothing consisted of a loose pair of pants that folded over at my waist and a fitted top with long sleeves and a hood. I made my way to my bedroom door and peered over my shoulder out the window towards the tree line. Whatever was watching me was still there, lurking; I could feel it.

I closed the bedroom door behind me, made my way to the bathroom, bushed my teeth then went into to the kitchen. Edel and Ada were sitting at the table with Marcia and Jane.

The laughter and chatting came to a halt when I entered the room.

"Nora!" Edel exclaimed, "Sit my girl, and meet our friends, Marcia and Jane."

Both women had dark, wiry, curly hair, icy blue eyes, and prominent freckles that seemed to spill over their noses and down their cheeks. Marcia's hair was more of a salt-and-pepper color like Ada's. Their lips were full and their smiles wide.

I reached my hand across the table and shook their hands. Marcia trailed her eyes to my forearm where a bit of my binding tattoo peeked through. I pulled my sleeve down self-consciously and took a seat.

"Marcia and Jane are dear friends. Marcia and Edel are around the same age, except she's a descendant of Miksa."

"Miksa, one of the Seven, the Bering Sea, right?"

"That's right, my dear," said Marcia. "See that Jane, she's just a few weeks old in our world and she knows our history better than you do!"

Jane rolled her eyes, taking a sip of her coffee. "Too many names, too many dates. It's, like, impossible."

"Ay, what am I going to do with you?" Marcia nudged her daughter.

"Where did you get that outfit?" Ada asked, touching the fabric of the hood.

"Aston gave it to me earlier."

"Earlier? Did Aston stop by?" Ada asked raising an 'I'm-on-to-you' kind of eyebrow in my direction.

"Well, earlier as in, last night when he stopped by. Training clothes." I tried correcting myself.

"Hold your horses!" Jane blurted out. "Aston Boxam? You're training with Aston Boxam!" Her jaw dropped.

I looked to Ada. "I suppose so?" I felt silly not knowing his last name.

"She is," Ada smiled.

"Oh now come on! That is *so* not fair! How is it that she gets here and gets a trainer like Aston, and I'm stuck with, no offense Mom, but I'm stuck with my mom."

"Excuse me, babe, but I think I'm pretty hip for my age." Marcia brushed her hair over her shoulder.

Everyone laughed.

"So everyone knows Aston then, huh?" I asked Jane.

"Know Aston? Girl, he's a pretty hot commodity in our world, especially for us *young 'uns*, as I like to call the under-a-hundred crowd. Let's just say you didn't get tangled up with some average guy." Jane winked.

"You're killing me, Jane! Have I taught you nothing about our history?" Marcia blurted, slapping the table with her hand. She looked to Ada and Edel. "Honestly, can you believe our lineage is going to be left to these kids!" Marcia looked at me. "Aston and his sister Lia are descendants of Amena who settled in the Black Sea. They are a little over a hundred years old." Marcia narrowed her eyes to her daughter. "Maybe a hundred and twenty-four, I believe, this year."

"Age-shmage. The point is, he's a babe." Jane pulled her full lips back, cracking a smile.

"Oh," I said, shocked to hear his actual age.

"We age slowly dear," Marcia looked at me, "obviously, since I'm going to celebrate my twelve-hundredth birthday this year!"

My jaw dropped.

"Twelve-hundredth? Seriously?"

"I know, I know my dear. I look a ravishing forty-five wouldn't you say, Ada?"

Belts of laughter erupted.

Jane threw her hands up. "See Nora, save yourself the sanity, and don't even bother with it all."

"Excuse me for asking, but why the age gaps? Between your generation and us? I was told Jane is my age right? I'm assuming what, seventeen or eighteen?" I asked a very obvious question in my mind.

"Seventeen. My birthday is in October." Jane winked again. She had a very playful demeanor.

"Excellent question!" Marcia said. "When we all heard that Alexo and Rebekah had gotten together and that they were expecting *you*, we all thought that things were going to become better for us, finally safe to bring children into our world. We believed that Alexo would change the ways of the Lamians and maybe even the Elders, but that wasn't the case. The Elders were furious, and punished those who conceived with humans." She looked to Edel and Ada. "And heavens forbid if your child was born on the night of the rare blue moon that year. So we all hid, ran, giving birth in hiding and raising our children in secret until they were old enough, trained enough to protect themselves from the Lamians. We were once abundant in population, Nora. But if you heard the story of the Elders, then you would know about the wars, deaths, and unexplained disappearances of Sereni men and women. The short answer to your question: fear. Fear is why we waited for so many years before bringing you chickadees into the world." Marcia pinched Jane's cheek.

"And your husband?" I asked, suddenly regretting the question, unsure if something terrible had happened to their family.

"Oh Barrett, he's out making his rounds, strengthening protective shields and tracking down the movement and patterns of Lamians to keep us safe," Marcia smiled.

I felt relieved to hear he was alive.

"Marcia and Barrett are Guardians. They are two of several who are left in these islands protecting us." Ada said. "Jane and Katia, like you, are in training to become Guardians. They really risk their lives for us, Nora."

"Don't sweat it," Jane smirked and Marcia slapped the back of Jane's head. "Training, child of mine. You are not a guardian, yet."

"Strengthening protective shields?" I asked, trying not to laugh at Jane and Marcia's relationship.

"A protective shield is an invisible force that we can create around locations like safe houses. We've been working on your home, actually. It takes quite a bit of magic and power to shield a safe house, but I believe, based on Barrett's and my conversation this morning, it's coming along!"

A small ticking timer near the oven dinged, and Edel stood up to fetch warm scones from the oven. She handed each of us a steaming lemon poppy seed scone.

"Where's Yael?" I asked.

"Fishing with my eldest daughter, Katia," Marcia said. "They will be back later on."

I thought of Eben and Nolan.

"If you haven't noticed, she is a DIY kind of girl. She got that homemaker green-thumb farming soul from her father. He loved working the land." Edel looked down at her mug, smiling.

This was the very first time I had heard anyone, aside from Yael, mention him. Ada placed her hand on Edel's. There was an uncomfortable silence for a brief moment.

"So," I said, filling the silence. "What about Eben and Nolan, Ada? Are they going to shield their cottage?" I asked.

Ada's face went white.

"Oh dear," Marcia said. "You didn't?"

"I couldn't hide it from her forever. Eben and Nora met on the beach and were growing close. Nora also wouldn't stop asking about Eben. What was I supposed to do?" Ada bit the inside of her cheek.

"Eben? Who the heck is Eben?" Jane asked.

Marcia leaned back in her chair.

"You have just endangered your family, Ada!" Marcia hissed.

"I know!" Ada said. "I know."

"Endangered?" I asked. "I think it's great Ada has reunited with her family."

I bit into my scone.

"Great?" Marcia asked. "Have you picked up on *nothing*, girl? Nolan is human. The Elders could care less about reuniting a family. Once they know, that is if they don't know already, they will come for them - or *you*, Ada!" Marcia crossed her arms. "How many times have you gone to see them? Were you careful? What about your scent and the Lamian trackers? You know we can't shield a human's house, there isn't enough old magic living there to do such a thing. You can't just make any house a safe home, Nora. It takes centuries of magical properties, the walls live and breathe our energies."

"I know, I know, I know," Ada said. "I have only gone twice so far, and I have been careful."

Marcia rested her chin on her propped arms.

A knock came from the front door, and we all jumped a bit. Ada turned even whiter with fear.

I was the only one who stood up fearlessly to open the door.

It was Aston.

16

"You look ready." Aston gave my outfit a nod, his lips tugging into an inviting smile.

"Come on in, Aston," Edel's voice echoed from the kitchen.

Aston smiled, and I stepped aside, letting him in then closing the door. Marcia stood up and embraced Aston, and Jane bashfully waved, her coy demeanor gone. A touch of pink entered her cheeks. I smiled. As Ada had predicted, I really enjoyed Jane and her personality.

"Good morning ladies," Aston said, looking around. "So, where's Barrett?"

"Out working, the usual," Marcia smiled, taking a seat again.

"Of course. Well, thank him for the work he did on my grandfather's island."

Marcia waved her hand in the air. "Anytime."

"So, you ready to train then, Ms. Stone?" Aston asked.

I nodded.

"Take care of her, Aston," Ada said.

"Always, Ada. Always."

"Oh, and Nora." Ada handed me back the necklace, the clasp already fixed. "You can thank Edel."

I nodded in Edel's direction. Aston's hand touched my lower back and nerves burst in my insides. I turned, following him towards the front door.

"Nora!" Jane called after me.

I turned around.

"It was really nice meeting you. Would be great to hang some-time. There aren't many of us young 'uns around." She winked at her mom.

"I'd like that," I smiled back. "See you soon then, Jane. Nice to meet you, Marcia."

"Likewise babe!" Marcia waved.

Aston and I walked down a path in the woods until we came to a beach with a small dock. At the end of the dock rocked a boat. He assisted me into his boat and started the engine. It rumbled while we backed up, then we took off, leaving Stone Isle behind. I felt like a raveled mass of both excitement and nerves. Aston's boat had a lot of power and appeared to be very expensive. Its polished wood-work was dark and gleamed. It was lined in black with slick white seats, and a radar system sat in the middle of the dashboard between Aston and I. Leaning over, I put my hands into the water and saw the word *Frauscher* written along the boat's side. The sea was calm this morning and the boat moved quickly over small crested waves in the middle of the dark chilling water. Aston looked over to me and smiled. He flipped a switch and the boat filled with music. We sped along lost in thought listening to different artists, some I knew of, until I felt Aston's hand grab mine. He had folded his chair up and playfully yanked me out of my seat sliding me in front of him. His arms wrapped around me, and he placed my hands on the steer-ing wheel.

He trailed his lips along my neck as he slowly walked me through all the mechanics of the boat, allowing me to drive. Our bodies stayed pressed together as we sped towards the unknown destina-tion. I tried to keep my focus on maneuvering the boat and not let myself get completely submerged into his body, but it was difficult.

Before long a little island appeared on the horizon.

"Is that where we're headed?" I asked.

"Yep." Aston again pressed his lips against my neck and then moved one of my hands to a lever, pulling it down. The boat began to slow and we coasted in and alongside a dock. Aston tied up the boat, then held a hand out towards me assisting me onto the brittle old dock.

The dock led to a stone filled beach.

Assuming that we were going to head into the forest for more protection, I began walking towards it, marveling at the beauty of this island. I was half way across the beach when Aston stopped me.

"We're going to train here."

"In the open?"

"We're safe here, but I'm going to do a quick run around the area to make sure. These islands have been uninhabited for hundreds of years. They are called Les Îles Oubliées, The Forgotten Islands, and there have never been sightings of Lamians here before."

Aston took off.

The Forgotten Islands. Whatever inhabited—or *had inhabited*—these islands also eventually became forgotten. The pebbles and stones scattered across the sand were intermixed with seashells, sea glass, and pieces of old driftwood. I made my way into the forest. It was like a dream; everything shimmered from the night's storm. The leaves popped in vibrant shades of green, the dirt smelled rich and damp, and the tree trunks were dense and thickly covered with old bark and moss. These woods had an old soul, an old spirit. I ran my hand over a soft patch of moss. For a moment I felt lost in a forest of glittering earth tones. I stood quietly waiting for Aston's return. I snapped my gaze towards an unfamiliar sound. The hairs on my arms stood on end. Were we alone? I began to feel the paranoia creep back in—the uncanny sense of being watched?

"Aston?" I whispered, amidst luscious ferns.

Silence.

I felt eyes watching me, burning into me. I heard the subtle sound of weight pressing on the earth again and I froze.

Stop being so paranoid, Nora.

I decided to make a run for the beach where I should have stayed. I stood up quickly and turned, slamming into Aston's body trying to sprint. My heart jumped into my throat.

"Aston!" I gasped.

"Whoa there, you okay?" His hands gripped my shoulders settling me in place.

"Uh, fine, I just freaked myself out. Easy to do these days."

Aston had taken off his shirt and was now wearing nothing but black pants, his chest broad and pale. White scars lined his right shoulder and trailed across his chest and perpendicular to his ribs— from Lia. Every muscle was distinguished and defined. I traced his scars with my eyes.

"Your scars…" I ran my fingertips along the raised skin.

"Lamians." He looked down and grabbed my wrist, turning it.

"I've noticed you have some of your own." The small scars Lia had left from the Elders' incepting my mind were still there, white, raised, and sensitive to the touch.

"Fresh?" he asked.

I lowered my hand, turning my gaze towards the ocean peeking through the trees.

"Come on, let's train then," he said, noticing my distance in conversation.

We made our way back to the beach.

"Right," said Aston, "I need to advance you as quickly as possible. Time is always ticking, and I must make sure you can controllably walk before you can confidently run."

I swallowed hard at his words. His words made it real, they made everything real.

"You need to learn and learn fast. We don't have much time."

"Much time for what?"

"Until Sebastian sends more Lamian trackers your way. He wants you, and he wants you alive."

"Who is Sebastian?" It was frustrating to feel as though I were still on the outside of so much looking in. "This is the first I've heard that name."

"Sorry. I keep forgetting. Sebastian's the leader of the Lamians." He then held up his hand to quell a tide of questions I'm sure he could see in my eyes.

"Nora, yes, there's a lot I could tell you about Sebastian, but Ada can tell you just as much, or Edel for that matter, and neither of them can train you like I can. We should make the most of the day and train. Okay?"

Is he hiding something?

"Yeah, sure. Let's train."

The seed of paranoia that had been lodged in my stomach started to germinate into something like panic. My hands began to sweat as I felt the fragility of my life.

Aston began to show me some footwork he felt was necessary to learn. He taught me to quickly move out of the line of an attack with minimal effort. Once I felt confident with the footwork, we began to add speed. We moved across the beach, trailing our feet and kicking up sand, darting and making contact with one another here and there. It turned into a heated dance, a dance of intimacy, existence, and dynamic movement. After a few hours, we began to add some hand striking to our training.

A few hours more and Aston picked up two long pieces of driftwood and he began to teach me movement with a weapon. I enjoyed moving with a weapon and learning to strike and attack. I began to feel confident until Aston knocked the stick from my hand and pinned me onto the sand with force.

"Just keeping you on your toes, Nora." The sun was low on the horizon.

"Okay! Not so hard!" I squeaked as Aston locked my left arm behind my back, leaving my neck vulnerable. My throat cocked to one side, exposed for any Lamian's instant gratification.

"Right here." Aston dropped his stick aside and ran the tip of his nose along my skin, inhaling. "Right here is where I would twist your neck until I heard a break, or sink my teeth into your vein and enjoy your intoxicating life source." He held me with an absurd amount of force. I winced at the thought of breaking someone's neck, and I hoped I would never have to hear that sound. Aston's lips ran down my neck then a discomfort of pressure as something hard—like teeth— dragged along my skin.

My chest tightened.

"Get off!"

"Make me," Aston hissed.

I wiggled anxiously, beginning to panic.

"Control your panic, Nora." The pressure of his teeth pressed even harder into my neck. My veins pulsated, my temples pounded, and my twisted shoulder throbbed.

"Get off!" I gasped as his weight began to crush my lungs.

"Dig deep, Nora. You're going to have to do better than that!" Aston growled.

His heart was racing, and I could feel hunger vibrating. His arms and fingers tightened to the point of suffocation. I held back the oncoming tears of fear. I became angry and afraid. Was Aston losing control? He wouldn't attack me, would he? I shook my shoulders only to feel his grip grow even tighter.

I yelled in frustration.

"Come on, Nora! Let it go!"

I gasped breath after breath.

"Get off," I angrily hissed through my teeth.

"No!"

"*Get off!*"

Aston flew back into the sand. His lips were pulled back into a satisfied smile.

"That's it! Yes! *That's* the emotion I was looking for!" He got up, shaking the sand from his pants.

"That's it? Are you insane? You almost lost control, I felt it, Aston!"

I was shocked to see him about fifteen feet from me now.

"No Nora, I never lost control. I pressured you into feeling yours. I speculated on the possibility of you having energetic powers, and they are hungry to obey your commands. Your eyes..." He interrupted himself.

"What about my eyes?" I asked, frustrated.

"I thought I saw them shift color for the first time, but maybe not." He rubbed the bridge of his nose, pleased with my accomplishment.

I thought that would be the end of the day, and I was hungry—hungry for what? I was not sure anymore. Aston however, wasn't done. He bent over, reached into his bag, and handed me a glass bottle of water. I took it from him, without releasing my gaze. I still felt angry, annoyed, and afraid. Was Aston really in control of himself? I twisted the top off and took enormous gulps, embarrassed by the sound I was making while swallowing between gasps of air. After I emptied half the bottle, I handed it back to him, wiping my lips with my sleeve. I pulled off my long sleeve shirt. I had a tank underneath and invited the cool breeze coming off the ocean.

"Glad I brought another one."

Aston glanced at the sun, gauging how much light we had left. Deciding that we could go on for one more round, he reached into his pocket and took out a red blindfold similar to the one he had given me the previous evening, then closed his eyes as he tied it around his own head.

"By cutting off one sense, we can train our other senses to rapidly improve. The reason we do this is to train our body to instinctually continue moving, quickly and confidently and with precision, no matter what senses we've lost touch with. Think of this as fine tuning our instrument. Now I want you to attack me."

"Why do I have the feeling that you are about to show off?"

Aston smiled and lifted his hand to me, beckoned me to attack. Feeling bizarre, I went ahead and threw a mild punch towards the side of his ribcage. To my surprise, it was immediately blocked. He grabbed my arm before it could even make contact, twisted it behind my back, spun me around, and locked me against his chest. Again my neck was exposed and I was unable to move. I squirmed, trying to loosen his grip, but he kept me clamped against his torso.

"Okay Aston I get it, quickness and precision, now let me go!" I blurted, annoyed, as my wrist, still caught behind my back, thrummed in pain. This time, he gently released me before I could get angry enough to throw him off. He took off his blindfold and pulled me in, bringing his face closer to mine.

"This is serious, Nora. Our fates are woven together. And I don't regret that. But I have to teach you these tools because I need you to stay alive. You die, I die." He turned his face towards the sea as if the thought pained him. "And, I may not always be there to protect you, but I will feel everything and experience everything."

I nodded, and he released me, turning me around and handing over the blindfold. I smoothed out the soft piece of fabric in my hands.

"I guess I would feel it too if anything ever happened to you."

"At first, this is going to be difficult," Aston said, pushing my loose hair back. "But try to not get frustrated. It only prevents an outcome from going your way, okay? I'll take it easy on you."

Aston winked, and I lifted the soft fabric to my eyes, but before giving into darkness, I pushed one side of the blindfold up and took a final look at him.

"Listen, Nora." His voice strung through my ears as the hairs on my arms stood on end.

"Smell, Nora. All abilities are tools, extensions of you." A warm exhale traveled down the side of my neck as I inhaled, smelling the air around me. He *was* alluring.

"Feel, Nora." There was a sudden shock to my system as his hand slid into my shirt and pressed over my heart.

I froze.

"Now find me," he said. "Just like before."

Then, he was gone.

I touched my chest, but his hand had vanished along with his presence. I flared my nostrils in hopes of finding his trail. Nothing.

After a few moments of tenacious concentration my ears flooded and awakened to the world. The water was the first sound to become crisp, and I could hear each individual wave smack the beach. Next, the trees came alive as they gently swayed in the wind and insects marched along their branches. A bird ruffled its feathers as it cooed safely in its nest. I began to hear rustling sounds coming from the forest. Animals were scurrying, and I heard their hearts thumping as their noses and ears twitched in attention. Then I heard it—a strong heartbeat that was not mine. Aston's? His heartbeat slowly became louder, bringing me comfort in a world of darkness. I listened, memorizing its rhythm. Suddenly something about the rhythm changed, and a second heartbeat introduced itself, it was double the speed of Aston's, then a third blended with a possible fourth. My ears began drowning in the echoing of hearts.

Is he somehow trying to disorient me?

I caught the sound of the animals fleeing from the shoreline, heading deep into the forest. Wings of birds were expanding and taking flight.

No, something's not right.

I could smell fear, hunger, and anxiety dancing through the air. My heart skipped and my mouth became bone dry.

I reached for my blindfold but before I got ahold of it, a hard blow swept across my face, almost knocking me off my feet.

I let out a sharp cry as another blow hammered into my ribcage. I spat blood and reached out my arms, angry and disoriented, lost in a world of darkness and pain. That's when I heard Aston scream.

"NORA, RUN!"

As soon as I got to my knees, something bashed into my stomach, knocking the wind out of me, and I fell backward onto the pebbled beach. I scrambled onto all fours, letting out a gasp for air as my mouth began filling again with blood. I spat blood and tore off my blindfold, looking up to see three Lamian trackers, similar to the ones who attacked me the night I ran with Vivienne.

Two were aggressively going after Aston and this one, a sickly looking female, was towering over me. Her skin was rough and hard, like dried, cracked leather. Her eyes were yellow with disease and violence. Thick liquid strung the corner of her thin mouth as it screamed.

She lifted her foot to smash my face, but I rolled away just in time to watch her foot sink into the pebbly sand beside my face. She wrapped her hand around my shoulder and her brittle nails pierced my flesh. I screamed in pain as her nails dragged down my arm. The smell of my blood spilled through the air, and for a split second, it caught everyone's attention, including Aston's. They were hungry. They had been starved so they'd be aggressive, and this was the first time in what looked like months that they would be able to feed. Her stomach was sunken into her ribcage, and her black pupils were dilated to the size of quarters.

You need to fight, or you will die! The alter ego in my mind surfaced.

I leaped to my feet and took up a defensive stance that protected my bleeding arm. I swung towards her face but missed. She was too quick and tossed me right back to the ground.

She grabbed me by my hair and yanked me back up to her eye level. She snarled and exposed her sharp pointy teeth, attempting to sink them into my flesh. The pressure in my chest began to build and a low growl escaped my sealed lips. I raised my leg and smashed my foot into the side of her caved-in abdomen, sending her flying into the sand. This riled her up even more, and she scrambled to her feet, wildly clawing the ground as she ran towards me. Aston had grabbed her mid-air. He threw her to the ground and pinned her wild body with his knees. In a terrible fluid motion that seemed almost second nature to him, he reached down and wrenched her neck until there was a sickening crack.

The other two Lamian trackers took off, disappearing into the woods. My knees were weak and I was lightheaded. Aston sprinted over and took me into his arms before my knees gave out. I leaned over and puked. He pulled the loose hair away from my face.

I opened my mouth to speak, but no words came. I was in shock. Blood stained my skin. My shoulder throbbed and a surge of energy swept through my body as I began to uncontrollably cry and shake. Aston pressed me against his body. I stayed there, shivering with adrenaline. I could smell blood, vomit, and salt. My chest heaved as he calmed me down.

"Shh, it's okay, Nora. We need to move. We can't stay here."

I was hyperventilating.

Aston's arms swept under my body and picked me up, and he began to carry me to the boat. He walked stiffly, still tense and alert.

"I am so sorry, Nora. I had no idea." Aston repeated in a low voice as he scanned the tree line with black, furious eyes.

"My shirt!" I yelled, remembering my long sleeved shirt that I had left on the beach. We both turned to see that it was gone.

A look of panic, a kind of fear I had never seen before, spread across Aston's face.

"Nora, get in the boat now!"

I ran down the slippery wet dock as he quickly untied the rope and we both pushed the boat away from the dock together. The engine flared up as he flung the prow around and hit the throttle. We sped through the water as fast as the engine could go, and I held on tightly to the railing and the cushion of my seat.

"What is going on?" I yelled over the howling winds as salt water sprayed my face.

"Trackers! They are Lamian trackers. They are fast, angry, hungry and following the orders of Sebastian. Their appearance is what gives them away. They look worn, abused, and starved. Sebastian has been breeding them for generations. They have gray wolf ancestors. Shapeshifters. And they are highly trained to track and hunt. They're hunting you. You have just become the most exciting piece of their game."

At these words, I leaned over between my legs and began hyperventilating again. Aston didn't slow down.

"They have a tremendous sense of smell. It's only a matter of time before they know where you live and where you have recently visited. They will not stop until the scent of your clothing brings them to you."

My hands began to shake and my chest tightened, restricting my airflow. Pain pierced my bloody shoulder. I quickly grabbed it, squeezing as hard as I could in hopes the pain would subside for the moment. My hand was stained red, and I winced as another searing pierce ran down my arm.

"Where are we going?" I shouted over the rushing ocean and roaring engine.

"Edel's home." Aston eyed me, and I knew what his expression meant.

All I could think about was Ada, Edel, Yael and their beautiful home. Everything was quickly turning into a nightmare. The only thing I could think of doing at that moment was to send Yael thoughts.

–Run Yael, grab Edel and Ada and run, Lamian trackers are coming!–

–Run Yael! Run!–

I kept chanting, rocking, and repeating this over and over in my mind.

–Run Yael! THEY ARE COMING!–

I was unsure if Yael could even receive my thoughts this far away, but I wasn't going to give up. We slowed down as we pulled into the dock where presumably Edel's boat sat rocking in the waves.

–RUN YAEL, THEY ARE COMING!–

All I could do was scream thoughts. I felt helpless. I wanted to jump out of the boat and run to them when suddenly I heard Yael in my mind.

–Nora! Nora! Where are you? Help!– She was screaming and choking.

Quick cuts of her mind began flashing. I could see everything around her: fire, smoke, her little hands crawling across a ground of debris. Suddenly something broke, smacking her body out of the way.

–Nora...–

Her voice sounded fainter.

"Aston. There's a fire and smoke. I can hear Yael screaming. She needs us. She's alone!"

Pressing my hands against my ears, I dug my fingers into my temples. The world felt like it was spinning. Yael was pleading and crying, and the screeching of the Lamian trackers filled the air. Yael was trapped underneath something heavy. I could see their feet, shuffling close by. Aston grabbed me by my hand, tearing me from Yael's mind, and we began to sprint towards the house back up the sandy path. We ran as fast as possible as I tried to focus, but I kept returning to Yael's pain and fear. The smell of smoke permeated the trees, and I shook off Aston's hand darting down the trail to the home, but before I broke through the tree line, Aston caught my arm, yanked me back and slammed me up against a tree.

His eyes flickered between the home and me. Flames engulfed the cottage. The fire spat and lapped in unpredictable directions. Hot ash rained through the air, and the sounds of shattering glass, popping stones, and cracking wood bounced around the woods. The once beautiful stone home looked like a massive bonfire. I was hot and out of control, my hands shook. A small vibrating growl began tingling my throat, and I had an overpowering desire to rip into Aston for pinning me against the tree and keeping me from Yael and my family. The demon inside me trembled and I stretched my neck. Aston locked eyes with me, and for a moment, challenged my demon.

"Nora! *Control it*! Control your demon." He shook my shoulders. I swallowed hard and shrugged him off of me. This time, he removed his hands and held them in the air in a gesture of backing off.

"Stay here, do you hear me? I have to keep you safe." Aston ordered, and I looked back at him with tunnel vision. All I could think of was Yael. I nodded, turning my focus back to the burning home, back to Yael's thoughts.

"Nora," he carefully touched my shoulder, and I whipped my face in his direction. He looked as if he was afraid of me. "Please. Do not follow me. They could still be here."

My eyes softened and began filling with tears. I couldn't hear Yael anymore.

"Just go."

Aston's hand covered my mouth before I could say anything else. He left me and ran towards the flames. I squeezed my eyes shut and listened harder for Yael, but I couldn't hear her anymore.

–Come on Yael, stay with me, come on!–

A wall of flames erupted in Aston's face. I gripped the tree nervously digging my nails into its pliable surface. I squeezed my eyes shut trying to find Yael. When I opened them Aston was gone; he had found a way in. I waited for a sign, for anything. Pops and bangs came from within the once beautiful sanctuary. The home was beginning to collapse. My eyes flitted back and forth across the gamboling fire.

Aston, where are you? Come on, come on, come on!

I pounded my fist into the tree. The anxiety of waiting and being of no use was unbearable. I was ready to take my first step into the open, to do something instead of sitting there useless with my heart heavily pounding against the knot in my throat, when I saw movement. Aston broke through the flames shoulder first with someone small wrapped in his arms. When he reached me he handed over the draped, wilted body. Yael.

He fled back into the home and disappeared as I collapsed to the ground with her overheated, lifeless form in my arms. She was no longer breathing. I pinched her nose, forcing air into her lungs, but got no response. I began pumping her chest over and over again between breaths, but nothing was working, not a single response. The tears that I had been fighting began spilling down my cheeks and onto Yael's face. Crying, I continued giving her air and pumping her chest, something I had learned should work in the human world, forcing air down her throat, and screaming thoughts to her.

—Yael, please. Yael, wake up. Stay with me. Please! Yael, wake up—

Another loud bang came from the home when, finally, Yael let out a shallow cough. Instantly I stopped pressing her chest and helped her sit up. She began to cough louder. Her eyes slowly opened and they focused on my face. A sigh of relief swept through me, and I held her pressing her head into my chest. Her face was black from ash and her arms were cut and burnt. I was rocking her back and forth in my arms when I saw movement from the clearing. I stopped rocking and froze attentively, watching as Aston burst through the wall of smoke and flames with someone else in his arms. Ada.

Leaning Yael back up against the tree's sturdy trunk, I stood up, ready to take Ada into my arms but, unlike Yael, Ada was awake, and she reached out her hand to me.

"Nora, you're okay," she said between coughs, then folded over in pain.

Aston gently sat her down against the tree next to Yael. Her forehead was split open and her arms and neck were clawed and torn. Bite marks trailed along her neck and down her legs as she opened and closed her eyes, drifting in and out of consciousness.

"Ada!" I yelped. She opened her eyes again.

"Shh!" Aston hissed warningly.

"Stay with me Ada." I lowered my voice.

"What do I do?" I looked at Aston for answers. The gash on Ada's neck was bleeding heavily. The blood trailed down her collarbone, and I caught a hint of its sweetness. This took me by surprise. I pressed my hand against her neck, and Aston ripped off a piece of fabric from his shirt and tied it around my face like a handkerchief covering my nose. He knew.

"Control your thirst, Nora. I can see it in your eyes," Aston whispered into my ear.

"I would never!" I spat back angrily.

"*Quiet*! They were just here, and more could be on their way. I killed the Lamian tracker I found feeding off of your aunt." Aston pointed to Ada's legs, his eyes black with anger and maybe even hunger. My stomach turned uncomfortably as the scent of blood turned into sweet aromas.

The inside of her thigh was gashed open. I felt sick again and swallowed hard at the rising hunger. A hunger that came from deep inside me, a hunger my Lamian demon was feeling. I looked at Ada's face, her head was tilted down, and her eyes closed again. Instinctively I slapped her across the face. Her eyes flung opened and she looked up.

"Everything okay, dear?" she asked in a raspy voice. Ada had no idea what was going on.

"Please Ada, stay awake and focus on me!" I said, holding her cheeks between my palms. I looked up at Aston for some kind of guidance.

"Keep her awake, we need to get her out of here. She's weak and needs to generate blood. She's lost a lot."

Yael reached her hand up and grabbed my arm. She did not need to think anything for me to know what her eyes were asking.

"Any sign of Edel?" I looked to Aston again.

"No," he said, searching the perimeter.

Yael was looking like she was going to faint any minute. As her heavy eyelids slowly fluttered I lightly tapped her cheek.

"Wake up!"

She opened her eyes and stared at me.

"We need to get them out of here," I said.

"I see someone." Aston retreated a bit behind the trunk of the tree, and I tightened my hand around Yael's arm nervously.

Sure enough, a figure was walking around in a disoriented manner through the clouds of thick smoke. It was Edel. She slowly limped and wobbled, making her way towards our general direction. She must have seen Aston. As she got closer, we could see that she was soaking wet and bloody. Aston ran to Edel and picked her up, quickly bringing her back to us. Yael became more alert when she saw her mother.

—Mommy— She reached out as Edel collapsed, holding her daughter to her chest. Ada was beginning to look more aware, her eyes tracked faster as she started looking all around frantically until she finally saw the home in flames. Aston took my hand and pulled me up; my body was trembling. We all watched as the fire consumed everything. Ada winced with every pop and bang, watching as the smoke and flames crumbled walls and shattered windows. Tears cleared paths through the ash that covered her face. Edel and Yael didn't watch, they stayed wrapped together with their eyes tightly closed, but I could hear Yael's thoughts, and she was screaming in pain.

Aston and I moved them all quickly back to the boat, and when we got to the dock, I took one last look back at the black smoke rising over the tree line and filtering into the dusk-tinted sky. Next came a haunting crash that echoed through the forest, sending a flock of birds into the sky, and I knew that the roof had finally caved in. The backbone of the home had finally broken.

We all sat in silence listening to the eerie requiem of sounds.

Aston pushed us away from the dock, and I couldn't look at anyone, not yet. This was entirely my fault.

I could see the gears spinning in Aston's mind; he was unsure of where to go. We puttered around the now-calm waters offshore.

It was Ada who broke the wounded silence.

"Head north," she said.

17

The skies had become morose, and thick gray clouds reflected the ominously dark sea. Ada quietly guided Aston through the dour waters, leading us to a small island where a house appeared through the twilit fog beyond the waves. The windows of the home glowed warmly, and a steady stream of welcoming smoke billowed from a stone chimney. Ada had said nothing apart from giving directions, though she showed muted expressions of immense pain at every droplet of salt water spraying over the sides and soaking into her wounds. Her skin had become paler, and her eyes were murky. We began to slow down, easing alongside a wooden dock. The island was still and quiet. I stood, ears perked, scanning the grounds with wide eyes. I was the first to step foot onto the wooden boards, and Aston passed me each person, one by one. A screen door swung open and then slammed. A woman in a velour purple robe stood on the porch, staring cautiously in our direction. She looked nervous and interested at our arrival but kept her distance. Ada and Edel leaned on my shoulders and we hobbled together, the walking wounded. I quietly winced every time Ada pressed into the gashes on my shoulder where the Lamian tracker had planted its rusty nails. Aston carried Yael. She looked like a small, limp rag doll in his arms. As we reached the end of the dock, the woman who watched us with careful hesitation widened her eyes in recognition and she bolted over to assist us.

"Inside. Inside, quick!" She spoke in a low, smoky whisper, frantically looking around.

Helping us all into her home, she banged the screen door behind her then turned and pressed the other end of her nose against it, scanning the horizon through narrow eyes, concerned that we had been followed. Satisfied, she slammed the wooden door, which made me jump. The door was lined with five deadbolts and a sliding chain lock. Something looked oddly familiar about her, and I watched as she twisted the first bolt and the other four locked themselves. She slipped the chain lock in place, and then pressed her eye against the peephole, checking the perimeter once more.

"Into the kitchen," she instructed, waving us down a hallway as she tightened the sash on her robe.

Once we all had entered the kitchen, she scurried off down another hallway, and I could hear the slamming and locking of doors, windows, and shutters. She zipped from room to room, pulling every curtain closed and turning off every light in the house. The only light available came from candles and the fireplace. She reappeared from the shadows and quickly walked over to help Ada, who was most in need of assistance. She had straight pearly white hair wadded up into a fat bun on the top of her head. Her body and features were long and thin, and her eyes had a hint of lavender. She looked up at Aston, who still held Yael in his arms as if she were shocked to see him standing in her kitchen. She pointed in the direction of a couch for Aston to lay Yael on. I watched him gently place her body into the down cushions, then grab a blanket from a nearby basket and tuck her in while pushing the sweaty hair from her forehead and wiping soot from her cheeks with a rag he grabbed from a nearby table. Once she was set, Aston knelt beside her and began to speak quietly. Yael nodded as she held his hand tightly, then fell into a deep sleep.

"Thank you, Iona," Edel whispered.

Iona. I recognized her as the woman who'd saved me and brought me back to Edel's. Iona pulled out a chair for Aston and beckoned him to sit near her. She filled a large wooden bowl with water and poured in coarse sea salt that looked like snowflakes, along with a few other powders, ointments, and herbs from apothecary jars. Iona held her hands over the water, mumbling words under her breath as she peeked in my direction from the corner of her eyes. The water began to slowly swirl, and aromatic steam rose and wafted through the air. I smelled rose and sandalwood and instantly felt calmer. Iona grabbed one of the flour sack towels from the pile that lay on the table and submerged part of it into the water. She dabbed Ada's forehead and the other open wounds on her body. Ada hissed and flinched in pain each time the towel made contact with her skin but Iona didn't seem sympathetic, and she watched Aston and me with daggers in her eyes.

"What happened?" Iona's voice was harsh and dark, spewing concern.

"We were tracked," Aston said.

Iona eyed him carefully and then looked at me. "Were you followed?"

"I'm not sure," I replied, unable to confidently confirm anything.

Ada's hands and feet were beginning to tremble and seize, gasping every time Iona pressed the rags against her wounds.

"Why is she trembling like that?"

The veins along Ada's hands and throat began to turn black and web beneath her skin.

"Lamian venom. Why didn't you say something right away?" Iona spat. "It has begun attacking her nervous system."

She stood up and rushed over to her apothecary cabinet to mix an antidote for Ada. She held the small glass against Ada's lips, but Ada refused to drink it.

"Come on Ada, you must drink this. You must!"

Ada's eyes turned black and her hands shook. The darkening veins along her neck now bulged and I could hear her heart pounding out of control.

"It's the venom. Aston, help me!" Iona cried.

Aston bound Ada's hands behind the chair and grabbed her body, restricting her movement.

"Come on, Ada. Open your mouth!"

Iona shoved her fingers into Ada's cheeks, forcing her jaw apart. Ada snarled and hissed. Iona poured the foaming dark liquid into her mouth and forced her to swallow. Some liquid escaped from the corners of Ada's mouth trickling down her neck. I took a step back, frightened. Her black eyes were darting back and forth between Iona and me before they rolled back in her head. She then gave a scraping gasp for air and her eyes returned to normal before her body melted into the wooden chair. Her head and shoulders rolled forward, and Aston caught her before she toppled over.

"Your venom," Iona looked at me, "Lamian venom is toxic and dangerous. If not treated right away," Iona sighed with relief at the instant recovery Ada was making, "it will kill you. Its properties are meant to disorient, paralyze, and kill. The invasion of the nervous system is the last phase; she could have died."

Iona checked Edel's body and then Yael's to make sure they hadn't been bitten.

"Were either of you bitten?"

"No, we weren't," said Aston.

"What exactly happened?" Iona asked anxiously.

"I'm training Nora," Aston said.

"You? And why on earth are *you* training Nora?" I could feel a tension between Iona and Aston.

"Because we are bound, and it's his job," I spoke. Both faces turned in my direction. Iona's expressed shock and Aston's discomfort.

"Venomous teeth? Failed to mention that during training." I sneered, tired of being in the dark.

Aston turned back to Iona, "And today I decided to take her to one of the Forgotten Islands to start combat training."

Iona then noticed the blood on my shoulder and I covered it with my hand, lowering my gaze.

"We were on our last round of training when three Lamian trackers emerged from the woods and attacked us."

Iona dipped another flour sack towel into the warm salty water and handed it to me as she listened carefully to Aston.

"Those islands have been empty for at least a hundred years." Aston sounded frustrated.

"Sebastian's trackers must be growing in number and covering more terrain," Iona said. "And if they are rapidly growing in numbers, you and I both know where the numbers are coming from."

"Where? From where?" I asked.

"The mainland," Aston said.

"Humans," Iona added. "They are turning and training humans. Most likely they're snatching people who have already been forgotten or cast away from the world; homeless, runaways, the mentally ill."

"I killed the one attacking Nora."

Aston's words caught Iona's attention.

"The other two took off, grabbing an article of Nora's clothing."

"So, the hunt has begun." Iona's voice sliced through the silence.

"As soon as we realized what had happened, we immediately started for Edel's, but we were too late." Aston glanced in Ada's direction.

"On the contrary, Aston. You were both in time and saved these women," Iona corrected him, her tension between them softening.

My throat burned as I replayed the events in my mind. Iona did not take her eyes off me.

"You okay?" she asked.

Uncomfortably, I nodded my head. I wasn't, but there wasn't much to be done about it. I sat still, dabbing my shoulder with the rag. The thought of the Lamian tracker's face close to mine caused my chest to tighten and my defensive muscles to fire. My hands remembered the feeling of its leathery, worn skin and goosebumps pricked down my arms and legs at the thought of it ever touching me again. Pressing the rag hard to my wound, I forced pain to interrupt the unpleasant images in my mind.

Iona dipped the rag again in the water and pressed it against Ada's neck. The wound the rag had been on was now sealed, and I looked at my shoulder to find a similar effect. The longer I kept the rag on the faster my gashes healed, and I watched as my own skin began mending itself. Remarkable.

"Are you some sort of medic?" I asked Iona, watching the wound seal.

"I'm what you call a healer," Iona said, smiling. She looked around the room at the lot of bandaged and broken women. "It was only recently that I decided to come out of hiding. Ada and Edel sent for me explaining that you, Nora, had returned and that, upon that, protection was crucial. I waited for many years knowing that one day our indolent world would start shifting and gain back its old magnificence." Iona looked at me with hopeful eyes, and I couldn't look away, interested in what she was going to say next.

Aston stood up and walked over to check on Yael.

"Sebastian is training an army and becoming powerful once again, and they are coming for you, Nora. Then the rest of us."

"Since you are the daughter of Alexo Stone, you are the forbidden life that became, and you are the one they have been searching for, for seventeen years. You are the rightful heir to Queen Lamia's throne, meaning you can control the Lamians, and Sebastian wants you destroyed for that."

"The Elders too, Iona. I know the prophecy."

"Oh good, good. So you aren't as ignorant as when I first met you then." Her eyebrows furrowed. "As long as your bloodline continues walking this earth, he won't stop hunting you. Killing you will be a victory he has sought after for many years. He is a dangerous man."

I remained quiet.

"What did my father do wrong exactly, except love my mother?" I asked.

Iona looked at Ada with concern. Perhaps she was wondering why I had been kept in the dark for so long, why I had never been prepared for this world. I wondered the same thing. Ada said nothing.

"Your father was the most powerful Lamian, aside from Queen Lamia, to ever exist," Iona said.

"That much I know," I hissed anxiously.

"He was also the former *leader* of the Lamians."

"And that much I *guessed*." I could feel my anxiety souring into anger. "So he was the Lamian leader, and he fell in love with my mom, broke some stupid law, and then vanished."

Iona remained tranquil and poised as she sat up a little straighter in her chair.

"Alexo fell in love with your mother and, in doing so, turned his back on all he once stood for, breaking the unbreakable edict which forbade any such behavior with a Sereni. The line of pure power was derailed and the Lamians turned to a new leader: a very dark man named Sebastian Stone, your uncle, one of the original three sons of Queen Lamia and Keto.

"Your father is still the most powerful being our worlds have ever seen, but Sebastian grew to resent his brother's powers. Your father has a unique ability to manipulate and control the elements. Without lifting a finger, Alexo can burn entire villages to the ground, ice over the ocean and change the winds. He is also an unparalleled Shapeshifter, like his father."

She looked down at the bowl of water and waved her hand over it, and steam rose again. I remembered opening the wall of flames for Aston. That was when I realized that Iona was speaking of him in the present tense. Instantly, my mouth became dry.

"He's alive?"

"Once Sebastian gained power, it took he and an army of Lamians, most of which died in doing so I may add, to track down your father and lock him up behind enchanted walls for all eternity. The enchantments disable any abilities a being may possess. Alexo, himself, designed the entrapment. Over the course of time, it weakens a man, stripping him of power, stripping his or her soul. Killing them slowly. From that day Alexo was captured, our lives here were no longer safe. Most of us had hopes that the unity of Rebekah and Alexo meant positive change for us all, but instead we had to flee to different parts of the world, scattering like animals before a storm. Most went north towards the arctic weather, many settled in Alaska, Russia, Nova Scotia, and other more remote locations, hiding our children and keeping them safe." Iona dipped the rag into the warm water again and lifted Ada's arm, pressing it on her forearm where more bites had penetrated her skin.

"We could no longer live on these islands. We waited seventeen years for you to come back, Nora. Ada took you into hiding, which was the right thing to do." Iona glanced at Ada, reassuring her of her decision. "She concealed you until you were old enough and strong enough to come back and take your mother's place. You are the only one who can defeat Sebastian, for you are his blood. The only one who can control the Lamians, because you are the heir."

I leaned back against the wooden chair and her last words hung in the air.

"Me?" I breathed. "You want me to fight a man who is thousands of years old and dangerous? You want me to finish what my mother and father apparently started? To fight Lamians and kill Sebastian, take my place as heir to what, the Lamian throne? Become Queen of the demons! Then what? Control the Lamians and kill them all? You're telling me that my father is still alive, rotting in a cell somewhere, and no one has done anything to save him!" My mind was exploding in every which way, heat filled my chest and my veins pulsed wildly. "No! This is far too much to deal with! I need to find my father, Ada!" I shot her a look of anger and pain. Had she known all these years that he was alive?

"You must!" Iona's voice boomed through the kitchen, causing Yael to stir in her sleep. Aston rushed over to her.

"It is your legacy, Nora. Your path is already laid out, and you must fulfill it. The prophecy says that during a blue moon a child will be born. She will become the hidden child and emerge from the ashes of darkness. Her bloodlines pure, strong and powerful. The hidden child will be the end of destruction, the end of our pain, and will return us to our haven. You are the hidden child. You are the prophecy! The Elders and Sebastian know this and want your head for it. You have the ability to end the Lamians, to end even the Elders. Do you understand *now* how important you are to this world?" Iona's tone rose with every word.

I pushed myself away from the table and stood up, needing fresh air. I felt like my chest was caving in, and it became harder and harder to breathe. My hands tingled as the veins in my wrists throbbed.

I looked at Aston and saw concern in his eyes. I turned to the oval mirror on the wall and almost fell backward when I saw myself. My eyes were black the way Lia's were on the night we went to see the Elders. My face was paler than usual, the veins on my neck were dark and protruding, and my lips were tinted blue as if lacking oxygen. I looked like a demon!

"You are Queen Lamia's grandchild." Edel's voice broke the silence as she acknowledged my appearance.

"Eleanora," Ada's pained voice tried to speak.

I did not face them. My fingers twitched.

"You are the *only* person who can save us." Ada coughed and began choking on what sounded like fluids.

I felt Aston's cold hands on my waist, and he apprehensively turned me around to face him.

"I give you my life. I will protect and teach you everything I know. *Everything.*"

"We will protect and teach you until the time comes," Iona said. "But in the end, it is you who must bring peace and safety to our world, just you."

Yael rolled onto her side. She was awake, watching us quietly from the couch. She was the only one who didn't have a glimmer of fear in her eyes when she looked at me—at this demon I had become. Even her thoughts were silent. I loved her, and I had wanted to do nothing but protect her from the moment I laid eyes on her, but I had no clue why or how. Something deep within me, maybe a part of my soul, had latched on to hers. I looked back at Aston, whose eyes were subtle amber. Everyone was quiet, waiting for my response.

Pressure began building again in my chest, and the flames on each candle were rapidly flickering and cracking the more anxious I grew. Unexplainable things began to happen around Iona's home. The pots that were hung in the kitchen rattled and the china in the cabinet chimed as they began shimmying slowly towards the floor. Aston's hands moved to my face and I began feeling afraid and angry. I wanted to get out of this house. I needed to go outside now. The windows one by one obeyed my inner desire of breaking free. They flew open one by one, smashing their shutters and shattering glass all over everything. The metal of the deadbolts on the front door twisted and unlocked. I watched the front door fly open— there in front of me was my escape.

My anger subsided and the winds calmed themselves. A long, bluish-gray feather floated down and landed on the floor by my feet.

I bent down and took the feather, examining it. Its texture was silky and striped, and its tip was dark. I remembered the feathers in my mother's desk, they were similar to this one, and the feathers that are wrapped in Ada's hair. The small ceramic cup in Edel and Yael's home held two of these feathers.

"We all have one." Iona's voice broke the silence, and I could see the feather wrapped in her hair. "That one is for you. It is a sign of your familiar, your spirit animal. The Gray Eagle is the totem of the Sereni. A feather arrives when a siren is ready, ready to accept his or her fate. Some legends hold that a Gray Eagle was somehow involved in the magic that bound the blood of the Goddess to that of Lamia herself. Some even believe that for every siren soul there is a Gray Eagle familiar attached to it. All this to say, Eleanora Ada Stone, that this is your time."

I tightened my hand around the feather, looked up at Iona, and said simply, "Fine."

18

Standing ankle deep in the icy cold Atlantic, I felt captured, frozen in time. I thought about the Pandora's box of reality Iona had opened for me. I tucked the long feather into my hair, pushed up my sleeves, and leaned over to splash my face. The sensation of the water on my skin was relieving. The screen door opened and closed, but I had no desire to turn around; I was not ready to see or speak to anyone. Whoever it was stood on the porch, silently watching from a distance.

"Nora?" Edel's voice broke the uncomfortable silence.

She was leaning and holding herself up against the front banister. Her right leg was wrapped and blood had begun seeping through the white bandages. She attempted walking towards me; it was painful to watch. She winced with every step. Reluctantly, I made my way to her. She looked relieved as I approached the porch.

"I know it has been a lot to take in. I do."

I rolled my eyes. How could anyone *possibly* understand what the hell I was going through? Edel's eyes were still and green as ever as they watched me.

"And believe me when I say that we all understand the position we have put you in. We need you. There is no future for us, for Yael, or these islands without you." Edel forced a smile through her pain.

I didn't respond. Wrapping my arm gently around hers, I assisted her back inside.

The interior was back in order when we entered. The windows were closed and the broken glass seemed to have mended itself. Papers that once covered the floor's surface were back in their original piles, neatly stacked. It looked as if my turmoil had never passed through. Ada was sitting at the kitchen table, speaking with Aston and Iona. Yael was again fast asleep on the couch. Her body gently twitched in a field of nightmarish dreams. Edel hobbled in my arm, and I guided her over to the kitchen table where Aston immediately stood up and slid out a chair for her to sit. Instead of sitting back down, he put his arms around me and pulled me into his chest. I listened to the pulsing rhythm of his heart and felt the rise and fall of his chest beneath my cheek. It was a rhythm that comforted and relaxed me. I cradled my arms within his. I felt safe there, hidden, and wanting the curtain of the Nora Show to remain closed.

"You have the heart of a lioness," Aston whispered into my ear before releasing me.

Without another word, I took a seat. Aston's hand found mine under the table, and I squeezed it tightly, scanning the faces of the women who sat across from me like a panel of silent judges.

"Sorry about the mess," I said.

"Never mind girl, never mind. We have more important things to discuss now!" Iona cleared her throat.

The night was long, and before I knew it the sun had begun to rise. Splashes of warm red and yellow light filled the home. My brain rattled with endless hours of storytelling, facts, questions, history, and legends of the Sereni race in general and my prophecy in particular. Iona had spread books across the kitchen table showing me charts, historic timelines, and old photographs of Iona, Edel, my mother, and Ada over the past hundred or so years. It took all the effort in the world for me to hand her back those photos. Tears lined my eyes as I stared at pictures of my mother smiling proudly. There was even a photo of her linking arms with Aston's parents who, I learned, had died as well. Aston's eyes vaguely flickered in color when they fell upon his parents and, for a second, I thought I saw the corner of his mouth twitch before he changed his focus to Yael.

She stirred in her sleep as a warm streak of light fell across her body. My life was on the verge of making sense, or at least I felt like I was scratching at the surface. Through the escaped Lamian trackers Iona was certain that Sebastian now knew that Aston Boxam was training me, and this could only mean one thing; that the Sereni were preparing to fight. Sebastian would take his time, train, map, plan, and attack appropriately as he saw fit. This news left me incredibly afraid. My life was going to become a minefield, and I would have to walk through it with fear and caution behind every step.

"Why don't we just move and avoid such a war, leave the islands and never come back, find a new home somewhere far away from what feels like a suicide mission for me?" I asked out of sheer panic and anxiety.

There must be a corner of the world that we could call our own. That was not an option of any sort, however; because, Iona convinced me, unless they are stopped, they will never stop, and we would never find that utopia.

I had no idea how I was going to become the missing key to ending this war, but I had to allow for the possibility. So many people were relying on me, the hidden one. The weight of prophecy sat heavily on my shoulders.

~~~~

The next four weeks Aston and I spent training, day in and day out. We would rotate and find new training spots every couple of days. We couldn't stay in one place for too long for fear of being tracked. Most of the time we trained on the island that Iona lived on. We occupied her home until Barrett and Marcia safeguarded the lighthouse home at Alexander Point and we could move back.

Iona discovered that Ada had been visiting Eben and Nolan on a weekly basis.

"Are you insane?" Iona hissed at her one night. I slept near a vent that traveled to the bedroom Iona shared with Ada and Edel.

"I know, I just…"

"Ada, they will *kill* them! Couldn't this wait? You don't want to end up like me, and bear the pain Edel and I had to face. Both my Nicola and my boy hung, drained, then burned for me to watch! Do you remember that horror?"

I heard Iona's voice crack as she choked on her own words. "Does Nora know?"

"Yes, she does," Ada whispered. "I had to tell her. The two have already met. Of course, there was an instant attraction, an unexplained connection. They are family, they are of the same blood, the same life source. You could see it growing in her eyes, she couldn't let the idea of Eben go."

I felt my cheeks flush thinking about the night at the bonfire once again.

"So what do we do now?" Ada asked.

"I don't know, but he's going to have to know, and I think it's better that it come from you than Nolan. One must be in the presence of power to birth their own, and you have now been using your abilities here Ada. If he's been exposed to you, it's only a matter of time before his abilities begin to show. Look what happened to Nora; it only took that wench, Vivienne."

"You're right, I know you're right. When we move back to Alexander Point, and I have a safe house to protect him in, I will tell him." Ada seemed to be hoping to buy as much time as possible.

"Until then, we need to keep the two of them safe."

"They will be watched." Ada sighed, "It's all that can be done, for now."

I had thoughts of Nolan and Eben dangling from nooses. I closed my eyes, trying to shake the horrific image, fearing for their safety, wanting to escape and bring him back in the middle of the night. I hadn't considered their safety to that degree. I hadn't thought about what the Elders would do to them or how they would punish Ada. It was a selfish action.

Over the course of four weeks, my abilities were becoming more powerful and easier to control. I was now able to compartmentalize and isolate each ability, engaging and disengaging them when needed.

> *My name is Eleanora Ada Stone. I am now living on Stone Isle, Maine. I am bound to a man for all eternity. I am not human, I never was. I have abilities. I am a siren. I am a demon.*
>
> *I am dangerous.*

My known abilities, aside from speed and hearing, were dark telekinetic forces—from the Queen herself—and heightened smell. I had mind connection with Aston because of the bond and with Yael, though the reason remains unknown. And like Aston and Lia, I have venomous Lamian teeth.

~~~~~~~~

"Bite the rabbit."

"No!" I squirmed like a child as I held a beautiful, snow-white rabbit in my hands.

"Nora, you have to understand what your venom can do! You need to feel and see it and understand why we do our best to never bite unless we have to!"

"No Aston! I am not going to kill it! I already witnessed Ada almost die, isn't that enough?"

"Bite the rabbit, Nora. It has to come from you; watching and doing are two different things."

"No!"

"Fine, maybe I will take you into town and human scent will tempt you more." Aston raised an eyebrow in my direction.

I held the rabbit; there were tears in my eyes. Its eyes were dark and wide, for it knew I was a predator, knew that it was about to meet its end. I could feel its little heart fluttering my hands, and I listened to the quick ins and outs of breath, watching its nose twitch.

"I'm so sorry," I whispered into its soft ear before I bit it.

My teeth sunk into its flesh, piercing through muscle, tissue, and veins. The rabbit's body stiffened and then went limp in my hands. Blood stained the white fur and coated the inside of my mouth. The taste was...

Sensational.

Oh, my god!

The once repulsive hints of metallic copper turned into sweet seductive aromas. I wanted more. I leaned over and bared my teeth, but Aston knelt down and looked me dead in the eye.

"Just one bite, Nora."

But I wanted more, and I curled my lips over my teeth, ignoring Aston's instruction.

"You must learn to control yourself. It's a challenge and it won't be easy, but you need to be able to control your desires and emotions. Believe me, it's a long road."

This was the first time I had ever tasted another's blood and it was divine.

"It's easy to lose yourself to it. It's easy to allow it to take over your mind. It is a never-ending hunger that your father has passed on to you, but you must not chase it, for it is impossible to catch. Don't give into it."

I squeezed the rabbit in my hand, hissing and swallowing the burning sensation in my throat, ignoring the twists in my stomach that told me I was being deprived of succulent satisfaction. I felt the weight of the rabbit's limber body in my hands. Its ears flopped to one side and its paws were lifeless. Its brown eyes that had moments before been filled with fear had softened, and then I noticed its nose beginning to bleed. Its relaxed ears began to twitch and its hidden claws pierced into my skin. It shivered and began trembling the way Ada had done in Iona's home after the Lamian tracker attack. I dropped the rabbit onto the ground, upset at what Aston had made me do. The white rabbit twitched and shook, squeaking and fluttering until, as quickly as a light switch could be turned off, it dropped dead.

I walked off without saying anything, and though I knew he was keeping his eye on me, Aston gave me half an hour of space before he approached me.

"We should keep training."

"Yeah," I said. "Sure."

"I won't ask you to kill again, Nora," he said. "But you needed to experience that. Better now than later, and better a rabbit than someone."

I wrapped my arms around myself and said nothing.

"Killing and tasting blood is a slippery slope," he said.

"Is that what happened to Lia?"

"Perhaps."

Lia had vanished. She had disappeared from Aston's life completely and hadn't been seen since the night of the human killings. Her disappearing act concerned many. She could be anywhere and with anyone; her motive and intentions dark and twisted, her lust for power strong and her hunger for blood toxic. I knew the reason she had vanished: me.

19

Spring was coming to an end, and I welcomed the warm summer air. I held my glass of sweet tea, taking in the morning sun and the salty breeze from the front porch, listening to the many wind chimes Iona had around her garden and hanging from various trees. Her plot of land held an element of magical charm. Yael and Iona were out in the garden burning a small pile of branches and dried leaves they had collected and raked. The charred scent wafted through the air, and I was flung back to the memory of watching Edel and Yael's home burn to the ground. My stomach twisted, and I clenched my jaw. The glass slipped through my hands and broke on the ground, ice and glass chips pricking my legs.

Ada cracked open the screen door and peeked out. "Everything alright?"

"Far from it."

We both knelt on the porch, cleaning in silence.

The reminders were everywhere. The punishing memory of the Lamian trackers was behind every breath I took. My skin remembered holding Yael's overheated body. If we'd arrived any later, Yael would have been burned alive or crushed by a collapsing roof. I remembered Ada kissing the hand of death as she was being aggressively fed upon and Edel's eyes engulfed with what looked like endless pain. I could barely stand the memory. I'd had good and bad days since the fire, and today was turning out to be a bad one. Iona called it Post Traumatic Stress Disorder.

"We all have it to some degree. Being a Sereni or Lamian isn't the easiest path. Sometimes I envy the humans. Everything seems simple for them," Iona had said one evening as she tended to the wood burning stove in her kitchen.

"Thinking about the fire, aren't you?" Ada stood up cupping the bits and pieces of sharp glass.

"Have you been over to see Eben and Nolan recently?" I asked, keeping my eyes on the floor.

"Iona thought it was best that I avoid tracking fresh scent toward their cottage, and I agree. If we want to take every ounce of precaution in protecting them, I need to keep my distance."

"What if they are already in danger? What if—"

"Don't worry, no news is good news, right? We'll be able to move home soon, I promise. Perhaps going for a walk will help you clear your mind? Just," she paused, "be careful."

Ada disappeared back into Iona's home.

We were all waiting patiently to leave Iona's home and journey back to the old lighthouse at Alexander Point whenever Marcia and Barrett gave us the go-ahead. Iona's home had started feeling cramped, and it lacked the space for the five of us to continue on comfortably. Marcia and Barrett had been feverishly working on preparation and protection before we moved back home.

I stood up and headed to the forest. Yael and Iona stood up and watched me enter the woods. I stuck to a small winding animal trail that wove in and out of trees. I continued feeling hazy, my mind constantly being sucked back to the fire. I could smell the smoke as if it were yesterday; it haunted the forest. I roamed the woods numbly.

My mind flipped through an endless slideshow of memories of the Lamian trackers on the Forgotten Island and the fire. It was as if I had relapsed into shock and the reality hidden behind the adrenaline had finally sunk in. I wanted to be home. I wasn't even sure where home was or where it existed, but I wanted something to call my own badly, a place to hide. The photograph of my mother continued flashing through my mind. It was the only image I had of her and it had been reduced to ashes.

I was surprised to find tears emerging. She hadn't visited my dreams recently, and I wanted so badly to dream of her again. For her and my father to tell me I was going to be okay. I wanted to lie in the warm spot where she was sitting and breathe in her lavender aroma, to feel her hand running through my hair and watch how my father held her in his arms. My father, alone in some cell on an island that I was never allowed to visit, was still alive. I had been burdened with the knowledge that he was somewhere out there, trapped by Sebastian who was no doubt waiting for the right time to use him as bait. I pressed my hand over my face.

Pull it together, Nora.

My mind filled with buzzing sounds that began to cloud my hearing. I noticed that I was plowing through ferns and that, at some point, I had veered from the path. I began frantically searching for it. I had walked a long way into the woods and could no longer see the home, hear the ocean or smell the fire. Anxiety began to creep in, raising my heart rate. Sweat beaded on my forehead, and I fell into a state of confusion and disorientation, walking aimlessly in what felt like circles. My body temperature spiked, and I had begun to feel hot, thirsty, and uncomfortable. I needed to get out of the forest. I was beginning to feel trapped in a cage of paranoia and fear. Trapped on these islands that were beginning to feel like prisons. I heard rustling behind every shadow, and a thick blanket of clouds covered the sky.

I tripped on uneven ground and fell against the trunk of a tree, gripping it for a moment, trying to breathe through the panic that blistered through my body. I caught a hint of an animal's fresh kill and my fingers started to tremble. I frenziedly tried to breathe. I felt my insides turning, and the hunger I'd experienced when I bit into the rabbit returned. My thoughts and vision were clouded by the scent of blood.

I wouldn't release my demon, not here, not alone. My heart was racing, my breath shallow and rapid, but I continued moving in endless woods. I could hear every animal's pitter-patter and scratches, breaths and heartbeats, the ruffling of fur and feathers. I was being swallowed by the forest, swallowed by my own fear, swallowed by my own mind. The trees were alive and the sensation that I was being watched, being followed, was there. My eyes darted around the woods but saw nothing. Whatever it was was out there, lurking and hiding in the shadows. My throat burned, and I began to hear a faint howl that disappeared and reappeared.

What was wrong with me? Biting into that rabbit's neck had released an itching addict, craving its next hit of blood. My pace quickened to a jog, and then from a jog, I began panicking and sprinting as if I were being chased. I ran without knowing where I was headed, lost in a world of blurred green. A bomb was ticking away and counting down the minutes until it shattered everything that was ever me. I heard a loud squawk and looked up. I stopped and dropped to my knees. The bird landed on a branch high above me.

A crow, midnight black with lustrous oily feathers, watched me, shifting its weight. Its eyes were black and smoky. It watched me carefully when I began to hear voices hissing and dancing through-out the forest. The bird's eyes stayed fixated on me; the longer it held its gaze the louder the hissing voices grew. It was the Elders. Their gaze was upon me. They used the birds, they hid in trees, they were watching me. I am not alone.

"What the hell else do you want from me?" I screamed at it. I picked up a stone and threw it in its direction. The bird flapped its wings, hopping to another branch, its smoky eyes still fixated.

"Kill me already! Do it! Take what you want from me!" I grov-eled, picking up another stone and tossing it in its direction again. This time the crow shrieked, then took off.

Tears erupted, and I held my burning throat and chest. The more I cried, the more the pressure valves opened and the more the emotions that I'd been bottling up spewed out. I was scared. It would only be a matter of time until Sebastian was ready for me. How were my hands going to change the pattern of this world? How could I vouchsafe the lives at stake and calm the waters when I couldn't even control myself?

The scars on my shoulder pricked. The weight of the world was swallowing me and my heart ached, beating as though to tear itself apart.

Breathe Nora.

Breathe.

I stayed anchored to the ground. The sky growled with another storm rolling in off the sea. I closed my eyes, partially hoping to stay lost in this forest, waiting for the rainfall to wash me away.

Two hands then grabbed my torso and rolled me over. I was picked up and cradled in a pair of strong arms. The heartbeat was slow and steady, and I didn't need to open my eyes to know who it was. I stayed there wrapped in his arms being rocked back and forth. Gradually I began to calm down.

"Breathe," Aston said, holding me tighter. "Breathe."

I tried. I tried so hard to breathe. I was fighting to breathe. My lungs were desperate for oxygen. I couldn't shake off the images that were burnt into my mind. Every day I wondered if I would return from training to another home that had been burned to the ground. Aston sat there holding me until I gained the strength to look up at him. My eyes must have said everything.

"You can do this, Nora. Fight through the hunger and control your mind. You were born to be here with us. You were born to be more than you have ever imagined."

He sounded so confident in me.

"They are watching me," I whispered, my eyes fleeting around the trees.

"Who?" Aston turned his head.

"The Elders. They are using the birds. I felt their presence and I faintly heard their voices." I stayed guarded within Aston's arms.

"Yes, well that wouldn't surprise me. They have the ability to host their sight through others."

I pressed my head into his chest again and froze.

"Come, let's get out of here," he said lifting his gaze to the trees. "There is something I want to show you."

He grabbed my hand, helping me up, and we ran back to Iona's home.

Aston led me to his boat which was floating at the end of Iona's dock. He turned on the engine and I closed my eyes, resting my head on my arm. We slowly pulled away from the dock and headed towards the horizon. The sky was overcast with iridescent gray clouds, and we were going in the opposite direction of the storm that painted the distance with dark moody shades of gray.

Wherever it was he wanted to take me, I'd go.

20

Water was misting my face. I reached my hand into the spitting sea and enjoyed the stinging sensation as the white water hit my fingertips. We continued traveling across the vast endless blue surface. There were no islands or landmasses of any kind in sight. In the distance, a pod of whales breached the surface. Giants of the sea. Aston continued to occasionally look back, and I gazed towards the horizon keeping my eyes on the whales until they disappeared into the abyss of dark waters. My eyes were swollen. Aston slowed down the boat and the engine droned. We were floating in the middle of silent dark waters.

"Why have we stopped?"

Aston pointed towards the horizon.

"Watch," he said.

I looked in the direction he was pointing and watched as a small island *appeared* like a mirage in the distance. Aston increased the engine power and we headed straight for it.

The small landmass came to life, its silhouette distinct and real. Aston smiled and brought us gently onto a sandy beach. He took off his shoes and stepped into the water. I slipped off my shoes and he lifted me out of the boat and set me down, thigh-high, in the ice cold water and velvety sand. Waves lapped against my legs. The island reminded me a little of Iona's place, empty and peaceful. We began making our way onto the beach. Pebbles and tiny shells decorated the shore. I took a few more steps when my heart rate spiked; it resembled the Forgotten Islands where we'd been attacked. I quickly took a few steps back, and a lump built up in my throat, making it difficult to swallow. I stared at the tree line and began to panic.

"Nora, Nora, it's okay here," Aston's hand grabbed mine. "You're safe. No one can find this island but me."

"What do you mean?"

"My grandparents left this place to me." He looked out at the forest.

"They left you a *vanishing* island?" I whispered, not taking my eyes off the vegetation surrounding me. I expected a Lamian tracker to appear at any moment.

"Well, it only vanishes because Marcia and Barrett recently put a protective shield around it. I've wanted to bring you here for weeks, but I wanted to ensure your safety and the safety of this island first."

There was a rustling of leaves and the hairs on my neck stood on end, but before I could run a brown fox trotted out onto the sand, stopped, looked at us, then scurried back into the bushes. I struggled to pull my heart from my throat.

"A safe house or location can only be seen by those with Sereni blood. It has a shield the way Iona's home does, the way your home soon will. I am the only one who knows it's location; not even my sister knows about it, and it's important she never knows." His face turned grim for a brief moment.

"You're the first person I've ever brought here." He looked at me and smiled as if this should please me in some fashion. "I thought you needed a place to get away. You've been dealt a lot of cards lately, and the weeks of intensive training were bound to break you down at some point. To be honest, I was surprised how long you lasted."

Yes, this is what I needed, a place to hide. I looked at him with eyes that broadcast my fear, exhaustion, and gratitude. He met that gaze and kissed me unexpectedly. He held me tightly in his arms, and once again I felt this net of safety cast around me. He pulled back half smiling.

"When I feel antsy or stressed, I run," he said.

He darted off into the woods. After a stricken moment of panic, realizing I was left alone on another beach, I began to run.

The island is safe, I reminded myself, and for the first time in weeks, I felt free again, running through the forest unafraid of what might be. I was lost in pure bliss.

The island was splashed with a variety of luscious greens. Running made me forget about everything. I began to feel alive, and I spread my arms open like a soaring bird. Unsure of where it came from, I burst into laughter that echoed throughout the trees. I couldn't remember the last time I had laughed, *truly* laughed. I lost my footing and took a spill, rolling into soft moss and island ferns. I lay with my arms outstretched against the spongy ground. Aston was immediately on his knees by my side, assessing if I was hurt.

"You okay?"

My smile was the only answer he needed; I was more than okay. Being on this island removed the heavy weight that had been over-powering my soul and brought life back into my eyes. I realized that I could stay here forever and that no one but Aston would ever find me. The thought was infinitely comforting.

Aston laughed at my moment of giddiness and lay beside me. He tried to roll over me, but I pushed him off, got up, and ran. I wanted to continue running. His voice yelled my name, and then the chase began. Adrenaline and lust filled every inch of my body, and I broke through the trees into an open field where a flock of birds, hidden in the tall wild grass, took flight. Aston was still in the distance, and I locked my gaze on him for a moment until he disappeared. I slowed down to a jog, stopping at the edge of the forest I was about to reenter. I scanned the sea-like field waving in the breeze. My fingers wrapped around a tall blade of grass and I ripped it out of the ground, slowly wrapping it around my finger, waiting for him to appear.

"I know you're there," I said. "I can feel you watching. I can feel your hunger, Aston."

Closing my eyes, I breathed in every scent of every flower. The sun was beginning to break through the clouds, and finally, after what felt like weeks, its warmth penetrated my pale freckled cheeks. I knew I was safe here. Fear was unnecessary on this little island. We were hidden.

I paused, listening to the sounds of the island. I could hear animals scurrying and insect legs marching along endless blades of grass. I listened to the lively ecosystem of the island. A bird whistling and ruffling its feathers, the sound of a small animal breathing, and something below scratching and digging. A stronger heartbeat floated into my ears.

He was behind me.

My body became rigid as two arms quickly wrapped themselves around me. Warm air made its way down my neck, and I bound my arms around him, sealing whatever it was that we had. His hands trailed their way from my stomach to my hips. I turned. His face was close to mine, and his eyes were dark and filled with hunger. I hesitated, touching his face with my fingers, outlining his prominent cheekbones. My world was quiet. I felt nothing but this moment, a moment I hoped would never end. This island sparked life into my aching soul, and I realized that my definition of home lay within these arms.

Aston touched my face with his nose, I smiled bashfully and pushed him, but his arms stayed locked around me. He brushed his lips over my cheek.

I realized then that killing the rabbit had not only released my hunger for blood—it had also set off a gradual loss of control when it came to Aston. It awoke my demon, and left me raw and open to the seductive lure of the senses.

Aston moved his lips by my nose and over my closed eyelids until they worked their way back down and pressed gently against my lips. I grabbed the back of his shirt, and he firmly pulled me in by my waist, holding me as close as he possibly could. My heart fluttered like monarchs breaking into the sun. My knees weakened, and I moved my hands through his dark hair.

I wanted to stay hidden here, lost here, forgotten here. The thought of going back to reality pained me. I didn't want to go back through the protective glamour that shielded us. I was afraid of what was waiting for me out there. Here I was a secret, scuttling unseen along the ocean floor. Here I could be alive. Here Aston and I could be lost with one another. A crow somewhere in the forest squawked, reminding me of the Elders of the prophecy, of reality. I couldn't stay here forever. I pushed Aston away.

"What's wrong?"

"I'll never be able to escape them," I took a breath.

"Who?" He traced his fingers over my forehead then brought his lips to it.

"The Elders, they will find me no matter where I hide."

Aston pulled away, "No matter where," he confirmed with a sobering nod. "But right now, those hags aren't here. So for a moment, let's forget it all. Come."

He led me by my hand, and we took off into the woods. My stomach twisting in fluttering knots and my legs tingling, I followed him once more through the trees with a coy smile permanently marking my face. This time, we ran slowly, weaving in and out of the tall pines and stepping in every patch of moss we came across until we broke out into the sunshine of another beach. There on the edge of the forest was an old home.

The house appeared to be on its last legs, but it had an immaculate view of the untouched water. The paint on the sides of the wooden structure had peeled off with time, and the once tall Victorian windows were partially missing their glass. The stone chimney was still intact and the wraparound porch was warped and missing the occasional floorboard. Through the ruins, I could envision this to have once been an elegant home. A smaller structure stood behind it—perhaps an old stable of some sort—consumed by thick green moss.

"My grandfather built this place himself. It was one of their hideaways, on my mother's side. Not even my parents knew about this location. I found the coordinates disguised in a journal my grandfather left me in his will." Aston said. "Well, now it's mine. One day I'd like to rebuild it and make this island my home the way they did for some time." He took me by my hand and led me inside.

"What were they hiding from?" I asked.

"Everything I shared with you in the story. The Elders, the Children of Lamia, and your father."

"Oh, right." I had forgotten the monster of a man my father was before he had met my mother.

It seemed as though the thinnest breeze would collapse the walls of this old home and I pulled back, uncertain, but Aston reassured me it was safe and opened the front door. The doorknob looked just like the one on my mother's bedroom door, elaborately carved with ivy and birds. Everything inside the home was ghost white, for sheets were draped over the furniture and lamps.

Spiders had made homes in every corner, and the only light entered from the broken windows, casting the rooms in a haze of filtered light and dust. I ran my fingers over a wooden surface and made a mark that could possibly last a lifetime.

A small mouse surprised us, dashing across the keys of an old piano and diving into a crack in the wall. It was then I caught a glimpse of something shimmer from under a white sheet. I reached and grabbed a corner, pulling it with caution. The sheet slipped to the floor in a cloud of dust. I coughed loudly into my hands, wiping my eyes. When the dust settled, I saw an old chandelier. The crystal teardrops danced in the sunlight. The light poured through the crystals and speckled the room with tiny lights. Aston and I squinted at the astonishingly blinding moment.

Aston then disappeared, and I could hear his footsteps and the creaking of floorboards coming from upstairs. Following the sounds, I made my way up a wooden spiral staircase and found him in the first room I turned into. This must have been his grandparents' room. Their bay windows had a breathtaking view of the sea. The brittle rose wallpaper was curling off the walls. Aston stood by an ornate dresser and opened the top drawer. He rustled through it for a moment before pulling out a wooden music box. When he opened it, a few notes escaped. Aston pulled out a tiny velvet sack and shut the lid, placing the box back in the drawer. He poured the contents of the sack into his hand—something black.

"Turn around."

I did.

I felt his hands unclasping my necklace, adding something to it. Then a cold heavyweight slid down over my collarbone and landed in the middle of my chest. I looked down at it, and my jaw dropped. It was a smoky black stone, cut like a rough crystal. Lost for words, I let the weight of the stone sink into my chest. It fit perfectly with my mother's charms. Lifting my hands, I went to remove the enchanting stone, but Aston stopped me.

"It's a gift," he said with a serious tone in his voice. "Black tourmaline. My grandmother once wore it, said it protects one's soul from outer dark forces. I want you to have it."

"I can't accept this, Aston. It was your grandmother's, a family heirloom. You don't just give heirlooms to—" I wasn't even sure what one would call us. I touched the stone. I could feel the instant energy radiating off it within my grasp. I let go. He closed my fingers around it and pushed my hand back against my chest.

"Its magic is real Nora. Guard it well." He said with a smile, his eyes darkening with every breath.

I sat at the edge of the bed, holding the stone in my hand. It was beautifully daunting.

"Aston," I whispered.

He stepped closer.

"Sometimes I fear that we only feel this way for one another because of the bind. Would you even look at me the way you do if we weren't bound? Is this something that can last? Is what we feel a fabricated emotion the Elders gave us?" I looked at my bind then up at him.

Aston pushed me onto my back and leaned over my body.

"I *would* feel this way," his eyes darkened even more, "with or without the bind. Do I feel I could lose control, want to lose control, with you because of our bind? Sometimes. Some nights I want you more than you could ever imagine. You have a part of my soul, Nora. That is unmistakably true. And my hunger continues to grow stronger for you every day, my demon rousing to latch onto yours."

He kissed my neck, trailing his lips over my collarbone. He slid my shirt up, revealing my ribs and stomach, then lightly moved his lips along my ribs. I understood what he meant. I had become aware of it when my eyes shifted to darkness and I could feel them in this moment changing. I began to squirm, wanting to feel him, knowing that I would die without him, that he would die without me. There was something seductive to that thought. His hands gently tugged at the loops of my jeans so he could kiss my hipbones. I couldn't resist, and I pulled him on top of me, planting my lips on his. Our bodies entwined. My cheeks were flushed and our hearts tribal and primitively beating in sync. The weight of the tourmeline heavy on my chest. Then a brash moment surfaced. I wanted to lose control, now.

He stopped, feeling my desire. He pulled his face away from mine and ran his fingers through my hair. I sighed, feeling disoriented and confused.

"Why?" I whispered.

His dark messy hair outlined his pale face and his bottom lip was a deeper shade of red. His eyes were no longer amber but dark and filled with hunger and lust, reflecting mine. I watched as he bit his lower lip.

"Why did you stop?" I propped myself up on my elbows flustered with emotion.

He pressed his lips intensely into mine.

"We need to wait. I'm not sure what will happen," he said, "how our abilities will react to one another, and this isn't the time to start adding more variables to the mix."

"Right," I said somewhat breathless.

React? We're bound for crying out loud.

I rolled onto my belly, watching him as he ran his fingers up and down my spine. Aston's eyes showed regret at the moment of lust and giving in to our seductive cores that had fleetingly passed, but then the look fled as he curled his lips back into a smile.

"You are truly unlike anyone I have ever met," he said.

"I'm sure you've had your fill of many to know that then."

"I've been alive for over a century Nora," Aston smiled, rolling his eyes, then stood up, pulling me off the bed.

21

We arrived later that day at Iona's, but before we'd even left the boat, we knew we'd find it empty. The front door stood curiously unlocked, and Aston insisted on entering first. We made our way into the kitchen, and I inhaled, flaring my nostrils and feeling my eyes widen as my ears gently twitched, searching the air for familiarity.

"We're alone," I whispered, relaxing my tense muscles.

Aston looked at me suspiciously.

"What?" I flicked my hand in his direction to dismiss his suspicion of me being a shapeshifter. It hadn't happened yet, but there was a good chance I'd inherited the trait and most people's first shift happened unexpectedly at a time of physical or emotional distress. Shapeshifting wasn't something Aston—nor *anyone* we knew—could train me in.

The living room was empty. The couch Yael had been occupying was stripped of its sheets and blankets. I noticed that nothing of Yael's, Edel's, Ada's or mine was left in the house. On the kitchen table, I spotted a folded paper weighted down by a sea shell.

Nora,

It is time, like I promised earlier. We went back to Edel's home to see if we could salvage anything from the fire. While you and Aston were away, Marcia, Barrett, and the girls swung by saying that all the appropriate protection has been organized and we will be able to go back to Alexander Point this evening. Jane was bummed to learn she had missed you and wanted me to let you know that she'd like to hang out with a fellow 'young' un.'

Love,
Ada.

I placed the note back on the table and looked at Aston.

"They went back."

It is unsafe to revisit a location where a Lamian tracker attack has happened. They are territorial creatures and always retrace their own steps, especially if they believe that anything valuable to a person was left behind. Sebastian was well advised. He would know that eventually we'd return to collect bits and pieces of the life we once had there. We anxiously took off, back to the boat and back to the nightmare I had been fighting against in my mind for over a month.

We arrived, and I could still smell the smoky residue that the fire had left. It lingered amongst the trees, masked the moist grounds, and hung in the stale air. Aston and I did not bother running this time. We walked quietly down the sandy path until the smell of the old fire masked absolutely everything, burning the inside of my nose and causing chills to run down my spine.

"You okay?"

"Yes, it's just that I can still smell the smoke as if it were yesterday."

Touching the dark stone that now hung around my neck, I took a deep breath and we exited the trees together.

There we stood, eyes wide open at what was not. All that remained of Edel and Yael's beautiful cottage were piles of rubble, charred stones, burned wood, shattered glass, ash, and a broken family picking through the debris like refugees, trying to piece back their life. Yael was organizing a small pile of things she had salvaged and piled on the ground. She didn't say anything when her eyes met our gazes. She must have hated me at this moment more than anything in the world. I was the reason she was picking up the remainders of her prized kitchen and gardening tools from her former home. Iona was there with Ada, helping her move a large beam out of the way to reach something. Edel, with an arm full of charred, wet, and mossy items walked over to Yael. No one spoke, all were lost in their burned memories and broken hearts.

I walked over and began rummaging through the ashes. Aston stayed close by my side.

"Quite the scene," he whispered, and I nodded.

We were carefully stepping over a pile of ash when something in the debris caught my eye. I knelt down and gently pushed some broken pieces of wood and glass off a rectangular piece of paper. It was my mother, sitting there smiling at me as if none of this had affected her. Even with a few burnt edges, she still shone radiantly.

I handed it to Aston, feeling lucky. It was the only thing I wanted, and he looked at her for a moment.

"I remember her, you know. I only met her a handful of times, but I remember her." His eyes glazed with memory as he handed back the photo.

I couldn't have hoped for more luck than finding the photo, but somehow I also found my mother's feather, slightly singed on the edge, and the remains of the quilt that had once lain over my bed.

Marcia and Barrett paid a visit between sweeps of the area, making sure we were still in the clearing of Lamian trackers. I overheard them saying to Ada that there had been little activity and sightings of Lamians and Lamian trackers on the islands. This worried them, for it perhaps meant that Sebastian was beginning to prepare them, give them missions.

At dusk, we had managed to collect quite a few items and pile them in Ada and Aston's boats. We were satisfied that we'd salvaged all we could, and after Edel and Yael took a moment in the clearing to say a final goodbye, we got into the boats and headed for the lighthouse. I was excited to be back in my mother's room, but part of me began to feel anxious, worried that since the Lamian trackers had my scent they would eventually follow it to the lighthouse. I couldn't bear another home being burnt to the ground because of me. Ada gently shook her head in my direction, addressing my worried eyes.

Iona further assuaged my fears when she explained that Marcia and Barrett had put a similar protection shield over the home similar to the one around hers. They would also be trading shifts with their daughters and another two Sereni, who I hadn't met yet, to keep a constant watch.

"Our world is coming alive once more." She smiled at me with warm gray eyes.

"More Sereni are coming out of hiding and joining us because of you, Nora." She looked out into the distance. "Something is beginning to happen, something feels different."

My shoulders instantly felt heavy again, and I wanted to go back to the vanishing island. I nestled myself in between Iona and Aston, clamping my hand around my stone. Aston noticed.

The sun set quickly as the boats sped through the water, and just as we were about to reach Alexander Point, the lighthouse turned on. It glowed eerily, and we could hear strange humming noises as it made its rounds. The old white house at the end of the bridge stood empty and lifeless, just as it had the first time I rode in on the ferry with Ada and Eric Turner. Both boats glided alongside the dock and were parked closely together. When the engines were shut off, no one moved. Something unfamiliar was stirring in the night air. We all sat in silence, listening carefully. There was something or someone moving around in the boathouse. No, not one, but two beings; I knew they weren't animals, but were they Lamians? I carefully listened but couldn't make out anything from the rustling sounds and shuffling feet.

Then I scented blood. I quietly stepped out of the boat and stood there in the dark, facing the boathouse at the end of the dock. Aston tried to grab my arm, but I yanked it out of his hand.

My heart pounded in my throat, which burned with thirst. My body went cold and my cheeks tingled. I heard Edel gasp at the sight of me, at the sight of what I could easily turn into when I allowed my darkness to consume me. My eyes were locked on the two shadows casually making their way back and forth across the boathouse window. My mind clouded with the scent of sweet blood and the smell of a charred home. Hunger began to consume me.

Kill them, Nora, you can do it. It's easy Nora. Let me help you. Kill. The hissing demon voice was back after its long silence. *Tap into what makes us so powerful Nora. Use me!*

"Don't do it." I heard Aston's voice. "I can smell the blood too, but the more you give into the darkness, the more it will change you, consume you.

"No," Aston said to Ada when she attempted to grab my hand. "She is too strong. She must learn to control herself. She needs to do this, alone."

I swallowed. I heard them, but inside my head, the voice was powerfully seductive. Its whispering promises created a warm sensation in the deepest part of my belly, summoning a hunger that was hard to ignore. I licked my lips, smelling the air, and like a lion in a cage, my eyes paced back and forth, watching the figures' silhouettes.

"You're more powerful than that, Nora," Aston said. "Don't give into it. This is a real test. Don't do it."

My body became tense as the scent of blood wafted again through the salty air. It was sweet and intoxicating, delicious and rich. A low growl escaped the back of my throat.

"Nora," Aston's voice had become stern. "Don't do it. Don't follow your—NORA!"

I gave into the scent, the hunger, the fiery burn blistering in my throat, the demon inside me whispering *Kill* over and over.

"Nora no!" I heard Ada's voice, but I couldn't stop myself. I tore down the dock with Aston on my heels, but I wasn't going to let him stop me. The drive for blood hardened in my mind, killing every last ounce of sensibility, propelling me towards the thing I wanted more than anything at that moment: blood. I'd been denied it from the rabbit. To pierce my teeth again into flesh, to rip through fibrous muscle and tissue, that was all my dark instincts wanted—what the demon in me wanted. I ran into the boathouse baring my teeth. Two figures dressed in hooded cloaks saw me and began to run.

Ah, the chase. Listen to their fluttering hearts Nora, listen to how quickly they are producing blood and how agitated their muscles are becoming. Kill them. Strike.

The one figure fell, tripping over a pail on the ground. It tried to scramble to its feet when my hand wrapped around its ankle and I dragged it back, throwing the body against the wooden wall of the boathouse. The voice was right. All I could hear was blood pumping, a heart fluttering and muscles contracting in fear. Hair covered the face of the being as it balled itself up against the pressure of my fingers squeezing its neck.

"Stop!" Aston ordered from the other side of the boathouse.

"Oh come on, Aston," I flung my hand up and Aston flew against the opposite wall, "as if you don't know the desire, the thirst. As if you never experienced this feeling of wanting nothing more in the world. Satisfying your demon, your deepest desires," I hissed in his direction.

Aston quickly stood up and I could feel the veins in the body's neck pulsating against my fingers. The figure was beginning to gasp for air, its fingers scratching the wall behind it in a plea.

"You're right, I *do* know that feeling, Nora, and it is an incredible feeling, but you can't give into your demon like that. You can't kill your *friend* because you'll never be able to forgive yourself." Aston hissed back.

His eyes were black and watching the thin body's legs twitch and kick in mid-air.

"Let her go, Nora! Now!" Aston charged over, ripping me from the figure.

The body dropped like a rag doll to the ground. Aston pinned me to the boathouse wall. I growled.

"You're right," his eyes vicious and black, mirroring mine. I jerked and he slammed me harder into the wall. We were demons challenging one another. "I *want* to give into the darkness, satisfy my deepest desires, especially with you. Ravage you and taste your soul like no other, but we need to learn to control it, learn to channel it, learn to use it in the best light, learn to enjoy its seduction because this is something we will have inside of us forever."

Aston was shy of hissing when he pulled back the corner of his mouth in a sinister smile.

"You're a wild one, Nora." He let me go. "You okay?" he asked, turning and crouching down to the girl hidden in a cloak. She winced and kicked her legs in Aston's direction. I took a step back, trying to comprehend what had just happened, digesting Aston's words. Who was it? The thin body stood up off the ground pushing ringlets of hair from her face.

It was Jane.

My heart dropped to my stomach as she gasped for air. Blood was trickling from her nose and her body shook with adrenaline.

Aston turned around. "Good for you, you didn't kill her."

"Why? If you knew it was Jane, why would you let me attack her? I could have killed her!" I was angry and heated.

"Because you need to learn self-control. I may not always be there to stop your hunger."

"Hey, Nora," Jane's airy voice broke through the wheezing.

"What are you doing here, Jane? Are you out of your mind? I almost killed you!" I felt angry and grateful at the same time. "Jane!" I pounded my fist against the rocking chair. "I'm sorry," I whispered.

"Hey! No harm done girl, okay? Sorry for suddenly having a nosebleed. My mom said I have the thinnest veins in the world, so I can't exactly always time them right. And what am I doing here? Protecting this joint. You're welcome, by the way."

"You were lucky it was us," Aston said. "You would have died if it was a Lamian or their trackers. You need more training before being left in the field, alone." Aston crossed his arms.

"Thanks, chief!" Jane cleared her nose. "Tell that to my mom."

I heard the rustling of feet and noticed the other person slipping back into the boathouse to see what was happening. She looked like Jane, but older. I could see the fear still lingering in her green eyes, and I knew I must have looked like a monster. Jane wiped the blood from her nose on her sleeve and waved the other girl over.

"Katia, this is Nora. Nora this is my sister." Jane sounded proud introducing me even though I'd nearly just killed her. Katia nodded but said nothing.

"Jane, I am so sorry! I really am. It's something I'm working on," I said, looking at the blood still seeping from her nose. The color was rich and the sweet candy smell of copper began lighting the fire once more in my throat. I covered my nose with my arm.

Aston leaned into me. "That is your friend. Battle your demon, Nora."

I shook him off my shoulder. "I'm fine!"

"Oh, it's okay, Nora! No harm done!" Jane smiled and her teeth were stained red from her nosebleed. "See, I'm alive!"

I looked away.

"Hi Jane," Aston said.

Marcia and Barrett entered the boathouse on one end, and Yael, Ada, Iona and Edel the other end.

"We really need to work on your control, Nora." Iona's voice was stern. "You can't just allow your demon to take over. Two people have almost died now!"

I looked down, feeling both vexed and embarrassed.

"So this is the famous Eleanora," Barrett said. This was my first time meeting him. He stood tall, with broad shoulders and a thick dark beard. His eyes were a dark blue and his skin olive. "Thanks for controlling yourself. I am fond of my daughters. I don't know if anyone has ever told you this but you look—"

"Like my mother, I know."

"I was going to say your father. He and I crossed paths once many years ago, and believe me when I say he is not someone's path you want to cross." Barrett smiled.

Marcia looked at Jane, who was patting the last of the blood from her nose.

"Oh baby, are you okay?" Marcia sounded rightfully concerned until she saw the blood on Jane's sweater. "All over your new sweater Jane, honestly!" She shook her head in disappointment.

Jane shrugged her shoulders again.

"It's my fault," I said

"No, Nora. Jane should not have been dilly-dallying here in the boathouse to begin with when I asked her to run the perimeter of the property again." Marcia's head cocked to one side as she put her hand on her popped hip.

"Sorry," Jane rolled her eyes and looked at me.

Barrett, Marcia, Jane, and Katia all walked to the boats and helped bring in what we'd salvaged from the fire. It wasn't much and the ten of us got it all inside in one trip. Once inside, Barrett and Marcia immediately disappeared with Jane and Katia to strengthen the perimeter shields.

It was dark now, and I watched as the lighthouse beamed as far as it could over the ocean. It felt great to be back at Alexander Point, great to be back in this old white house, and great to feel the cold handle twisting in my hand as I opened the kitchen door. Like she had the first night there, Ada lit a few candles until we got news from Barrett or Marcia that lights could be turned on. When Jane returned from her rounds, she was the first to notice the stone hanging from my neck, even in the dark, and her eyes widened.

"That wasn't there the first time we met!"

I tried tucking it under my shirt.

She looked at Aston then back to me, narrowing her eyes, questioning us.

"Yes, he gave it to me," I hesitantly answered her gaze.

Jane winked.

Once Barrett and Marcia were done protecting the perimeter, they gave us the okay, and we turned on the house lights.

"What exactly is a protective shield?" I asked Barrett who stood at the kitchen door staring into the night.

"An enchantment that alters and confuses scents, making it impossible for anyone without Sereni blood to see the location, in this case, your home and property." Barrett eyed me. "It also has the properties of altering memory and disorientation."

"Why could the Lamian trackers find Edel's home then?" I asked keeping my voice down so only Barrett could hear me.

"Shields need to be strengthened on a regular basis Nora. In Edel's case they had weakened. And having such a strong scent to hunt and track by didn't help seclude the location of her home either."

I turned my gaze down.

"Nora?" Ada's hand grabbed my arm. "Would you like to show Yael the rooms?"

I nodded, glad she had pulled me away from the guilt Barrett had rested on my shoulders. I took a box from Yael and led her upstairs. Jane, Aston, and Katia trailed behind us. One-by-one we went through the bedrooms. I wanted Yael to have the one she'd be the most comfortable in, and of course, she chose my mother's room because she liked the elaborate doorknob. I told her that was

fine if she didn't mind sharing it with me, but she quickly changed
her choice to the room across the hall.

–No offense, but your dreams are too creepy– she explained,
moving towards her new bedroom.

Aston, Jane, and Katia helped Yael bring up the rest of her
charred pile, and as they helped her clean and organize her new
room, I stepped away, excusing myself to the bathroom. My attempt
to act casual didn't fool Aston, who threw me a concerned look as I
escaped. I ignored him and walked to the end of the hallway closing
the door gingerly behind me.

I turned on the faucet and splashed my face with shockingly
cold water; the water heater hadn't caught up yet. Pulling a small
crocheted rag off a hook, I soaked it and allowed it to rest on my
neck for a moment before passing it over my arms. I wanted to sink
into the numbing liquid, to somehow submerge my entire body
and simply go numb. I stood there supporting my weight with
both arms against the sink and observed my reflection. There was
no mistake this time; my eyes were a brilliant color. They did not
change when I blinked; they remained a deep, cold, glacier blue.

Releasing my hair from its usual nest, I rubbed the back of
my scalp where the hair tie had been tugging. My hair fell longer
this time, ending just below my ribcage, and it looked wavier and
richer. No longer a dull brown—more amber, or chocolate. I ran
my fingers through my improved locks and closed my eyes, breathing in the salty air that had been held hostage in my bun. I pulled
the photo of my mother from my back pocket and tucked it in the
mirror between the glass and frame. I pressed my fingers to my
mouth and then touched her cheek as if I could somehow kiss her
through the paper. Taking one last look at my reflection, I opened
the door and exited.

I didn't hear anyone's voices anymore and assumed everyone had
gone downstairs. I walked quietly down the hall and entered my
mother's room. The bedsheets were cool and soft, and the mattress

was welcoming. It felt as if I could close my eyes and instantly drift to sleep. I wanted a moment to myself, a moment where I could run, or breathe, or be still. I wanted a moment where my dreams were just dreams again and my nightmares didn't blossom into reality. I lay still, remembering that the album Ada had made me with all our memories had been lost to flames and ashes. Ada was the closest thing I would ever have to my mother, to memories of childhood, to childhood lessons learned and laughter.

A light tapping entered my thoughts, and I turned to the door where Aston stood watching me, waiting for permission to enter.

"Come in," I sighed softly.

Aston closed the door behind him and lay in bed with me, pulling me into his arms. No words were exchanged. My hands were in his and our fingers intertwined. The voices of all the different Sereni coming from downstairs started vanishing one by one, but no one came to bother us, no one came in to say goodnight. Maybe Ada assumed I needed the time alone. Soon there were no sounds left in the home at all.;I could hear bedroom doors shut one by one and the kitchen door lock. Aston pulled me in closer to his body.

"I broke her heart. I promised her I would protect her, and I broke her. She doesn't deserve this kind of life."

"Who?" Aston whispered.

"Yael." I gripped him harder, my heart, filled with stones, now weighed down into my chest. "I am the reason for her pain, for so much pain, for as long as I live. For every gift comes a curse." I spoke, repeating what Ada had shared with me about our bind. "No matter what good I do, what good I attempt to do, darkness will follow."

"This is the sacrifice of life Nora. This is the balance, there is no good without evil." Aston breathed into my hair.

22

The beating sun poured through the windows and pulled me from my dreams of wolves running through endless fields of primrose. The sounds of glasses clinking and cabinets opening and closing downstairs reminded me where I was. Rolling over, I found myself in an empty bed. Aston was gone. I pressed my face into the spot where he had been, then touched my necklace. The stone, along with the charms, were tangled in my morning hair. I rolled back over, stretching with a smile. The door opened, and Ada came in placing a cup of steaming tea on the nightstand beside me.

"It feels nice to be back, doesn't it?" she said, pushing my hair off my shoulder when she noticed the new addition to my mother's necklace.

"I wish it were under different circumstances," I replied grimly listening to Yael and Edel move around in the kitchen.

"Where did you get that? Sit up, let me see it!"

I sat up and pulled the charms out of my hair, then fixed the gold chain so that the clasp was in back. Ada touched the stone and looked at me.

"I know this stone." Ada lowered her voice as if she were fleetingly surfing her memory.

"It was Aston's grandmother's," I said, looking down at the stone, a tinge of pink entering my cheeks.

"Sigfrid," Ada smiled. "That was her name."

"It's Black tourmaline." I pressed the jagged angles of the stone between my fingers. "He said it protects one's soul from outer dark forces or something."

I gave a quiet laugh.

"What's so funny about that?" Ada sipped her tea.

"What's funny is that I am a dark force." I dropped the stone against my chest.

"Nora," Ada sighed, tilting her head to look at me, "There is no light without darkness. Learn how to use it to your advantage, don't hide it, control it."

"I'll try." I gave her a crooked smile.

"It's a remarkable stone," Ada said, unable to take her eyes off of it. "He must really love you." She smiled. "I *knew* it!" She slapped her leg as if she had just won a bet and nearly spilling her cup of tea all over herself.

"You did?"

"Oh, I just knew that the two of you would develop feelings. It was inevitable." She let out a girly sigh.

"Well, even if you haven't, he's definitely made up his mind about you." Ada pinched the end of my nose with her fingers.

"Ada, can I ask you something?"

Ada took a slurp from her too-hot-to-drink tea and nodded her head. My cheeks began feeling warm as I tried to decide how to phrase this delicate issue.

"What happens to abilities when two beings...um, well let's just say—*connect?*" I had no idea how to ask this question, but I was worried enough about what Aston had mentioned yesterday on his grandparents' island.

The color of Ada's face quickly flushed to scarlet. "You mean like *connect*-connect? Nora, you and Aston aren't 'connecting' yet, right? We haven't even had that talk! Oh my god, am I too late? I am such a bad guardian." Ada seemed to be having trouble swallowing her tea.

"No Ada!" I said nervously. "No! We haven't…*connected*." I couldn't even look at her while saying the word now.

"Oh thank heavens, there's still time!" She put her tea down and flopped onto her back as if suddenly exhausted with emotion.

"Ada!" I said, exasperated. "I was just curious. Well, what happens?"

She sat up on her elbows and looked at me. "Well, I guess you should know in case the 'connecting' ever happens in your life, which—being a Sereni and a Lamian—it will, probably a lot."

"Ada!" I raised my voice an octave, embarrassed.

I'd never be able to use or say the word 'connect' again without remembering what it now meant between Ada and me.

"When two beings with abilities connect…" Ada paused for a moment, rolling her eyes as if she couldn't believe we were having this conversation. "Their abilities then bond as well. Meaning that you and Aston—"

"Ada!"

"What? It's the best example I have at the moment, Nora. Where was I? Oh right, meaning that if you and Aston connect you both will take a piece of each other's abilities. Which ability is shared is out of our control."

"But we're bound! What difference does it make?" I asked, not making eye contact with her.

"It makes all the difference, Nora. Yes, your souls are bound, which is rare and profound, granted, but when something like this happens you can actually share abilities. What if you are a Shapeshifter? What if suddenly he can mind-connect with Yael? Understand? Do you see why the Elders forbid us to get involved with humans? Can you imagine, humans running around with abilities? It's dangerous for them and in turn even more dangerous for us." Ada stood up and sternly looked at me. "And if you two plan on connecting, Nora, use protection. Even teenage Sereni with abilities can get pregnant." Ada turned and started for the door.

"Does Nolan have abilities from you?" Then something else dawned on me. "Wait, what about Yael's father?"

Ada paled.

"Yes," she said. "And yes, which is why the Elders killed him, and I fear the same fate will happen to Nolan if they ever find out."

"Wait." I stopped Ada again from exiting. "Eric Turner. Is *he* human?"

Ada smiled, "No, he and his wife Mary are also descendants of the Seven."

"But, don't they interact with humans? I mean he's the captain of the ferry, right?" My brow furrowed in confusion.

"There is another ferry a few miles south of his that the humans use. They don't know about Eric's services."

She gave me one last look, then stepped out.

There were only a few items of mine left here from the last move, but I had to make do with the slim pickings. I'm not a girl who likes shopping, but at this point, I'd be willing to go. I needed clothes.

I sighed and quickly dressed, throwing on a gray circular scarf to hide the stone around my neck so it wouldn't draw any more attention. I headed downstairs to find the kitchen full of wonders. Edel and Ada were standing by the sink. Both looked withdrawn, and I thought fleetingly for the first time about the responsibility they carried around with them each day. Aromas from many different flavors of tea sifted through the air, and on the table there was a bowl of plump blueberries, rich in color. I took a handful and their skins stained the tips of my fingers.

"Good morning," I said. Yael wasn't in sight so I imagined she must have stepped outside.

"Ready?" Edel asked me.

"Ready for what?" I replied grabbing another handful of berries.

"Oh, I arranged a young 'uns day for you, Jane, and Katia. The girls are dying to hang out with you, and I figured you could use a day to get away and make some more friends? Don't be mad, it was last minute last night, and the girls said you went to sleep." Edel smiled.

"I'm not mad at all. Sounds nice," I smiled back.

"Here," Ada turned around and opened a drawer. "Some cash. You girls are headed to Stonington, so maybe you can do a bit of shopping?"

I pocketed the cash and hugged her.

"Thanks, Ada."

A rapid knock came from the kitchen door; it was Jane, rapping at the glass window. She opened the door.

"Hello everyone," Jane smiled. "Glad you can hang today, Nora. Katia is in the boat waiting. Shall we?"

"Have fun, girls. And be safe please," Edel said.

"Oh, Nora! Here, I almost forgot." Ada handed me my cellphone. "You'll have service on the mainland. I added the house line under *home* and Marcia's number because she will be out and about in that direction with Barrett and Iona. I bet it'll feel nice to turn that thing on again."

"I don't know," I said. "I kind of liked the whole no-phone-zone lifestyle." I followed Jane out the door. "Ada, when Aston swings by, tell him that I'm sorry for ditching training today. A girl's gotta be a girl some days. Love you."

"I will, love you more." Ada and Edel watched us make our way down the dock where Katia was waiting patiently in the boat. "Move it! Come on girls, we have to be back before sundown."

We hopped in and sped off heading towards Stonington. Jane and Katia, who apparently went all the time, were excited to take me to all their favorite stores. Katia's driving, however, wasn't as smooth as Aston's and I arrived exhausted, feeling more like barfing than shopping.

The harbor was filled with fishing boats of all colors, and Jane pointed out the tall lighthouse that was flashing like the one at Alexander Point. The water smelt of rotting fish and made a large gulping sound as Katia tied up the anchor. We secured the boat with a thick rope and grabbed our bags. The docks were filled with fishing crates piled on top of one another. The lingering scent of spoiled bait and chum was repulsive, and I was glad when we quickly escaped into downtown Stonington.

Stonington, Maine, turned out to be a very quaint town, filled with old historical buildings and little motels. We spent most of the early afternoon floating in and out of stores, having lunch at a little café Katia loved because the deli boy was attractive.

"Sucks, doesn't it?" Jane said to me, as we watched Katia shamelessly flirt with the boy over the counter.

"Meaning?" I asked, taking a bite of my sandwich. For a moment, I began to feel human again.

"Meaning *that*," she twirled her thumb in their direction, "will never work out."

"Oh, yeah that is pretty sad. Why doesn't she look for a Sereni instead?"

Jane snorted and shook her head. "God, so many families are in hiding right now; between that and the disappearances, guys in our world are few and far between at the moment. They're out there, just spread all over the globe probably. You lucked out." Jane winked. "Although, I heard rumors that another family moved back to the islands and that they have a son our age, but Ma won't give me details, says I have a big mouth. I won't know more until their home and its location is safe. Other than that we've only got humans to tease and flirt with. I will say, those girls may not have abilities, but they're pretty lucky with the selection of fellas." Jane winked again, this time at a guy passing by with his girlfriend in hand.

"Nice, Jane." I took a sip of water.

"What? It's like the only action I get." She then blew him a kiss when he looked back over his shoulder at her. We both laughed.

We all managed to buy a few things here and there. I was pretty much on the hunt to enhance my limited wardrobe, which worked out nicely when we found a consignment shop we all loved. We loaded up on flannels and jean shorts. Jane found herself a new pair of Converse runners, and I found myself clogs and Keds.

"Seriously?" Jane said. "You wear shoes like that and you get a guy like Aston? Katia, what the hell am I doing wrong!"

Katia just laughed.

The humming sounds of street lamps beginning to turn on filled the air. Couples linked arms, and I could hear their intimate conversations as we passed them on our way down the street, people-watching and enjoying our ice creams on our way to the harbor.

"Things look simple here," said Katia. "People smile, complain and laugh. Children beg, parents discipline, couples kiss, and all live their lives unaffected by the knowledge that a world that could end the entire human race is only a boat ride away."

"Shh!" Jane nudged Katia.

"What? Even if they overheard us it would be chalked up to something else." Katia sounded fatalistic. I appreciated that even Katia and Jane who were born into the Sereni world knew how odd it could all sound.

The sounds continued, growing louder and louder the more I watched and listened. Waitresses were beginning to take orders; matches were struck and candles were lit; cashiers rang up customers; tongues licked ice cream; heels slammed onto stone floors; paper bags were opened and stuffed with purchases, and cellphones buzzed with static.

I dropped my ice cream unfinished in a trashcan and cupped my hands over my ears, trying to block out the layered sounds, wanting to be back on our quiet island. My senses were suddenly being overloaded with nonsense information I couldn't handle, sort, or register.

Jane and Katia both noticed my spiraling anxiety attack building and grabbed me, pulling me into a quiet alleyway before my emotions could take over and cause something to break, shatter, or bleed.

"Breathe. You okay?" Katia asked curiously.

"Her senses got overloaded," Jane said. "No matter, you are safe, okay? We need to go anyway; the sun will set soon."

I began to miss the quietness of our home.

"Humans are oblivious to how much noise pollution they cause, huh?" Katia smirked. "Come on, let's get back to the islands."

My body started to feel warm, and a lump grew in my throat. We reached the docks. Something was starting to feel peculiar.

"Do you guys feel that?" I asked Jane and Katia.

"Like a lump just lodged itself in the back of your throat?" Jane said not looking back at us.

"Yep," Katia said. "Something isn't right."

Suddenly my back jean pocket started vibrating and we all jumped. I quickly grabbed my phone.

"Let's have it then, come on." Katia eagerly asked.

"Yeah, what's it say?" Jane added with worry in her eyes.

I looked up at the both of them standing there anxiously.

"It's for you Jane." I handed her the phone having already read it.

Jane – It is up to you and Katia to protect Nora right now. There has been Lamian sighting north of the islands and from what we understand from an inside source they are making their way to Alexander Point. We are unsure if they know the safe house's exact location. Find Iona, get Nora home quickly. Love – Mom

"They're coming for you," Jane whispered.

23

The dark clouds began to roll in over the ocean, and the waters started to move violently. Rain lightly began to fall, and people were scurrying to either hop into their boats or run into the nearest store for shelter. Jane, Katia and I stood there, iced-over in fear of the unexpected and dread at what lay waiting for us beyond those dark tumultuous waters back on the island. Jane and I jumped as bony fingers grabbed our shoulders. It was Iona.

"I see you got the message from your mother," her eyes stared at the wet phone screen in my hand. "All three of you are coming with me," she said in a rushed tone. "Move."

"Where to?" I asked, but Iona did not answer me.

We ran to her boat.

"Wait, what about *our* boat?" Katia yelled.

"Get in my boat, Katia. We can get yours another time," Iona said in a tone that would brook no debate.

Once piled in, we took off into the storm. The water was choppy and dark, but its fury did not bother Iona one bit. You could tell she had grown up maneuvering sea crafts through this type of stressed northern Atlantic water. The three of us held on for dear life as we went up and down, occasionally becoming airborne as we launched over the whitewater crests for almost an hour.

The water was rough as we finally approached Stone Isle. The lighthouse was already in full swing, humming and vibrating through the wind.

Two figures stood waiting at the end of the dock. Ada and Edel. We pulled up, aggressively rocking side to side, and they frantically helped us out.

"Into the house!" Edel yelled. "Move!"

"Nora!" I heard a familiar voice breaking through the sounds of rain, wind and waves.

"Let's go!" Iona yelled.

"No! I heard my name." I yelled back over the stormy winds and rain. I looked around wiping my eyes and face with my sleeve.

"Nora!" I turned again and there, beyond the dunes was Eben.

"Eben!"

"Who is *he*?" Jane anxiously asked tugging at my arm to move towards the house.

"Oh my," I heard Iona say.

Ada looked stunned, and she followed me. I ran down the dock and across the grounds into Eben's arms, embracing him. He was cold and shaking.

"Eben, what are you doing here?"

"Ada told me to stay away until she came back, but I needed to see you. I needed to talk to you."

"Eben!" Ada's voice broke into our conversation. "Eben! You *can't* be here, not now. It's too dangerous."

Ada was right. If the trackers smelled another half human in our midst, Sebastian would think we were doing exactly what he was doing and building an army of our own. Not to mention that the Elders could found out that Ada had been hiding a son. I feared the consequences.

"Look, Eben, Ada is right. This isn't —"

"I can't go back!" Eben yelled in desperation his voice cracking. "I can't go back! I can't go back! Don't make me go back!" He continued repeating. His body was shaking in fear when I caught the scent of blood, *a lot of blood,* more than a bite of a rabbit, more than a nosebleed. I looked down and his sleeves were saturated in blood.

"Ada," I quietly hissed, taking a step back from Eben.

"What happened?" Ada then lifted his hands, seeing what I had seen. "Where is Nolan?" Ada's eyes were wide with fear.

"They took him!" Eben's voice gasped for air, trying to fight back tears and anger.

"Who took him, Eben?" I asked.

"I don't know!" His eyes were bloodshot and his eyelids dark.

"What did they look like?" Edel asked, stepping in. Everyone on the dock was now watching us.

"Three of them, cloaked, and then I felt—"

"Paralyzed?" I finished his words.

"Yes."

The Elders.

"Eben, why are your arms covered in blood?" There was desperation in Ada's voice.

Eben began to roll up his sleeves and there, across both arms, a message had been carved into his skin. I clasped my hands over my nose and Ada began to shriek. I could barely take the smell of his blood. I felt my insides churn and my demon stirring from its slumber, awakening to the scent of sweet, syrupy blood.

"Nora, your eyes," Eben said.

"I can't be here," I said, afraid I would lose control, but I stayed long enough to read the message carved into his skin, an arrow pointing up and a crooked H was cut into both his arms.

"Tiwaz. Hagalaz." Edel hissed. "Sacrifice. Banishment."

Ada screamed into the howling wind as Eben's face streaked with heated tears.

"They killed him, didn't they?" he yelled "Because you came back, now he is dead, isn't he? I hate you! You threw us to the wolves! You left us unprotected! Why? Why couldn't you stay away!"

Marcia and Barrett grabbed Ada and pulled her heaving body towards the house, and Iona and Jane grabbed Eben, but he wasn't done.

"Didn't they?" he screamed into the storm at Ada. "Why couldn't you have just left us alone! Why Ada? Look at me!"

Ada was speechless and in her eyes I could see her soul shatter.

"Eben!" I said. "We don't know if they've killed him. If they didn't kill him in front of you, then there is a chance he may still be alive! Look at me!" I had wrapped the scarf I had around my face and tried to relax my desire, my hunger.

Eben's cheeks were bright red, and his bloodshot sage-green eyes were violent and angry.

"There is a chance," I said. "Okay?"

"Then we need to find him now. You!" he yelled to Ada. "You better find my father! You better fix this!"

Ada never turned back to look at him.

"We can't do that right now, come inside," Jane said pulling him into the home.

Eben jerked his hand from mine, and through the rain, I caught the scent of sweet mouthwatering blood again. I ground my teeth, swallowing the itch, the thirst.

"Come inside, Eben. You aren't safe anymore!" I ordered him. This time, he listened and followed me up the hill and back to the white house.

Marcia and Barrett stopped at the perimeter of the property and held their hands up, whispering incantations to make sure the protective shield was closed and strong. As the shield reinforced itself, all I could think of was Aston.

Where the hell was he?

Everyone entered the home except me. I waited, watching Marcia and Barrett as they worked on the shield, listening to the deep electronic drones of the spell at work. Once they were done scanning the perimeter, they came towards the house. As they passed me on the porch, Barrett grabbed me by the arm and pulled me inside.

"Inside, my girl," was all he said. The door closed and locked itself behind us.

Iona and Edel were soaking Eben's wounds in the kitchen sink that was full of mineral scented water. He already looked more relaxed, relieved.

"What did you give him?" I asked

Eben reeked of oaky whiskey.

"A really strong and responsive tonic," Edel said evasively. "Something to calm his jumpy nerves."

Yael was in the living room, wrapped in a chunky blanket with her head resting on the arm of the couch. Rain and wind were now slamming into the windows. Next to Yael sat Katia and Jane, both of whom were wrapped in towels Ada had given them. Ada handed me a towel. Her eyes were deep with sorrow and pain. I wrung out my hair, then patted down my soaked clothes. Edel looked out the windows, scanning the property, and every now and then Eben howled in pain. Iona and Marcia stood beside me. Ada vanished.

"Where did Ada go?" I asked.

No one said anything for a moment.

"She's upstairs. She needs a bit of time." Edel whispered.

"Oh jeez, I dint mean'ta upset'er," Eben said, starting to slur his words. He flung his massive arms up in the air, splashing whiskey everywhere. "I mean I guess I did but—"

"Shh, it's okay, Eben. We'll talk about it later," Edel said as she began rubbing an oily ointment on his skin. The skin healed, but the message was scarred onto his skin.

"It won't go away?" I whispered in shock to Edel.

She shook her head and spoke under her breath, drawing me aside. "The Elders use very powerful dark magic. The best I could do was stop the bleeding, which from the looks of these markings wasn't meant to stop. The characters on his flesh ran deep. A few minutes more and he might have bled to death."

My stomach jolted as I looked at the bloody water in the sink.

"See? All better! This girlie is brilliant at what she does." Eben held his forearms up to me with pride, and I caught Edel wearing a half smile.

"Yes, yes stay still!" Edel bandaged his arms.

"How much *tonic* did you give him, Edel?"

Eben's head bobbed around for a minute and crashed into the counter, where he began snoring loudly.

"Enough," Edel said. "Come on, I need help. Let's get him upstairs to the spare bedroom." Barrett picked up the stocky six-foot-tall boy and carried him upstairs, while Yael ran ahead opening the door and turning down the bed. Ada emerged from her bedroom. Her eyes were red, and she looked right through me.

For every gift, comes a curse, I reminded myself. I had wanted nothing but for Eben to have his mother back, for Ada to be reunited with her family and in turn, I may have just killed Nolan, and endangered Ada and Eben.

—I should have never encouraged her to visit Nolan and Eben. This is my fault—I looked at Yael.

—It would have only been a matter of time before the Elders came for them Nora, with or without your involvement—

Yael squeezed my hand, and we all left the room except for Ada, who sat down beside Eben. I watched her kiss his hand and push back the hair from his forehead. Eben stirred in his sleep.

"It's better if he sleeps through this," Marcia whispered before exiting the room. "We don't know what we're going to run into, and he's not trained yet. I'm sure this is a lot for him to even consider taking in right now. Yael will watch over him, she is far too young to enter the field."

"Do you really think he has abilities?" I asked, knowing all too well the magnitude of what lay ahead of Eben.

"I do. He could see the safe house, couldn't he?" Marcia put her hand on my shoulder, "The tonic Edel gave him included a melatonin-based potion. He'll sleep for a good long while."

I cast a glance back at the room then followed Marcia downstairs.

"The rain will make it difficult for them to see," Iona was saying as she stared out the window.

"Them? As in more than one?" Katia asked.

"We have to assume so. It's not often they travel alone. They're pack creatures. And I fear Eben was not careful when trailing his scent here."

My palms began to sweat. I was not ready for this moment just yet, though I doubted I would ever be truly ready. I had hoped Sebastian wouldn't order an attack for at least another two months until I'd had time to train more fully. I needed Aston. I couldn't do this alone. My heart started fluttering out of control, and my chest tightened, making it impossible to breathe. I needed Aston to be here. Panicking, I began to take a few steps back, away from everyone. Maybe I could run away, leave the islands, and never come back?

–You can't leave us, Nora!– Yael's voice broke into my mind, –You can't! We need you. I need you, and Eben needs you–

I responded telepathically.

–I'm scared! I don't want to be the reason anyone in this room gets hurt anymore. Look at Eben, Ada, your mom, and you! I can't do this without Aston, Yael. I need him–

–It's okay to be afraid, Nora. But you're not alone. You are strong and as ready as you can be. You vowed to always protect me, to always be here! Remember that? You have everything you need inside of you. You have always had everything you needed inside of you to survive, just waiting to be used–

She was right, I did promise her. I could have left the night of the fire, but I made the decision to stay here and fulfill the prophecy. I was to be the keystone to their survival, which meant I had to somehow end a conflict that had waged for over three thousand years, if it could ever be resolved. I looked back at Yael and her eyes were like darts piercing into my mind.

–I'm sorry I ever thought that. I made a promise to you, and I'll stay–

Yael's eyes relaxed with relief, and I made my way over to her. Wedging myself between Yael and Katia I pressed my hand against her warm cheek. I would not let anyone hurt her. She did not deserve any more pain. Lightning illuminated the home, casting shadows across the walls, and I felt Yael's body stiffen in my arms.

–Someone is coming–

I looked down to find her eyes had become wide and full of fear.

"Someone is coming," I said to the room of anxious bodies.

Listening hard through the storm, I began to faintly hear the noise Yael heard. Feet racing and splattering through the wet forest grounds caught my attention, and closely behind them another set. There were two Lamian trackers headed in our direction. My stomach knotted. It was me they wanted, not anyone else, just me. I had to do something. I couldn't just sit here, listening to them getting closer and closer. I stood up and casually paced the room. The stone against my neck began to grow warm against my skin. I could feel its energy moving.

Then my knees buckled at a flash of a man's silhouette, his cloak ripping through the air as he turned. I couldn't make out his face, but it was clear he wasn't a Lamian tracker. He was a Lamian, however. Was it Sebastian? Was he personally coming for me now? Who was the second? Aston? I grasped the back of a chair in a bid to stay upright. Something wasn't right. My stomach cramped in a surge. I had to go to them. Something deep inside wanted me to run. It was telling me to run, now. Edel glanced curiously in my direction.

"Are you okay? Did you see something again?"

I shook my head, lying.

–Yael, I need to leave–

–You promised! –

–I just have to Yael, something isn't right. I need to go. Please just trust me–

Yael's thoughts became blurred and frantic as she thought she might never see me again, but she made no move to warn the others.

I edged closer to the kitchen door trying not to draw attention to myself. Trees and blinding rain flashed through my mind. They were getting closer with every minute, every step. I waited, almost in pain at the strain of it, for the sky to let out an enormous bang of thunder that would shake the house—that would be my chance. Edel kept her eyes on me the closer I got to the kitchen door. I needed a distraction desperately.

Then it came; Yael clapped her hands over her ears, and at the same time the lightning and thunder ripped through the sky and pierced through the home. This was it. I slipped out of the kitchen door and ran.

I heard Ada scream my name as someone restrained her and slammed the door.

I broke through the humming shield of the home as energy surged. I listened and ran towards the sounds. I looked back and the house had vanished behind a protection of trees and rain. I heard the feet closing in and I ran faster. Something was wrong. I could sense someone needing me, desperately.

Energy spread through my body. It was dark now, and my vision was blurred in the sheeting rain, but my hearing and my sense of smell were heightened. I began to pick up scents as I made my way through the trees, then I stopped in my tracks. Something smelled familiar, but it was masked by an odor I didn't recognize. I knew I would meet the running silhouettes soon. I sniffed the damp air. I heard the rushing water up ahead, and I remembered when I'd first chased Vivienne. I didn't stop this time. I picked up speed and flew over the massive body of water that was in as much turmoil as the raging sky. On the other side, I stopped once more, listening carefully. The stone hanging around my neck began to generate heat against my skin.

Something was off; the feet were no longer in motion, and I heard a man's voice begin to scream in pain.

"Stop, boy. You don't know what you are doing! Let me explain!"

There was a growled response but I couldn't make it out.

They were close, hidden behind the curtain of trees nearby. Smelling the masked familiarity, I took off quietly in their direction, then stopped on my heels when I saw two dark cloaked figures, one leaning over another man's body.

"The bond!" said the prone figure. "My God, you're bound to her? Listen to—"

Aston?

I felt a pain shoot through my right hand as Aston shattered the jaw of the man with a blow that would have killed a human being. I could sense the blind fury coming off Aston through the bind. I saw him pick up the Lamian and hurl him into a tree. Sebastian? Bones broke and the Lamian fell to the ground, broken. I could smell the sweet scent of blood again. My eyes darkened with thirst.

"You think you can get to her through me?" Aston's voice was thick with rage as he landed a vicious kick that drove all air from the Lamian's lungs.

The Lamian staggered onto his hands and knees, shaking his head.

A garbled gasp that might have been "Please" came from the wretch, but Aston came down on his lower back and grabbed his head.

"Go back to hell where you came from," hissed Aston, and there was a familiar dark glee in his voice.

Lightning struck, illuminating the man's face for an instant before Aston snapped his neck and wrenched his head around backward and then drove it into the mud.

I screamed in horror. Aston whirled around, and his eyes were black and violent the way Lia's had turned when she'd first seen me. He rushed to me, but I ran past him to the ruined shape in the mud. All my senses told me he was dead. I fell to my knees.

"No, no, no, no," I repeated, turning the now lifeless body over.

"Nora, don't go near him! He was instructed by Sebastian to bring—"

I let out an unearthly wail and grabbed at the shoulder of the dead man, shaking him.

"What are you doing? We have to get back to the others. More are coming."

I couldn't stop wailing.

"Nora?"

He was at my side then. Terrified. What I said then he couldn't make out through my sobs.

"What? Nora, we need to go. I don't—"

"He was my father."

The news staggered him, and I could feel the horror and confusion run through him. "No," he said. "That's not possible."

"It's him," I said.

"Alexo? No. Nora, that can't be. Alexo is practically a force of nature. He could have killed me."

I held up my arm then, the one with the etched mark of our bind. "No, he couldn't."

Somewhere in the woods, a wolf loosed a long mournful howl, and when I howled in response, I became utterly lost.

I can only piece together what followed in dark nightmarish frag-
ments. I remember holding the body of my father. And the rain.
And becoming hysterical when I found blood on my hands. I
remember being carried into the house at some point, by Barrett
perhaps; the faces of Edel and Ada, Marcia and Jane; how different
my screams sounded inside; Yael weeping inside my head; a warm
bath and a strong tea that tasted of something that made my vision
swim; Ada sitting by my bed; and Aston—Aston standing in the
rain, his form dwindling to a silhouette, then disappearing into
the woods.

24

"Your father left you a letter. Marcia found it in the pocket of his cloak," Ada said, early the next morning.

I could hear paper rustling in her hands. I wasn't sure if I could hear his words at the moment, but Ada did not read anything. I remained still, staring at the wall and listening to the rain. I heard Ada let herself out of the room. The storm had calmed down, but the rain was still tapping aggressively at the panes of glass. The sound blocked any thoughts from entering my mind. Both mine and my mother's bluish-gray feathers sat on my nightstand; Ada must have put them there and I squeezed them in my hand. It gave me an odd sense of comfort.

The dreams I had woken from haunted me. The images were brutal and bloodthirsty, shifting and replaying in exquisite detail. The bloodlust that had washed over me before the lightning had revealed the face of my father was not forgotten.

I wiped my face on the sheets and kicked off the thick comforter. Cool air washed over me. I tried not to hate Aston. I tried to forget the images, to leave them all behind. My feathers had fallen to the ground. Picking them up, I placed them back on my nightstand where Ada had left the letter. I had no intention of reading it yet. I felt the heavy weight of the stone Aston gave me around my neck. I rolled back over, hoping that sleep would take me back, but it never did.

The dark shadows of my room disappeared as the sun rose steadily peeking through the lingering stormy clouds over the island. My eyes ached and burned. I lay still, not speaking as Ada entered and exited the room throughout the day. Hours passed, and my body remained numb. I was not hungry or thirsty. Yael brought me snacks here and there, but they went untouched and eventually were taken back down to the kitchen. I wanted nothing.

Aston had disappeared, leaving me with only one image: that of his silhouette vanishing into the night.

Eben visited once in a while. He looked different, older, and tired. His eyes reflected heavy knowledge of a world he had never expected. The scars on his arms were still prominent.

"Nora?"

He ran his hand over my shoulder and down my arm.

"Look, I know you need time, Nora. This is all really new for me too. I just wish you'd come around. I need you."

As night fell again, so did the nightmares, interrupting the little bits of sleep I was able to wrangle. Images of bloodshed and Lamian trackers kept sifting in and out of my dreams. Images of my mother and father would appear and disappear. The tracker who'd attacked me frequently visited my dreams. Her leathery face and shrieking voice caused me to wake up gasping for air between and screams. Every time I closed my eyes, I submerged into a subconscious sea of pain. Heavy paranoia began to take up home in my mind. I'd wake up thinking that someone was in my room, hoping to find Aston, but always finding nothing.

Aston had only been protecting me. I was not angry with him for the death of my father. However, by the second day, I was angry with him for leaving me to suffer alone.

And the angrier I grew, the stronger the demon inside of me grew.

25

The midmorning glow of the sun convinced me to open my eyes, but it was a mistake. I was rewarded with sheer blindness. Ada entered the room. She looked surprised that my eyes were opened and sat down beside me.

"Good morning."

Without replying, I rolled over. Her soft hand ran up and down my back. I was beginning to feel like I had a massive hole in my chest. I grieved for the loss of a father who'd been lost to me my entire life. I grieved too over my separation from Aston. Every day he didn't show his face meant another night filled with nightmares, screaming terrors, surfacing demons. Every day the hole grew deeper and darker.

"Nora," Jane whispered one day, "Aston will come back. He's having a hard time coping with what he has done. He never wanted to hurt you like that, ever."

After the fifth day, I woke up to a morning with rain lightly tapping the window. I opened my eyes to find Ada once again in my room, but this time she was hanging a black dress on a hook and placing a pair of black flats on the floor. An outfit fit for a funeral. She flattened out the fabric with her long delicate fingers. I'd never seen the dress before and knew she must have gone to the mainland and picked it out for the occasion. Two large brown shopping bags sitting side by side on the ground caught my attention. They were filled with new clothes, one bag was what I had purchased in Stonington, and the other from Ada. She finished with the dress and sat down on the bed.

"Baby girl, you have to get up today. You have to eat something. You're beginning to look pale and weak."

I put my hand on hers and closed my eyes as she played with my hair.

"Edel and I took care of all the funeral arrangements, but we cannot put Alexo's body to rest without you." She swallowed the words and kissed my cheek. "We'll be waiting for you downstairs, okay? Please get up. For him."

Then she left the room.

I slowly curled my body to the side and began to sit up. The letter Alexo had brought for me lay untouched on my nightstand. The envelope was a cream color and thin, the handwriting matched that of the letters he had written my mother once before. On the other side, it was sealed with black wax and stamped with the letter S, for Stone. I peeled the wax off and took out the folded piece of paper that matched the envelope. A black feather fell out and landed near my feet. I picked it up and began to read his last words to me. My eyes skimmed the lovely scripted handwriting and I felt numb.

Eleanora,

I hope this letter finds its way safely into your hands. There are a million things that I want to say, but I only have so much time to write this. Let me start by saying how proud I am of you. How proud I am to hear your name being spread throughout the islands. How proud I am to know you are strong and growing even stronger. You must be incredibly beautiful, the way your mother once was. I know a lot has been changing for you and that Ada has brought you back to a world you had no idea about—but belong in.

She is a brave woman and loves you, Nora. She has given up much to protect you. I hope you know this by now about your aunt. After all the favors she has done for your mother and me, well, I would never know how to repay her sacrifice. You have come home during a very dark time, Eleanora. Perhaps one day there will be peace amongst the islands once more, but so long as Sebastian continues to lead the Lamians and the Elders continue on their path of cultivating powers and controlling the Lamians, I am afraid the darkness will continue consuming our world, and your demon will be as vibrant as ever.

Never give up, Nora. Never stop fighting, never isolate yourself, never stop having faith in the bodies that love, protect, and surround you. They are your source of power, your roots to grow stronger and, first and foremost if you find love someday, love until your heart stops beating. I still love your mother. I still see her every single night in my dreams, and I will never stop loving her, nor have I ever stopped loving you.

I love you my little Eleanora. I always have and always will.

Your Father,
Alexo

I folded the letter back into its creases and pressed it firmly against my chest. My lungs began to heave as I fought back the approaching tears. The black dress hung there, a reminder of its purpose. I stood up and ripped it off its hanger, angrily threw it against the wall and let out a scream of pain. I put the letter back into its envelope and hid it in the desk, slamming the draw. I placed his feather with my mother's and mine on my nightstand. Three feathers lay together, symbolizing my once family. I turned to face the black bundle of fabric that lay on the floor. I took off my nightgown, but before I could put my dress on, I caught my reflection in the old mirror. My body was thinner and bonier than normal, dark circles shadowed my once-again murky gray eyes, my cheeks were slightly sunken, and my skin tightly hugged the bones that bulged beneath.

I turned back to the dress. Ada had picked out a tasteful dress with black lace shoulders. It hid my emaciated form within its folds, and I stepped into the black leather flats on the ground. I looked in the mirror once more. My reflection was a reminder of loneliness, of pain, anger, uncontrollable darkness and death. I was a soul waiting for the war, sitting in the silence, and feeling my demon beginning to grow and press the walls of my body until I might break. I grabbed the feathers and the small spool of blue thread from my mother's desk and left the room. The hall was empty and the silence eerie. Not a sound came from any corner of the home. As I made my way down the stairs to the kitchen, I could hear everyone holding their breath, waiting to see if I would have another outburst or do something unexpected. They were all sitting still with sorrow, fear and concern in their eyes.

There were Edel, Yael, and Ada, all dressed in black outfits similar to mine. The mood was somber; the type of event we were about to attend would have been painfully clear to any onlooker. Eben emerged from the living room dressed in a dark gray suit.

"Ready?" Edel spoke in the most soothing voice she could muster.

"No," I said looking to Ada. "Can you please wrap these feathers in my hair before we go?" Ada nodded. and I sat at the kitchen table silently, feeling her hands comb through my hair and pulling small strands that she braided, then began to wrap in one feather at a time. I ran my fingers around a knot in the pine table waiting for her to finish.

"There," she said smoothing out the rest of my hair. "You look beautiful."

Edel opened the kitchen door and led Yael out. Ada followed suit, then Eben and I began to trail behind Ada.

"Nora," he said. "When you disappeared, I came here every day looking for you. I knew something was wrong. I could feel it in my bones, in my body. Wren and Joe continued to hound me about forgetting you and moving on, and then one day out of nowhere Ada came to visit. Everything became clear that day. I understood why I was so drawn to you, so confused about you and wanted nothing more than to be with you."

"Eben, I'm sorry I never came to find you. I should have, I wanted to, but I wasn't allowed."

"Hey, it's okay. I get it now."

"What about Wren and Joe? What about yours and Nolan's disappearances? Someone is bound to look for you right?" I rubbed the scars on my shoulder.

"I know. Apparently the Knox Country Sheriff came to the house when Edel and Ada were there. Ada used her ability of persuasion and the next week I read his obituary in the paper." Eben's eyes glazed over with heavy confusion and sadness. "I withdrew from my high school and told Wren and Joe I was leaving town for a while to stay with family." Eben looked out the window and sighed.

He smiled with great sadness in his eyes. I knew that attending my father's funeral was like attending one for his as well. For all we knew the Elders had already killed Nolan, but Ada refused to have a funeral for an empty casket.

"There is still a chance," she'd said to Edel one evening. "There is still a chance he could be alive. The Elders would make his death a statement and I will not give up on him."

Eben had been dealt a tough hand, and the constant changes were overwhelming at best. I knew exactly what he must have been feeling.

We piled into Ada's boat, and she drove us to another island near Pond's Point. Three other boats were already there tied in. Aston's was not one of them.

I felt sick.

Ada pulled alongside the dock, and I stepped out and walked towards a man dressed in black. It was Eric Turner, and next to him stood a short, heavyset woman. She wore yet another black dress with black lace gloves and a black-netted headpiece that covered part of her face. I assumed it was Eric's wife, Mary of the famous chocolate ganaches. She pounced on me engulfing me within her arms and bosom. Both Mary and Eric expressed how sorry they were for my loss, but I said nothing in reply. A thank you did not seem appropriate because it was not something I was thankful for in any way. On passing, I heard Mary whisper to Edel, "I cannot believe he's been alive all these years! How devastating."

Something in the pit of my stomach twitched and I ground my teeth angrily. All these years. All these years and no one tried to save him? All these years and no one cared to save him.

Eric and Mary guided us down a gravel path through the woods to an area where the trees parted. There, beside another tombstone, lay a dark wooden casket. Marcia, Barrett, Jane, and Katia were standing beside Iona. Another man and woman, accompanied by a young man, stood beside Barrett, and a woman I had never met before stood beside Jane and Katia. She was striking; a tall, thin woman with wiry gray hair that twisted into tight spirals and sprung in all directions. She wore a long black flowing dress for the funeral tied around the waist with a thin brown belt. In her hair, wrapped in golden threads, were three eagle feathers. Her hands were covered in silver rings that felt cold as she grabbed my hand and looked me over. Her eyes were honey-brown—like Aston's. She smiled then released me.

Eric Turner stood at the end of the casket and spoke words of farewell.

"He was a man of change. A man who believed in those around him. A man who was living proof that one can change. He strove to live life in the light. A man who protected those he loved and believed in. May your demons finally be released and your soul, your light, set free."

After a moment of silence Eric, Barrett, the older gentleman, Eben and the other young man lowered the casket into the ground. Mary sang a glum funeral song while tears streaked her cheeks. The rope lowering the casket into the ground made a low grinding sound against the cold earth. Muffled tears came from Ada as Eric gritted his teeth holding tightly on to the rope. I broke into Yael's mind and found she was reliving the moment she'd seen me brought back into the house the night my father died. It was the last thing I wanted to see, and I wished I didn't have the ability to hear or see into her mind.

We each grabbed a small handful of dirt and tossed it into the hole as gaping as the one that had grown in my heart. One by one everyone stepped away, leaving me alone by the grave. I stood there lost for words, numb, and broken. Seeing the casket topped with dirt, and knowing the man inside had died in the mud in front of my eyes, my hands began to shake, and I turned to Ada, barely able to see her through my tears. Ada nodded her head in my direction, telling me to take as much time as I needed, and left towards the docks.

It all came and went so quickly. I was just covered in this man's blood holding his lifeless body in my arms, and now he was buried six feet underground.

The tombstone planted at the head of the grave said:

Alexo James Stone

Through my blurry eyes, I noticed there was a second tombstone next to my father's grave that read.

Here lies my love
Rebekah Gabrielle Stone.

My mother's body was buried here alongside my father. They had ended up together, side by side in the end, in a small safe haven where they would rest in peace for all eternity. I touched the three feathers wrapped tightly in my hair. The idea comforted me. I knelt down between both headstones. I'd never seen my mother's grave before, and I leaned over, tracing her name with my finger. I had nothing to offer them. I wished I could have left something behind. I looked to the foliage around us. Like the magic I had conjured as an infant in my parent's arms, I summoned leaves of fern. The tears stopped and my heart mellowed to a slow rhythmic pace as I fashioned two wreaths from ferns and old brittle ivy. I watched as they finished twisting and braiding themselves, then gently landed by my knees. I picked them up and placed one against each tombstone.

"Nora?"

I quickly spun around to see who called my name. The young man who had accompanied Iona stood in the shadows watching me. I wondered how much he had just seen.

"I was sent to tell you that the boats are ready."

I stood up and brushed off my knees, following his lead down the winding sandy path back to the docks. I looked back at the secluded glen where lay my family: my mother and father, together. *Goodbye.*

I looked back one final time, and I thought I saw movement in the woods, I stopped for a longer look, but whatever it was had gone.

"I'm Collin by the way." The young man had an English accent. His hair was blonde and his eyes were a dark blue. He smiled, but I didn't smile back. I said nothing, and we quietly made our way back to the boats.

"Right, well, I am sorry for your loss, Nora. Really I am," he continued politely with his hands clasped behind his back. We boarded the boats.

Ada and I sat quietly. I felt as if I had buried my heart alongside my parents. We all journeyed back to Iona's home where she had an array of food and refreshments. Eating was not on my mind lately, but I did take a glass of the punch she'd made and sat on the front porch alone. The screen door creaked open behind me.

"Can I sit with you?" It was Jane.

I looked at her and nodded.

"I'm sorry about your dad."

I wasn't sure what to say, and neither did she, so we both sipped our punch and quietly kept one another company.

"I've missed you. I know you need time right now, but I just thought you should know that Katia and I miss your company," Jane smiled. "No one has seen Aston yet either. I thought he would maybe show for the funeral, but I can't imagine the weight he is bearing right now. Don't worry, he'll come back Nora, I know he will."

I did not need to imagine the weight Aston bore, I felt it, every moment. I looked down into my glass of punch and swirled the juice.

No one had seen or heard from him since the night in the woods. Jane stood up and went inside, asking me if I wanted anything to eat, and I said no, thanking her. As soon as the screen door closed it swung back open and Collin stepped out with the older couple from the funeral. He bit into a sandwich that was wrapped in a napkin. He chewed loudly, and I couldn't help but focus on the sound of food mashing around in his mouth.

"Eleanora," the older man said with a thick English accent, "this is my son Collin, and my wife Veda, and I'm Jon. We just wanted to extend our condolences and to let you know we are so very glad that you and Ada have rejoined us."

"If you ever need anything," Veda said, "please sweet girl, don't hesitate to ask." The couple went back inside, holding hands, but Collin remained.

The sounds of food mashing around grew more and more intense, causing me to almost scream as my heart rate quickly rose. Then he swallowed and leaned against the front porch banister looking at me. He was making me incredibly uncomfortable.

"How are you doing?" he asked.

"As well as expected," I said, trying not to look at him or focus on the sounds of the sandwich again being pulverized by his teeth.

"You're a lot prettier than I thought you'd be," he said.

Are you serious? I shrugged my shoulders baffled at his statement. "Err, thanks?"

"No, I mean, I guess I didn't know what to expect when I was told I was going to meet you. Sorry, that may have come out wrong. It's just I've never met anyone who was part Lamian before and—oh never mind." He smiled at me, displaying perfectly white teeth.

"Do you and your family live on the island?" I asked, dismissing the attention on me.

"We do. We just moved back actually, this week. We had to leave for a long time. Veda was terrified of staying around the islands, but since we got word you were back, we came back to join you, support you." He took another bite of sandwich.

"How old are you?" he asked.

"Seventeen," I said.

"Nice." He smiled again. "And the other lasses inside?"

"You mean Jane and Katia?" I raised an eyebrow at him. "Jane is seventeen and Katia is twenty. How old are you?"

"Turning a hundred and ten this year."

"Oh, not much younger than Aston." I looked away.

"Aston," he said then paused for a second as if weighing what he wanted to say. "Yes, that's right. You know, we spent some years together when we were little tykes. Haven't seen him going on over sixty years."

I thought you said you'd never met anyone who was part Lamian. I decided I didn't like Collin.

He took the last bite of his sandwich. "So do you know if Katia is seeing anyone?" He leaned against the railing.

"I don't think so." I narrowed my eyes in his direction.

"Great. Well Nora, it was nice meeting you."

Collin tucked the napkin in his back pocket and made his way into the house.

The hours passed quickly, and before I knew it, the sun was descending and Ada, Eben, Edel, Yael, and I were piling into our boat to head home. Marcia, Barrett, Katia and Jane piled into theirs; Veda, Jon and Collin in another; and Eric and Mary turning in another. I had yet to meet the other lady, Helen, whom I learned was also a healer who had moved in with Iona.

"Helen is Iona's sister," Ada told me.

As we sped across the waters, darkness fell. The clouds had subsided, and the stars shone brightly in the clear night sky. When we docked, we all stayed in our seats a while, silently admiring the beauty of the heavens, until Yael's head began bobbing with sleep. Ada and Edel took her to the house, while Eben and I stayed in the boat.

"You okay?" Eben asked.

"Yeah, I just need some time alone." I tried to sound as pleasant as possible.

"Okay, I get it. Well goodnight, Nora," Eben said, taking the hint and heading up the dock towards the white home.

I lay down on the long seat and stared up at the sky painted with night expressions. I touched my charms and the stone Aston had given me, wondering what was going to happen. How long would it take for Sebastian to come after me himself? Was I to face him alone, or would Aston come back? My heart was splintering.

The boat gently rocked side to side, and I felt my heart throbbing as my chest started heaving once more. I wanted to feel alive, I wanted to sink beneath the waves and listen to nothing, feel nothing. Standing up, I pulled off my black dress and stepped out of my shoes. I stepped up on the seat, my skin illuminated in the moonlight. I stared into the black ocean, stepped up again, one foot and then two to the side of the boat, sucked in my breath, then plummeted into the dark water. The icy liquid shocked and stung my skin, overloading and blocking out all my senses at once. I felt the water envelope me while I sunk for as long as I could stand before opening my eyes to the burning sensation of salt. I pushed myself even further down with my arms, and my hair wrapped around my neck and face. My skin looked paler than normal beneath the surface in the shafts of moonlight that filtered through. I kicked up to the surface and took a sharp breath, noticing I had already drifted a bit from the dock. Diving under, I kicked both my legs and glided how I imagined a mermaid would, feeling weightless as I twisted and spun. This was my first time in the ocean and the experience consumed me.

The sensation of freedom from the shackles I had been tied to on land had been released. I was free. Under the surface, I did not just watch my father get buried, I did not suffer the pain of rejection from the man I possibly loved, I did not have the weight of pain, fear and responsibility of an entire race on my shoulders. If I could, I would have stayed beneath the waves forever.

I closed my eyes again and felt something quickly swim by my feet. Its rubbery body slid against my legs. I opened my eyes in panic, looking around, but nothing was there. I desperately needed air, and I kicked my way to the surface and gasped. The current had taken me quite far from home, and I took a breath, ducking back under so I could swim quickly towards the ghostly white dock. This time, two bodies brushed the side of my legs. I stopped and looked around, then began to kick harder when I finally saw something, a black shape—no, multiple shapes in the distance swimming towards me. I panicked, my heart beating faster, and I reached my arms back and kicked in the opposite direction, but the small black shadows were closing in quickly. I turned as the first hit me and slid across my ribs. The hit was surprisingly soft but instinctively I swung my arms out to hit back at the shadow. I wasn't sure what they were, they moved too fast. There was no way I could out-swim them; if they attacked me I was going to have to fight back.

My panic grew as I watched the little dark shadows encircling me in the water. Suddenly, as if it triggered an attack, at least ten more shadows began emerging from the dark waters and making their way towards me. There was no way I could win this. I closed my eyes, afraid, but nothing came, nothing hit me nor bit me. I opened my eyes again and yelped in surprise, sending bubbles from my mouth. I was five feet under water and floating face-to-face with a seal, actually with an entire pod of seals. They were gray and spotted. The one closest appeared to be older with wrinkles lining its eyes. It floated gracefully as it watched me curiously with its wide black eyes. My lungs felt as if they were about to collapse and I was left no choice but to swim to the surface, watching beneath me as the seals followed.

I broke the surface gasping for air, and all around me seal heads popped up. The seal closest to me flared its whiskers and exhaled, splattering water on my face. Letting out a burst of laughter, I noticed other seals watching me with the same benign curiosity. Taking a deep breath, I sunk back into the salty world and the same seal met me nose-to-nose below the surface. The others crowded around me, and I began to feel a bit anxious. Perhaps they weren't as harmless as I had thought. The larger seal must have sensed my panic and it moved even closer to my face touching its slimy cold nose to mine. I reached out my hand and gently stroked its belly. Its face slipped past my nose and nuzzled against my neck. The sensation of its skin against mine was bizarre.

Without warning, a few began pushing me with their noses and the leader began swimming away and back to me. They wanted me to follow them, but where did they want me to go? At this point, they weren't giving me a choice, though I was terrified of swimming farther from shore. I visited the surface to take in more of the salty night air, then dropped back in. The seal looked at me steadily, its eyes warm, welcoming, persuading me that I would be okay, and so I decided I'd risk it.

The pod swam off with me trailing behind. Every time we came up for air, I saw myself further and further from Stone Isle. The lighthouse eventually disappeared and I was lost in the dark waters of Stone Isle Bay. I realized I could swim a lot faster than I'd thought. I began to move fluidly without effort and was able to swim almost as fast as I could run, only coming up for quick short breaths here and there. I kept up with the pod as they surrounded me, taking me somewhere, somewhere far, somewhere unknown. The one I assumed to be the leader finally slowed down and turned its head to look at me. It beckoned me to the surface.

The pack had brought me far out into the ocean where nothing was familiar, and as we rolled around in the waves, waiting for something to happen, I noticed a beach nearby and then heard voices. I quickly dropped my face half way under water. I stayed as low as I could and watched four figures walking along the shoreline.

"What do you *mean* you can't find him!" The voice was male and full of angry authority.

He raised his hand, and another man was forced to his knees in agonizing pain. His cries spilled over the ocean, but no one came to his rescue.

"Unfortunately, you are no longer of any use to me. Shame, I really had high hopes of your loyalty to help see this plan through."

The man on his knees let out a grueling scream as his neck twisted then snapped. I gasped, swallowing a mouth full of salt water and began to choke. Then other faces quickly turned in our direction. I took cover under the water and held my breath, hoping I would not attract any more attention. A seal jumped into the air, distracting them by barking and bellowing. Out of air, I was forced back to the surface, but I kept my head low with only my mouth above water. A woman spoke.

"Seals Sebastian. Only seals feeding. Nothing to worry about, my love."

Sebastian looked in our direction curiously, and then took the woman's hand in his. I caught a glimpse of the hooded slender figure. It was Lia. They left the dead man's body and walked up the beach.

So this is where Lia had disappeared to, she had joined the Lamians, she had chosen the dark path. She had become involved with Sebastian.

"Our babies will be thrilled tonight," I heard her say, and then the fourth figure, slight and female like Lia, let out a grim slightly maniacal laugh.

"Quiet!" Lia snapped. "Go tell Jean Felipe that Alexo has gone missing, and send out a pack of our most starved, immediately! We want him back, dead or alive!" Lia hissed. The girl nodded and scurried off into the woods.

"Don't worry love," Lia reassured Sebastian. "We'll find her." The two stared out across the ocean. "I want her blood as badly as you do, along with that weak link of a brother of mine." Lia's tone had slid from a slight hiss to a downright snake-like tone. "I should have killed him when I killed the rest of the Boxams."

"We mustn't forget, my dear," Sebastian said, "the Elders will cultivate her powers first. This is our agreement, and we must obey our elders. You were wise, my love, to pledge your life to our kind."

"Since birth, I knew what path I wanted to walk. I would never suppress the greater power within, the power of Lamia's lineage."

Lia turned sharply and the two disappeared into the woods. A moment later howling sounds filled the night air as five wolf-like creatures, Lamian trackers, trotted onto the beach and began ripping the man's body apart. They were newborn Lamian trackers, still transforming into their full potential. Some still had tattered remnants of their human clothes on their bodies. I looked at the seal and dove back into the water, allowing them to lead me back through the currents towards home.

When we got there, the pod escorted me to the dock. They stayed behind as the leader swam closer to me. I hesitated for a moment and then swam closer, kissing its white spotted nose. Turning, I climbed the ladder and pulled myself up onto the dock. The air had grown cooler, and I held my body as I watched the pod swim into blackness. The leader stopped right before vanishing and looked at me before it dove back into the sea.

That night was the first night I dreamt of the ocean and its dark shadowy waters. I was swimming alone when I saw the shadows of the seals return. I waited there patiently, and their shadows grew into those of hungry Lamian trackers. I kicked and swam as hard as I could through a field of shackled floating bodies. I woke up swinging my arms and legs in a bid to free myself from my tangled blankets. I sat up, looking around and orienting myself. I was in our home, in my bed. I was okay.

I lay back down and thought of the last day Aston and I had spent on the vanishing island. The last day we'd been together. I rolled over as warm tears formed and fell from my eyes. I missed him. I felt safer with him. I wanted him back, I wanted to be back home.

Aston, please come back.

If you can feel me, please, please come home.

26

Darkness was beginning, just as the Elders had told me it would. I felt alone, unloved, abandoned. Vulnerable as a rabbit with an injured leg facing down a black-eyed, hungry serpent.

Life at Alexander Point drifted by in a blur. The more days that passed by without Aston, the more I began to fall into a state of absentmindedness; my soul was beginning to lose its light. Jane would occasionally try and keep me company, but my misery must have been uninviting. Pushing everyone around me away, including Katia and Jane, I sat alone and hungry in a way no food could satiate. My body began to look as pale as white marble, and my eyes took on a darker, murkier color. I knew I was dying.

Eben was beginning to spend a lot of time with Jane, who was slowly training him, teaching him everything she had learned when she wasn't in training herself. A search party was sent out to find Aston. He could be in trouble, my state only reflected his, and neither could not survive without the other. My mind was becoming intoxicated as I replayed dark events over and over: Sebastian and Lia, Aston vanishing into the wood, the death of my father, the message on Eben's arms, and the Lamian trackers tearing apart that man on the beach.

I had told Ada about the seals and visiting the beach where I saw Lia and Sebastian, but she barely batted an eye. "We need to take care of you right now, Nora. I will speak with everyone about what you saw."

My demon whispered to me through the darkest hours each night, hissing and growing stronger, wanting to hunt, to kill, to break free from control

"You're fading fast, Nora," Ada whispered into my ear one night when she thought I was sound asleep. "Please come back to us."

I pretended to stir in my sleep so she'd leave. I felt iced over and frail. The hole in my heart continued to grow, and I continued to relive the nightmare in which I had a gaping dent of blood in my chest. *Aston will return in the morning*, I would tell myself each night before falling asleep; he would return and the pain would disappear. My thoughts became obsessive. No one knew what to do with me anymore. I screamed in pain throughout the nights, listening to my demon, feeling phantom, searing burns on my arm where Aston and I had bled during the binding ritual. The longer he stayed away the worse the burning had become. Edel, Ada, and Eben would watch over me carefully. Yael was no longer allowed to see me. She was kept from me. I had become a plague.

I am lifeless.
I am empty.
I sleep in fields of nightmares.
I struggle to breathe in the dead of night.
My demon grows hungry.

My only chance for survival was Aston's return. The search parties continued to come back empty handed. He had taken something from me when he left; a part of my soul. I needed to be near him, to regenerate, to heal.

"Where are you?" I would scream into the night.

He'd rather keep his distance as we both perish.

Lies Nora! Do not believe what others are saying! He will return! I know he will! I found myself hissing these words in the dead of night.

There was a constant dark tennis match in my thoughts, and I started talking to myself, comforting myself, answering myself, yelling at myself, and scolding myself as my demon volleyed back and forth. I came out one day to Ada about the demon and voices in my head. I was afraid of my own mind and body. I was in a war with myself.

"It's getting bad," I overheard Iona say outside my closed door. "We need to find him, or we could lose them both. Their destruction depends on her."

Edel labeled it as an inner demon of pain, Queen Lamia's seed, the root of my creation. She explained that because our souls were bound, the longer Aston kept his distance, the weaker either party would become, and the more pain and suffering we both would endure as our demons became stronger.

Iona's words resonated in my mind during the nights. I had never felt so helpless, so desperate and so alone. Our only chance to survive was to be together—this I *knew* to be true. My suffering was not only my own but was also a reflection of the turmoil Aston was experiencing. Even our nightmares blended together, every moment of fear, pain, discomfort, and loss of control was doubly strong. What was happening to me, to my body, to my mind? Edel feared I was beginning to slip into a state I might never come back from. She and Eben would switch with Marcia and Barrett and head out after nightfall in search of Aston, to bring him back, but they always came back empty handed.

Screaming and loud banging came from my room in the dead of night as I released fits of rage. Anger and hate grew within me, and I noticed my eyes becoming darker and darker. I was beginning to feel like a rabid animal, caged. I opened the drawer where I had stashed the letter from my mother and father and ripped it apart. I watched slivers of paper spread across my floor. I was angry to have been led into a trap by my parents, to have been left to fulfill an ancient prophecy that may very well kill me, to have been given a demon, and to have returned to this godforsaken island.

My bones became more prominent on my frame. I was vulnerable, a perfectly weakened creature ready to be killed by the first hunter who found me. Sebastian was coming. I could taste blood and smell it in the air from miles away. I lusted for it, craved it, starved for it, and was denied it. I was under constant supervision. My windows and door were barricaded after I made an attempt to break free, to hunt Aston myself.

"This is for your protection!" Ada yelled through tears while Eben and Barrett bolted the door. "It's only temporary!"

Eben would come periodically to my door and remind me of how I was when we first met. Iona would force tonics down my throat as Ada and Barrett bound my arms and legs. They wanted to keep my demon at bay for as long as possible until they found Aston. I was spending my days in confinement and darkness. My veins were dark and my eyes permanently black; even the whites were gone.

I started wishing for death.

"Let me go! Let it take me!" My eyes rolled into the back of my head. "I can't do this any longer. Just let it kill me!"

I wanted to be released from the pain, from my demon, and from this life. My body temperature began to drop. I was cold all the time, and there was nothing Ada or Edel could do to warm me. In the mirror, I ran my hands over my bony hips and did not recognize myself. I was turning into a Lamian, into the reflection of my demon as it consumed me from the inside out.

"Leave me! Get out of me! I want you gone!"

I lifted the desk chair and threw it against the mirror, shattering it into long, tooth-like shards. The only thing that did not change about my appearance was the Black tourmaline stone that hung from my neck, cruelly reminding me of Aston. Its heat scarred my chest, but I refused to remove it. Its magic contributed to protecting me from my dark self.

I could vaguely remember what his kiss felt like, what it meant to lay with him, to fall asleep in his arms.

I have lost you, my dear, the only one I would die for. I cannot go on doing this without you. Come back to me, please.

Nightmares absorbed me. That night I dreamt of the Elders. I was back in the snow, this time, barefoot and naked, with only a cloak draped over my frail body. The three hooded figures hovered over me.

"You think this is a dream?" hissed Nephthys. "It's not a dream if you can feel *this*."

A stinging sensation paralyzed my body in the snow. My skin burned, and I watched blood begin to stain and soak through all that was white around me. Beautiful, elaborate red snowflakes began to fall from the sky.

"You will die, and we will come for you soon if you don't correct the course you are choosing." Nit hissed between breaths. "We need you alive!"

The three continued to surround me.

Milda touched my cheek and said, "Let us show you."

I snapped my teeth at her as painful pins and needles spread through my limbs.

White noise flooded my ears, and I saw myself on my knees in the snow before the Elders. Edel and Marcia were forcefully restraining Ada as she thrashed in their grips and tried to save me. Eben and Yael were missing. I looked nothing like myself. My body was sunken in, my hair gone, and my fingernails rusted over like that of the Lamian tracker who had ripped open my shoulder. My breathing was quick and short, and my skin looked like cold veiny marble. I turned to look at Ada one last time and mouthed, *I'm sorry*. My teeth were sharp and stained with blood.

Milda lifted her hand, and before I knew it, my head fell and rolled in the snow. My body slumped to the ground, and my necklace with the charms and the stone slid across the icy surface and landed beside my feet. Aston was next. His shackled form was dragged out of the woods and executed beside my broken form. Nit lifted her hand and both our bodies became engulfed in flames. Kneeling down, I touched the stone and awoke gasping, my heart thrashing. I reached up to touch my hair and found it still there. I looked at my hands and my nails were normal, I ran to the window and opened it, desperate. But they were barred. I banged the iron bars.

"Damnit!" I hissed wanting cold air.

The Elders were warning me, warning us.

I pulled my comforter over me, begging for sleep to take me, for my demon to call me to rest and then leave me alone. The beginning stages of sleep started to sweep over me when, without a warning, I heard the creaking of my door hinge. It had been left open. I then felt a weight push down the end of my mattress.

I flung up, looking towards the end of my bed. There, in the darkness, was the silhouette of a man sitting at the end of my bed.

"Aston," I whispered.

I pulled back against the headboard, thinking this was another hallucination. My bind began to prick and burn. The longer I sat, the more real he looked; I watched his shoulders rising and falling with every breath. He sat there, quiet and guarded. Slipping back down to a curled position I stayed frozen, waiting for something to happen. Waiting for the hallucination to disappear or for a sign this was real. My heart began to wrench again. He'd been gone for two months and then, in the dead of night, he reentered my life, unannounced and without warning.

"Did the Elders come to you too?" I whispered into the cold night air.

He was real.

"I know what I have done. I know you will never forgive me. I didn't know how to deal with the pain I had inflicted upon you," Aston finally said. His voice was quiet and dampened with sadness as his words hung in the still night air. "I have lived over a hundred years on this planet and I have been able to compartmentalize almost everything emotionally, except this. Except hurting you. I was unprepared for this."

There was silence. I wanted nothing but to have him back in my life. I needed him. I wanted him so badly that my heart felt as if it would explode, felt as if my lungs would collapse and my throat would catch fire. I was weak without him, slowly perishing within my own skin. I had allowed my demon to consume me, to control me, to hurt me and to haunt me. My demon needed his to survive. Yet, there he was sitting right there, an arm's reach away, and I couldn't find a single word. Not one.

"Have I broken everything we are?" he asked. "Perhaps." He paused. "I have driven a dagger through your heart and I have severed ties of trust." He spoke so frankly.

Pushing myself up to a seated position I stared in his direction, but he had yet to face me.

"Look at me!" I spat angrily.

Aston didn't turn around.

"The Elders *did* come to me." The tone of his voice was void of emotion. "And they warned me."

"I know *you*, Aston. And I know you didn't know who that man was," I said.

I wondered if he was right—could everything that we had have fallen apart as quickly as it came together? Did every laugh and kiss die that night, along with my father? I stared at my legs.

No, this can't be right. It can't be. This isn't how it's supposed to go.

I was *not* supposed to lose the man I was bound to. I reached towards him and grabbed his shoulder. His flesh felt real in my hand, but he didn't move. Like a board, he stayed cold and rigid for a few more minutes before standing up and facing me for the first time. His eyes were heavily lined with dark circles, his cheeks were sunken in, and his eyes, like mine, were black. I could tell that his soul was broken and his demon consuming him. He'd felt every ounce of pain that I had suffered. He did not smile and could barely look at me. After a moment, he turned and began to walk out the door.

"Haven't you had enough pain?" I cried.

His soul was bound to mine, and he felt every terror and night tremor, ever bit of the anger. He slept through my dreams and relived the monsters that attacked me in the dead of night. He was dying the way I was.

"Aston!" I gasped. He looked at me, piercing me with his violent eyes.

He slowed down his breath at the sound of my desperation.

"Why? Why do this, Aston? Don't go."

"Nora," he stopped and narrowed his eyes, "the Elders sent me after Alexo. They deceived me. It was part of their plan, all this was part of their plan and I'm done being a pawn in their game to bring you pain."

My heart stopped. "What?" I whispered sitting back on my heels.

"I had no idea who the Lamian was that I was hunting. They kept that information from me, but they told me a powerful one was on the move to kill you and I needed to protect you. They set me up. I am a monster. I should have known, I should have!" He said these words with such regret and hatred.

I watched his hand reach for the knob. Blood rushed to my head and I stood up on my knees.

"Aston!" I shouted. "You *cannot* leave me again! You can't! You promised! Remember?" I pounded my fist into the mattress.

The door wrenched itself from his hand, slammed itself. My abilities were already gaining control with him near.

My words trailed off and I felt my chest heaving. "Please." I was begged now, my voice shaking. "Please." Tears began to fill my eyes.

He finally looked at me again and I sat there, scared. The tears swept through their barrier and lightly rolled down my cheeks.

"Why on earth would you want me after what I did? I murdered your father Eleanora." Aston waited silently for an answer, and when I didn't have one he continued. "The Elders were furious when they learned you were dying—*we* were dying—and they paid me a visit," he said. He pulled off his shirt and turned around. His back had fresh scars, gashes where they had punished him. I stepped off the bed and made my way over to him. His scars were still red and blistered. His body was sunken in like mine. I grabbed his arm and turned him around. I had felt these lashings in the middle of the night, the insanity the pain had driven me to was an indescribable one.

Together we were demons—his eyes like mine, his veins like mine, his mask of exhaustion and pain like mine. A montage of every memory I shared with him slipped across my eyes. Lying in the forest with him on his island one more time, running through the woods with him one more time, making my way through the old enchanting home one more time, feeling him put the tourmaline around my neck one more time, fighting with him in the rain one more time and kissing him *one more time.*

"Why?" I said. "Because you introduced me to myself, because you embraced what I am? I am at home in your arms, because you are my forever…" the words trailed off, and I knew my face was red. "And because I love you. I love you in whatever form you take."

I narrowed my eyes at him. I hoped that that was enough. It needed to be enough for him to stay. I released my clammy hand from his arm.

"And I would wait a million years for you," I said through tears. "You and no other."

My breathing slowed down along with the pace of my heart, and for the first time Aston did not look composed. He seemed lost for words at my outburst. He appeared, for a moment, almost human. I stayed quiet after letting those words escape my lips, and then fear began to grow in the silence. Aston stepped closer to me. He ran his fingers along my hairline and down the side of my neck. I could smell hunger again in the air.

"I have waited for what has felt like a hundred years to hear you say that." His eyes shifted back to their sweet honey brown under his bruised eyelids.

I stared at his pale lips.

"You are my *everything*, Nora," he said.

"Please," I said. "Please, don't *ever* abandon me the way you did, not under any circumstance, not under any amount of pain." I sunk back onto my heels and stared at him.

"Forgive me. I will never leave your side again."

I pulled him in, hesitating at first, but then he grabbed my face and I kissed him.

My body felt a wash of relief as my inner demon quieted, then slithered back into its dark hole. Aston leaned me back onto the bed until my head touched the pillow. This kiss was different from the rest. It sealed our confessions and our promises and mended our wounds. He rolled over onto his side and pulled me against his body. His lips kissed the back of my neck and made their way to the tip of my shoulder. Our fingers intertwined, and he held me there until my eyes closed. For the first time in what felt like years, I slipped into a dreamless state, a place where our bodies could heal and regenerate.

The next morning, when the warm sun bathed my face, I opened my eyes half expecting to find that Aston had left at some point during the night, half expecting to find it had all been a dream, but I found his arms right where they had been when I had fallen asleep, wrapped around me.

"It's unlocked!" I heard Edel's voice full of urgency. My bedroom door cracked slightly open, then quietly closed. I shut my eyes, pretending to be asleep, listening to it creak open again and close once more. I knew it was Edel and Ada peeking in to see what nightmarish scene they were about to encounter when I heard Ada suck in her breath at the sight of Aston.

"He came back," Ada whispered to Edel.

I felt him shift in his sleep and then unexpectedly roll over, taking me with him.

"We have an audience," he whispered with a smile.

I was still lying on top of him when the bedroom door cracked open once more. This time, it slammed shut.

"That we do," I said.

I smiled at him. It felt like my heart would burst. "You look—"

"Better?" he said. "You too. The color of your skin has returned, and your eye color."

He pulled the white sheet over the two of us, and we stayed there looking at one another, lost awhile in a world of white bliss. I sighed, resting my head on his chest.

"I'm afraid to get out of bed with you," Aston said.

I kissed his forehead. "Why?"

"Reality. I'm afraid you will come to hate me, resent me. I'm afraid of what more the Elders have in store for us."

I looked at him and touched his cheek.

"No." I looked at him more seriously. "I do not hate you. There is no life without you."

Our hands held each other, and we stayed there soaking up the minutes until we both knew it was time to face reality—time too for the other members of the household to exhale. We rolled out of bed, and I pulled on some black leggings and a large knit cotton shirt. I took a few deep breaths, stretching my arms into the air. Aston's hands found their way to my stomach and up along my sides.

"I've missed you. God, how I missed you."

We made our way downstairs together, and right before we turned the corner of the banister and entered the kitchen, I stopped and squeezed Aston's hand. The idea of four sets of eyes turning to us with expectant wondering made me a little nervous. But as it turned out my fear was unfounded.

It was twelve sets of eyes.

When Aston and I stepped into the kitchen we were greeted with a wall of uneasy silence from the assembled gathering. Ada, Edel, and Yael were there, of course, as was Eben. But Iona was there too along with her sister Helen; so were Jane and Katia, and Marcia and Barrett. Veda and Collin were in attendance as well though there was no sign of Jon. As they gazed at us I caught a clear glimpse of the fear I had caused them.

Ada looked ragged with concern. I walked over to her and she stood still for a moment before flinging her arms around me.

"I'm sorry," I said.

"I thought we were going to lose you, Nora," she confessed into my ear. "For a moment, I thought we only had so much time left until—" Ada swallowed and choked back her tears. She pulled away and embraced Aston. "My boy, I am so glad you are okay."

Aston hugged her back.

"I'm sorry *about everything*, Ada."

"Shh," she pressed her fingers against his lips, "what is done is done. We laid his body to rest, and you were only doing your job by protecting his daughter." She smiled and embraced him once more.

Jane stood up. "I'm just glad you're back, Nora," she said clearing her throat. "And the *you* you, not the creepy version of you!"

Eben sat silently eyeing Aston, emotion and confusion flickered in his eyes. This was the first time he had laid eyes on him.

I grabbed a cup of tea, and Aston and I slipped out of the kitchen and made our way down the path to the stony beach where Aston held my hand. We walked in silence, listening to the water crashing onto the shoreline. We reached the end of our beach, and

Aston picked up a stone then flung it into the water. We watched the smooth stone skip once, then disappear into a wave.

"Where did you go after," I paused instantly choking back tears. I couldn't say the words. My father's lifeless body flashed across my mind.

"I needed time and distance to think, come to terms with the fact that I was being used as a pawn in their game." He looked at me as his hair wildly blew around in the ocean breeze.

"The Elders?" I asked. A tear rolled own my cheek landing on my hand.

"They summoned me to an old, tired lighthouse on Cross Island." I felt a chill across my shoulder.

"That's when they gave me the job to hunt the man who, I would eventually learn, was your father."

There was a moment of heavy silence between up.

"I felt like I was dying without you, Nora."

"I know," I said, trying to communicate how very much I understood.

We both took a seat on the sand.

"I also came to learn that they are controlling the Lamians. We can't trust them."

I wondered how I would tell him about Lia and Sebastian and what his reaction would be.

"They have Nolan," he said. "We'll have to tell Eben."

"You saw him? He's still alive?"

"Barely alive. I am assuming Eben is Ada's son."

"Yes, but how did you—"

"I just finally put two and two together. I'm assuming they are keeping Nolan alive to control Ada when the time is right."

My heart dropped into my stomach like I was pitching off the top of a roller coaster.

"They also told me something about Lia," Aston said.

"I saw her the other night!" I blurted, anxious to get it off my chest.

He looked at me sharply. "What do you mean you saw her the other night? Where? I've been going crazy trying to find her. The Elders refused to give me her location. They said that she has made promises and decisions she cannot reverse, and that—" Aston stopped speaking.

"That *what?*"

He looked at me. "That only one of us, Lia or I, would come out of this alive."

"I saw her with Sebastian," I said.

"You saw Sebastian and you escaped?"

"Well, he didn't see me." I felt odd knowing I had to explain the seals. It made me sound like a crazy person, but I went on and told him what had happened that night, disregarding how strange it sounded rolling off my tongue. Aston listened quietly and didn't once make me feel as if I had lost my mind.

"It's good to know you're a strong swimmer."

I could tell he was trying to avoid the painful thought of his sister promising her loyalty to Sebastian.

"Okay forget it, I don't want to talk about her anymore, I can't." He swallowed and stood up pulling me to my feet and into his arms. "She made her decision and I have made mine, to protect you."

27

The energy in the home had changed drastically while we'd been outside, and I knew the brief reprieve from fear had ended. We stepped back into the kitchen, and the beautiful morning had come to an end. Ada's tone was alert as she asked Aston and I to follow her into the next room.

I filled my cup with more steaming hot water then followed Edel and Iona into the living room where others were already seated around the long wooden coffee table.

"I am truly sorry to end a well-deserved relaxing morning with unpleasant information, but we currently have a situation to discuss."

Ada reached into her pocket and pulled out the letter Alexo had written to her. I had completely forgotten there was a second letter. My stomach plummeted at the thought of shredding the only two pieces of paper I had from my parents.

"I knew it was time to read this letter when you explained to me what you saw, Nora." She was referring to the island where I had seen Sebastian and Lia.

"We all have read this letter already, some of us several times, in fact, and I think there is some important information we need to consider."

Ada handed it over, and I opened the crinkled envelope that had once been sealed with wax and stamped with an S. The last memory of my father spoiled in my mind. I pulled out the thin paper with worn creases and silently read it while Aston read over my shoulder.

Ada,

I know it has been some time, and I do hope this letter finds you well if in fact it finds you at all. Rumor has it you have returned and brought back my Eleanora. A day doesn't go by that I don't think of you both. I thank you for taking her away from here for as long as you could. I wish I could have vanished from this place with you both, but Eleanora would have been in even more danger than she currently is in.

I have been under close watch by Sebastian ever since my convicted treason and captivity, and I am afraid that these chains and bars do not allow me to get out much. I have not felt freedom for almost eighteen years. The prison on Cato Island is a place I would not wish on anyone. The island here has not changed, but the thought of you and Eleanora near has given me new strength. I hear through the chambers of the prison that there has been a treaty between the Elders and Sebastian. I believe it promises protection under the Elders for the exchange of power and the destruction of the Sereni race, starting with Eleanora and Aston. They fear the prophecy will come true.

Lia Boxam also paid the island a visit and sought a private meeting with Sebastian. She offered herself to him, to become his mate and to help bring strength back to the Lamians in numbers. She has given birth already to three children at once. Three boys. Sebastian is using her to grow his lineage, his power, to have heirs. I also learned that Sebastian summoned an ancient and dangerous witch by the name Inessa to the island. She performed dark magic on Lia, cursing her to produce Sebastian's heirs within a few months—monstrously speeding up the process of development. The entire island could hear her scream in agony for two months straight as those damned demons grew in her womb. Even through the pain Lia has promised him as many sons as she can possibly give. This has pleased Sebastian. She is to be Sebastian's queen, rewarded with power and authority in the Lamian world.

You can imagine my shock when I heard these chains of whispers spreading rapidly throughout the cells. I was summoned right away by Sebastian and given the task of finding Eleanora and bringing her to him. I only obliged to have my shackles removed and to feel freedom once more, but I will never turn my own blood over to him. I've planned on delivering these letters and seeing my daughter's face again, though I know that when I return empty handed I will be killed. I am weak, Ada. This cell has been stripping me of my abilities. I don't stand a chance against Sebastian. To have one more moment with Eleanora would be worth being burned at the stake.

The world is changing quickly, Ada. With Lia's assistance, Sebastian has been hunting and taking humans. He then tortures and twists them, forcing them to become Lamian trackers. I can hear them screaming, howling, and hunting in the evening outside my barred window. I can hear them being whipped, starved, and trained to kill. Anyone who does not want to follow in Sebastian's shadow is killed. I fear for every being out there. Sebastian wants to repeat history, Ada. He wants to fulfill what I stopped the day I met Rebekah. He wants to end your life, Eleanora's life, and the lives of all who oppose him. He is building an army, Ada, to make sure he does not lose. I have never seen a rage like the one in his eyes. With the Elders giving him a false sense of power, he is ready to attack.

Please protect her, Ada.

Forever your dear friend,
Alexo

Aston's composed body tensed as he came to the last line. I was afraid to move my eyes from the letter. His skin radiated the heat of rage. I could not imagine the pain of a sibling betrayal at this level. The letter matched perfectly what I had seen the other night on what must have been Cato Island. I had been to the island, I had seen these wolf-like creatures, and I had heard Sebastian's voice.

Aston picked up a pillow, pressed it against his face, then took a deep breath and ripped it in half. Goose feathers spilled through the air. Lia was now on a confirmed enemy list in his mind. She had chosen the path of a Lamian, and she had given herself to the demon, Sebastian. Iona stood up and waved her hand. We all watched silently as the feathers recollected and refilled the pillow, and the fabric mended itself. Aston was leaning against a window, his hand pressed against the frame as he stared out towards the sea. Iona attempted to touch his shoulder but stepped away when she felt the ferocity radiating from him.

"I was so stupid to have left you this exposed, Nora, so stupid. Sebastian could have attacked you at any moment, any!" Aston's voice hummed in an intense angry whisper.

I said nothing in response.

"The Elders are right. I will have to eventually kill my own blood, and I *will* kill her."

Everyone in the room remained silent, and I could hear Katia, Jane, Eben, and Yael quietly listening in the kitchen. Yael must have read the letter through my thoughts.

"I was a piece in their game."

I knew he meant the Elders.

No one in the room moved. Ada stared at me as I stood up and walked over to him, tangling my hand in his. He looked at me, and his eyes had shifted to black. I moved closer and he pulled me in. I was not afraid of his demon, just as he was not afraid of mine. The difference between Aston and Lia was that Aston was able to culti-vate and control his demon, something that I still struggled with. I could hear his heart racing, but I was not afraid of his energy.

"I know what I have to do," Aston whispered.

I knew exactly what he was thinking, but I was not certain how to respond. He was going to start hunting Lia and try to intercept her and Sebastian's army before they found me; to prevent her from providing Sebastian with more demonic heirs. He would kill her first then hunt her children.

"Let me go with you, Aston."

"You know I can't do that."

"No! You said you would never leave me again, no matter the circumstance. You *promised*," I hissed angrily.

Aston sighed giving in to my demand. "You're right. Besides, you're the only one who has been to Cato Island."

I heard Marcia gasp. "What! What do you mean you have been there? When? How? We are so potent to them—how did you escape alive?"

"I've seen the Lamian wolves as well," I said, trying to sidetrack the conversation. I didn't want to talk about the seals or Lia again, but I didn't have to. Ada stepped in.

"Nora was guided there one night by the gray seals," Ada said, proudly looking me dead in the eyes.

"Saltwater," Edel said. "It helps mask your scent, not completely, but it helps."

"You've seen the gray seals?" Katia sounded amazed. "But I thought they were only stories, rumors, legends."

"No, they're real alright," I said. "As real as you and me."

"The big question, Nora, is whether you could lead me back there," said Aston.

"Not a chance," I said.

"Look," he said. "If we're going to—"

"No, I mean I wouldn't be able to. I was simply following the seals around me. They led me there, then led me home again."

"Then I guess you'll have to find them again, tonight," Edel spoke.

"Yes, I guess I will."

Things were about to get very dangerous. If we were caught, the war we'd been preparing for would begin. I was ready.

As the sun was setting, Marcia and Barrett went out to reinforce the protection of the home, and Katia and Jane began making runs around the perimeter testing the strength of the shield. Eben wouldn't hear about staying inside, so he was warned not to venture far from Jane, while Collin—who was also from a family of Guardians and had been one for over seventy years—ran with Katia. Yael was under house arrest for her own safety, and Iona and Helen began mixing ointments for the possibilities of wounds during an attack. As for Edel and Ada, they sat in the kitchen plotting and contemplating with Veda and Jon the possibilities of Lamians attacking and where it might fall. The only issue we would have this evening was my safety. Was the risk exposing myself at sea alone a wise one? Probably not. Aston wanted to come with me, but I wanted to recreate familiarity for the sea creatures. We basked in the sun's final moments as its glorious streaks of orange and reds melted into dark hues of midnight blue over the ocean.

"You gonna be okay?" Jane asked.

"Let's hope so, huh?" I smiled at her.

"Yeah. Look, you were trained by the best, so just be careful, and don't do anything stupid, okay? I kind of like you as a friend." Jane smiled and wrapped her arm around me.

It was time.

"May I walk you to the end of the dock?" Aston asked.

I nodded.

"Remember, Nora, at any sign of trouble, any sign, I will be right beside you, okay?"

"Thank you."

"Nora!" Eben ran over, shoving past Aston. "Don't do this, please. I was thinking about it, and I just feel like it's a bad idea," he pleaded.

"Eben, I have to. I have to do what I need to in order to keep this family safe—all those people watching us right now, including you. If I had the choice, I wouldn't want to be me right now."

"Please, Nora," he grabbed my hands, and I could feel Aston's breath shorten, "don't go."

"I *have* to," I smiled, trying to ease his nerves.

Eben pulled me in and squeezed me so hard I could barely breathe.

"Just come back, girlie, okay? Please come back, I need you." I saw Jane over his shoulder smiling with tears running down her face. Eben released me and I made my way back over to her.

"Why are you crying? Thought you were a tough girl," I said, grabbing her arm and pulling her in. She embraced me and whispered in my ear.

"Please, be careful, Nora."

My stomach twisted, and I quickly walked away before I changed my mind.

Ada was waiting at the beginning of the long white dock. She squeezed my hands and kissed my forehead, unable to form words. Edel stood beside her but said nothing, only winked at me.

"I'll be back soon, okay? Don't look upset. This is what I'm meant to do, right? I was trained by the best, I am able to control my abilities now, I got this," I tried reassuring Ada.

Eben made his way back over and held onto his mom's hand for the first time. She leaned on his shoulder and the two walked back towards the house.

Aston took my hand.

"Nora." He paused before we stepped onto the long white dock that had begun to resemble a plank. "I just wanted to tell you, I love you."

"Everything will be fine." I squeezed his hand.

"Say it back, Nora. I need to hear you say it."

I didn't hesitate. "I love you too, Aston."

"I feel like I have no power once your head goes below that surface, and I'm afraid of losing you."

We reached the end of the dock, and I turned. Aston brought me in and kissed me in front of everyone. All eyes were watching the both of us.

"I love you," he whispered.

Next, I took off my robe and stood there in a black bathing suit. I looked at Aston one last time, then dove into the water and disappeared under the dark liquid. The temperature of the water had changed—this time, it was much, *much* colder. Goosebumps formed, stinging as they spread across my skin. I began swimming out to sea, trying to remember where I had been when I first saw the seals. Whenever I came up for a breath, I looked back to see Aston. He'd wave for confirmation that I was still okay, and I'd wave in response to let him know that I was. Then I'd dive back under and swim around some more.

Where are you guys? I thought, swimming around. *Come on.*

The sea was dark and silent. The moon was blanketed by clouds so its light wasn't able to shine through the surface. I floated in an eerie world of infinite apprehension. I came up for a quick breath and then dove back into the water. They had to be somewhere, but the waters were still until I began to feel the currents starting to change. I resurfaced and waved to Aston that I was fine.

"Nora! Come back! A storm is starting to move in!" Aston yelled from the dock, pointing out to sea.

I waved my hand again, signaling that I was fine, and turned to look where he was pointing. The waves were beginning to grow, and I began kicking my way back to the dock when I suddenly felt something glide along my stomach, catching me off guard. I yelped and immediately submerged myself below the surface to see what it was, and there, floating in front of me, was a wide-eyed seal. My fear dissipated and was replaced by anxiety. I placed my hand over my racing heart as its rate dropped. The seal watched me curiously.

I pointed out to sea. *Please*, I thought, *take me back to Cato Island*.

I watched it bob its head amiably. Could it hear my thoughts? Suddenly it saw something behind me, and its dark eyes became filled with protection. The seal's mouth opened and it hissed baring a row of sharp teeth. The approaching figure was moving fast and the seals protectively began to encircle me. Aston. A seal with a wrinkled snout shot out to attack like a little silver bullet.

–Stop! No!–

The seals stopped in their tracks and looked at me with fury in their eyes. They began to retreat and leave as if I had betrayed their trust.

–Wait, no, please! Please, we really need your help–

The larger seal stopped and turned, staring at me with anger in its face.

–Please, trust me. We need to know what is happening–

It encircled the two of us, assessing Aston reluctantly. Then it took off with the other seals following. Aston looked at me and

I nodded. We followed the pod out to sea as they led us back to Cato Island.

The storm grew worse, and by the time we arrived at the island, massive waves were blocking our view and crashing overhead. Aston searched around while the seals stayed below the surface. I scanned the beach but saw nothing. I wanted to head back. The waters were beginning to terrify me. Aston put his hand over my mouth just as I opened it to speak. People were walking on the beach. I could barely identify them, but I knew Lia and Sebastian were present along with fifteen or twenty Lamian trackers. We watched as Sebastian placed his hands on Lia's stomach and then leaned in and gave Lia a kiss. I could feel the water ice and tremble around Aston. Was she already expecting again?

"Traitor," he spat darkly under his breath.

Watching curiously, we then saw another being exit the forest and take off Lia's fur coat. She moved jerkily; her ankles were chained—she was enslaved. Lia had a personal servant and personal supplier. Her arms were bruised and lined with bite marks.

Lia looked at Sebastian. "Make sure our young ones are fed the purest blood we have."

Lia then turned to the waters where she began to lead the Lamian Wolves towards us. "To Stone Isle!"

This startled us, and the seals began swimming furiously.

"Swim!" Aston looked at me with fear in his eyes. "Swim!"

We went back under the surface and began swimming as fast as we could away from the beach. That's all the confirmation we needed; they were indeed planning on attacking tonight. Alexo's letter was a true warning. My heart raced, and the seals swarmed around us, staying close by. We glided through the icy liquid. The leader stayed closest on my right. Were we leaving a trail? Could they track under water? We swam deeper into the dark ocean. We didn't know where we were heading, but we both had put our faith in the hands of these oceanic creatures. The water began to grow even colder, and I knew we were headed in a direction that was far from home. I slowed down, but the seals started aggressively pushing me with their noses and Aston's hand tightly grabbed mine as he pulled.

–This isn't the way home!– I tried to communicate out to the leading seal, but there was no acknowledgment; it continued on even faster.

Its eyes were filled with fear, and I began to pull Aston the other way. I wanted to go home. We were continuing to swim farther and farther out into open sea. Aston tried grabbing me, but I continued slipping out of his grip.

I watched as the seals began to scatter, except for the leader and a few stragglers. They were fleeing from something. Aston and I both turned as the smallest of the seals came out of the shadowy depth, swimming as fast as it could, flying right by us.

There in the dark water shadows began to grow like in my dreams. Aston pointed to his nose. They had latched onto our scent, like sharks hunting a trail of blood. I looked at Aston, who mouthed, *Move*. We swam as fast as we possibly could, coming up for air only when direly needed. It was during one of these brief surfaceings that I saw it.

Stella.

"Eben?" I gasped, seeing his boat come flying through the water.

"Eben!" I screamed.

He spotted us and swung the sunfish round. Aston and I climbed onto the boat, and he asked us to duck as the boom swung out of control.

"Are you insane?" Aston yelled.

"If saving your asses is considered insane, then yes, I guess I am."

The seals had begun thrashing through the water alongside the boat.

"Follow them," I yelled. "Follow them! They're leading us away from Stone Isle!"

Eben maneuvered the boat quickly amongst the battering sea. "You shouldn't have come, Eben! Why did you follow us?"

"I couldn't let you go, Nora. I had to make sure you were okay!"

The waves towered over us as we whipped through the stormy sea. The sails snapped and bowed capturing strong gusts of powerful wind. Eben kept as close to the seals as he could. Lia and the trackers were far behind us now, but nevertheless, their shadows were visible occasionally breaking the surface for breath.

The deep water disappeared without warning and the belly of the boat scraped against rock and sand. We jumped out, scrambling away from the water. We were back on the same beach where the Lamian trackers had first attacked Aston and I. These were the Forgotten Islands.

"Eben, you need to leave right now. Hide in the woods! Go!" Aston ordered.

"Yeah right, man. You left her once, how do I know you won't leave her again?"

Aston was at a loss for words and the tension that had struck between the boys was profound.

"Alright, then," Aston finally said. "Stay, but get behind us."

Eben stepped behind us and took his stance. I stood there nervously. My fingers twitched. The three of us waited.

"Breathe, Nora. Just breathe," Aston said.

I began to hyperventilate. The veins on my neck rapidly pulsated and my eyes shifted color.

"Look at me, Nora!"

I looked to Aston, but my eyes continued flickering between the ocean, Eben and him.

"Nora! You are strong. You are trained! You are the daughter of the two most powerful beings known in our world."

My breathing was becoming heavier with every breath I took.

"Do you understand me, Nora? You can control anything with your mind. Anything!" I looked at Aston, panicking, as bodies began to float and break through the surface. The seals must have attacked them, trying to help our odds. The water washing ashore had turned a muddy red color. Then, one by one, Lamians began crawling out of the blood-stained surf.

One Lamian tracker tossed a dead seal from its mouth, like a sack of potatoes, to the ground. My heart stopped as I saw its face: it was the leader. My stomach tightened in anger. I projected my thoughts as far as I could possibly imagine them going.

–YAEL, IF YOU CAN HEAR ME WE ARE UNDER ATTACK! ON THE FORGOTTEN ISLANDS! YAEL! UNDER ATTACK! ON THE FORGOTTEN ISLANDS, YAEL!–

Lia crawled out of the water, leading the Lamian trackers. They hissed and snarled in our direction, clawing at the sandy earth and snapping their jaws. Lia held out both her hands and the trackers stopped, growling as they watched her for the command to attack. Her eyes were no longer the honey brown they had been when I first met her, but murky and black. Her skin was no longer delicate like porcelain but hardened and cold. I could see the veins in her arms and hands pulsating. She looked nothing like the Lia I had once met. She looked lifeless.

"Tsk. Tsk. Tsk. My dearest brother, is this *really* the path you have chosen? You could have walked with me to an eternal life of power." Her voice hissed like a rattlesnake as she spoke.

Aston's body tensed up.

"Instead, you decided to waste it on—" she paused, noticing Eben standing behind Aston. "Well, well, look what we have here, Ada's son. Oh, this is too good!"

She looked back at Aston. "This is the kind of company that will surely lead you to your own grave. Disappointing, if I do say so myself."

Lia spat at my feet, and I heard Aston snarl.

"I trusted you, Lia. I believed you could change, that you could see life the way our parents did and the way I do!"

Lia chuckled at Aston. "And then what, dear brother of mine? What, decide to continue fighting someone greater than us? Wait around another seventeen years for the promised one to save us? No! I can save myself, thank you. Sebastian will save us!"

The creatures howled in unison at Sebastian's name. Lia looked pleased.

"I had a choice, and I chose to be with and to follow Sebastian! He appreciates my powers, believes in my powers, and enhances my powers!" I could see Lia becoming angrier as the conversation continued.

"You're right, Lia! I can see you have traded, sacrificed even, your beauty for power!"

I followed Aston's eyes and saw the bite wounds above Lia's elbows. Suddenly I understood: she had become a source as well; her power was fueling the new trackers. They were all feeding off her blood. She was Sebastian's secret weapon because he would do no such thing as supply non-pure bloodlines with his blood. He needed someone powerful and willing to do his bidding. I looked at the trackers and saw that they all had amber-tinted eyes, like Lia once had.

"How are the kids?" Aston continued egging her on. "Expecting again? You know Lia, I never thought of you as the mothering type."

"I have an army, Aston! What do you have? A Sereni in training and a mutt!" She hissed in hunger. "Now come on! Hand them over, and we will spare you. We will offer you eternal protection in return."

Lia's words reeked of lies as she stood there, her neck twitching, her teeth grinding as she waited for Aston's answer.

Yael's voice broke into my mind.

−Nora! They're coming! They're coming!−

When Aston didn't answer her, Lia smiled.

"Fine then! Have it your way. It's a pity to have to kill my own flesh and blood tonight, really," Lia said sarcastically.

"Just like the pity you had for our parents and grandparents when you murdered them," Aston said. "How long Lia? How long have you been spying and working for Sebastian?"

"I do what I need to for the greater good, Aston." Lia raised both hands, signaling the trackers and they started closing in slowly. Aston, Eben, and I took our stances. The closest Lamian tracker leapt into the air and Aston slammed its body to the ground, cracking its bones.

"Kill them!" Lia screamed. "Except for *her*, we want her alive."

Her black eyes burned into my flesh. She watched as her Lamian trackers began to close in on us. She watched and stayed back. Before I knew it, claws and teeth had sunk themselves into my flesh. I screamed in horrendous pain, hurling them off of me, ribcages cracking, necks snapped and limbs torn off. The battle had begun. Aston killed Lamian trackers left and right and, to my surprise, so did Eben. I heard Ada's voice, and both Edel and Ada emerged from the water accompanied by Marcia, Iona, Jon, Barrett, Veda, and Collin. They joined in the fight as they ripped apart the Lamian trackers one by one. Lia scanned the beach.

"KILL THEM ALL! ALL OF THEM!" Lia commanded and the Lamian trackers began to move faster and faster. "But leave her to me. I like to play with my food." Lia began to make her way right to me.

One tracker with yellow eyes caught me off guard and pinned me to the ground. I heard Lia snarl at the tracker, throwing its body aside. "I *said* leave her to me!"

Lia dug her knee into my chest, restraining my arms and legs. The corners of her mouth pulled back unveiling her bloodstained teeth.

"You said they wanted me alive!" I aggressively wiggled, trying to break free from her grasp.

"Oh they most certainly do, but I won't kill you, Eleanora, just taste you."

Her eyes were black.

Then her teeth sunk into my throat and she began pulling hard. I tried tapping into my energetic powers but my vision was beginning to double with the pain. I was gasping for breath when Aston ripped her off of me, tossing her aside. I tasted blood in my mouth. The entire beach was painted red. I rolled over to my side then stood with my hands pressed against my throat. I was losing blood and a lot of it. Lia watched with interest, cackling. Aston fought with Marcia to keep the other ravenous Lamian trackers away from me. Eben grabbed ahold of me, pressing his hands into the gash to slow down the bleeding. My body trembled at the sight of Lia, at the sound of her laughter echoing in my ears, and at her serpent-like eyes. The scent of my blood filled the air, and Lia's nose flared in utter delight.

"My my, what a delicious flavor you have. I can see now why my brother is *so* attracted to you." I watched Lia lick her lips, savoring what she had tasted. "Don't let that bind fool you, girl. There is so much more that he wants from you. So much he will take from you!" Her laughter faded as I scanned the beach.

All around me, the people I loved were shedding blood for me, fighting for me. I lay there fixated on a Lamian that was latched onto Ada. I wanted its heart to stop. I wanted it to bleed and to feel pain, the pain I was suffering as I pressed my hand over Eben's as he applied even more pressure against my neck. Blood seeped through our fingers and I felt the warm liquid running down my chest. Ada screamed in agony as Barrett stabbed the Lamian tracker in the back with a knife, then cracked its neck.

"Iona, come get Ada. She needs medical attention now!" Barrett belted.

"Nora!" Aston yelled. "Come on Nora, stay with us!"

"Save them." I looked at Aston, then closed my eyes.

I was back in my dream of running with wolves, running and killing. Streaks of blood splattered along my coat and across my face. Marcia's shriek pulled me from dreamland. I watched as a wolf emerged from the surf and took to the beach. It was white with gray streaks across its face and back.

Suddenly, I felt the wild uncontrollable urge to kill. My body arched in agony, my hands and feet curled with pain and I felt an uncontrollable transformation take place. Next, I was snarling and ripping apart the bodies of Lamian trackers.

"No, it can't be," I heard Lia hiss angrily in disbelief.

I dropped a crippled tracker from my jaw and made my way slowly towards her, snapping the air and snarling. Lamian trackers continued to attack me as I approached their leader, their *queen*, but the other wolf and Aston held them off. I was ready for Lia, ready to end her life. My black paws were splattered red with blood. Blood dripped from my teeth as I swiped, snarled, and killed, gradually getting closer and closer to Lia. I was sinking my teeth into their bodies, jerking them around, flinging them in all directions. The other wolf did the same. We both howled towards the stormy skies moving side by side.

Lia looked at me in horror as the gray and white wolf dropped the last Lamian tracker on the beach, placed its large paw on the tracker's chest, and tore off its head. I stopped when I saw her beginning to retreat, her eyes black with fury. I pounced, grabbing her body within my paws and pinning her down to the ground. Lia kicked and cursed. She had become weak from supplying an army with her blood; she depended on their protection.

"Do it!" She hissed, her nails digging into my sides. "Remember what I told you when I first met you, *kill when the moment presents itself.*"

I removed my paws from her body and took a step back. She scrambled in disbelief and stood up.

"Weakness, just like my brother."

Lia turned to escape into the water when I attacked her from behind. She screamed and I sunk my teeth into her neck and severed her head from her body. I heard a gasp from Marcia.

–I like to play with my food too–

The other wolf and I howled towards the dark heavens. Lightning and thunder streaked the night sky.

Every last ounce of energy I had left escaped through my throat, and I buckled, falling to my knees, whimpering. I was bleeding out. I watched as Eben and Aston hovered over me, pressing their hands into the side of my neck. I looked at Aston one last time, catching my reflection in his eyes. I was a black wolf, a Shapeshifter.

Then everything went white.

28

I woke to droning hums and the feeling of salty wet rags draped over various parts of my body. The stinging was severe and refreshing all at once. My vision was cloudy, and all I could make out were gray shadows hovering over me. The sounds of howls rang in my ears and masked the faint echoing of voices.

"She's going to be fine," a woman said.

The echoing was so bad I couldn't distinguish who was speaking.

"She lost a lot of blood and has gone into shock. We need to stop the infection. Nora, Nora, can you hear me?"

My body remained hardened. The Lamian venom seared through my veins.

Another woman spoke. "She's listening. She is trying to figure out what is going on, and is in a lot of pain, she cannot move."

I knew this voice was Edel's—Yael must be near.

"Fight, Nora!" A deep voice echoed in my ears.

"Take it out of her! More tonic! Give her more!" a frantic woman's voice screamed.

My eyes began rolling back behind my fluttering eyelids. White light faded in and out. Convulsions swooped over my muscles, and I began screaming, hissing, and trying to break loose from my bound limbs. This insanity was not me at all; it was Lia's venom—Queen Lamia's deep hooks fighting to stay in my body, to take me home to the demon rooted within me. Aston forcibly restrained me while

Iona poured the tonic down my throat. Yael's voice in my mind was panicky with fear. My veins hardened, my teeth hammered together between screams, snapping and snarling. Finally, my body had had enough. It could no longer take the pain. I let go.

Whiteness led to nothing.

I was back on the island, standing with Aston, walking silently through the old home. No words were spoken. We only held hands and floated through empty space. The warm sun turned his eyes to a honey brown, and we were safe and in love. His hands touched my cheeks and then he looked me dead in the eyes.

"Stay with me, Nora."

Of course, I will stay with you, I thought. *How silly.*

"We need to leave this island now. It's time to go home."

I pulled my hand out of his, not wanting to leave. This was home. *He* was home. I wanted nothing to do with going back to the pain and fear.

"Nora, we need to leave!" he yelled at me as he shook my shoulders.

"No, I will not go back. No!" I closed my eyes, wanting to stay, grabbing onto the furniture like a child throwing a tantrum.

"Wake up, Nora. WAKE UP!"

I am awake! I opened my eyes, about to scream when his eyes turned to black and he grabbed my jaw the way I had seen him once do to Lia.

"WAKE UP, NORA!"

An intense buzzing of voices flooded my ears again, and my eyes could no longer see anything.

"WAKE UP, NORA!" I felt a surge of energy as if my whole body had been slammed against a wall.

There was whiteness, then gray shadows, then Aston's mouth, screaming at me. I wanted to be back on the island. I wanted to be with Aston. I wanted that to be my home. Aston's face disappeared. *Where is he? Where did he go?*

"You promised you would never leave me!" I screamed into the space of white light and shadows.

"Nora! Nora, baby, I'm here. Please stay with me!" Aston's voice filled my ears.

Another powerful shock shook my body, and I rolled over and threw up.

My vision began adjusting, and I stayed there, keeled over the side of the bed. A cold rag wiped my face. Vomit continued to work its way up my throat, and when I finished, I was rolled over to my back and I lay there, still. The bright white world, filled with shadows and voices, began to come into focus. The first face I could see was that of Aston's as he stood over me.

"Welcome back," he smiled and wiped my forehead with a rag.

"That was the last of the venom," Helen's voice spoke.

Shoes shuffled across the wooden floorboards, and then Ada's face came into the picture along with Jane, Collin, Eben, Katia, and Yael.

"Everyone out! Out, out, out! She needs space." Iona's voice left no room for debate, and everyone shuffled out, with the door slamming behind them. Aston stayed. The room was unfamiliar and didn't look lived-in, a spare bedroom somewhere.

"Where am I?" I asked.

"You are safe. You are in our home," Iona said as she and Helen looked down at me.

"How are you feeling?" Helen pressed the red tinted rag against my forearm, and I let out a moan as she dabbed and pressed various cuts as she worked her way towards my neck.

"Ouch!" I snarled sharply, and my moans turned into growling sounds.

"Alright pup, alright," Helen smiled removing the rag. "Take a breather."

"You were *amazing*, Nora," Aston said with a lower tone of voice. My ears were still ringing heavily.

"You turned," Aston whispered into my ear. "You're a Shapeshifter, Nora, like your father."

"You've lost a lot of blood," Helen said. "And then you went into shock and—"

And what? And what?

"And we almost lost you. Your heart failed. She almost killed you." Aston finished the sentence, then went silent.

"But you are now back and need to rest," said Iona. "You need to regenerate."

I saw her hand Aston a rag, then smile at me. "You're in good hands, my dear."

Aston pressed the rag against my neck and the lower part of my ribcage. The stinging was becoming tolerable, and I watched him as he dipped the rag into the familiar wooden bowl and pressed it against my wounds.

"I turned," I whispered, faintly remembering what had happened. "I'm a Shapeshifter."

"A beautiful, dark one." Aston put his hand on my forehead, and I was back on the island watching a large black wolf with hungry eyes staring back at me. Then I saw the second wolf, the white and gray one snarl and attack a Lamian wolf. Aston removed his hand.

"But, who was the other wolf?"

"Me," Edel whispered from a seat in the corner of the room.

"Edel?"

She walked over and looked into my eyes. "Yes, I come from a long line of Shapeshifters. When you turned, I wasn't able to hide my secret anymore. Aston is right, you are a beautiful creature."

"That's why you can communicate with the seals, hear Yael, and follow scents," Aston said. "You have heightened senses because you're a Shapeshifter. And a powerful one."

Edel nodded. "And the reason why you have become so attached and protective of Yael is that she eventually will become one of us. She will be a part of our pack."

"Yael too?"

"With time, yes," Edel answered.

"How did I turn back into my Sereni form then? I thought shifting was dangerous and sometimes irreversible," I asked, short of breath.

"It can be, but we turned back together and you did just fine. You may not remember, though. You were floating in and out of consciousness by then," Edel said. "But it's not as dangerous when you are aware of the transformation, aware of your power."

"Lia." I looked at Aston. "I killed her."

"You did." He glanced down at me. "You were brave."

"Nora, you need rest. You need to regenerate your blood and energy to heal." Edel pressed her hand over my eyes as she whispered enchanted words that lulled me towards sleep.

My throat felt stiff, and I listened to Aston's beating heart as my eyes began to close.

"Don't leave me," I whispered.

"Never." Aston's voice echoed in my ears.

I had no idea how long I had been asleep, but when I awoke, I was alone in my bed at Alexander Point, and in my nightgown. My muscles ached, and a painful headache pinched my temples. The window was open, letting the salty air roll the curtains in and out. My neck hurt, and I pressed my fingers against my wound, only to find there was nothing except five cold long scars from teeth. On my nightstand was a vase of flowers. My necklace lay beside it on the wood, the gold chain and charms nesting with the black stone. I caught an overwhelming hint of floral scents and sat up. I held my breath. Arranged on every flat surface and across the floor were maybe a hundred vases filled with peonies, wildflowers and foliage. Pushing off the comforter, I stepped onto the floor and took a deep breath. My room smelled like a forest painted by spring. I tiptoed my way through the vases and caught a glimpse of an envelope attached to one. The handwriting on the front was Aston's. The envelope was heavy, and as I opened it, a note and an iron key fell out.

Nora,

My world has changed since the moment I first laid eyes on you. Life has no meaning without you. You are the reason my heart beats the way it does. You are the only one I want to share my life with, and the only one I call home. I could never bear to lose you the way I almost just did, again.

You are my everything, my forever, and I will love you until my heart stops.

Aston

PS. This key unlocks the home on my grandfather's island. It's yours.

I stared at the key in my hand. The home, on the vanishing island? I stared around the room filled with beautiful aromatic wonders and grabbed my necklace from my nightstand. Opening the door with the key tightly clenched in my hand, I headed downstairs.

Ada was the only one in the kitchen, and when I appeared she sprinted over to me, practically tripping over a chair in her hurry to throw her arms around me and squeeze me tightly. Tears flooded down her face and slipped down my shoulders. I tried calming her down, and after what felt like an hour she had relaxed enough to tell me through tears how she had thought I was gone, how she had almost lost me, how scared she had been on the beach when I turned, how terrifying I was, and how Edel and I had saved everyone.

Everyone had escaped with only flesh wounds. Ada broke into sobs again when she finished talking, and I kept reassuring her I was okay. Every time she released me from her grip, she would fling her arms around me again, afraid to let go. We stayed like this until she collected herself, then I showed her the note and the key. She read through it and began sobbing again. This time, the sobs were exaggerated.

"Why are you crying again? I'm okay, Ada. I'm here. And I'm alive!"

"Because now," she said through renewed sobs, "now you're going to leave me."

She'd managed to stretch the word *leave* out into three strangled syllables and *me* into two.

"Oh my God, Ada," I laughed. "I'm not going to lea-ea-eave you-ou!"

She wiped her face and looked at me.

"He loves you, Nora."

"I know he does," I smiled.

"Go to him. He's waiting for you."

I looked over her shoulder and out of the kitchen window. There he stood, leaning against the railing, watching the slate blue ocean moving calmly. I stood up, kissing Ada's head and handing her a napkin before I headed out to see Aston. I opened the kitchen door and carefully closed it behind me. He turned, and for a still moment in time we looked at one another, smiling. Once I remembered to breathe, I ran across the porch and jumped into his arms, wrapping my legs around his waist.

I was home.

I held onto him tightly, never wanting to let go. I looked up into the sky and my familiar, a Gray Eagle, screeched as it flashed its wings by the sun. It soared and then vanished into the dense evergreen forest. I pulled back and kissed Aston.

"I love you." It was all I could think to say. I whispered it over and over into his ear.

~~~~~~~~~~

There is a time and place where your nightmares will begin to resurface and every inch of your body will shiver like a silver aspen in the wind. Every shadow you've left behind your closed eyes will suddenly know your name. Where then do you run and hide from your demons?

Sebastian and his forces were recovering from the shock of losing Lia and most of their army of Lamian trackers. We knew that the *next* time they attacked, my deepest nightmares would resurface. Sebastian was out there counting his losses and planning for a greater war. He would personally come for me next time.

The Elders have been exposed to us in a light only some believed to be true for years. They controlled the Lamians, and they were *their* Elders as well. We knew we'd see them sooner rather than later, but one thing I knew was that I would never have to fight them alone.

My fate was here, and I was ready to accept what I must do, who I must be, and those I must protect.

The skin on my arm began to tingle and I watched as dark ink spread across my forearm creating the same Sereni symbol Ada had once shown me on hers. The Elders were watching.

> *My name is Eleanora Ada Stone. It is June 14th, my birthday, and I am eighteen years old. I live in a world of secrets and abilities. I have a demon seed planted inside of me.*
>
> *I will fight.*

ACKNOWLEDGEMENTS

A HUGE THANK YOU TO:

My husband, Ian Dory, for his endless, love, support, and faith; Lisa and Jon Dory for always believing and supporting me in my endeavor; my mother Irene Charvet for being the world's best mom and always cheering me on: I love you more, Mom. My brother Jonathan, thank you for endless inspiring conversations; my sister Kimberlee R. Molineaux for twenty-five years and counting of endless friendship and always telling it to me straight; Jackie Hueftle for taking the time to comb through my first manuscript; the Ridgley Family, Olivia, Marcia, Derek, and Keegan for always being there as family, here's to the stable table and family dinners; Jamie Marie Fischer for being there to photograph and capture the milestones in our life. Shannon Claudio for fanning the spark of ISLE; Olivia Hendrick, for taking the time to read and review ISLE; FriesenPress and their incredible staff, without you ISLE wouldn't be where it is today.

Thank you, thank you, thank you.